As Dawn Approaches

John Reid

ISBN:0994752709
ISBN-13: 978-0-9947527-0-3:

I would like to thank the following people:

Sarah Main Ellis for encouraging me to write this book and for finding time in a very busy schedule to edit and proofread the book which is greatly appreciated.
Joe O'Rafferty, my musical soul mate for allowing me to borrow the book title from the song of the same name which he wrote.
And last but by no means least, my lovely wife Mandy for her love and support.

My unconditional love and gratitude to you all.

Introduction

A year or so ago I was reading an article on a website when I came across an extremely interesting comment by John Reid. He had written an e-book entitled "The Organic Economy", the title sparked my interest as I teach economics in university. Having only been able to download one page of the document, I contacted John as he was kind enough to leave his email address. I wrote asking for the whole e-book, which he sent me immediately.

I was enthralled with this book, firstly because it was pleasant to read and mainly because this was the very first time that viable, possible answers too many of the world's problems were proposed. This in itself was rather a revelation as it is terribly easy to destruct rather than construct. I live in a country that is known for its truer-than-most "direct democracy", however, I am of British origin and we, the people, can see what "democracy" means in most nations today – centralized government where most parties are convergent, different entities of the same side. The book was informative and interesting therefore I uploaded it onto the university intranet for free access to any person who may be interested. I contacted John to inform him of this news and to enquire whether he would be penning a book about the organic economy. I was disappointed that he had decided against it, because I think his e-book can fundamentally change people's vision of a newer and better system for everyone.

As Dawn Approaches

After a few weeks I was contacted by John who enthusiastically informed me that I had been "the catalyst" that had encouraged him to write the book, the emotions I felt were rather dramatic as it was quite a revelation to be told this. Not many months later I received the whole book which John asked me to proof read, this was a extremely exciting episode of my life, being able to read his book and have some input, I cannot express how much this touched me.

The information this book contains including the viable solutions for taking the responsibility for our own management, making us question why so many areas of our society are imbalanced. John's writing style is pragmatic and direct. He takes you on a journey that will fundamentally and categorically change your life.

Everything in life happens for a reason and there are no coincidences, things are meant to happen, because nothing truly goes away until it teaches you what you need to know, whether this is positive or negative, until we as people hear and listen to that message it will simply come again. So what is it that stops us as human beings form hearing or listening to that message? It is simply one thing FEAR. Fear of the unknown. Fear is the most destructive of all emotions, it stops us from advancing, progressing, loving, changing, or even grabbing every opportunity with open arms and in the end we only regret the opportunities we have never taken. So where is this leading us? I believe this is leading us into a system that works for no-one except the privileged in society where everyone else lives in an illusion, believing that they could possibly one day be privileged too, effectively an illusion. We need to wake up and realize there is another way.

Gandhi stated, "Be the changes you want to see in the world", so why should it be up to everyone else to change rather than "me"? This is where this book is primordial, because it is the idea of a better, fairer system a new model of a society created of the people, by the people and for the people. This is where I know the crux of the matter lies- the power of the people to create and change a fairer more positive world for everyone, with everyone's participation where we are all equal.

"You never change things by fighting the existing reality. To change something, build a new model that makes the existing model obsolete." Buckminster Fuller

Here is this new model. Read and Enjoy!

Sarah Main Ellis

Professeure chargée d'enseignment HES (Haute Ecole de Gestion, Neuchâtel, Suisse HES-SO)

Teaching Professor (The University of Applied Sciences HES-SO of North Western Switzerland)

Contents

CHAPTER 1

1 – The Wedding

"I now pronounce you Man and Wife, you may kiss the bride," said the Pastor as the newly wedded couple embraced in a loving kiss, the first kiss as man and wife, a kiss to remember always.

Outside the stone church confetti rained down upon the happy couple as snap happy photographers shot from almost every available angle. Late June in Southern Ontario was a safe bet for good weather and today it didn't disappoint. The afternoon sun shone warmly upon the excited wedding crowd. The Bride and Groom made their way slowly toward the awaiting Limousine and with a farewell wave entered the luxurious vehicle. Cheers arose as the chauffeur closed their door and again as the car pulled smoothly away to where the wedding portraits were to be photographed.

"Mommy, where's Daddy?" asked eight-year-old Sarah Jenkins.

"He should be here soon," replied Sarah's mother Annie, then continued "Daddy had to go to a call today because someone else couldn't go."

"Ok, but he missed the best part, didn't he mommy?"

"I think so Sarah," said Annie.

Annie Jenkins was happily married to Toronto Paramedic Mark Jenkins and they had two children, ten-year-old Brandon and eight-year-old Sarah. It was Mark's old school friend James Young who had just married his long time sweetheart Julie Sanders and Annie knew well that her husband would not want to miss this day. The wedding guests made their own way to the banquet hall where the reception was to be held and waited until they were allowed to locate their appointed tables.

2 – The Cottagers

"Watch this!" thirteen-year-old Paul Hagel said to his friends as he launched himself off the wooden dock, compressed his body into a ball and crashed into the lake, bottom first, as a human bomb, creating the intended splash in the process.

"How big was it?" Paul asked his friends after he surfaced.

"Not bad," said twelve-year-old Jared, waving his hand horizontally over his head.

"Not as high as the one you did this morning," ten-year-old Phil added.

The three boys were enjoying the lake, swimming in the cool clear waters of the Georgian Bay section of Lake Huron and diving off the dock making the biggest splashes possible.

Each year their parents, who had been friends since before the children were even thought of, spent as many weekends as possible at the family cottage of Jerry Hagel, the oldest of the friends.

However, it just seemed that every year these long awaited weekends away from the hustle and bustle of the daily rat race where becoming harder to arrange. Maybe it was the busy work schedules, the kids sports or a combination of both, but when they did all manage to escape the 'hamster wheel' of life and spend a weekend together at Jerry and Andrea's cottage it just made it that much more special. The fact it was the July 1st. Canada Day weekend was also an added bonus as they all loved setting off fireworks into the starry night sky. The husbands had driven into town to pick up gas for the barbeque and stock up on beer and wine while the wives stayed back at the cottage watching over the kids, enjoying the sunshine and natural beauty of the Lake.

Jerry's family cottage sat back about a hundred and twenty feet from the water's edge and twenty five feet above water level, the mothers could easily keep an eye on the boys at the dock and their sisters who played on the small sand and gravel beach that sloped gently into the crystal clear water beside the dock. The cottage had 4 bedrooms which was perfect before the children came along but now things were a little tight, a compromise that bothered no-one, they would erect tents too if that is what it took and it likely will in the near future as the kids grow older. Anything to break away and relax from the hustle and bustle of stressful urban life, to 're-charge the batteries' so to speak.

The wives were enjoying a cup of freshly brewed coffee on the old cedar deck which overlooked the dock area, busily catching up on the latest and greatest of each other's lives. The ladies had always got along well with each other and had over the years become firm friends.

"Hey Paul take it easy, you're bigger than Andrew!" Jerry's wife Andrea shouted down to the dock as Paul was trying to push the younger and smaller Andrew off the dock and into the water.

"Ok Mom," replied Paul, but he told Andrew in a quieter voice, "I'll get you later!"

Andrew, laughingly said, "You wish."

The boys were also good friends and loved to see each other and enjoy the cottage and lake, especially with their fathers who would take them fishing, water skiing and wakeboarding. The old eighteen foot bowrider boat had certainly seen better days but she could pull a water skier with 6 other people in the boat and that was all they needed.

"Hey I've just had a promotion at work," Natalie said to Andrea and Rose with a big grin as she wiggled in her dock chair, both hands wrapped around her coffee mug.

"That's fantastic," said the other two women.

"So, what is it you are doing now then?" Rose asked.

"Much the same as before really, just that I am now the 'go to' person in the office and I train the newbies."

"Well that's good to hear," Andrea continued, "and you like it there too, don't you?"

"Yes I do, I feel very lucky to be honest. So many people hate their jobs but I love mine," Natalie added.

"It's a big company you work for isn't it Natalie?" Rose asked.

"Yes and forever growing it seems. We have just bought another big company in Europe too."

"These big corporations, it seems like they are gradually taking over the whole world," Andrea sighed.

"Hasn't it always been that way?" Rose asked.

"Well yes, but not on such a scale, the corporations today are so large, so...."

"Powerful?" Andrea offered.

"Yes, so powerful," Natalie replied nodding.

"You would think that if things keep going the way they are then there will only end up being one giant global corporation that owns everything!" exclaimed Rose.

"I don't think you're far wrong there Rose, I heard that the mainstream media, you know, all the TV stations and newspapers are now owned by just a few corporations, when it used to be owned by a hundred different companies," added Andrea.

"I don't know, it's all over my head," Rose continued, "I

know nothing about business."

"Anyway how are things at the tax office Andrea?" Natalie asked.

"Don't ask," replied Andrea.

"Why, are they working you too hard?" Rose added with a wink.

"It's always busy and we do have a huge workload but it's not that."

"So what is it then?" Natalie prodded.

"Well, you remember I told you last year that things changed?" Natalie and Rose nodded in agreement as Andrea continued.

"It's different now, things are different, the atmosphere is different, it just isn't the same as it used to be," Andrea said with a shrug.

"Why is that?" asked Rose "New boss or something?"

"No it's the way we go after people now."
Rose laughed out aloud "What, the taxman goes after people now, so what's new!"

Andrea said quietly "Yes, of course the taxman always comes after defaulters but it's the way we are doing things now. I really don't like it, it's so un-Canadian."

"Oh, in which way, why is it un-Canadian?" asked Natalie.

"It's the way we go after the small people, people who don't have money and the small businesses more than anything."

"Well I don't like the sound of that at all," exclaimed Rose.

"Are they going after all those corporations that don't pay their taxes too?" Natalie asked.

"That's another part of what I don't like," Andrea said, "The corporations seem to be a law unto themselves. We do go after them but they don't take us seriously, they have so much power, I think they have so many people in their pockets that they can get away with almost anything.

As Dawn Approaches

"No, my problem is how we now go after the little guy, the person who hasn't the money to defend themselves and the small businesses, it's unfair to these people who are doing everything they can to build a business and earn an honest living. We are ruthless to these people, that is what I mean by un-Canadian. I know the IRS in the US are known for such tactics but we never did things this way before, before the bombing."

3 – The Judge

The Crown pub in Toronto was typically busy for a Thursday evening. The after work crowd had had their couple of drinks and left and now the local regulars were beginning to fill the place, except for one person, one after work regular who wasn't in any great hurry to make his way home on the subway.

The Judge liked The Crown pub, liked the staff especially twenty four-year-old Jeff Summers, the trusty barman. Being a regular he also knew the owner, Jeff's uncle, Jack Finlay quite well.

Sometimes the Judge would have a pint or two, sometimes a pint and a Brandy, and then make his way home, for the Judge was a widower and hadn't really anything to go home to. His only child Sabrina was now a thirty four-year-old school teacher who was happily married to David Sinclair, a computer systems analyst with whom she bore two children, five-year-old Samantha and two and a half-year-old Gareth. The Judge's wife Harriet had passed away over three years previously but did get to experience the joy of her only grandchild Samantha, who sadly would probably never remember her doting grandmother. Occasionally the Judge stayed longer than the usual couple of drinks and ate at the pub too. Jeff knew from experience that when the Judge ate there he would almost certainly be staying for a while longer and would also be consuming enough Brandy to warrant a taxi home instead of negotiating the subway to the North York region of Toronto. Tonight was one of those nights for the Judge had just asked Jeff for the menu.

The Judge wasn't a court room judge but an immigration Judge, his responsibilities included interviewing, preparing and testing applicants for Canadian citizenship. But to Jeff the Judge was "The Judge" and that was that. He and the Judge often had interesting chats about the state of the world, politics, economics and things that made the headlines in the news. Jeff respected the Judge's opinions, knowledge and wisdom for he was a learned and experienced man. The Judge also made it clear that he also respected Jeff's opinions. The Judge was an open minded and fair man.

The Judge sat at a two seat table while eating his meal of fish and chips, one of his favourites

"Fish and chips, there just isn't another dish quite like fish and chips," the Judge said to himself.

"Fish and chips and a decent pint of beer."

The Judge had eaten at some of the finest restaurants in various cities around the world but a good plate of fish and chips couldn't be beat. After finishing his meal the Judge relocated himself to his favourite seat, a bar stool in front of the Guinness tap where he would be able to talk to Jeff in short snippets of conversation while Jeff served his customers. Their talk would almost certainly include the upcoming Federal election which was happening the following week.

"How was the fish and chips?" Jeff asked the Judge, careful not to call him Judge audibly in front of the other customers. The Judge preferred to blend in and not stand out in any way, he was a modest man.

"Excellent as always," replied the Judge, "can never tire of a decent plate of fish and chips."

"What's your take on the election next week, majority government again, have the pollsters got it right this time?" Jeff said while pouring a pint of Guinness.

"Tough one to call really," said the Judge.

"You would think the Tories would be out for sure after the scandals and wasting of taxpayer money," Jeff added.

"Yes, but the voter is a fickle animal, it certainly isn't a bet I would like to take," replied the Judge.

"I don't mean to pry but which party do you think is best for the country and the people, I mean all the people, everyone, I try and look at the bigger picture myself and not the party lines and their own ideologies?"

The Judge took a sip of his fourth Brandy, savouring every drop then replied "You know Jeff, after all my years I can only come to one conclusion."

"And what is that?" Jeff asked in earnest.

"None of them," the Judge replied in dismay, Jeff could see the Brandy's were hitting home but he liked this because the alcohol loosened up the Judge and he would now be more open than when sober.

"None of them?" Jeff spat back "I thought – yes sir what can I get you?" Jeff had to break away mid-sentence and serve a customer.

The pub was filling up which left Jeff little time to talk to the Judge but he wanted to hear his opinion.

A customer asked for a Guinness, Jeff took a pint glass, walked over to the Guinness tap and spoke under his breath to the Judge, "I must admit I am surprised to hear your answer about the parties. I hear that a lot from people but I didn't expect to hear it from you, Judge."

"Yes I know, I never would have thought I'd be saying it myself, upstanding member of the Government, citizenship Judge, a trusted and long serving civil servant."

"So what has made you think this way now, I must admit I am beginning to feel the same way but I come from a family with strong beliefs in our system and institutions and my Father drummed it into us that we must always vote because so many died to allow us the privilege, it's what our democracy is all about, the vote isn't it?" Jeff asked.

"That is true, many did make the ultimate sacrifice for our freedom today," the Judge said guardedly as he realised he had set off something in Jeff. The judge raised his glass and said "and may God rest their souls."

The Judge was always so careful about what he said because he knew people viewed a Judge differently from most other people even though he wasn't a court room Judge.

He always took his position in society seriously and that also meant treading carefully when consuming alcohol. However, he had had so many conversations with Jeff over the course of the last eighteen months or so that he felt completely at ease with him. He then decided to be straightforward with Jeff, what the hell, he was retiring in a couple of years anyway and he knew big changes were coming.

"But," continued the Judge "Things have changed, changed a great deal since the Second World War…"

Jeff could see another customer getting ready to call him for a refill.

"Changed, in which way, what has changed that makes you think that there isn't a party that is worth voting for, is it something to do with the bombing?"

"No, not entirely, things were heading in the wrong direction for my liking well before the bombing." the Judge replied.

Jeff served the customer and returned to the Guinness tap to continue the conversation with the Judge.

"When you say things were heading in the wrong direction, what do you mean?" asked Jeff.

"Back in the day, most politicians did care, most of them genuinely did the best they could as our representatives, democracy was for the most part alive and well, could you top me up while you're here Jeff?"

"Coming up," replied Jeff who poured another Brandy for him. "There you go, so, as you were saying?"

"Yes, yes, where were we, right, politicians used to represent the voter, the taxpayer, as they were sworn to do but over time the emphasis gradually shifted away from what they are supposed to do to becoming representatives of those with money, huge sums of money."

"You mean corporations?" asked Jeff.

"Mostly, yes, corporations and what you may call the elite," answered the Judge.

"Elite?" Jeff replied.

"Yes, the ultra-wealthy families, the bankers, surely you've heard about these things Jeff?"

"Well yes, kind of," Jeff said hesitantly, "it's just that, that to hear it from someone like you, it's a bit of a surprise to be honest, I mean, people talk about this stuff but I don't think they really believe it."

"Well they should start believing it because it's true, many of our supposed representatives have long ago sold themselves out. They don't really believe in our systems either, they pay it lip service and they just take what they can get while the going is good."

"All of them?" asked Jeff.

"No, not all of them, but the majority for sure. It's all a game to them Jeff, all just theatre, most of our politicians, well the top ones, the cabinet ministers are in actuality some of the best actors on the planet and the better actor you are the further up the ladder you go," the Judge said nonchalantly.

"Actors," Jeff said. "Well that does make sense now you've said it."

"Think about it, TV cameras and microphones in your face, having to be ready with quick sound bites that can fit broadcast scheduling, failing to do that alone will sink your political career in a hurry. To be fair, an honest politician barely stands a chance and the sad truth is people are so conditioned to hearing the slick presentations and sound bites that they equate it with being a good representative. Just look at the US and how slick their politicians are, they have to be because the media, over the years, has distorted what a good representative or politician is. The image, the acting, the sound bites are what makes good news and over time the people have also bought into it just as they always do because the media teaches people how to think, sad but true Jeff, people have no idea how brainwashed they are from the media, especially the TV."

"So are you saying it's the media's fault?" Jeff asked.

"No not that it's the media's fault, the media has evolved in its own way into the monster it now is which has had an overall effect on just about everything including how our politicians behave in front of the cameras. It has become so important today for political leaders such as cabinet ministers to be really good actors, it's just the way it is today and I feel that because of this we may have been denied, let's say, better leadership."

The Judge was opening up now and Jeff was lapping it up, opportunities to hear the opinions of someone like the Judge were rare.

"Ok, so you are saying the media has changed politics to some degree Judge."

"Yes it has forced a different type of leadership on us, but that isn't the worst of our political problems."

"So, what is the worst of our political problems?"

"The problems, well, the voter feels so disenfranchised by today's politics, that nothing will change, that his or her vote doesn't make any difference, so they don't vote. The net effect of that is the politician can be ever more nonchalant which only serves to drive more voters away. It almost gives the politician more licence to do whatever they wish."

"But they have been doing that for a long time anyway, surely Judge, I mean people know only too well that political promises are broken so often that it's a farce."

"Yes true, but it only serves to exacerbate the problem and doesn't help in any way. But that isn't the worst problem. The worst problem we face is Globalisation, especially at the Federal level," the Judge said.

"Yes please!" cried another customer.

4 – The Wedding

Annie Jenkins and her two children Brandon and Sarah had been seated at their banquet hall table long enough for the novelty of the professionally decorated wedding reception hall to wear off despite Annie's best attempts at engaging the children in how nice things looked and how smartly dressed most people were.

"Where is he?" Annie asked herself, "he should have been here by now, the kids are getting bored."

"When is Daddy coming Mom?" Sarah asked, the third time in forty minutes.

"Like I said, he will get here as soon as he can Sarah – oh! hold it, there goes my phone, that must be him now."

Annie was correct, Mark had just called to say he was on his way. He had already been home and changed into his suit and would be there in about fifteen minutes.

"Thank God for that," Annie thought to herself. It wasn't that she couldn't cope with the kids, the kids were good really, just a little bored which is to be expected and they hadn't yet had the chance to meet other kids their own age at the reception.

It was just that Mark had been working long hours and she was really looking forward to letting her hair down with him, having a few drinks, some dancing, something they hadn't seemed to have done for a while now.

Money was tight these days and money for entertainment was sparse, so tonight was a very welcome relief.

"Daddy!" cried Sarah, as Mark navigated around nearby tables to reach their's.

"Hey Buttercup," cried Mark "You look gorgeous, you all look gorgeous."

Teenage boys may not appreciate being called gorgeous but Brandon knew what his dad meant.

Mark kissed Annie and Sarah, hugged Brandon then sat down to catch up on the day's events thus far.

Annie began telling Mark everything had gone to plan as she filled his glass with white wine from the bottles allocated to the table.

"Ok, that's you updated, how was your call?" Annie asked Mark.

"Nasty," Mark replied "double shooting, neither made it."

"Was it gang related or something?" Annie asked.

"No, it was a drug raid gone wrong, police broke down their front door and ended up shooting the husband and wife, the husband died immediately and we lost the wife en route to emergency."

"Oh my God, another one, what's going on with the cops these days, are they trigger happy or something, it never used to be like this, don't they train them properly these days?" Annie replied.

"Yeah it's getting out of hand, not just the shootings but the harassment, I always supported the police but they're way over the top now," Mark added.

"Ever since they brought in that bullshit anti-terror law after the bombing, things have gone downhill, I hardly recognize this country now," Annie cried.

"Yeah it's true Annie, things have changed in a big way since the bombing. I see it in the police more and more, the aggression, it's in your face."

"But why, why be like that with people who have nothing to do with terrorism?" asked Annie.

"And in today's case, people who were actually innocent," said Mark.

"Innocent!" Annie said in shock "They were innocent and were killed by the police?"

"Yep," Mark said slowly shaking his head in disgust, "wrong house again, the cops said they didn't raise their hands quick enough."

"And they shot them," said Annie closing her eyes, "that could have been us Mark, or anyone, Jesus are we safe or what, what is happening to our country?"

"If this would have happened three or four years ago there would have been an investigation, people would have been fired or disciplined or there would have at least been something to satisfy the public that it was a one off mistake, but not today, nothing will happen to the cops who murdered these people," Mark said in disdain.

"I really don't like how things are today Mark, it worries me, what kind of world are the kids growing up in?"

"I know, I know," Mark replied, "me neither, it's bad enough seeing what happened across the border, the way the US went after the Patriot Act, the police state, the TSA, Homeland Security, NDAA and all the spying on their own people, don't get me started."

"Yeah ok let's discuss this later, we've your old friend's wedding to enjoy and boy am I going to enjoy it!" Annie said with a big grin as she topped up both their wine glasses.

5 – The Cottagers

"Anyway, that's enough of my complaining, I think the kids are probably ready for lunch," Andrea said as she jumped up from her chair.

"I'll make the rolls," Rose said as she made her way inside the cottage to the kitchen.

"Great," Andrea replied, "and I'll make the drinks, coffee, tea, juice ladies?"

"Juice for me please," Natalie replied.

"Me too," said Rose.

Andrea called down to the children to begin making their way up to the cottage for lunch while Natalie waited on the deck for them to come. Rose had just finished making the last ham and cheese roll when the men showed up.

"Perfect timing," Rose said to them as they walked into the kitchen, "lunch is served."

"Awesome," Jerry responded, "cheese and ham rolls too, we should have these more at home Honey," Jerry said to Andrea.

"Yes Dear, you say that every time we come here," Andrea said with a wry grin.

"Then why don't you make them then?" Jerry said under his breath as he winked at Ron and Nick who were sitting down with a plate of rolls.

"Hey, I heard that!" Andrea scowled at Jerry as everyone else sniggered or smiled.

"You did?" Jerry said mockingly with a big cheesy grin.

"Here take some chips with you too," Andrea passed Jeff a medium sized plastic bowl full of regular chips.

"Chips, don't you mean 'flab flakes'?" said Rose.

"Flab flakes!" replied Natalie as she and Andrea laughed at the name. "Where did you get that name from? But hey you're not far wrong Natalie!" asked Andrea.

"A friend of mine, she's a bit of a health nut and calls them flab flakes. She says you may as well lick them and stick them straight onto your hips and thighs!"

Andrea and Rose looked at each other then Rose said. "I think your friend has a point, don't you agree Andrea?"

"Yes but I love the darn things, they're so yummy."

"Me too," offered Rose.

"I know, I know, but I only eat them on certain occasions like being up here at the cottage or parties. I don't even buy them for the kids or I would eat most of them myself," Natalie replied.

"Did you get everything guys?" Natalie asked the men.

"Yeah we got it all," Ron replied "busy today too, seems like everyone decided to come up this weekend."

"Didn't run out of beer though did they?" Rose said cheekily.

"Er, no, and they know better not to," Nick responded.

"Remember that time they did run out?" Andrea said.

"Don't remind us," Jerry said shaking his head, "it was horrible."

"Well we were ok though," Andrea said grinning "we had plenty of wine didn't we ladies?"

Rose and Natalie both nodded as they had just taken a bite of their food.

"Coming outside guys?" Jerry said to Ron and Nick.

The other two nodded and followed Jerry out to the deck, sat down and began eating. Jerry broke open a case of beer and handed one each to Ron and Nick, opened one for himself, took a big gulp and said, "Ron what's going on with the police these days?" Jerry asked Ron because he was a veteran Toronto police officer.

"What do you mean?" Ron said while chewing his food.

"In the city, in Toronto, the cops have such an attitude now," Jerry replied.

"It's a tough job at times Jerry, sometimes you have to be an asshole when you're dealing with the kind of people we have to deal with," Ron replied.

"We all know it's tough Ron and I was always the biggest supporter of Toronto's finest but sorry, I can't call them that anymore," Jerry said shaking his head slowly.

"I have to agree with Jerry," Nick chipped in.

"We've known you Ron for all these years and we're, well I'm sure you're a fair cop. I understand you sticking up for your own but c'mon, we're old buddies here, you must know what I mean," Jerry said.

Ron sat there looking slightly defeated and knew he couldn't keep up the facade much longer, not in front of such old buddies as Jerry and Nick.

"Yeah, I suppose I do guys, it's just that it's hard you know, hard to accept the force I love and served for the last 14 years is heading down a path I don't like...one bit, in fact there are many of us who feel the same way, veterans who have seen the changes, police officers proud to wear the uniform, proud to serve and protect. Now we are feeling more and more like a public enemy, people avoid us like the plague now, I used to love meeting and talking with the public, it felt so good, the job satisfaction, actually it wasn't like a job at all, I loved it."

"Understood," Jerry said, "didn't think or appreciate how it might affect you too, suppose it's natural for a genuine decent cop to feel that way."

"So what's it all about Ron?" Nick added, "what is the agenda, something is going on, someone is instigating all this bullcrap, for some unknown reason."

"Wish I had the answer Nick," Ron replied, "but all I know is for some strange reason we are instilling fear into people, for what purpose, at this time I have no idea."

"Why would anyone want to do that, to instill fear in the public, it's the public that pays their wages, what have they done to deserve that!" Nick said, obviously annoyed.

"And where does it all lead to?" Jerry added "there must be some kind of end game, an agenda of some kind."

"As I said guys, I don't know for sure and if you find out please let me know," Ron answered.

"Ron you said you don't know for sure, so you do have some kind of idea," said Jerry.

"Look guys I don't want to go messing up your heads with gossip, there's always a lot of gossip at the station and most of it is garbage so until I know for sure, there's nothing to say," replied Ron.

"Aha! not so fast Ron," Jerry replied, "we're not letting you off the hook that easily, this is me and Nick you're talking to here and we ain't taking that as an answer, you have an idea so let's hear it."

"Look guys, I'm not trying to avoid telling you it's just it may be bullcrap," Ron answered.

"Me and Jerry can be the judge of that and it won't go any further," Nick said to Ron.

"Look, I don't want to get into it because to be honest I don't really believe it myself," Ron replied "It's too wacky for me."

"Ok, just tell us what the talk is and we can make up our own minds," said Jerry.

"Ok, ok," Ron began, "Do you guys ever follow anything online or do you get all your news and information from the mainstream media, the newspapers, TV etc?"

"Are you kidding?" Jerry replied, "mainstream media is owned by a handful of corporations that are all in it together, we don't get real news, I know it's all controlled propaganda, Andrea feels the same way too."

"Me neither," added Nick, "stopped watching TV a couple of years ago, it's all garbage, I get my info online, found some websites I like, get to learn about a ton of things you'll never see on TV or in the newspapers, even though the powers that be are gradually censoring the net and removing websites deemed radical or too critical of the government."

"Oh ok, good, I didn't realise," Ron sighed, "this will make it easier then because you are probably more awake and aware than most."

"Things started to change a couple of years ago when the police in the US were really getting militarized, you know, when the US Army gave armoured vehicles to the police, even in small towns. Even then we all looked paramilitary and for no other reason than to scare people in my opinion."

"Yeah, noticed that in a hurry," Nick said.

"Me too, I think that was when it all seemed to change," Jerry added.

"It did," Ron said, "felt good at first all geared up but then it hit me, what the hell are we doing, we don't need all this, this is Canada."

"Agreed," said Nick as Jerry nodded in agreement.

"Well, talk among some of the guys, nothing official though, just talk, well, you know how it seems like we are losing more and more rights and freedoms, new laws coming at us every week, control of the Internet, banning protests and all that?" said Ron.

"Well, yeah, but I think we all know about that," Jerry added.

"Ok then get used to it because we are on a one way trip," Ron said.

"One way trip?" Nick asked.

"Yes," Ron said, "have you ever heard of the long term goal of the UN, what North America is supposedly going to look like, how it will be?"

"Is this something to do with Agenda twenty something or other?" Jerry asked Ron.

"Bingo!" Ron replied, "you surprise me Jerry, how much about UN Agenda 21 do you know?"

"I read about it online and seen a couple of videos too I think, but that was a while ago," Jerry answered.

"I have heard the term before but never paid much attention to it," Nick added.

Ron continued, "There are videos explaining what it's all about and how things will look in the future and it isn't pretty. Basically they want to herd almost everyone into cities, have people living in tiny apartments in high rises."

"Why?" Nick asked.

"They call it sustainability, they want us all away from nature, from wetlands and watersheds, we will be confined to cities, crammed in tiny apartments like sardines," Ron continued "they want to control all our food and water, there is a document called Codex Aliment... something, I can't recall the name but it spells out how our food will be controlled."

"So the police are becoming more and more paramilitary and aggressive because of this?" Nick asked.

"I don't know Nick, I'm not sure, I could be completely wrong but that's the talk among the guys and some of them have contacts, friends and family that kind of back some of it up, or so they claim," Ron offered.

"Don't tell me this is all part of the One World Order or whatever they call it?" Nick said.

"Maybe, as I said, I don't know for sure," Ron added, "but ever since the bombing things have definitely gone from bad to worse, I really don't enjoy it anymore, in fact it crossed my mind to get out."

"Wow!" Nick said in surprise, "never thought I would hear you say that, things must be getting bad then."

"So the hiring of thugs in the police and the aggression is to do with this?" Jerry asked Ron. "As I said, I don't know for sure but if that was going to happen then it would be far easier to control people, to move them and everything. If they fear you it's.....easier," Ron said dropping his head and speaking low.

"I don't think you're far off," Jerry said.

"There is also talk about the collapse of the dollar," Ron added.

"Yeah we've all been hearing about that, well, those of us who get their news online, as far as the mainstream media goes everything is just fine," said Jerry.

"And there's always the threat of World War Three breaking out in the Middle East or Russia. Something is going to give sooner rather than later, and we know how bad things are in the US, they are pretty much a dictatorship now and who could have ever predicted that a few short years ago?" Ron said.

"Yeah, hear ya Ron, so if that's the case then the cops are getting ready for rioting, looting and all that fun," Nick said

"I believe that is very likely to happen but I don't believe that is the only reason the police would go rogue like they are, there must be more to it all," Jerry replied.

"Yeah, I agree," said Nick.

"Ok, changing the subject just a little, talking about the dollar collapsing, the way things have been going, the control, the laws, the loss of freedoms especially since the bombing and the draconian terror laws they brought in which to me seems a little too convenient, are you guys as pissed off as me with what is going on, how we are being ripped off and everything, the bank bail-ins, the corruption, the corporations owning the politicians and calling the shots?" Jerry said.

"Of course Jerry," Ron said, "it's ridiculous, but people are so busy trying to work and pay bills they don't see what is going on."

"I think that's changing though," Nick added "after the latest round of censoring of the Internet so many people made noise, I think it hit a nerve and people are beginning to get ticked."

"Yeah who would have thought that they would have done that, censor most of the internet, I mean c'mon wake the hell up people, what does that tell ya, history freakin repeating itself or what. Are people that dumb they think the things that happened in the past can't happen again? Ask the people in Pakistan and Yemen, hell even Iraq if they think the good ol' US of A is a civil nation and that goes for Canada and the likes of the UK," Jerry's passion was rising, "sorry guys but folk must have their heads buried so deep in the sand they can't see their own country being stolen from them in front of their own eyes."

"Doesn't surprise me at all," Ron said, "and they will keep at it until we are like China, with a totally censored and controlled Internet which means the end to free information flow and as we already know the mainstream media is basically involved with it all so our chance to organize any form of opposition in any way is over."

"Holy shit," spat Nick, "we have to do something, we have to fight this or we are finished."

"I don't know about that!" Ron replied

"I like your attitude Ron but what makes you say that?" Nick said.

"The collapse of the US dollar is highly likely, ten years ago we wouldn't have dreamed this could ever be possible and now we are talking about it like it's a done deal," Ron said shaking his head slowly in disbelief. "When the collapse happens or something like a food shortage happens, that will be the opportunity we need, the opportunity to take back control of the country," Ron said.

"You are almost saying the collapse will be a good thing Ron," Jerry said.

"I think common sense will tell you it will get ugly, real ugly and real quick too and it will take some time to recover from it, for sanity to prevail, but long term if we can get together we can rebirth the country with a new system which works for the people," Ron said.

"I'm impressed with that little speech Ron, where did you get that from, those ideas, you were never the activist type?" Jerry asked.

"Have you heard of 'the book'?" Ron replied.

"'The book'?" Jerry and Nick both spoke together.

"Yes, 'the book', it's all in 'the book', the book that's been making the rounds online," Ron answered.

"What book is this, not the Bible, you're not religious Ron?"

Smiling, Ron replied, "No not the Bible, it's..."

"Guys there's more rolls here if you're still hungry," Andrea called from the kitchen window.

"Ok Honey we're coming in," replied Jerry and the men went back inside to finish lunch.

6 – The Judge

Jeff was in his element and served the customers hurriedly so he could spend as much time with the Judge as possible.

"Globalism, so how does that affect our leadership?" Jeff asked.

"The astounding power of the globalists, some things have gone downhill politically in line with the globalists increase in power."

"In which way do you mean, how has globalism affected leadership?" asked Jeff.

"You have to understand how a leader, be that a President or a Prime Minister, is really a short term figurehead while the globalists, the corporations and central bankers have been around a lot longer. They play a long slow waiting game so that most people can't see what is going on around them and in that time many leaders come and go."

"Ok," Jeff said, "and what effect does that have on leadership."

Jeff had a higher than average understanding of politics due to a healthy interest but he couldn't work out where the Judge was going with this, the globalist angle.

"As I said earlier Jeff it's the overwhelming power of the

globalists and when they want something they get it. No-one stands in their way, no-one can stand in their way because they are so powerful."

"So the leaders of countries cannot stand up for themselves or their country because of the power of the globalists?" said Jeff.

"Correct and even worse, in many cases the.......no I've said too much already Jeff, I don't want to be the one to introduce you to things you don't really need to know and are probably better off not knowing," the Judge knew it was too late, the Brandy had loosened his lips way too much for his liking but the horse had left the stable, no point trying to close the stable door now.

A somewhat taken aback Jeff said, "no, it's fine Judge, I can handle anything you say, I'm a big boy now."

The judge replied, "Of course you are, but you must understand that the vast majority of people would have their…. bubble burst if they learned what really goes on around them and how things really work."

"Sure I understand but like I said, I can handle it Judge, so please continue what you were saying," Jeff said earnestly.

"Ok, where was I….?" the Judge asked.

"You were saying that the globalists are very powerful, it affects leadership…"

"Right, right," the Judge had recalled his train of thought, "I was saying that the globalists are so powerful that the actual leadership is chosen by them!"

"They choose the leaders, like our Prime Minister or, no, not the US President, no way?"

"See Jeff, that's why I didn't want to talk about that, bit of a shocker isn't it?"

"Yeah, are you sure about that?" Jeff asked the Judge, not that he didn't believe him but this was something Jeff had never considered.

"As I said, things are not how they appear. Now your eyes are opened to that, you may want to search out that information online and learn what you can, before it all disappears due to censorship."

"But isn't the Internet just full of baloney?"

"It's full of everything Jeff, just need to learn how to discern and use your internal BS meter, and you probably won't find answers anywhere else, certainly not in the mainstream media, they only tell you what they are allowed to tell you."

"But we have a free press, we are a free country Judge, why don't we read about the power of the globalists?"

"You will," replied the Judge, "but not to the extent of the control they have over things such as governments."

"Why is that then?" Jeff asked. "Because the same globalist network or club or cabal if you like, own the media Jeff which is how the news is so controlled. We in the West naively think that we have a free press, free as in open and truthful reporting, investigative journalists keeping watch for our nation's best interests. That was how it used to be before globalist power structures bought up the media."

"Jeez, I would never have thought that could be possible.....I see now what you mean about having your bubble burst!" Jeff said in disgust.

7 – The Wedding

Mark Jenkins was thoroughly enjoying himself at his long-time friend James Young's wedding. He could relax now after a trying day at work and couldn't wait to let his hair down with Annie between the dance floor and the bar.

Mark was also waiting for the right moment to congratulate his newly wed friend but as often happens the man of the moment seemed forever in conversation with everyone else.

Mark asked Annie if she wanted something from the bar and told her he would also try and congratulate James.

At the bar Mark ordered two light beers, he and Annie were thinking alike, they both knew they would become thirsty from dancing but also wanted to remember the evening.

"Mark buddy!" James had just excused himself and broke away from a group conversation when he saw Mark at the bar.

"Congrats man," Mark said from the bottom of his heart as he and James embraced in a vice like hug.

"Thanks Mark, so glad you could make it, I didn't see you at the church and thought you weren't coming," James said.

"Yeah, apologies James," Mark said as they let go and faced each other, "I'm really sorry pal but I couldn't get out of a call, you know how it is sometimes in my line of work."

"Of course bud, of course," James replied, "but I was so glad to see you here in the hall, just wouldn't be the same without you, it means so much."

"Thanks, at times my job can really suck!"

"You couldn't get off on a Saturday then Mark?" said James.

"I had booked the day off of course, but they were short-handed and a big emergency happened today which meant I was obligated to go in."

"Oh what was that, a pile up on the highway or something?" James asked.

"No, I don't know if you heard about the shooting incident in Toronto, no of course, you wouldn't, you were getting ready for your big day," Mark corrected himself.

"No I haven't heard anything except wedding talk today," James said with a big smile.

"And rightfully so," Mark continued, "it was a police raid gone wrong, they shot and killed a man and his wife."

"Again!" James said visibly annoyed, "how many more times are they going to do that, something must be done this time, it's getting out of hand."

"I agree James," Mark said, "Canada is becoming more and more like the US, I am hearing talk of censorship now, the Internet, books, videos, how the hell can they justify that?"

"I know Mark, I'm hearing it too, the government says it's all for our own protection, the bombing is the excuse," James answered.

"Bullshit!" Mark spat, "that's all just a bloody excuse to clamp down on us and control everything, same as the Patriot Act after 911 and the laws they brought in in the UK after their subway bombings. If it didn't sound so insane you'd almost think it was done purposely, but for what? Why would the governments want us all locked down and everything controlled I

31

really don't understand it James, it baffles me."

"Yeah, well, it depends on what you know and where you get your info from but all that matters is the US and UK as well as some of the European countries have almost become dictatorships. I don't care what the reason is, I don't waste my time with all the theories Mark, I just want to stop it happening in Canada and make sure it can never happen in the future."

"Well said," Mark added, "I'm on the same page as are other people I know, they can see how they took over stealthily in the US, how the masses never saw it coming even though the alternative news outlets were screaming about it all along."

"Yes, one of the strangest things I've ever witnessed, the tyranny in the US and the UK for that matter. I would never have dreamed it could ever happen to countries like those. It was becoming so obvious, all the signs were there Mark."

"Yes I know, I watched it unfold too and whenever anyone tried saying the US or UK were going down the exact same path as Nazi Germany they were called nut jobs!"

"I know, I know," James continued, "the burning of the Reichstag, the twisting of laws to suit Hitler's objectives, the locking up or eradication of undesirables, political opponents and activists, the confiscation of guns, it's like deja vu," said James.

"Why couldn't people see it coming James, that's what gets me?" Mark asked.

"Most people only get their news from the mainstream media which is controlled by the same globalists so they won't ever learn of the things that are happening until it's too late, plus I think people just refuse to accept or believe that their own government would ever do such a thing," James answered.

"Too incredible to believe I suppose," Mark added.

"Yes that's about what I'm thinking too," James said.

"The issue now is what are we going to do because having seen what happened to those countries, we are heading the same way, same laws, same controls."

"Well yes we are, but more people than you may realise have also noted these things and between you and me there is a kind of underground movement going on, people, some in high places who value the country and people more than their 'masters' are planning a counter measure."

"Are you serious James?" Mark asked in astonishment.

"Yes but keep this to yourself, you know I am a consultant weapons trainer for the Canadian Military after I retired from the Army. Well that takes me to most military bases in Canada and some overseas bases. I get to mix with the officers and many are now good friends. They ain't happy Mark, they ain't ready to sit back and let globalists or whoever take over our country like they did to others."

"What does that mean James, a military coup or something?" Mark asked.

"Not a coup exactly, more of a protection against tyranny, a pro-active liberation."

"Ok but how would that work? I think I like the sound of the military stepping in and saving us from tyranny but what stops the military from becoming a Junta like we have seen happening for decades in third world countries?" Mark asked.

"Fair question Mark but the military people I know have no wish to run the country permanently, however, I do know they want to help ensure that what is happening now politically can never happen again."

"What do you mean by 'politically'?" Mark asked.

"The political systems we have had in place for hundreds of years are outdated, it was because of them that we find ourselves heading down the path we are on right now, it mustn't be allowed to happen ever again."

"Hold it, so what kind of system are they wanting to replace it with. How can we guarantee it isn't as bad as tyranny?" Mark said.

"I don't know if you have heard about an idea that's been

making the rounds for a while now, they call it.."

"'The book'?" Mark interjected.

"Yes, yes, 'the book'," James said enthusiastically, "have you read it Mark?"

"No not yet but I mean to, and after this conversation I will make sure I do ASAP. So 'the book' is that effective that the Military want to back the use of its ideas."

"Careful Mark, not the Military, the entire Military, just those who are extremely concerned with what is happening. It's an underground movement Mark, if it gets out what they are planning they could be in serious trouble. You will not have heard about it but the government has already fired two Generals and some other officers with the threat of imprisonment if they talk about any of it."

"Holy moly!" said Mark, "I had no idea all this has been going on, kinda makes me feel proud that Canadians, patriots, are ready to protect our country."

"Yeah me too but remember to keep it under your hat ok. You never heard it from me."

"Sure thing, but what bothers me is if the globalists managed to take control over the US and UK then how can our Military expect to hold them off, what's different?"

"It's tricky, the tyranny encroaches under the radar so to speak, it's stealthy and gradual so it isn't easy picking the moment. The moment must be chosen exactly right because they need the people on their side, they require their full backing or it will fail outright," James replied.

"That makes sense, my God this is going to be nerve wracking James."

"Yes but there is one other thing that would work too and would make things much easier."

"What's that?" Mark asked.

"The US dollar may collapse anytime soon and then be devalued and if that happens the country will be in turmoil. The

Military will be needed to impose martial law due to the rioting and lawlessness when people have no food and water.."

"And then they can step in and pave the way for a new system," Mark interjected.

"Bingo!" said James "that is what we are really hoping for."

"What kind of system are we talking about anyway?"

"Read 'the book' Mark the basics are all there, they actually make sense but they don't make sense if you haven't read 'the book'. Just read it, you'll see."

"Why's that?" Mark asked, "you've intrigued me".

"In a nutshell, we have all been raised in our various western societies since childhood through school and from our parents to believe that the systems we have are the best! We are kind of brainwashed to believe that this is the only way, the systems we know, the institutions we have grown up within, it becomes us, it is ingrained in our very psyches.
So, we can only comprehend things from that thought level, from this paradigm. The ideas will not make much sense when evaluated from your present beliefs," James asked Mark, "you can touch your toes Mark can't you?"

"Of course," Mark replied, he was a fit guy.

"Go on then show me, touch your toes."

"What now?" Mark replied in surprise.

"Yes touch them now, please."

Mark leaned over with legs straight and bent down and touched his toes "Like that?" Mark asked James as he straightened back up.

"Exactly, see Mark if I had asked a young child to do that he or she would have simply crouched down and touched their toes but you didn't, you assumed I meant touch your toes like you would for a doctor. See what I mean, it's programming, it's front and centre, it's a part of us just like our thought processes for the systems and institutions we were raised within, it's almost impossible to think outside the box voluntarily, unless you re-educate yourself or evolve past it."

"I get it, that was a neat example, so what, does 'the book' change your beliefs or something, how can it change that?"

"Read it, you'll see," James said.

8 – The Cottagers

The men stepped back inside the cottage and grabbed the last of the cheese and ham rolls, went back outside, sat down and continued eating.

"You got me thinking there Ron," said Nick, "I think I have heard something about a book but didn't take much notice cos I'm not really a book reader as you guys know."

"You guys really should read it, it changes your ideas about how things should be, you know, how the country should be run and all. It really opens your eyes, well it did mine and I know it has for lots of folk."

"What's it all about, politics?" Jerry asked Ron, "cos I'm done with those a-holes.."

"Yeah, politics, finance, banking, all the things which affects every one of us," Ron replied.

"Then I'm not reading that book," Nick said, "can't stand all that stuff, it's all garbage in my opinion, don't even bother to vote anymore, no point, they lie about everything anyway."

"No argument from me there," Ron replied, "but that's why you should read it Nick, it's only about thirty pages or so, you can read it in an hour or two and it isn't full of big words and things we can't understand, it's written in a way that anyone can recognize and understand."

"Trying to sell me on it are ya?" Nick said to Ron.

"No Nick, not at all, but it's something everyone should read, it has new ideas, fresh ideas no-one has heard of before, ideas that can change the 'garbage' as you call it."

"If it's so short then just tell us about it now," Jerry said to Ron.

"It doesn't work as well when you try and tell someone, much more effective when you read it yourself. The guy who wrote it said the same thing but after reading it I tried telling people about it and he's right, people don't get it unless they read it," replied Ron.

"I'm sure me and Jerry would get it, wouldn't we Jerry?"

"Sure we would Ron, c'mon tell us about it," Jerry added.

"Not going to waste my time guys sorry, I'll give you both a copy as it's getting harder and harder to come by."

Jerry and Nick knew when Ron meant what he said so they didn't pursue it any further.

"Ok Ron, if you won't tell us about 'the book', can you tell us why we should read it, why did you even bring it up?"

"Sure, I'll give you a quick rundown ok. There are many of us who don't like where the country is heading, we are going down the same road as the US and in a hurry and fortunately there are many who are waking up and seeing what is happening. Under the excuse of protecting people, the government has all but taken away our rights to privacy, we as police are almost a law unto ourselves and it's wrong.

"Take the protests in Toronto for example, we send undercover officers in among the crowds to smash windows and torch cars to make it look like it was the genuine protesters, then the police wade in and beat up innocent people and jail them, this is not the Canada we want to live in, we want our nation back and since 'the book' made the rounds it has given us some real hope.

"The ideas are completely different, ideas that make sense unlike the political nonsense we have been dealing with for most of our lives. We know now that we have a chance to have our country back and keep it the way we the people want it," Ron explained.

"And you got this from 'the book'?" Jerry asked.

"The ideas, yes, we have come to a realisation that one way or another, things will never be the same again. The Canada we know or knew is gone for good, we are either going to end up as a dictatorship within a One World Government or we take control and implement a new system, a system that will be much better than anything we have ever known."

"Phew, that sounds bitter sweet Ron," Nick said, "what a choice, heaven or hell, I know which I want and it ain't no dictatorship."

"Same here," Jerry added, "but how in hell are we going to stop the tyranny in its tracks and change the entire system, they won't allow that Ron?"

"It won't be up to them, it's up to us, the people, which is why we want as many people as possible to read 'the book' because once they have they will understand the power we have. The government doesn't have any real power, it's only an implied power which is given to them by the people but it works so well for them. But once a certain percentage of people understand it is they who actually have the power, then the government will be finished and the tyranny along with it.

"And another thing guys, the way things are going we won't have any money left for pensions, we won't be retiring, period.

"The system worked for a few years, some lucky folk retired with everything paid for and a good pension to live on in comfort. But the middle class is fast disappearing along with the manufacturing the globalists stole from us and you both surely know how dire the predictions are for the future, no pensions, no nothing, same across the western world, most countries are bankrupt now, so no matter what we think, major, major changes are coming, they have to because we cannot sustain ourselves at this rate.

"So, if we have to make major changes then hell, let's make changes that damn well work for us this time."

"Wow Ron, you are good! You should run for office or something, you have me convinced," Nick said as he raised his beer to Ron.

"Yeah right," Ron replied, "I'm getting you both a copy of 'the book' so read it pronto and let's get together at the bar so we can discuss it ok?"

"Ok, sounds good to me," Jerry replied.

"Me too, you won me over Ron, I'll read it too, you've got me interested in this now," Nick added.

9 – The Judge

"The media is one of the most powerful things in our lives, it shapes much of what we think, how we act, what we wear, the list goes on," the Judge continued, "so, having control of the media is to wield extraordinary power, the power to control what people learn and control what you do not want them to learn."

"If that's true.....man are we in trouble," said Jeff.

"Oh it's true Jeff and once you find your own trusted sources of real news online you will see immediately how much misinformation is sold to the public. For example have you heard of the Bilderberg Group?"

"If that's the group of business leaders that get together every now and then, then yes," answered Jeff.

"Ok good, now, if there were ever a news worthy event, an event which forges the directions of our governments, our planet and our lives, an event which shapes our futures and affects us all in some way, then this event would be the one. But it never made the mainstream news until recently after the alternative media did the job that mainstream media investigative journalism should have done, and even then it only gets a few lines.

"The Bilderbergers consist of the most powerful people in

the world including royalty, cabinet ministers, central bankers, trans-national corporation bosses and media owners. These people direct governments on how they expect policies to take shape, how they want the world to be, it was they who instigated the European Union and look how that has turned out, yes, several of the countries who threw away sovereignty to join the EU are now in huge debt and are being run by central bankers, how convenient, do you see how that works now? Allow nations to become virtually bankrupt then lend them bail out money on the condition they are basically run by the bankers, this was not a mistake but part of a much larger plan."

"My God Judge, I could listen to this all night, so you think the European bankruptcies and bailouts are by design?"

"Jeff, while you are checking out these things you will also hopefully find some speeches by US Presidents long gone that spell this out, just search 'presidents speeches about bankers' or something along those lines, then take a look at the world today and connect the dots."

"I will Judge, I will," Jeff replied.

"So, a highly significant news worthy event is kept out of the media, what does that tell you about media control? Didn't you say you went to the recent march against poverty Jeff and there were hundreds of other cities around the world also holding marches? But hardly any of it made the mainstream news?"

"Yes that's right, we were expecting to see it in the newspapers and on the TV but there was nothing really. Well now you've explained it that way it tells me the media can be controlled and I never thought that would be possible, in Canada I mean, I know they control the media in other countries that are more like dictatorships, but never in this country," Jeff answered.

"But that is exactly what is happening, there are really only a few corporations and people that run the entire world. They are so powerful that they own most politicians. In fact you could say that governments are merely agents of the corporations Jeff."

"Ok you have shattered my bubble now Judge, I would never have thought it was that bad, politicians or government being agents of corporations, but now you've said it, it actually makes some sense, it answers a lot of questions about why our leaders make some of the decisions they do. You know what I mean, the Prime Minister or one of his ministers keeps telling us a certain deal is great for us and we know damn well it's BS, yes that does answer some things Judge."

"Good, you sound like you understand. So picture this, the governments of two or more countries are in negotiations about trade and certain rights to do with industry and commerce, visitor visas, certain restrictions, that sort of thing.

"So, a powerful nation such as the US wants certain things, concessions from another country as part of a package of bargains but those favours are not for the American people, no, most of them are on behalf of the corporations, corporations incidentally that are transnational and have no allegiance to any country. Let's say Monsanto wants to sell its GMO seeds to a certain country, but that country knows its people will reject the idea. The US government being corrupt agents for Monsanto among others, use very persuasive arguments for that country to accept the seeds, the request will be part of an overall package which would also likely include some kind of financial aid or debt dismissal, the leadership of that country now has to sell the GMO seeds idea to its people knowing well they are not representing their people honestly."

"Ah so that is how globalism can effect leadership," Jeff thought aloud, "because the governments are agents for the corporations and leverage their own country's bargaining power..."

"And influence," the Judge added.

"Yes and influence to push the corporation's agendas," Jeff

whistled in realisation.

"Good man," said the Judge, "you now understand a very powerful piece of the puzzle, how leadership is affected by globalism. That is what I meant about the power of the globalists and how they can now use governments as their agents, their front men, their sales people in effect."

Jeff let the Judge's words sink in and the natural first instincts of fear crept into his mind, the initial feelings of helplessness which usually accompanied such revelations. Jeff felt an emptiness that he had never felt before, like he had been deserted, that everything he thought was real was now fake.

Yes, like most people he was skeptical about the government, he knew they lied about things but very little was perfect in this world and the system was as fair as it could be in the big picture wasn't it?

"So is that it Judge, the corporations have taken over and there's nothing we can do?"

"The central bankers too Jeff, don't forget about them, but to answer your question, yes, the good news is, there is hope."

"How, I mean what can we do, what hope could there be, isn't it too late?" Jeff asked.

"Not too long ago I may well have said the situation was hopeless," the Judge continued, "but I'm very glad to say I believe there is hope, real hope Jeff."

"A revolution?" said Jeff.

"No not a revolution, that wouldn't change anything."

"Why's that?" interrupted Jeff.

"Well, let's say that there was a revolution, hundreds of thousands of people marched to Parliament Hill and demanded the government stand down, then what, what would they do after that?"

"Form a new government or something?" Jeff said.

"But that wouldn't solve anything in the long run," the Judge replied "there is nothing to stop the same things from happening all over again, nothing to guarantee that the bankers and corporations would not be able to muscle their way back into control."

"Ok, I didn't think of that, so what could we do, what is the hope you spoke of Judge?" Jeff asked.

"We need a new way, a new system Jeff, I didn't think it possible, actually I never even gave it thought, another product of our environment like everyone else, almost impossible to think of a different way that hasn't been thought of before, that's how brainwashed we all are, but the present system must go as we can now see where it leads us."

"What new system Judge, communism or something, no, that isn't new, you said a new system?"

"Have you heard of 'the book' Jeff"?" the Judge asked.

CHAPTER 2

10 – The Global Situation

The western world is in a mode of great change. Not a naturally evolving change from the influences of such things as; technology, knowledge or science but forced change, coerced change.

The US, UK, Australia and several other western nations, nations that for many decades enjoyed guaranteed levels of rights and freedoms are now verging on dictatorships.

The majority didn't see it coming, people laughed at suggestions that their countries were heading down that path and ridiculed those who tried sounding the alarm bells. They simply didn't believe and couldn't conceive that what had happened to Nazi Germany could happen to them, no way, that was a long time ago, we are much smarter and far more sophisticated now and our politicians wouldn't allow that to happen.

Anyway, why would they want to do such a thing? Our country is a great place to live, everyone is to a degree free, as free as one can be within a society of millions of people so why would anyone desire the end of that, what possible reason could there be to ruin a well-orchestrated society that took generations to build?

Standards of living were the best they had ever been, well,

they were a few years earlier, then they did decline and decline rather rapidly too.

Income for a large section of the working population failed to keep pace with the ever rising cost of living. Manufacturing was all but lost to Asian nations and the middle classes were decimated.

Many European countries fell prey to the lending practices of the central banks and became either bankrupt or were in severe financial difficulty. Austerity measures forced on these nations by the bankers only served to worsen the plight of the people.

The bankers persistent lobbying of western politicians paid off and banking regulations were gradually removed allowing them the freedom to use their huge financial resources to run riot on the financial markets.

Their greed knew no bounds and as they invented new methods of making money, money which didn't actually exist, the bubble grew and grew until it finally, predictably, collapsed.

To make matters much, much worse for the people, the taxpayers were told by those they had elected that the banks were too big to fail and had to be bailed out by the people which robbed the nation's resources and wealth that had been honestly laboured for.

No sooner than they had received vast sums of taxpayer money, to rub salt in the wounds of the over-burdened taxpayer, the bankers were awarding themselves obscene bonus payments.

If the people had not been so complacent, had this been France in 1848, a revolution may well have occurred.

Never before had this happened. Bailing out banks that through their own fault, through their own pure greed, had landed them and more importantly, the people, in enormous debt. This was beyond capitalism, this was direct theft from the people.

The power of the bankers could now be plainly seen by all. They did not flinch at the debt they created, they had no concerns about the undue strain and hardship they had foisted on the working people.

It was now clear, that along with the mega-corporations, they owned the politicians in every nation, fascism was now firmly in place.

The world really did become run by the bankers and corporations, much of which was ultimately controlled by long time generational families, the 'elites' as some would refer to them. No longer did most western governments run their nations, they had been reduced to taking their orders from corporations and bankers on behalf of the elites. What else would any sane person expect when politicians are allowed to be bribed and lobbied by such powerful interests.

11 –The United States

Of course, the noticeable changes in people's lives began after September 11th, 2001 when the commercial airliners were hijacked and New York and the Pentagon were attacked. It all made complete sense at that time, the Patriot Act, the loss of some rights and freedoms for a safer country.

But it didn't stop there, the rights of Americans were gradually rescinded as intrusions into privacy increased. The NSA were exposed for recording every conversation made by phone and for storing all texts and emails. If you have nothing to hide then there's nothing to worry about, they used to say. Then they used past information against people, it was child's play, anyone criticizing the government, state or politicians in any way were quickly arrested on charges trumped up from past conversations which were fed into software which could re-arrange your words into whatever crime they wished it to fit. Technology is wonderful and helped send many innocent people to the FEMA camps for an extended stay until you were 'in agreement with everything about the state'. You would never again criticize the state or anything to do with it, technology is wonderful, amazing how you could go in as an activist and come out a fervent supporter of everything you fought against, how did they do that?

The various police forces throughout the country looked increasingly like special forces soldiers as they equipped themselves with armoured vehicles and battle-zone type dress. Police recruitment focused on the more aggressive personalities and lower IQ's. Constitution free zones were in force which denied people's basic rights, initially within one hundred miles from any border or coastline, but soon became nationwide. Privacy was just a memory, for everywhere people went they were being watched, listened to and monitored. Technology that could sense everything you wore, your temperature, your mood and listened to everything you whispered was installed in street lights, mall lights, parking lot lights and public toilets, there were hardly any places unmonitored. Drones monitored everything and made the first kill of an American citizen on US soil, soon after which, drone kills on US soil became commonplace, but still the majority of people did nothing.

People had to carry identification cards at all times or they would never make it past the thousands of checkpoints. The police and military were allowed to stop and search anyone for no obvious reason and the TSA (Transportation Security Administration) harassed travellers at bus and rail depots as well as at airports. FEMA camps had been previously built in every state and could hold many thousands of people, and had begun to do so.

Over time, Republican and Democrat Presidents gave themselves more and more powers by awarding themselves increasing executive authority. The NDAA was a game changer as it allowed the Military to detain indefinitely, without trial and to execute an American citizen. And still the people did nothing. Abuses of power became the norm. Fear was the 'order of the day', it worked so well, a buzz cut cop, TSA, Homeland security, border guard or any other thug in battle-zone dress, armed to the teeth barking orders always got their way and it got worse, quickly. It started with abuses of power such as over aggression in searches and arrests, then it sank from strip searches to sexual assault then by using fear of arrest and jail, rape became common. Those in charge of the various forces and security services turned a blind eye and some actively encouraged it because it amped up the fear factor and made them feel like demi-gods, they became so feared that no-one dare report them or challenge them.

How could this have happened to a people who had known freedom just a few short years before? Everything was in place to detect, detain, incarcerate or exterminate a terrorist and no-one complained because they felt safe, those laws were for foreigners not us, for terrorists not Americans, until, they gradually redefined the description of a terrorist. At first they called it 'soft' terrorism which applied to those such as anti-government activists especially war veterans, they went hard after those they feared would be the most effective, who could inflict the most damage in turning people against the oppressors and people respected veterans.

They also had a big thing against those who stored food, water and other essentials in preparation for a shortage, seems they don't want anyone being able to look after themselves, they wanted everyone dependent on the State and didn't want anyone giving others ideas of how to be independent. The term 'terrorist' for American citizens was gradually introduced into the American psyche by Senators, Congress men and women and the mainstream media. New terms such as eco-terrorist for those who protested against corporate destruction of the environment and domestic terrorist for those who questioned the government. What had only a few years earlier been fully accepted as free speech was now a terrorist threat according to politicians and the police. People realised they had better be careful about what they said or texted on their phones or what they wrote in emails for fear of being branded a terrorist and 'disappearing' as had been reported in the mainstream media.

Looking back only a few years it seemed impossible this could happen to the USA but fear had crept in stealthily and people began slowly changing their social habits and more tellingly, what they communicated.

For years the government had tried unsuccessfully to ban gun ownership but to many Americans this was a constitutional right they would not cede and would die fighting for. As unemployment and poverty increased, millions were using food stamps and homelessness became epidemic as those who were laid off and fell a little behind in their mortgage payments were evicted. Police shooting of unarmed people became commonplace and the killers were never prosecuted. People were being shot and killed or injured from situations such as police SWAT house raids for minor infractions and overzealous arrests for things such as refusing to give a name.

The dire economic situation in the US coupled with the ongoing police brutality made the nation a powder keg just waiting for a spark to set it all off. In Washington DC of all places, the 'spark' happened, the ignition source for the powder keg, a black man shot in the back fleeing from a police checkpoint, set off a series of riots. Fires blazed in several cities, entire streets were engulfed in flames and they resembled hell itself. Entire shopping malls and plazas once stripped bare of all useful goods were torched.

What purpose that served, one can only guess. Mindless vandalism, hormones, anger, the decades and generations of racial tensions, being raised in ghettos, the endless feeling of there being no hope? Regardless, this was the catalyst the government needed to implement martial law as the rampant looting and rioting could not be contained by the police. The Military were now the authority in every city and larger towns. Many by this time believed the government had purposely created the food shortage to enable the enacting of martial law.

The President had postponed elections and made herself

the supreme authority with all decisions being made at the White House. The Senate and Congress were suspended until further notice and any anti-government speech or action was swiftly dealt with under the domestic terrorism laws. It was now quite apparent that the laws were really introduced for this day and had little or nothing to do with genuine terrorism. A couple of years earlier the government had tried confiscating guns by using a United Nations mandate for global gun confiscation. The UN had equipment, foreign troops and even tanks and were trained to go door to door to confiscate people's guns but the ensuing uproar was completely miscalculated by the US government and a revolution almost erupted.The government knew then the only way to remove the guns was after martial law was in effect.

However, after martial law was imposed, the American people were told to voluntarily hand in all of their guns and weapons including bows and crossbows. They had six weeks to do so and those who did not and were discovered were arrested and detained by the Military as a terrorist. Many would not give up their guns as they had pledged citing their right to defend against tyranny as put forth in their constitution. In some areas there were those who headed for the hills but not all could evade the drones which could count the hairs on the back of a hand from 5 miles away, at midnight, and liquidate the person they were attached to.

Martial law decreed that no-one could leave their home vicinity without permission, they did so on the threat of incarceration. This mainly applied to the larger towns and cities as there were too many isolated areas to monitor until better technology would be available. The known weapon owners who did not voluntarily bring their weapons to the local police or military after the grace period were arrested and detained but their families were not told where and did not realise the plan was that they would either never see them again or if they did, that person was never the same person again but a mere shell of the person they were. The state had methods and technology which re-arranged the brain to whatever the kind of person they wished you to be. Technology which had been perfected decades previous. It was always beneficial to return the detainee back to their family and friends where they became the perfect spy albeit unknowingly to the person, for they had no idea they were doing what they were doing, technology is wonderful.

The US was now all but in the grip of dictatorship even though the propaganda fed to the media always called the martial law a temporary but necessary situation. Even with all this happening around them, there were some that still believed in the government, in the state, and chose to believe this was for the common good. The Internet and social media, long the bane of politicians, bankers and any other people or groups that were caught in the act of stealing from or misrepresentation of the people, had been almost fully under the control of the government or its agents for some time. The people now could only receive news from the mainstream media which was fully controlled propaganda as it has been for decades. Now the fascist (corporate controlled) government had a free reign to do as it wished without fear of incriminating videos and pictures showing up on social media and angering the people. The governments had privatised many services which gave them a degree of separation. When there was an outcry about privacy violations or poor service the government were more or less off the hook.

The government was in full control and was not going to go back to any form of democracy, ever again, for even if they wanted to their own masters would never allow it, for this plan has been in the works for a long time and they were well on the way to a One World Order, one government, one army, one currency and a horrifying reduction in world population. In fact, just as is chiselled in stone on The Georgia Guidestones.

As Dawn Approaches

When did the realisation of a full blown tyranny happen, what was it that finally 'flipped the switch' in everyone's heads to wake them up to the unfolding nightmare, the glaring reality that they had not learned anything from the past, that they were far too sophisticated to allow this to happen?

It was the moment that dawned on them that they could no longer say "No". They no longer had rights.

However, there were many thousands of true patriots that were now in full fight back mode and underground networks were being set up all over the US, the power of human fortitude and survival should never be underestimated.

12 – UK, Australia and Europe

The UK, Australia and certain European countries including Germany, France and Italy fared no better. Looking back one could see the patterns, the same erosion of rights and freedoms, the increased surveillance and monitoring of everything written or spoken using the Internet. Some brave people did try to start up a new internet that was intrusion proof but by that time governments could get away with almost anything they wished and those responsible were caught and locked up as a deterrent to anyone else who had similar ideas. Again the preposterous rationale being national security, which of course by this time almost everyone knew this to be a nothing more than a convenient smokescreen.

The police dressed and acted as para-militaries and most of them believed they were on the 'right' side but little did they know they were mere pawns in a game against humanity itself. Those that realised this kept their mouths shut for they knew there were only two sides and woe betide those who found themselves on the wrong side. It just all happened so fast that many good and caring people were swept up in the tide of control under the guise of civil obedience and maintaining law, but began quietly questioning themselves if what they were doing was right. Such thoughts though, can become unsuppressible.

The same things happened to these countries as what occurred in the US but in different ways, sometimes more subtle, sometimes not but again, by the time most people became fully aware it was too late. Without access to an open internet they couldn't spread the news quickly enough and organize against the tyranny, smaller areas of cities and entire towns were picked off and fully controlled by the Military and police as martial law took full hold of the nations. Martial law was usually invoked after the many protests against police brutality, loss of rights and freedoms including the right to protest and to bring attention to government inaction to aid the less fortunate. It was always announced as a temporary measure to protect people and property from rioters and looters but it was anything but temporary and the mainstream media, the propaganda wing of the state did everything it could to sugar coat the situation.

13 – Asia, Africa, Central and South America

Generally the tyrannies were focused more on the western countries, countries with highly organised states, for these were the nations whose citizens were to varying degrees highly enmeshed within its frameworks and subsequently very dependent upon it, never realising just how dependent. China had always been in almost full control of its people and North Korea continued to rule with an iron fist.

Russia had become allies with China and it was unclear if the hidden hands behind the western tyrannies would form an uneasy alliance or go for all-out war with the winner taking all.

The poorer countries such as those in Africa, the Far East, Central and Southern America were considered easy game to be picked off when the time came. Such countries were also good for corporate business as they could easily be goaded or even forced into a war they did not want and could not afford. Either way the elites made huge profits supplying both sides with arms. Mossad, MI6 and especially the CIA were masters at regime change and stirring up a good old war.

The Middle East continued to be in turmoil and the talk of World War Three was a constant theme in the mainstream media, however, it had not yet happened despite the best efforts of the US, UK and others.

The unmitigated disaster of the war against terror, especially in Iraq, was plain to see and had only served to be the catalyst for further generations of it as young men and women who had witnessed their mothers, fathers, siblings and spouses being shredded by bombs and munitions had only one goal, to kill westerners, just as westerners would do if the tables were reversed.

14 - Canada

Canada, although bordering the US, surprisingly did not follow the exact same path and for some reason tyranny took a longer journey. It could have been the demographics, the huge land area with a relatively small population, or just that she was thought of as an easy target once the US was fully controlled. Possibly it was down to the Canadians themselves, they always did pride themselves as being different from Americans and this tended to create an insular and somewhat quiet but defiant resilience. Whatever it was, Canadians still had a modest amount of freedom, for now at least. However, even though the main stream media only aired or published highly 'sanitized' news and often used crisis actors to play the parts of everyday people in interviews, Canadians were waking up fast to what was going on around the world and to their neighbour, the US. A bomb did detonate outside the Israeli Embassy in the nation's capital Ottawa, which was blamed on Muslim extremists. This enabled the Canadian Federal government to enact new anti-terrorism laws which, similarly to the US, further encroached on Canadian's rights and freedoms.

In general it felt like a giant noose was closing in on the world, surveillance in all forms became increasingly intrusive. The police and any other persons with 'authority' always treated people as guilty of something which instilled the desired outcome, fear. Internet freedom was diminishing at an alarming rate and every day websites were blocked, especially those which questioned anything about the government or state. Protests were basically outlawed effectively eradicating free speech.

15 – How Did They Pull It Off?

One of the biggest questions for those who could see what was going on was, "why couldn't people see it coming?"

In fact it boggled many minds how so many people were so complacent. It would appear that most people would rather believe their government than face the daunting prospect of reality. Cognitive dissonance and normalcy bias was the order of the day. Maybe the almost religious reliance on the mainstream media was a factor. Most people had to have their daily supply of news from the newspapers, television or both, and never questioned its authenticity. Yes, they all said much of it was hyped up or even made up but that never stopped the faith, the daily fix of useless or dangerously misleading information. Couple this with the fact that true journalism had long been neutered and no news outlet would go against the government line and the recipe for effective propaganda was complete. Dependence on the state was also a likely factor. The state had become so enmeshed in people's lives that they were almost as one. This had the effect of blinding people to actually refuse to think the State could be anything but benevolent. A huge mistake.

The march toward tyranny appeared to coincide with the spread and use of GMO foods. Dr. Henry Kissinger once said "Control the food supply and you control the people". Many nations refused GMOs but the corporate agents (the US and UK governments) used every dirty trick in the book to coerce other nations to accept GMOs whether they wanted them or not. Kissinger or Dr. Evil as many call him would lose no sleep over hundreds of millions of people being used as guinea pigs for GMOs, him being one of many of the 'elites' who refer to the elderly section of the 99.9% as the 'useless eaters'.

16 – Those That Could See

There were a number of people who had, as they say, 'woken up' and saw the mainstream media for what it was. These people received their news from various internet sources and often it was the complete opposite of what was being broadcast and published by the mainstream media. The 'awakened' people further educated themselves watching various videos and reading articles which would never make the mainstream media and which increased awareness to what was actually going on around them and how the world really works. It was claimed the 'awakening' process was painful, frightening at first, realising the world is not the world you thought it was. Then anger would set in and you would try and 'wake' others which was a waste of time and usually led to people thinking of them as having 'lost' it. Once you are awake there is no going back, they said. It was very difficult watching those you loved or cared for believing in the system, the media, the politicians too to a great extent.

It also became crystal clear how powerful 'culture' really is. Culture programmes us far more than we realise and defines the boundaries of society including how we think, how and what we communicate and who with. A culture's boundaries are the virtual mental prison bars which keep the masses from thinking 'outside the box' as they say, an indispensable tool of those in control. Yes, this too became apparent to the awakened as did the irony of the self-policing of the virtual mental prison by those within it, those who ridiculed the awakened who thought 'outside the box', which intimidated the 'inside the box' thinkers from asking questions. Yes, an unexpected but invaluable tool indeed.

17 - A Glimmer Of Hope, Real Hope

All through the journey toward global tyranny there were still hundreds of thousands of people who understood what was going on and attended marches and protests. Most of these people had another thing in common, they had all read 'the book', in fact before the tyrannical-bound governments banned all anti-government material, 'the book' had really made the rounds and a good percentage of people in many countries were either familiar with, read or seen videos about 'the book' and the new ideas it offered. Canadians were no different and had longer to familiarize themselves with it, in fact, as in most other countries 'the book' was well received by people in all walks of life, in all disciplines and occupations.

'The book' was the subject of University lectures and papers and news stories. It made many well read articles and people warmed to most of the ideas it contained. The writer of 'the book', who was a guitarist with the alternative music group Synners of Truth, helped organize and headline music festivals to promote humanity, freedom and democracy in its name and the festivals became so popular it became a major worldwide tour. Although this was never reported in the mainstream media around the world, such was the far reaching control of those who really controlled things.

As Dawn Approaches

As various governments tried to supress 'the book' and its ideas it naturally became even more sought after and attractive to those who could see the approaching tyranny. For now, several major nations were firmly under control but the damage was done, the cat was out of the bag, the horse had bolted from the stable, the seeds of new ideas had been sown and an idea whose time had come, had come.

For this time was different, it was not about protesting a war in a far off land or marching against destructive corporate ambition. This time it was about them, their families and loved ones, their fellow man. People could smell that nauseating stench of fear, they now knew how those poor folk in far-away lands felt, waking up each day to oppression, knowing there were no longer laws to protect you and not knowing if you would be taken away for good, never seeing one's family again. The time was now 'fight or flight' time and there was nowhere to run, but, fuelled by the thought of winning back freedom and of starting anew with a system which eradicated the possibility of this ever happening again, the patriots grew in strength, in numbers, in courage, in belief.

'The book' had spawned a quiet 'movement', just people who wanted to discuss its ideas, people who could see the end of the present systems and who understood it was these systems which allowed the present situation to happen. The situation of having their country and freedom stolen from them by a very, very small group of powerful people. They could see that the power these people enjoy stems from money and position and by eradicating the means to exploit these, they could take back their country. The new system made sense because it was all about the people and it had the effect of galvanizing people from different backgrounds. It was effortless, just a new way of thinking, no revolution, no violence, just a new idea percolating through the population. As strange as it sounds, just a change in belief. Concerned politicians did try and condemn 'the book' but even they knew it was too late. Whatever defence they tried to use for the present systems it became blatantly obvious that they were flawed, one only need look at the alarming reductions in democracy and freedoms to see there was no stopping the march toward control and tyranny.

CHAPTER 3

18 – The Sleeping Giant Stirs

"Good to see you Richard!" The General said to Colonel Richard Wainright as he let him in at the front door of his elegant home and shook his hand.

"So glad you could make it, come this way and meet the others, how was the drive?"

"Very good, thank you Sir," the Colonel replied as he followed the General along a passageway adorned with old paintings of military men in various poses.

"No need for formalities here Richard, Ben will work just fine," said General Benoit 'Ben' Rousseau, a highly thought of Canadian Military strategist from the province of Quebec.

"Yes Sir, er Ben," replied Richard.

Colonel Richard Wainright was born in Vancouver, British Columbia in 1969 and was the eldest of three children born to Georgina and Captain Harold Wainright (Retired) of the Canadian Army. As a military family the Wainrights had moved around as warranted by wherever Captain Harold Wainright needed to be stationed. Richard followed in his father's footsteps who had also followed in his father's footsteps and had never really had any particular location he would call home, not that that bothered

John Reid

Richard for the nomadic life was all he knew and he felt fortunate that he had lived in different countries, seen many things and met different people. Having said that though, Canada was where Richard's heart lay, he loved his country deeply and served her proudly. He had not yet married but knew he would when the time was right. Richard was enjoying a successful career in the Canadian Army and had risen through the ranks to Colonel in a relatively short period, being one of the youngest Colonels in recent history.

Richard had partaken in some form in both Gulf Wars and had spent time in Afghanistan after 9/11 in one capacity or another, sometimes in exchange programmes with the US or UK militaries.

Even though a proud military man, Richard retained his core beliefs that ideally peace would reign across the planet and one day there would be no need for war. Over his years he could plainly see that war was the result of the ambitions of only a few men, and those ambitions were not about security, redress or genuine grievances but greed, and he and his military brothers and sisters as all other militaries, were merely playing the role of policemen and women for the central banking cartel and the multi-national corporations. 'War is a racket' as Major General Smedley Butler, at one time the highest ranking soldier in the US military once said and Richard's own research proved this to be the case. History as we have been told is just a convenient facade for the truth behind all the wars. But today things have taken a turn, the profiteers behind war are now coming for the grand prize, 'everything'. Richard could now see the end game, the plan unfolding and as a soldier he would not lie down and let this handful of anonymous psychopaths take his country which was happening across the rest of the western world.

The General lived on a modest estate near Ottawa, the nation's capital, with a walled and gated century home comprising of 10 bedrooms and probably as many bathrooms. The house and associated buildings sat on 50 acres which were farmed by a local farmer and also included a picturesque river which ran through twelve acres of the property. They entered a larger room which was more like a small hall where at least twenty five men and eight women, some in military dress which consisted of Army, Air Force and Navy uniforms, were standing with drinks in hands and talking in small groups. The atmosphere was warm and sociable and Richard was introduced to the group by the General.

Richard also discovered there were four high ranking police officials present, as a proud and patriotic Canadian he was impressed how the word had spread and how it appeared that all the main areas of concern to him were covered.

Many who served in the Military were alarmed at what had happened to the US, UK and other nations. Some had very quietly begun sharing their concerns with colleagues and an underground movement gradually came into existence. Recent events proved they had to be very careful as the top command were firmly under the control of the one world order psychopaths and had forced the retirements of two high ranking Generals under the threat of being fired under falsely fabricated accusations.

This occurred because the Generals in question had been under suspicion of plotting a coup in the event of martial law which was in essence true, however, the coup was not intended for military control but to assist in combating the approaching tyranny of which they wanted no part. They were Canadians, strong and free and would do everything to maintain that. Alas, there was a 'patriot' among them who reported what was happening to his superiors and the Generals were outed. This was followed by a memorandum to all military personnel that any form of anti-government action would be deemed as traitorous and subversive and would result in dismissal with loss of all privileges and benefits including pensions. Those threats however, paled into insignificance to the true threat to personal freedoms, rights and a nation under tyrannical rule and if anything helped to fuel the interest in an underground network of true patriots unwilling to hand over their beloved nation to unelected bankers and corporate psychopaths.

Richard was invited to join one of the groups which consisted of two men and a woman and they shared information on their respective backgrounds and careers and also how they heard about this particular 'underground' movement. Gradually other guests appeared and much to Richard's pleasant surprise three well known and publicly recognizable, high ranking politicians entered the room and were introduced to everyone. Even more heartwarming was the fact these politicians were from two of the three main parties proving their allegiance to their country and her people and not just their own political parties, which is what this was all about. Then he saw two famous TV personalities enter the room, one male and one female who were long time national news anchors for the CBC, the Canadian Broadcasting Corporation, and well respected across the nation. Through the course of the evening Richard was introduced to various military, police and political people and also four professors from Ontario Universities. Richard found this all to be more than he expected, so many well placed people who like himself were proud to serve and work for their country and refused to serve corporate interests and central bankers. They knew well what was going to be coming and they were prepared for it. These people, like Richard were truly serving and protecting their country and her people but probably never thought it would one day be in the form of protecting Canada from her own government, albeit a government forced along a certain path.

Richard couldn't help but chuckle to himself when he realised he was a part of a pseudo Bilderberger group but instead of plotting to rule the world, this secretive group were plotting the Bilderberger downfall, in Canada at least for now, but this group truly believed that once other nations saw how Canada fared under a new system free of central bankers and corporate controlled government (fascism), they would clamour to follow suit and the complete demise of the psychopaths would be well under way.

"Attention please Ladies and Gentlemen," announced the General, "let me begin by saying a big thank you for attending tonight, I understand the difficulty with all of our schedules to all meet at the same time so again, thank you everyone." The General paused while a round of applause filled the small hall then continued.

"As you are all aware, our friends in other nations, especially those to our immediate south have fallen victim to the ambitions of a group of people who have used the central banking system and concentrated corporate power to completely control their governments which have almost become tyrannies. Canada has to a degree been left out of this but we all know it is coming and coming soon.

It is now clear that the systems of government and finance we have lived within for many decades, the systems we thought served us all fairly well are doomed to fail. Not in so much that the systems themselves are badly flawed but that they are open to abuse from nefarious human traits and elements.

"It has taken many years but gradually and stealthily the central bankers and trans-national corporations have in effect taken full control of many nations in their quest for a one world order. Many learned and well positioned people including American Presidents have, over time, warned of this but those warnings went unheeded. I think you will agree that it is very difficult to envision a different way, a new system geared to inhibit those with such monstrous ambitions, but fortune has favoured us and we do have the blueprint for a new way forward that has captured our hearts and changed our beliefs.

"We here are all familiar with 'the book', the book which opened our minds and changed our beliefs and gives us a solid framework with which to rebuild our systems in a truly democratic way.

I can honestly say that this is one of my proudest moments as a Canadian. We have among us here tonight, true patriots willing to risk everything for our great country, patriots from various backgrounds joined by a common purpose, to save our nation and keep her strong and free."

The General paused for another round of applause then continued,

"This meeting was called to share our ideas and to be prepared, for the moment is fast approaching when we spring into action and save this great nation. We are through our various and extensive network of patriots, fully aware of events in real time and will know when to 'push the button' so to speak. Most of you here are already well versed in your respective roles and what to do when the codeword is given but for those who have just joined us, all the necessary information will be provided tonight. As you can understand, we have planned almost everything, which is imperative for our success."

Richard was very impressed by the extensive organization of this planned takeover, no, takeover was the wrong word, custody or stewardship, yes stewardship was a better word, stewardship until the new system is firmly in place.

The General continued. "As we have discussed, timing is of the utmost importance, the timing of the moment we act, which is just after the expected announcement of martial law in Canada. Martial law is expected to be declared when the coming food shortage is announced. There will not actually be a real food shortage but the government will tell Canadians that there is and food will stop being supplied to stores causing starvation, rioting, looting and all the other criminal activities we know will happen. That is when we make our move, sometime just after martial law is declared. The Military is expected to already be in place due to government foreknowledge of events and will not look out of place as martial law is announced. We will then take control and announce from all the major TV stations what is happening and all information about what we are doing will be shown every hour.

"We also know that approximately 12% of Canadians have also read 'the book' and a further 14% are very familiar with its contents which will be available to everyone to read. We feel it is far more effective for people to read 'the book' as we know the effect it has and does so in short amount of time, well, quicker than we can explain it all I would suggest. Most importantly the new constitution of which you have all agreed to, will be shown to the nation through all media sources which is to be voted on within one month. This will hold off the UN from declaring our action as a coup, they will not like it but that is not our problem."

The General pointed over to a man and woman standing side by side.

"Our top rated news anchors here tonight who need no introduction I'm sure, will be the chief spokespeople for the transition. As we are well aware, most people only believe things when they are told by trusted and familiar faces on television, so our friends here will be a major asset. Everyone here tonight will be given a copy of the new constitution which will always be open to amendments from the people for it will be the people who make the decisions regarding their country.

"The new constitution guarantees the rights of all Canadians and protects the nation from predators such as; the central banking interests and corporations responsible for the looting of our prosperity. We will also make it perfectly clear what the present government were planning to do and the tyranny to which we were to be subjected.

"Ladies and Gentlemen our patriotic actions will make history and we will need to be strong and resolute as the global machine and central bankers will be baying for blood at our door. These are desperate times and we must take advantage by forging all the changes we need at one time. This includes announcing our departure from the British Commonwealth and becoming a sovereign republic nation. The Canadian people need no longer be subjects of a monarchy which has no relevance to them."

The last two sentences caused a faintly audible gasp from some of the listeners, hearing that Canada would completely break away from Great Britain brought home the realisation and gravity of what was going to happen. This really was going to be a monumental change, but then again, "what does Canada really gain from being associated with Great Britain and her people, subjects of a foreign monarchy?" Richard pondered.

The General continued.

"We know there will be condemnation from around the world but that condemnation will originate from the orchestrators of the New World Order and their puppets. The Canadian Broadcasting Corporation CBC, will be the eyes and ears of the people and will be completely free to provide unbiased news and keep a watchful eye on all of our endeavours. It is imperative that a truly free nation has a truly free and unbiased national press. The CBC will be on the streets interviewing Canadians about their reactions and aspirations leading to the vote and this will be seen around the world so as to quell fears of a coup. Although we know the controlled mainstream media around the world will not be showing our endeavours in a favourable light, we also know the truth will filter through other means to the global populations.

"Our news presenter friends here with us tonight will be spending long hours on air to ensure Canadians of our intent and that there will be no food shortages after all. We also have a strong contingent of known politicians from different parties, who actually do care about serving the Canadian people and will join the new system as stewards of democracy. They will assist in any way they can with the transition and the implementation of the new system, including giving interviews for the media to help explain where we are at and how the transition is progressing.

"We have a vast network of patriots ready to fulfill their duty and help with the transition and we do not anticipate much resistance especially once the majority fully understand our purpose and that the transition is for their benefit.

"The most difficult thing, as I believe we all know, is coming to terms with a failed paradigm, that the only systems we know have failed us, that and changing one's beliefs to accepting a new way. But once that threshold has been crossed the people will fully understand and see the new way as the only way forward. They only need look at the United States, UK, Australia and other nations under virtual tyranny to realise this and the CBC will provide this information unfettered by any outside interference so Canadians can clearly see where they were heading under the present systems and government.

"Information packages will be handed out after this speech and I encourage as much sharing of ideas and information as possible so that we are all as fully aware as we can be, for we will all be responsible for disseminating and sharing the information we possess."

"As a footnote, there will no doubt be some challenging times ahead as we make the transition, do not lose hope, be focused on what the alternative would have brought us and be resolute in the knowledge that each day brings the nation closer to equilibrium. Take heart that our children, the next generation, will know no other system and will find our present corrupt models abhorrent and no different from the serfdom of yore. Of course everything we have discussed is to be kept secret until we make the announcement on air. I thank you all again for your presence and wish you all the best of luck with the parts you will play in this historic event in the name of freedom and democracy for Canada."

The speech was followed by a very enthusiastic round of applause and everyone were handed their information. The new constitution was included in the package but everyone in attendance knew what it consisted of already so they began exchanging the parts they would play and how they expected things to unfold.

CHAPTER 4

19 – The Cottagers

Three weeks after the weekend at the cottage the men got together at a favourite sports bar, as they did from time to time. They sat at a high table and ordered their beers.

"So what's new?" Jerry asked Ron and Nick.

"Nothing much," Nick answered.

"Nothing much with me either except I do have something I want to tell you both," Ron said.

"Ok, shoot," Jerry said.

"Yeah, hit us man," said Nick.

"Well, now don't go getting all worked up or nothing, but you remember what we were talking about back at the cottage, you know, 'the book' and the way things are heading in the world, that stuff?".

"Yeah, we remember," Nick said nodding his head at Jerry who nodded in agreement.

"Well, word is there will be some kind of martial law imposed on us in the near future but.."

"Holy crap Ron are you freakin serious?" Nick interjected, "things are getting that bad, this is really going to happen, I mean, what the hell are we .."

"Let me finish Nick, you'll be pleased to know we have a kind of movement, a silent movement of highly placed people who ain't gonna sit back and let our beloved Canada become anyone's servant, no sir, there are hundreds if not thousands in very strategic positions who are ready and willing to block any attempts to take over our country," Ron said.

"Holy smokes," Jerry sighed, "well that's good, I guess, I mean it's good we have people ready to fight back but man, this is some scary stuff you're talking Ron."

"No kidding it's scary stuff," Nick added, "what do we do Ron, what do we do, us, our families, what's expected to happen?"

"As I said, from what I'm hearing we don't have to do anything, just keep on living our lives as usual. The movement will block any attempt at martial law and control and bring in a new system," Ron replied.

"New system, now what kind of system would that be Ron?" Nick asked.

"Funny enough, it's gonna be based primarily on the same system I told you fella's about at the cottage, based on that 'book' I told you about, 'The Organic Economy', told you both you should read it, now you're gonna ain't ya?" Ron said with a grin as he chinked his beer off Jerry and Ron's beer bottles.

20 – The Organic Economy

About four weeks after the guys had met up at the bar, Andrea happened to be using the computer at home one evening and saw a folder on the computer desktop named 'The Book'.
"This must be Jeff's, is this that 'book' I keep hearing about?" thought Andrea as she opened the folder. They had no secrets and everything was shared on their computer. Andrea saw a PDF called 'The Organic Economy' and opened it. She began to read.

INTRODUCTION

This e-book will challenge your mind as it questions almost everything we are familiar with in our
societies. Are the political, economic and financial systems and the institutions that are firmly entrenched in our lives and minds serving us fairly? Do we enjoy true democracy, are we being gouged by the banking systems, is our political system representing us? In this book I give the reader my take on what I have learned and continue to see, and also how I believe we can greatly improve our lives with a fair and just system of economics. I ask the reader to keep an open mind, to bear with

me until the end of the book, as much of what I share will require some time to take in and digest.

Andrea was intrigued, "this must be 'the book'" she thought. Andrea had her own opinions about politics and finance and continued to read...

Edition: 1 March 12th 2014
THE ORGANIC ECONOMY

Through my life I have had many questions, questions that I did not really think I could ask people.
Questions that I probably thought would most likely be laughed off or scorned, so I kept them to myself, turned them over in my head and heart when driving or working away on something which didn't take a lot of brainpower, basically day dreaming, as we do.

Some of these questions pertained to our political, economic and financial systems. These questions seemed to come from a 'feeling' deep down that some things were just plain wrong!

Naturally most of us have similar thoughts each day when we receive the news, whether from television, print media or the Internet, and these are often part of the day's talking points with colleagues, family and friends.

We complain, we debate, we even get angry at times but that is where it ends, because what can we really do? Oh yes, we can vote for the 'other party' and hope they get into power at the next election, that is the fair and democratic way isn't it?

Then we sit back and watch the newly elected government break promise after promise, they lied, we have been taken for complete fools yet again.

We have become so conditioned to the lies, so conditioned to the same tired mantras of empty rhetoric such as 'hope' and 'change' that we bury our heads in the sand, hold our noses and carry on, let's face it, what can we do, how could we ever 'better' this system. It's ages old, tried and tested, surely there is no other way unless it is a radical shift to communism or something involving anarchy, and the vast majority certainly don't want any part of that!

After the Internet had fully taken root in our lives I decided to see if there were any other people who had similar thoughts to me. I quickly learned that the Internet was full of nonsense and full of the truth, one just needed to re-learn how to use discernment and critical thinking to figure out which is which.

I also learned that there are many people like myself with similar questions and many very good pundits and bloggers digging up important information that affects us all but often fails to make it into our mainstream news, therefore we are kept in the dark far more than we realise because we trust our media coverage and believe that it is comprehensive.

True journalism is one of the cornerstones of a free society, it plays a pivotal part in keeping us aware of what is happening and how our leadership is performing which enables us to have a level of control and helps keep things in check.

The mainstream media is now owned by a small group of immensely powerful people or corporations and true journalism, the kind that asks the difficult questions of our leadership has been all but eradicated leaving the alternative media as the only choice for true journalism and this is coming to light as viewing figures for television news stations and readership of print media continues to decline.

Therefore, the mainstream media are willing partners in keeping us in the dark and cheerleaders for our present political, economic and financial systems and this just further serves to cement our beliefs that there cannot possibly be another way.

In many countries governmental factions actively 'go after' anyone publishing the truth about
corruption or mismanagement. Edward Snowden can attest to that.
When this happens we know that that government is abusing its power and has things to hide even though that government is paid for by the people and should ONLY be working for its people, anything else is tyranny.

These things as we all know are commonplace in third world countries but sadly they are now firmly entrenched in our own countries, none being spared.

I was always an avid newspaper reader and follower of news on the television but as I gradually came to prefer the alternative media for my news, my routines changed.
What sealed it for me was a work contract that took me away from home and out of country for three weeks and I decided not to check on any news from my home region, province and country, just to see how much news and important information I had missed. It did, to be honest, feel quite strange and I did feel I was missing something.

When I returned home absolutely nothing had changed and I realised that even something as big as a general election (a supposedly worthwhile news event) would hardly be worth

As Dawn Approaches

learning about because, let's face it, what really changes, the same old, same old, just carries on, business as usual thank you very much!

From then on I rarely bought a newspaper and never watched the news on television. I saw it all for what it mainly is, mindless rubbish.
Once I broke away from obtaining my news from the mainstream media I found I began to research more and more things online, I began to uncover answers to my questions and a whole new world opened up to me.

I learned not to 'write off' someone because they said something I disagreed with, as most of the alternative news presenters do not follow carefully manufactured scripts but have the freedom to tell it as it is and often it is something we would prefer not to hear.

The immaculately turned out talking heads that present the news seem to give us the impression that everything they say is the truth, must be the truth, they've always told the truth haven't they? Well, no they have not. They are mere 'repeaters' and churn out whatever they are told to churn out, the news, as are most things in our lives, is controlled. We only get to hear what a certain few wishes us to hear.

From many of the websites I enjoy and resonate with I like to follow articles about our political,
economic and financial systems and especially enjoy reading the comments to try and gauge the feelings of like-minded people. People who are completely disillusioned with our systems and establishment and the gross unfairness of it all for those without the necessary money or influence to secure a privileged life.

What I learned from these comments is overwhelmingly that no one has an answer for the problems we face from our systems. It is like a mental roadblock that no-one can get past to envision a new way, a new economy that is equitable and fair to everyone, a truly humane way forward.

The best most can do is point out the wrongdoings, the corruption, the lies and deceit, but never any practical suggestion as how to really improve things for ALL of the people, except of course a violent revolution which never solves anything in the long run.

There are those who promote the peaceful type revolution of 'non-cooperation' which worked so well for Ghandi in removing British rule and that would be fine except,
"Ok great, we have peacefully overthrown the government....
now what?"

No-one appears to have an answer, it is like running into a brick wall, our brains just seem to turn off at the mere thought of proposing an alternative system even though we know in our heart of hearts that so many things are just plain wrong.

The way the politicians endlessly 'stick it' to us after promising they would be the ones who would make it a fairer nation, time and time again we hear the empty promises just to be let down again. It just does not work for us, yes it works for a privileged few and quite nicely by the look of it but it does not work for the vast majority, the majority that pays the most in taxes only to be let down time after time.

I don't say these things in jealousy of what others have, I wish no-one ill will and if someone works harder or longer hours or builds a business then they certainly deserve what they earn.

As Dawn Approaches

This is about the gross inequities of our present systems and the way our voices are ignored and now with the 'police state' that is rapidly taking over with more and more new technologies designed to watch our every move.

Wrong, wrong, wrong! Why should we pay taxes toward our own virtual prison, to be watched and listened to even in our own homes because that is where we are heading, if we allow it.

Most people know there are many wrongs with our systems, that those we elect and pay to represent us neglect to do so in favour of looking out for the best interests of corporations, corporations in the energy, food, financial and pharmaceutical sectors among others.
Corporations that should never have access to those WE elect to serve us, there are other ways for corporations to state their cases, but they spend billions in lobbying annually, again it's all about the money, money that buys power and privilege and tough luck on the rest of us without huge reserves of it to get our own ways to make more of it.

Corporations have grown so huge, wealthy, powerful and interconnected that the present political system is always under pressure to bow to them. These same corporations know no borders, have no affiliation to any one nation and have only one mandate, profit. The people, country, environment and resources that belong to each of us are merely expendable commodities.

These very same corporations have enormous leverage over those we elect and pay to look out for us.
Quite simply, we are not being represented as we should be.
One very important fact to be aware of is that the elite ultra-wealthy families that control much of the financial and corporate

world have been around for a long time, many for hundreds of years.

The Prime Ministers and Presidents we think of as the highest authorities in the land are merely
temporary figureheads of a nation and are no match for such families, sadly, it is often these powerful families and their offshoot organizations that actually choose that leader in the first place.
Our systems are far more rigged than you may ever believe and not rigged in the voters favour.

That does sound hard to believe but so does most of how things really work in our 'systems', which is why nothing will ever really improve by working within the same frameworks of our political, financial and economic systems. They simply do not serve us all fairly and never will.

The seemingly endless tentacles of the mega corporations and banking interests reach much further than most realise and are beginning to affect our lives in many more ways than before. Yes we hear about them all the time but again we tend to 'tune them out', we have busy lives, what can we really do about it all, can't someone else stand up to them and save us?

They try to sell us on globalisation and how great it will be for us all when the only benefactors are the corporations, central banks and certain elite families.
Firstly, they close our manufacturing plants and lay off hundreds of thousands of employees, to be replaced by the cheapest (almost slave) labour they can find, then tell us how great it is for us to be able to buy cheap products.

Corporations have zero allegiance to their employees in any

country they happen to do business in.

The executives have even convinced themselves that the only thing that matters is profit at almost any cost with complete disregard for humanity, the environment and the communities which serve them.

This attitude is one of the things that 'something inside' tells me is not only wrong but unsustainable in the long run. Use all the clever words you like to convince yourself that this is just the way it is, but wrong is wrong no matter which way you cut it.

The notion of us being fortunate to have access to cheap foreign products is a fallacy. When your sons and daughters go to college or university to earn a diploma or degree where will they find employment now?

The manufacturing plants that were closed down to enable ever greater profits not only provided jobs for production line personnel but Tradespeople, Engineers, Accountants, Business graduates working in Sales and Marketing, Human Resource personnel and the local contractors that supplied services to the plants.

Entire communities have been devastated in the name of higher profits when it wasn't necessary at all.

Therefore we are experiencing a false economy, cheap goods at first then the cost to the nation of high unemployment and lower consumer spending which costs more jobs. This puts the nations finances under stress which often means higher taxes and cuts to services to try and balance the books.

We are now seeing the results of globalisation. When a nation that grew to be wealthy and powerful loses its manufacturing industries what will happen to that nation? Well, look no further than that mightiest of manufacturing powerhouses, the United States.

High unemployment, record numbers of people using food stamps, record poverty, a country that is actually bankrupt except that its currency is linked directly to oil and that is only because of the enormous military threat they are to any others brave enough or dumb enough to challenge The Petro Dollar (Muammar Gaddafi of Libya being one).

So what is the real cost of globalisation to the USA, cheap goods in the short term, a country in ruins in the longer term, so much for globalisation being good for everyone. It is all about one thing and one thing only, higher profits at any cost.

Do you ever find yourself thinking "How much money is enough, when does enough become pure greed?"

THE IMPORTANT ROLES PEOPLE PLAY

It has always been said that people were never forced to work for low wages and awful conditions, they knew the wage and the long hours and there was always a long line of people ready and willing to take your job if you didn't want it.

To me that sentiment is disingenuous. No matter how much money a person has, if every person alive decided never to do anything for that person then that person would have a pile of money and nothing else, no workforce, no servants, no builders, no maintenance personnel, life would be almost impossible for them to enjoy.

The point being that people need people to enjoy a good standard of living and that goes for everyone.

Taking advantage of people with low pay and poor working conditions just because you can is pure exploitation but our society lauds them as good business people and that that is how you have to be to make it in business.

As Dawn Approaches

I disagree, from my own experiences I have seen first-hand how employees that are treated with dignity and respect will out-perform those under the 'whip' as they care about what they do and the quality of product that ships from the plant.

I believe that the vast majority of working people like to come home from a days work feeling they have contributed, that they feel valuable and appreciated.
Yes there will always be a few who take advantage and do as little as possible for as much money as possible but to me that is as unconscionable as the rich taking advantage of their positions, both are forms of greed and destructive to humanity instead of being constructive.

We all need to be in partnership with each other, help each other, instead of the dog eat dog attitude which we are told is the only way forward if you want to get ahead in life. Get ahead to what, a bigger house, a bigger car, more and more material things which are now cheap because your neighbours have lost their jobs to globalisation, where does it all end?
Common sense tells me that this attitude has a shelf life, it cannot sustain itself indefinitely.

After the previous section about corporations you may think I am anti-capitalist or anti-corporation but I am not.
I believe we need people with desire and drive and the will to work hard to build and grow a business and that those same people have a right to keep as much of what they earn as possible, there must always be incentives.

We have seen what happens when incentive is removed. As in the old USSR, nothing gets done and the country gradually falls apart.

The problem is when corporations become so big and powerful and use their power, influence and money to subvert our democracies for their own interests which include rolling back laws that protect workers and their rights.

Rights that were fought long and hard for because of the exploitation from the employers. Nothing has changed either for even today in our so-called civilised countries no sooner than employees lose union protection, they begin to lose their rights.

MONEY AND FINANCE

For many years I would read the newspaper or watch the television and when it came to things like inflation, lending rates, stock markets, trade deficits etc. etc.
My eyes would glaze over, in fact they still do but for a different reason today.

The first thing that would come to mind is how complex it all is, just looking at the skyscrapers the money people ply their trade in was enough to scare the pants off me.
I used to think how smart these people must be and if I knew what was best for me, to leave well alone, these guys are experts and I will never understand how money works, where it comes from, and how to make money from money.

I watched the 'experts' debate back and forth about which was the best direction the country should head for job creation, prosperity and growth and how they argued their points with all sorts of numbers and statistics.
These were experts that had university degrees and years of experience and even they could not agree on which economic policies were the best way forward.

As Dawn Approaches

Hold it a minute! If even the so-called experts couldn't agree then who is right? It seems there are no definitive economics, it boils down to opinions and which political party is in power!

So I spent time researching and learning about how the economy works and trying to find answers for things such as, why does our country have to pay billions in interest to a foreign bank when the country is hurting for services even though taxes are overbearing?

Why do I have to pay so much interest on my mortgage, why does everything go up in price, should towns amalgamate to save money and so on?

I wanted answers to my questions and explanations for why I felt so many things were just plain wrong.
Over time a picture began to emerge. It became clear why we are in such a mess and culprit number one are the central banks. Our countries un-necessarily borrow money from private banks when they could issue their own debt free currency.

The founding fathers of the US constitution knew this well and did what they could to stop the central bankers from controlling America's money supply, but by 1913 the US fell prey to the bankers as they weaseled their way in when the Senators should have been looking after the best interests of the people.
These same bankers were also behind the formation of the IRS, they were the ones that forced the US to tax the people on their earnings, when earnings were not supposed to be taxed as they are an honest exchange of energy, money for labour or work, a straight swap, no profit involved.

"I sincerely believe that banking establishments are more dangerous than standing armies, and that the principle of spending money to be paid by posterity, under the name of funding, is but swindling futurity on a large scale."
Thomas Jefferson, President of The United States (1801-1809)

We are grateful to the Washington Post, the New York Times, Time magazine and other great publications whose directors have attended our meetings and respected the promises of discretion for almost forty years. It would have been impossible for us to develop our plan for the world if we had been subject to the bright lights of publicity during those years.
But, the world is now more sophisticated and prepared to march towards a world-government. The supranational sovereignty of an intellectual elite and world bankers is surely preferable to the National autodetermination practiced in past centuries.—
David Rockefeller in an address to a Trilateral Commission meeting in June of 1991.

Why did Cyprus, Greece, Ireland, Italy, Portugal and Spain require bailouts from the central banks?
Only recently sovereign nations, nations that are now controlled by bankers, bankers that dictate how the governments will run their countries. Bankers that demand austerity measures while paying themselves obscene salaries and bonuses.

Sovereign nations that joined a European Union only to end up in a very short time as financial and economic failures, unless of course you are the bankers.

These nations that cannot take the necessary corrective measures to improve their economies because they gave up sovereignty by opting to adopt the Euro as their currency.

They lost sovereignty because they no longer have control of their own interest rates, they are tied to whatever the European Central Bank decides to set the rate at which can be extremely detrimental to a nation's economy.

I will never forget visiting family in Ireland in 2000 and learning that Ireland's economy was overheating, the Celtic Tiger roaring across the land while Germany was in a recession.

Ireland if it could, would have raised interest rates to slow borrowing and cool the economy and

Germany would have lowered the rates to stimulate their economy but both were tied to the Euro and could not help themselves.

Two different countries with two different economies heading in two different directions without the power to help themselves and now look at Ireland, her younger generation emigrating again to find a hopeful future.

Whichever way you look at it, the people of these nations were improperly represented by their elected leadership. Whether that be by borrowing too much money, spending too much money or both, the so-called leadership failed the people.

And the continuous push by self-appointed experts to amalgamate everything, towns into cities and countries into unions, such as; the European Union and the future North American Union of Canada, the US and Mexico.

This is extremely detrimental to the people as more and more people are represented by fewer and fewer representatives.

The result being we become almost invisible and our voices are not heard, another blow to an almost non-existent democratic process.

Now we have un-elected eurocrats making laws for countries that the people had no say in whatsoever.
Clearly such amalgamation leads to less say from the people and more control from the un-elected 'officials' and clearly that results in less and less democracy. Without true democracy we are at varying degrees just economic slaves.

INTEREST ON BORROWED MONEY (USURY)

People have been paying interest on loans for thousands of years and it is completely accepted as a system of finance and economics.

Why would anyone ever question usury? If you need money and someone has it to lend then they deserve to EARN a profit don't they?

Well, we are now witness to where things end up with usury.
In a relatively short time the money becomes concentrated in a few hands and these people then become extremely powerful.

"Give me the power to issue a nation's money; then I do not care who makes the law."
Mayer Amschel Bauer Rothschild.

Most people think that it's our politicians and government that are in full control of our country but sadly this is far from true. Money and greed are human weaknesses and most of us have our price. The banking families have spent hundreds of years angling things their way so that our very own governments un-necessarily borrow from them.

There is one inherent problem with interest on money and that is it can never be fully repaid, it is a self-fulfilling prophecy that it will all collapse because there can never be enough money in circulation to repay it.

The banks lend you the principle, but not the interest so where will that actually come from?
As all money in circulation is already 'debt' money (issued by banks in the form of loans) the only way to pay interest is with a growing economy, this means we need infinite growth which is impossible, it has to stop sometime and when it does the economy will collapse.

This system of finance is also what drives inflation and why the cost of goods keep rising, then we fight for more pay to be able to survive the rising costs. The entire thing is a rigged merry-go-round, or more accurately a spiral toward eventual collapse.

The real kicker is the so-called money that is lent does not actually exist, it is just numbers on computer screens. These bankers have managed to pull off THE BIGGEST SCAM IN THE HISTORY OF MANKIND!
They loan 'apparent' money to countries who then lend it to the people, who, by their honest labours, pay back principle and interest money that actually does have value!

When nations borrow money, the central bankers issue worthless 'fiat' money or 'credit', then turn on the financial and prosperity sucking vacuum cleaner and mop up the real money that people have laboured for, money with actual value.

This is why so much of our money and prosperity spirals

gradually upward and into the greedy pockets of the bankers.

Absolutely brilliant, I tip my hat to the ingenuity of such a monumental scam!!

It is the same as me giving you a blank sheet of paper and you give me back a pile of money, and you keep coming back time after time to do it again, genius, total genius!

The central bankers and banking families also have their greedy hands on almost everything we buy.
The interest that is paid back by manufacturers and farmers etc. is passed down to the consumer so we are always paying something to the bankers. The money gradually spirals upward into their pockets, there is hardly anything they don't have a piece of.

Your own bank is based on a pyramid scheme too. They can lend out much more (usually 9 times) than they actually have in deposits! They don't even have the money to lend you, it is all 'smoke and mirrors', just leveraged apparent money.

The world has been very cleverly manipulated into accepting all of this as 'the way it needs to be' with central bankers eventually being the sole supplier of the world's money!

Take a minute and ask yourself how then do we pay them back? With what do we pay them back?
Well, it is our 'real' money that the people of the country earn with their labours that pays them back.
So why do we not issue our own money and pay back our own country? Because our leaders over the years have been bought off, hoodwinked, blackmailed, whatever it took for them to accept this immoral system.

As Dawn Approaches

Canada where I live, is a stable country with huge resources and a good standard of living but has a debt (as of 2014) of over 600 billion dollars!

According to The Canadian Debt Clock, Canadians paid 33 billion dollars in 2007-08 just to service that debt. Currently (in 2014) each Canadian owes $17,000 each for their share of the Canadian Government debt!

Canada will never, ever pay this off completely and this also means that our children, even

grandchildren, are born into a debt they never asked for and will be paying for their entire lives should these systems continue.

I believe strongly that this should be totally illegal, it is immoral and inhumane to burden the unborn, to mortgage our children's future the way the politicians do.

Democracy ha! Sorry, that went out the window when you defaulted on your loans.

To compound matters, when things get tough and the economy takes a downturn putting pressure on the nation's finances, the rating agencies downgrade the nation's credit rating and the interest rate goes UP!

Pure gouging, pure greed and not an ounce of compassion.

Interest on loans is one of the main issues we have today. Extortionate credit card interest puts most people in difficulty. Yes, we have a choice not to get into debt but we are bombarded with commercials everywhere we turn, to buy this and buy that. This will make you feel good, that will make you feel loved.

The pressure to purchase is always upon us today and our banks keep raising our spending limits, they do not like customers who pay on time.

Edward Bernays, a nephew of Sigmund Freud, known as the father of public relations and a pioneering propagandist said the following;

"The conscious and intelligent manipulation of the organized habits and opinions of the masses is an important element in democratic society. Those who manipulate this unseen mechanism of society constitute an invisible government which is the true ruling power of our country. ...We are governed, our minds are molded, our tastes formed, our ideas suggested, largely by men we have never heard of. This is a logical result of the way in which our democratic society is organized.
Vast numbers of human beings must cooperate in this manner if they are to live together as a smoothly functioning society. ...In almost every act of our daily lives, whether in the sphere of politics or business, in our social conduct or our ethical thinking, we are dominated by the relatively small number of persons...who understand the mental processes and social patterns of the masses.
It is they who pull the wires which control the public mind."
Edward L Bernays

Basically we are all highly suggestible especially in today's age of mass media and concentrated
marketing and they know well how easy it is for us to fall prey to interest payments.

Usury is the biggest problem we face in today's society.
A sovereign nation has no need to borrow from any private banker whether native or foreign to that nation.

A sovereign nation does not need to charge ANY interest on

loans, now let that one sink in for a while and realise the positive consequences of that! It is completely life changing.

Once you understand how removing ALL interest changes the economy, the country, your finances and your life, you will see how it has been an un-necessary millstone around all our necks and amaze at how they managed to get our leadership to 'buy into it'.

Again, we have been so ingrained with our current systems, never really questioning them, just paying back interest like everyone else does.

"Well, it's the only way isn't it? No, it is certainly not!"

Usury is a leech on society, it drains our prosperity, the fruits of our hard work are gradually syphoned off until we wake up one day asking why the country has no money, why do we have to keep facing cuts in services, why do we keep seeing raises in taxes, why do they need to bring in new taxes on purchases and services, where did it all go so wrong?
One word, 'usury'.

There are of course many other contributing factors but usury is the standout culprit.
There are many excellent articles on bankers and how they weaseled their way into the power they hold and on interest and usury to be found online so please research further and learn more about this subject as it has so much influence on your life.

POLITICS AND VOTER REPRESENTATION

History tells us that our governing systems gradually evolved from various beginnings to what we have today and we are told this is IT!

We in the western world now live in democracies, it is fair and just, we can vote freely for the things we want and do not want in our societies.

This is it folks, you have the very best of the best today!

So, let's take a look at the democracy we are supposed to have.

In my case living in Ontario, Canada, there are 3 main provincial (Ontario) political parties. These parties are somewhat representative of the political spectrum in most western countries, namely right wing, middle of the road to left wing and left wing.

Being someone who takes an interest, I look at what those parties are standing for and which policies they wish to implement.

I always find that I like some of the policies of each party but do not like everything each party stands for or wishes to implement should they be elected.

Therefore I am left with the quandary of choosing the party I dislike the least!

Then after winning the election, I learn that the policies I did like will NOT be implemented and that they will introduce laws and regulations I do not like and would never have voted for!

Now what sort of democracy is that? Democracy in name only.

On top of that the elected representative gives the usual speech of how humbled they are to be selected and entrusted with our faith blah, blah, blah.

As Dawn Approaches

Then it's off to parliament or congress or senate to learn very quickly how things are actually going to happen.

Yes, our humbled representative (who may well really care at first) actually has very limited say in anything and must toe the party line.

Result for political system 1, result for real democracy 0.

Let's face it, why let an annoyance like an election disrupt the system, why interfere with a deeply entrenched 'old boy' network where the privileged few are always the winners?

Let the people vote, let them feel they are partaking in democracy. That will keep them satisfied but we know nothing really ever changes, we the privileged few win every time.

Another blow to this illusory democracy is the politically motivated media. I have witnessed time and time again when a certain party wins an election and proceeds to implement a policy that was a part of their electoral platform, that certain media will lambast them at every chance, even when elected in a clear majority.

True democracy? We are nowhere close to true democracy. Our voices are not heard, instead we are relegated to watching highly paid politicians act like imbeciles, our representatives displaying behaviour that we would not allow in a school.

They vote themselves salaries, expenses and pensions that verge on the obscene. They allow
corporations and special interests to bolster their election and campaign chests and try to tell us they are not biased toward that donor.

They allow the government to intrude into our lives with ever increasing surveillances which we the people actually have no say in, but foot the bill for. Who voted for that!

There are so many things the governments impose on us without our consent and the vast majority of those things are such that we would never allow if we had the chance to say so.

The governments act in a similar way to some of the large corporations that monopolise services such as; cable TV and telephone whereby they use 'negative billing'. Which means we will charge you for something you didn't ask for unless you actually tell us you don't want it.

The governments do the same by consistently nickel and diming us with new laws here, new regulations there and more surveillance everywhere. Big brother creeping into our lives more each day and as long as the complaints, the reader's letters and the pundits moan and gripe a little then that's just fine, the people won't march or revolt, they are too busy earning a living to do that, no, it's ok, we will continue to diminish freedom and democracy, it serves us so well.

The time is almost upon us where we will be monitored everywhere, even in our own homes as things such as; appliances, televisions and smart meters report back to the government WE pay for for our every move.

Who needs these intrusions? Why are these situations allowed, how can this be happening to the people, what right does the government have to do these things? Answer NONE!

They have NO such rights but by our complacency we the people

have inadvertently allowed them to do this to us.
And if you think this will make you safer please think again.

*"Those who would give up essential Liberty, to purchase a
little temporary Safety, deserve neither Liberty nor Safety."
Benjamin Franklin*

TRUE DEMOCRACY - APPARENT DEMOCRACY - NO DEMOCRACY

In today's world you could probably break the basic levels of
democracy into two categories:

APPARENT DEMOCRACY, which we have in most western
countries. We believe we have real democracy but a little
research and common sense tells you that this is not the case.

NO DEMOCRACY, this refers to the various tyrannies around the
world and includes the dictators.
I couldn't include true democracy because it doesn't yet exist.

In fact we in the 'apparent democracy' group, those who actually
believe we do have true democracy, will learn from some basic
research that the little illusory democracy we do have is rapidly
diminishing.
That bastion of freedom and democracy, the USA, even under
the control of a 'democratic' political party, have all but torn up
the American constitution.

The President continues to defy the very principles of the
founding fathers who tried their best to guard against
government tyranny by giving himself more and more executive
powers which bypass the checks and balances of the elected
representatives.

Then there is the NDAA. The President signed into effect, the right for the military to arrest and detain indefinitely, any American citizen, anywhere in the world without right to trial!

"I spent many years in countries where the military had the power to arrest and detain citizens without charge. I have been in some of these jails.
I have friends and colleagues who have 'disappeared' into military gulags.
I know the consequences of granting sweeping and unrestricted policing power to the armed forces of any nation. And while my battle may be quixotic, it is one that has to be fought if we are to have any hope of pulling this country back from corporate fascism."
Pullitzer prize winner and former New York Times Journalist - Chris Hedges.

The NDAA as with the Patriot Act and other security measures were adopted to deter and detain terrorists but the problem is the US government are gradually redefining what a terrorist actually is.

There is a creeping toward monitoring people who are anti-government, veterans and gun owners. They are beginning to use such terms as 'soft terrorist'.

Excuse me but being anti-government is a right of free speech, not grounds to be called a terrorist of any kind. How far will this go and where will this end?

The UK has hundreds of thousands of cameras monitoring the people and next to come is 'pre-crime' software which is supposed to know by the look on your face if you are thinking of

doing something illegal.
The police will then pull you in for questioning. Very much in line with the 'big brother' novel
1984 written by George Orwell.

The recent whistle blowing by Edward Snowden revealed how far the NSA, Canada's CSEC and the UK's GCHQ have infiltrated all of our lives with everything we say on the phone and write online being recorded.
If we allow things to continue on this path they will be able to go back and pull anything we
have said in the past and use it against us.
Edward Snowden took a huge risk and knew his life would be changed forever but he did what he felt as a US citizen he should do.
US politicians have called him a traitor, a traitor to whom?
Certainly not the hundreds of millions of taxpayers that have been spied on illegally! It appears that these people forget who foots the bill, it is the people they are spying on who pay for their own incursions of privacy, their loss of rights.

More worrying is that there are some in the US government that want Snowden executed.
I never thought I would see the day when Russia would give safe haven to an American for exposing his government's illegal activities!
This all just goes to prove that an unchecked government will stop at nothing when they have free reign to do as they wish.
Remember, we are all footing the bills for this, we are paying for our own invasions of privacy, by our silence we are condoning the diminishing of our rights and freedoms, we are allowing an encroaching tyranny.

Again, all of this is available online. I am not trying to scare people but I want to explain where we are heading and what happens when we give our power away to representatives who then abuse that power.

ILLUSORY POWER

"When the people fear their government, there is tyranny; when the government fears the people, there is liberty."
Thomas Jefferson

The people are not supposed to fear their government.
The government in a so-called democracy is not in any way supposed to be a controller of the people.
The government need be just a facilitator, a body of administrators taking care of the necessary business of enabling the smooth running of industry and commerce, the administering and distribution of funds to ensure those less fortunate are taken care of and assisted and looking after the nation and her people in general.

The people do not want or need to be 'governed' or controlled. We do not elect people to then have them control us. That would be tantamount to calling our version of democracy the right to choose which prison officer locks you up at night and watches over you.

Let's cut to the chase and understand we are all sovereign human beings, all equal regardless of which womb we originate from.

Just because some of our outdated cultures and customs espouse that some privileged people are higher up the ladder than others and that that makes them better than others is laughable today.

As Dawn Approaches

The divine right of Kings and their offspring has come and gone, sorry to be the one to spoil the party but we are all equal.

We are all flesh and blood, bleed the same colour and are sustained by the wonderful planet Earth.
Instead of dividing and conquering, we need to work together, we are all one, let us take that to heart and begin acting that way and the nation will be as one in unison with a focus on being good stewards of the country while we are taking our turn at the helm.

We are only here for a relatively brief period in history so why not respect the land and water, the nation and our fellow brothers and sisters and try leaving a better place than that we found it to be.

In truth our governments do not have actual 'power' but they assume they do have power by default because we allow them to believe they do.
It is a strange unwritten rule, an unspoken subject, the systems have been around for so many
generations which we are raised in and those who do question their power or authority are either silenced by the government in one way or another or shunned by the people as extremists, rocking the boat un-necessarily or just trouble makers.

Ask the government if they have power and they will tell you they are merely representing our best interests but most know this is not how it really is.

To give the illusion of power they award themselves ridiculous titles such as the 'right honourable' (British Commonwealth politicians), 'your worship' (Mayors), 'your honour' (judges).

As Edward Bernays knew, we are all so highly suggestible that the mere appearance of power has an effect on us and we subconsciously believe it to be true.

I will not get into Royalty and the titled people here except to say that anyone who bows and scrapes to another is merely lowering themselves instead of showing respect to another human being, and if you insist we are not all equal then you must delight in being treated as less than human because that is ALL we are, fellow human beings on planet Earth. Anything less is either self-imposed subservience or tyranny, you choose.

Again, I wish no ill will toward any human being but it is time for a new mindset of basic respect for everyone with no special cases for the privileged.

A NEW WAY, A NEW STRUCTURE
The present systems and institutions are so deeply rooted in our minds, so engrained in our psyches that we cannot see that there is another way.

Yet it is quite apparent that nothing will change by electing a different party. We have gone that route many times in the past but as we have seen, nothing really changes, at least not for the people.

Most of us are disgusted with our governments using our money to give to bankers who completely abused their positions and created financial disasters. Not only did they evade any prosecutions but sat back laughing at us knowing they are untouchable!

Then of course using OUR bailout money to lend to almost anyone but the people and to add insult to injury, also using that money for obscene bonuses! Someone pinch me and wake me up, this must be just a bad dream, it can't be real can it? Sadly, as we know, yes it is and it is just plain wrong!

This alone should be the final kick in the teeth of our present systems, they not only fail to represent us but abuse our hard earned money and set the scene for these abuses to happen again.
We are not represented. Period.

Quite simply, the entire system needs a clean sweep, a new structure based on every person having a say in how the country is run and how their lives should be. A system that serves each and every one of us as fairly, as equitable as possible.
A truly democratic way whereby WE have the power to say what we feel is right instead of giving our power away to people who fail to represent us.

A system in which WE actually represent ourselves. A system that we all partake in and can understand.
A system without politicians. There, I have said it, yes, a system without politicians!!

With the technologies and instant communication we enjoy today, politicians are now OBSOLETE!
We have no further use for them.

They supposedly take our concerns to parliament, congress or senate and argue among themselves whether or not action need be taken. OBSOLETE!

Political parties supposedly standing for certain values that we can vote for are now OBSOLETE!
We have no need or use for them today. The money and time

they waste bickering in ways a child should be ashamed of are over. Their time is over .

We the people can take care of things now and a far better job we will do too, at least whatever happens it will be down to us as we will have voted for it.
When the people take charge of their own countries and ways of life there will be no need for politics at all, just humanity, compassion and what is best for the country and her people.

Imagine that! A huge unnecessary part of our lives gone forever, politics, the game so lovingly played by those who take our money and power and hand it over to bankers and corporations, which continue to squeeze us in every way they can.
IT IS TIME
It is time for the people to be aware and fully participate in their's and their nation's best interests.
It is time for the people to take back their power and right the wrongs.
It is time for true democracy, devoid of greed and self-interest.
It is time for a completely new economic model.
It is time for that last final step in the evolution of democracy.
It is time for The Organic Economy.

THE ORGANIC ECONOMY

As we are so entrenched in our present political, economic and financial systems, what I am sharing with you may require a level of open mindedness and a willing to let these ideas sink in, to become familiar with and to understand the full implications of, for once you do you will see how it makes complete sense.

The irony is that our present systems are so distorted from servicing us, so unfair to the people, so undemocratic, that a truly fair and equitable system may appear radical!

What is an Organic Economy?

By organic I do not actually mean an economy based on organic foods etc. although I am a huge fan of organic foods, by organic I mean a real economy that uses real money instead of the phoney fiat 'Ponzi scheme' money or 'funny money' that almost every country in the world has been duped or strong armed into participating in by the banking families.

By Organic Economy I mean breaking away from a false financial system set up to benefit a very select few.
Breaking away from a system which sees the fruits of our labours drained away instead of being reinvested in our country where it so rightly belongs.

The Organic Economy will have no need for politicians. Every eligible voter will be required to vote by way of an encrypted message from their computers, phones or whatever devices are available to send encrypted information to a central system which will display the results after they have all been collected. I will elaborate later in this book.

The implications of an organic economy combined with a true democracy are enormous for the people.
History will certainly be made as the first nation to implement these ideas will clearly demonstrate how a nation and her people can truly prosper, enjoy abundance and live in peace, be compassionate, less materialistic and more conscious of the environment and more in tune with nature.

As other nations follow there will be less overall control by the world's 'leadership', the bankers and corporations, less wars and strife and more compassion and aid to our less fortunate brothers and sisters in lands and circumstances that only by pure chance we were not the ones born there.

We are ALL equal on Mother Earth. There is abundance for all when the people are in control instead of a select few.
The Organic Economy will be an 'interest free' economy for all money will be loaned by that country's ONLY bank.

There will be no reason for any of the other banks to exist unless people wish it but those private banks will not be allowed to earn interest should they lend money, for usury, the root cause of the world's monetary woes, will be completely abolished.

Savings in the bank will not receive interest as usury is abolished. Interest only serves to compensate for inflation anyway and The Organic Economy will eradicate inflation.

Why should someone make money just because they have money? This is where our financial problems began, this is where greed becomes master and those with money make ever more of it, use it for nefarious purposes and we gradually slide back down the slippery slope to where we are today.

Effort, enterprise and ideas deserve reward, not just the fact you have money.
Every loan will be interest free anyway so there will be no need to fall victim to the greed of others who will take your property and possessions if you struggle to make repayments.

To eradicate inflation, The Organic Economy will hold ALL prices as they stand at that time. There will not be any need to raise prices on anything we buy because our buying power will never weaken. This also applies to living accommodation, houses will be the same price when your children are ready to purchase their first home twenty five years from now.

Rents will be locked in as there will be no need to raise them when inflation no longer exists.
For those who do truly increase the value of their home there will be consideration for a fair increase in value but the criteria will ALWAYS be what is best for the country and her people as opposed to pure greed.

Wages are open for discussion but as taxes will gradually go down people will have more disposable income.
The eradication of interest on all loans in the economic system will also increase spending power significantly.

In a fair and humane society the focus will gradually shift from stressful material ambition to a more relaxed lifestyle whereby the people will re-learn how to fully enjoy life with what they have and to fully appreciate family and recreation.
These presently highly stressful times will be looked back on as we now look back on serfdom and peasantry.

As things currently stand we have no idea where our economies will be in twenty years, how much will a house cost, how much will college or university tuition be? We are all at the mercy of the bankers, growth, inflation and other un-necessary nonsense.

With an organic economy we will know exactly what things will cost because we will not be economic slaves to the bankers and usury which creates these problems.

Once the country is free from paying the extortionate billions of dollars of interest to the bankers, that money will stay in the country and assist the country in its lending to the people, interest free.

Once the people are liberated from the economic slavery of the bankers and they find they have much more disposable income due to the money saved from not paying interest everywhere they turn, they will spend more into the economy creating a demand for goods and services.

In The Organic Economy the people will call the shots instead of politicians who cater to corporations and other countries demands or wishes.

The people can if they wish, tear up international trade deals that favour the corporations and bring back manufacturing so that they have the jobs back that were lost with the corporate globalisation scam.
A single leader such as; a Prime Minister or President is weak when negotiating trade and other deals with super powers and central bankers, but a nation with every voter being its leadership is a formidable force and virtually un-breakable.

The people will decide if they want the country to be part of any international or global trade deals.
Anything which does not benefit the people and country can be rescinded by the people.
Credit cards will not be required as interest is abolished but the people will be issued debit/advance cards from the nation's bank.

Credit will be called advanced money, as that is what it is, an advance from future earnings.
The nation's bank will take care of all loans including mortgages and car loans and also offer lines of credit or overdraft protection. The rationale being that the bank will do whatever it

can to help the people as the bank is of the people.

Evictions because of non-payments of mortgages and rents will be kept to zero or the barest minimum.
The bank will do everything within fairness to keep people in their homes as this is by far the better way in the bigger picture.

Desperation and poverty can lead to crime and crime is far more expensive to society and in more ways than helping a person in hard times keep their home plus they will eventually pay it back anyway, just that the people's bank will be more flexible and caring.

Specially trained councillors will be on hand to help those in financial difficulty. They will help find work and other ways to keep them from losing everything should a situation become that dire.
The days of the cold, hard nosed banking business model will be a distant memory as everyone who is employed by the bank or any other administrative department for the country will be mandated to be of service to the people and her country at all times first and foremost.

To see a person be made homeless will be akin to seeing a family member or friend being made
homeless, we will all do everything we can to end the cycles of poverty, homelessness and desperation which affects us all in one way or another, often with drug and alcohol abuse and the associated crime to pay for it.

A society rife with crime and substance abuse is a sick society but this is not the fault of those who have made themselves wealthy by hard work, art or enterprise.

The problem is the systems we have now which do not work for the people.
The Organic Economy will address these issues as outlined here.

The term 'government' will no longer be used as will any other term such as 'authority', insinuating power and control over the people. Control over the people will not be real, implied or imagined.
This also pertains to the Police who are paid to serve and protect, the term 'force' is not necessary and will no longer be used.

The country and regions will be taken care of by administrators who will be highly trained and
knowledgeable regarding their duties to the people and country.

All employees of the nation will be well versed that their main obligation is always to the people who pay their salaries and to the country.
The present departments of government will be required but will not be called 'government'
departments.
All departments will be overseen by a panel of knowledgeable people who will also collect data which will always be available for the people to observe.
This data from all departments will also potentially be a part of the following years voting agenda list.
The various panels will oversee the departments to ensure everything is being done in the best interests of the country and her people. They will also be vigilant of any person or corporation attempting to buy favours or lobbying for projects which benefit themselves.

All requests from people, groups or corporations wishing to engage in any activity that may affect the people or their country in any way, will have to go through the proper channels that will be in place for those purposes and the people will always have the final say.

The over-seeing panels will always have spokespeople to relay pertinent information to the people and the spokespeople will rotate so as to inhibit the image of power. We are well aware of how impressionable we are to mass media and the repeated images and words of a person.

There will be a highly qualified emergency panel in place to deal specifically with immediate matters of high national importance such as international conflicts or disasters.
However, everything they decide will be made fully public and in the shortest period will be put to an emergency vote so the people can decide how they wish their nation to proceed.

IMPORTANT HISTORICAL NOTE

The reason I stress the removal of any naming conventions for departments which pertain to any form of 'control' (government, authority, force) is this.

We are very fortunate to be around to witness the history of the USA. A country which broke away from the control of Great Britain, or more accurately, the City of London and its bankers.

The founding fathers of the American constitution knew well the potential dangers of allowing private bankers to issue and control a nation's money.
They did everything in their powers to ensure the constitution protected the American people from private bankers but even with that protection the bankers weaseled their way in illegally in 1913 and created the Federal Reserve (a group of private

bankers).

At fault were the Senate who allowed this to happen. Any way you look at it, either the constitution or the representatives of the people failed them.

We are also witness today to how corrupt the American leadership is as the US is barely even attempting to hide how fascist it has become (fascism being government run by corporations).

I don't have time to list the litany of wrongs our governments undertake on a daily basis, wrongs which do not represent the best interests of the nation and her people. But they abuse this power to the point our governments are corrupt, have sold out to other interests and are rotten to the core.

We no longer have need for them, the voter will be the only person with true power.
Therefore we can plainly see that in a new economy such as The Organic Economy, we must not only ensure that the bankers are abolished permanently but that the power of the country must lie totally with ALL of her people and not given away to representatives of any kind, as it is only a matter of time before they are bought off and compromised.

Most people have their price and the bankers have almost unlimited wealth to offer. So to avoid a repeat of what happened to the US we entrust the leadership of the country to EVERYONE and everyone must be as aware and educated about the nation's affairs as possible. The power must always lie with the people.

END OF HISTORICAL NOTE

As Dawn Approaches

Every eligible voter will vote on the national agenda which will be presented every year. The voting agenda will be collated from all the main issues the various departments and the people have.
All issues will be discussed on the nations TV station and all other media so everyone knows what the main issues are and can educate themselves about them.
We will have debating teams discussing the pros and cons of any vote subject that may have deeper implications than at first thought so the people may have a maximum understanding of the issues they will be voting on.
Voting is done instantly from the people's computers, phones or any other communicable device. The vote list may be 20 issues or 120 issues, it does not matter how many are presented and requested by the people and the departments.

Voting will be open for one week of the year and every eligible voter must vote. We must participate in the decisions which affect us all.
At present, voter turnout continues to decline or stay at undemocratically low levels. This means the people are disinterested, disillusioned or just plain fed up with the system, that is when apathy sets in and the politicians assume more power and abuse their positions with little fear of retribution.

It is of the greatest importance that every eligible voter understands the issues and votes.
True freedom requires self-responsibility which in this case means everyone must vote.
Parliaments, halls of congress, senates, buildings which representatives presently use for their charades will be turned over to the people to be used as forums.
The people can apply and take their turns in these public and televised forums to make their points on issues they feel strongly about.

These issues have as much chance of being on the next voting list as any other issue so this will be an important democratic forum for the people.

These ideas are just a way to get things started. Such ideas, if the people will it, may evolve into
increasingly democratic systems not yet imagined, it will always be what the people will it to be through the vote.

Voting will be based on three choices; Yes, No and Uncertain. A significant number of 'Uncertain' votes likely means the issues were not discussed or presented in a fully understandable manner. The subject can then be re-addressed, examined and debated for the following years voting list.

Voting outcomes will be enacted as soon as possible by the administrators. If something becomes unpopular then it can be rescinded at the next vote the following year.

It will be seen that after some years the vote list will become increasingly smaller as the majority of people find equilibrium in their lives and most issues taken care of.

The Organic Economy requires no leaders, no one person or group will have any more power or control than one single voter. However, no matter how fair and equitable a nation becomes there will always be the few who lust for power and control. We must ensure that the new constitution guards against this at all times.

This will entail the careful placement and rotation of national employees such as; administrators to curtail any possibility of a 'power bloc' forming that may attempt a coup or to agitate the people against their own freedom and democracy.

Another important reason for the people to be vigilant of the nation's situations.

It only requires a short period of harder times such as a prolonged recession (should that happen) for seductive promises of jobs and more money to become attractive enough for some to protest for a new 'leadership'.

Once back in power the organic economy would soon be history and the people would very quickly once again become economic slaves to the bankers. The people must always be watchful.

Whistleblowers and those who witness actions or plans to undertake anything which is detrimental to the people and country will be allowed full freedom to express concern without punishment.

Journalism will once again be free to pursue and investigate within the laws of the land and to be the thorn in the sides of those who tend to abuse their positions.

Powerful corporations and monopolies, as with all issues, will be discussed, debated and presented for vote. This is not a manhunt for successful corporations but a fair and balanced look at whether or not the people and nation are benefitting from their presence.

The people will have full say regarding police departments. The police work for the people and mutual respect is paramount. Policemen and women who abuse their positions will be removed.

As The Organic Economy becomes fully appreciated there will be less and less crime, poverty and overall hardships for the populace.

Jail will be the very last resort and mainly for violent and sexual offenders that are highly likely to reoffend.

Community service and other forms of punishment and rehabilitation will be the way forward.
All positions of 'imagined' power such as; police chiefs will be subject to the scrutiny of the people.
They may still be appointed by a panel of knowledgeable administrators but performance will be monitored and the local people affected may at any time call a vote to remove that chief.

Judges will be elected and accountable and the people need only refer to them as 'Sir' or 'Madam' as opposed to 'Your Honour'.
Obscene gold plated pensions and perks paid for by the people will also be available for voting on by the people.

Recommendations can be made which are fair. The Organic Economy is not at all about anger,
retribution or payback, we must leave those attitudes behind us along with the greed so prevalent in today's broken systems.

Civil servants or national/provincial employees will not be attracted to those positions because of high salaries, jobs for life and higher than average pensions but because they actually want to help and serve their country and people.

Gradually, all people will be able to enjoy retirement with dignity as the country prospers with an organic economy.

The military will be required until most of the world adopts The Organic Economy but for defensive purposes only.
The military will no longer assist certain nations who use their militaries as policemen for
corporations that raid other nation's assets.

As the country becomes increasingly prosperous taxes will gradually decrease leaving the people with more and more

disposable income to spend.
This will also lead to lower and lower tuition fees for college and university students until it will
eventually become free.
Meanwhile there will be no interest on current loans.

New courses and degrees will be available that deal with national administration positions, again with the emphasis on what is best for the people and her country.

Eventually the country will be administered by very competent, fair and balanced employees with all our best interests at heart.

School curriculums will be adapted to reflect The Organic Economy. Students will be required to learn the basics such as; reading, writing and arithmetic, cursive writing and the 'times tables' but also encouraged to think critically.

They will also spend as much time as possible outside exploring nature and learning about the
environment and be encouraged some of the time to elect among themselves that which they wish to learn that day.

All natural talents will be encouraged and teachers will assist in exploring as many creative ideas as possible.

At the beginning of the organic economy era there will be many 'teething problems' but the next generation who will be well versed with it will grow into adults who only know of a system of equity for all, whereby no one person or group has power over others and that generation will never go back to the awful old system of politics, old boy networks and all the other systems of suppressing the people that exist today.

Those who wish to become teachers may stay in their respective schools for a period of time (two years for example) as paid mentors and tutors, to help the children and be with them to ensure their well-being and be observant toward negative behaviour such; as bullying and then working to eradicate it. This will help the school staff and give valuable practical experience to the teacher student in
preparation for university.

SMALLER COMMUNITIES

I discussed earlier the problems with amalgamation and how it eliminates democracy in all but name.
How the European Union is ordering once sovereign nations to what they can and can't do and how unelected eurocrats are making thousands of laws for people who never voted for those laws.
The big losers are the people and democracy.

The only way for people to have control over their day to day lives is to return back to community living.
Keeping communities in control over their own affairs, affairs that are specific to that community.
The present system of local representatives or councillors, in most cases, works for the people because they are community focused and the councillor lives among the same voters and is fully aware of the local concerns.
But there is certainly room for improvement and the locals can use the same voting system each year to address local issues. Therefore the councillors again would be more like administrators ensuring the will of the people is undertaken or enacted.

The annual voting system will eliminate any need for time

wasting politics and theatrics and we can observe with great interest as to how things evolve through the will of the people.

Local issues such as; new housing developments on land considered precious by the local people and other similar issues whereby the local people feel they are being 'steam rollered' by a corporate power, will be completely in the hands of those voters affected and they will have the final say.
Again, the defining principle being what is best for the people and the land.

A NEW CONSTITUTION

A country that adopts The Organic Economy will also need a new or modified constitution, a document that all the people agree is valid and will be the template compass for the nation to follow.

The main points for an organic economy are as follows;

To enshrine that the people's bank and only that bank will issue debt free and interest free money.
To eliminate politics - politicians are obsolete - annual voting by the people will replace them.
To eliminate usury in all forms - no more borrowing from central bankers - no more interest on any loans.
To cap ALL sales prices – inflation to be eliminated.
To ensure that no person, group or entity has any more power than any singular person.
To ensure that all national matters are made public as soon as possible.
To enshrine that what is best for the people and their country, their land, their water, is the basis for all decisions.
To ensure that the less fortunate are helped as much as possible with every possible effort being made to help them lead

productive lives.
To reduce or eliminate tuition fees for college and university students.
There will be many more items to be added but these are the most important I can think of now.
As with anything that affects the people and her country, everything will be voted on and agreed to by
the people. Additions and amendments can be proposed, presented and debated as with all issues
affecting the people.

QUESTIONS AND POTENTIAL ANSWERS

This is a most interesting section of this book. I have written this mainly with my own thoughts and
therefore have not addressed any concerns or questions raised about The Organic Economy (yet).
The one person whom I began to explain it immediately shook their head and said "Nope, can never
happen".

This is exactly what I expect to hear from most people because, as I said earlier, we are so entrenched
and so indoctrinated into our current systems that it is, for many people, almost impossible to think
'outside the box', to peek through the veil so to speak, and see what lays on the other side.

This is mainly due to our beliefs. Our beliefs 'filter' our perceptions and are the gate keeper of what we
think is possible.
Most of our cultural and customary beliefs are cemented into our psyches in the first seven years of our
lives and this also includes our 'systems' and institutions, our

ways of life that we learn from our parents, then teachers and so on.

These beliefs are all but hard coded into our psyches and anything that questions or threatens those beliefs can often be treated with hostility in its defense, such is the power of entrenched beliefs.

As I said earlier, when an accepted system is so distorted from servicing us, so unfair to the people, so undemocratic, that a truly fair and equitable system may appear radical!

Even if a new system is fair, it may be deemed radical or impossible because our present beliefs will not allow those thoughts to enter the mind.

However, an idea whose time has come is immensely powerful. Few would have ever thought that Gandhi could have achieved that which he did. The Indian people would never have thought they had the potential 'power' to remove the British Raj in any way, shape or form, but to do it with non-violence, with non-compliance, now that would seem impossible, but do it they did!

An idea whose time had come was spread by one man. The time had come, beliefs were changed, the mental barriers which guard the mind fell away and the people saw a new vision, a new way forward and nothing could stop that vision, such is the power of the people, people who have opened their minds and discarded the old beliefs.

John Reid

What was the biggest difference that people such as; Gandhi, Martin Luther King, Nelson Mandela and
the other brave souls who have made history by standing up to governments and militaries made?

Answer, they changed people's beliefs. Then history was changed. These people inspired the masses in
such a way that their beliefs were changed and nothing could stop that power.
When your beliefs are changed (with regard to governments) you will naturally find that you will 'lower
the bar' mentally to what you will accept and as you lower your own bar, the government
simultaneously loses power because the only power they actually have is the power we think or imagine
they have.
When a critical mass of people change their beliefs and cease to accept the government as a power, the
government will cease to be a government.

This is where we are today. We know things are so wrong and we merely need to change our beliefs that
we can live in peace, harmony and abundance. It is up to us, period!

I will also say unequivocally that the global power brokers, the controlling bankers and corporations will
understand exactly what I am saying. They know this is true and completely rely on the 'built-in' mental
barriers we are all victim to.

It is the only way they can successfully maintain their despotic grip on us. The mental prison we
unknowingly live within.

We are taught in schools how to think and critical thinking has no part in our curriculum. This is
intentional as the industrialists insisted on workers who were educated enough to communicate and
operate machinery but not to ask 'difficult' questions such as I have done in this book.

There is nothing quite as powerful as thought and the powers that be are well aware of this.
When the people change their beliefs and thoughts there is nothing a government can do to hold it back.
There is no need for revolution, merely evolution, evolution of thought, evolution of beliefs, evolution of
democracy.
So, I say to you the reader, if you find yourself putting up barriers to these ideas, to The Organic Economy, then please ask yourself which beliefs are behind those thoughts, try to identify their source and see what you discover.

Q – The government will not simply roll over and let this happen, how can this be achieved?

A – I agree, at present no-one with privilege and 'apparent' power will be willing to step down for The
Organic Economy to commence.
It will most likely be a replacement for a collapsed system caused by anything from a natural disaster,
global pandemic or war to a financial collapse which is looking ever more likely to happen in the near
future.
The people can then pick up the pieces and start anew. The most important thing I believe is that we

actually have a blueprint for a new system and this is why I am writing about an organic economy.
Without a new idea we would merely rebuild using the only blueprint we know, namely, our present
systems.

Q – What will happen to those currently in positions of 'power' and privilege such as politicians and senators?

A – Always keep in mind that these same people are also products of the same systems as we are, even
though many have had privileged upbringings and lives and many have abused their positions it is time
to start anew.

The Organic Economy will not be concentrating on the negative emotions, looking for revenge and
punishment unless the people decide that certain people need be punished. It will be time to move
forward in a positive manner looking to build bridges, to be inclusive instead of divisive.
I also offer that most of us in similar positions would find the human weakness for greed challenging to
deny.

I believe the fault lay mainly with the 'systems' and that in today's powerful global interactions that too
much power is in the hands of too few people.
The Organic Economy solves that issue as it will be the people who make the decisions.
I would suggest that those ex-politicians who display a true passion for the country and her people
would also be a valuable asset bringing extensive experience to

our over-seeing panels and stewards of
democracy.
There is nothing to fear for those who want what is best for all
the people.

**Q – The powers that be, central bankers and corporations will
never let this happen!**

A – Again, this is a belief from our present paradigm.
Of course the central bankers will do everything they can to
impede the progress toward true
democracy and economic freedom, to maintain and continue
their parasitical systems of usury over the
people but they will be no match for the people, people with a
new belief.
The nation will assemble the very best lawyers who will show
clearly that we have all been duped by an
age old farcical system of usury.
They will state the case that no country has the right to borrow
upon the backs of the unborn, natural
law would not allow that.
All laws can potentially be revisited by the people for vote and if
need be, they can vote down anything
that ties their country to any form of deal that is a proven
detriment to the country or her people.
Everything that happens to the country including threats from
the world's leaders and bankers will be
broadcast for the world to see.
The world will have a front row view of those who threaten in
the name of greed and control.
People around the globe are already aware and angry about
these things and in time, one by one, other
nations will also demand an organic economy.

John Reid

Q – Politically speaking, is The Organic Economy a socialist system?

A – No, as there are no politicians and everything is voted on by all the people it is an inclusive, apolitical, democratic, humanitarian system.

Being inclusive means everyone, which means taking care of the less fortunate, those in need and those
who fall on hard times, to those who are enterprising, build businesses and employ people, we will all
enjoy the freedom to pursue our own destiny without 'labels'.
If you wish, you could say there is socialism and capitalism, both are necessary in a successful and
prosperous country but these two labels have been at each other's throats for many years un-necessarily.
Politicians have had great careers on the back of these labels and it gets us nowhere in the end.
However, there needs to be balance and the people will keep corporate power in check as well as
wasted administrative spending.

Q – Is The Organic Economy about the redistribution of wealth with the rich being taxed heavily to subsidise the poor?
A – No, I believe there is confusion over the rich versus poor issue. We do not usually complain when a
famous artist such as a singer, actor or musician makes untold millions of Dollars but when a business
person does they are often thought of as greedy and callous.
Even if the rich were taxed at 99% (which the UK actually did at one time) this would not eliminate
poverty but would destroy incentive.
When the issue of poverty is mentioned it is common practice to

look straight at the wealthy but it is not
the fault of the wealthy. Yes, they can be exploitive and callous
but they need not shoulder all the blame.
The issue is really with our current financial systems of usury
which drain our prosperity leaving little left
for the less fortunate. The colossal impact of interest on loans is
such that it eventually ruins a nation.
With the abolishment of usury there will be enough money and
resources to take care of the less
fortunate.

**Q – You stated that there would be no inflation. How does
that affect the value of our money, and
how will it affect our imports and exports?**

A – When a currency is tied to a set value such as; a certain
amount of gold and inflation is kept at zero,
the currency will never de-value. Then as other currencies that
remain within the present system
experience inflation, their currency devalues against our
currency.
Even as other nations raise their prices because of inflation, this
will have a zero net effect for us as our
currency will always be stronger and enjoy increased buying
power.
Therefore, the cost of imports and imported raw materials will
not be affected, but exports will be
affected as they will be more expensive for other nations to buy
due to our stronger currency.
This can be addressed with subsidies from the nation's bank to
allow our exporters to compete.
The globalists have disdain for subsidies but the people will no
longer be held hostage by special
interests, especially those of foreign corporations.

John Reid

**Q – I have a good life, my wife and I both have good jobs that we enjoy, we have a nice house, two
cars and take vacations each year. The Organic Economy sounds good but how will it affect our lives, we don't really want to lose the lifestyle we have?**
A – Nothing that affects what you already have. You will have your jobs, cars and house and still take
your annual vacations but you will find as interest on loans (usury) is eliminated, you will enjoy a more
disposable income.
Then as the nation grows in true prosperity and taxes are gradually lowered you will enjoy further
increases in disposable income.
You will also enjoy increased spending power when you holiday 'out of country' as your currency
gradually grows in strength against other currencies.
You will be expected to vote each year on the issues presented by the people and the nations
employees as everyone will be mandated to do so. The success of an Organic Economy and true
democracy depends upon your annual vote.
Keep in mind also that the present systems are going to collapse one way or another anyway, it's just a
matter of time.

Q – I own a small business and employ five people, I have worked extremely hard to grow this business and want to know how the organic economy will affect me?

A – As a business owner nothing will change except the administrators will be looking at all of the 'red
tape' and cumbersome government agencies which cause so

much grief for businesses, with the idea of
streamlining things to make it as easy as possible for the business owner.
As with everything else that concerns the people and the nation, suggestions for improvements can be
presented, discussed, debated and added to the vote list to be ratified by the people.
One big difference will be the removal of usury or interest on any business loans. This will enable a
business owner to reduce prices to the customer or increase wages for example.

Q – Many people are concerned about the effects on the environment from projects such as; the Tar sands and oil and gas pipelines, what will happen to them?

A – As with any decisions it will be up to the people to decide. However, all details must be discussed
such as the cost of fuel if the Tar sands were stopped and other residual effects that may at not first be
apparent to everyone.
Every effort must be made to fully disclose any and all information and the possible outcomes of
terminating such projects so the people make informed decisions.
The new economy however, will provide research and development funds for alternative energy sources.

Q – How long will it take to implement The Organic Economy, it can't just happen overnight?

A – Any new system will have teething problems and there will be a huge learning curve as this will be

something that has never been done before in a developed society.
We have been subjected to so many methods of control over the past thousand years and longer that
even if takes ten to fifteen years before economic equilibrium is achieved, it will be worth waiting for.
However, I believe we will enjoy marked improvements in our lives within five years and equilibrium within ten years.

Q - What do people have to do to make The Organic Economy happen?
Do we organise, protest, march and rally because most people won't do that and it usually fails to
change anything anyway?

A - The most important action to take is to spread the idea as far and wide as possible as it applies to all
of the world's population.
Send this e-book to as many people as you think may appreciate it.
I believe firstly that it is extremely important that people realise there is another way so we can rebuild
using a blueprint such as; The Organic Economy after an economic or financial collapse.
Secondly, there is always the possibility that once people are aware of a far better system and they
become sufficiently disillusioned with the present systems, they may demand real change and from
there anything can happen.
What is important to note is the next generation, in ten years, will already be free thinking and rid of the
mental shackles of today's systems. They will only know one way of living and The Organic Economy will
be all they know. They will not want any part of systems such as

those we live under today.

Let's get this out to as many people as possible and plant the
seeds of thought, new thought, new ideas,
for the world is ours, all of ours.

"Every mind that is opened to these ideas is another puncture
hole in the balloon of control and
apparent power!"

END OF BOOK

CHAPTER 5

21 - A Mind Opened

Andrea was amazed at what she had just read and had certainly never read anything quite like it before. When Jerry returned from the park with the kids Andrea said "Hey I just read that PDF on the computer."

"PDF, what PDF?" replied Jerry.

"The one on the desktop in the folder called 'The Book', I take it that that's 'the' book I keep hearing about?"

"Oh right, that one, Ron sent it to me but I haven't got around to reading it yet."

"I think you should Jeff, it's something else, has some great new ideas," said Andrea.

"Yeah I will, we were talking with Ron at the cottage on the Canada Day weekend and again at the bar, he told us about a 'book' and that it could change things and stuff. I meant to read it too, as Ron also said things are gonna happen pretty soon Hon," Jerry added.

"Well it's completely changed my outlook," Andrea said, "I don't know where those ideas came from but I really like them and I think they could really mean something, you should read it Jerry. What did Ron mean about things happening?"

"Looks like Canada is going the way of the US after all, I knew it was too good to be true that we would be left out of what's going on in the world," said Jerry.

"You mean we are going to be taken over or something, soldiers in the streets, what's going to happen Jerry?"

"Ron said it'll never come to that Hon, there's a movement or something, lots of highly placed people will stop it from happening and then they will hold a vote so we can decide how we want Canada to be run, like it says in 'the book' you just read, a new system."

"Oh my God are you serious Jerry, if that happens....it would be fantastic, but are you sure we are going to be ok?" Andrea asked in shock.

"Yeah, yeah Babe nothing to worry about, let's face it we all knew something was going to happen but it's so hard to actually get your head around the idea. But Ron says things are in good hands."

"Ok, if you're sure about it then I'm ok with it, anyway, we can't go on much longer like this Jerry, the system is broke it's so screwed up, we have to change to some other way, we have no choice. 'The book' makes that pretty clear too so hurry up and read it Babe."

"I'm going to read it tonight Hon, soon as I've cleaned up, changed and ate."

Jerry did just that but by the time he had finished reading 'the book' Andrea was asleep in bed. Jeff was also surprised by what he read and looked forward to sharing the information with Andrea and some other people he thought may appreciate the ideas. Next morning at breakfast Jerry was talking to Andrea,

"I read 'the book' like I said," Jerry began, "boy oh boy my mind feels like it has been torn open."

"Mine too," Andrea replied, "never would have thought of those ideas."

"No, me neither, but it's really quite simple, it kinda makes sense doesn't it?" Jerry said.

"That's the crazy part, it does, it's pretty straightforward, kinda makes you wonder why we've put up with the garbage we've put up with all this time," Andrea replied.

"I suppose that's why he talked about beliefs and how we are brought up, only knowing one way, kinda brainwashed," Jerry added.

"Yeah, I suppose we are, not that it's our fault, how would we know any better?" said Andrea.

"We don't, or didn't until we read 'the book'," continued Jerry, "but now we can see for ourselves where this world is heading and we better smarten up pretty darn quickly."

"We should share this with as many people as we can," exclaimed Andrea.

"Never thought of myself as any kind of activist Andrea but I know my brother and his crowd will eat this stuff up unless they already know about it."

Andrea replied. "But that's the thing Jerry, if you get where the book is taking you we don't even have to be activists, it is all based on a change of belief, that's all it says it takes, evolve our beliefs."

"I don't get it, how can that change anything, surely we have to get physical somehow like at least march or protest or something," Jerry said.

"Yes I agree, or let's say I agree from my old way of thinking. My mind has been changed by reading 'the book' and I can now see the difference Jerry, my old way of thinking would never allow me to accept that changing a belief could change anything in the world but now I can, it makes sense to me, don't you see it?" Andrea asked.

"Yeah, yeah, I just realised I am thinking through things from my previous perspective, it doesn't add up when you do that, I kinda had it last night after reading it, maybe I need to read it again, I was really tired and it may not have registered properly," Jerry replied.

"I just realised Jerry, wow, that is what this entire thing is about, it's about us, it's about how we can change things, jeeze, the power we actually have to do that, I'm getting it now, it's all about perspective, which your beliefs control, that's what he said in the book, holy cow it's ingenious, we are ingenious, we just haven't been told yet!" Andrea said.

"I'm reading it again tonight," Jerry added, "this really is thought provoking stuff."

"Simple but powerful, more powerful than anything we have known Jerry, changing a belief, so simple but so easy to blind people from, I will have to let this sink in, it's life changing Hon, it really is," Andrea finished.

22 – The Judge

The rich voice of Pavarotti wafted gracefully through the house from the study. The Judge had showered and dressed and was putting on his jacket in front of the hallway mirror, he hummed to the music as he checked his tie and hair, then his watch, nodded to himself and exited the front door. The judge climbed into the waiting taxi and gave the driver the address, a twenty five minute drive north in non-rush hour traffic to Richmond Hill, another suburb of the greater Toronto area.

The Judge was looking forward to tonight, it was always an interesting and entertaining time at the parties of his good friend Anthony Carsdale, a barrister he had known for over thirty years. Tonight would be no different as he was aware that Anthony had a few additional guests who were major players in their own fields of education, law and politics. He also knew that everyone attending was in agreement that the world was heading in the wrong direction and that they would do everything within their power to prevent Canada from becoming a victim of the globalists, they had one other thing in common, they had all read 'the book' and were part of the movement. This event was one of hundreds of identical events being held across Canada on varying evenings with varying guests from varying backgrounds. The number of patriots involved across the country were in the thousands, and they were ready.

23 – The Cottagers

Jerry came home from work, kissed Andrea on the cheek while she was preparing supper and waiting on the slow cooker, then went straight to the computer. He wanted to read 'the book' once again, it had been bugging him all day and he wanted to take his time and make sure he understood the message this time. It appeared Andrea got something else, something deeper from it.

Just after Jerry finished 'the book' Andrea called everyone to the table for dinner.

As he was sitting down at the table Jerry said to the kids, "Hey guys how are ya?"

"Good thanks Dad," came the reply from the kids.

"Then that's great," Jerry replied eyeing his plate of spaghetti and meatballs.

"How was work Honey?" Andrea asked Jeff.

"Good thanks, same old same old, nothing bad to report," Jerry replied.

The family ate their meal and the kids asked if they could leave the table. It was the summer vacation so the kids didn't have any homework. After the kids had left the room Andrea spoke to Jerry.

"Let me guess, you just read 'the book' again?" she enquired.

"Yes I did, I get it now, it's hard to push all you've ever known to one side and accept something new but then again it isn't really, it's just about changing a belief as you said, I get that now, so difficult but so simple," Jerry replied.

"I learned something today," Andrea continued, "when you read 'the book' and get it, when you get the message, it changes you. I mean, you change a belief and you think nothing has changed but you have changed, so, your outlook changes, then you go try and tell someone about it and they cannot accept it, cannot accept that we can change it all. It's too much for them to accept. Then it dawns on you that they haven't read 'the book' and that I would have thought the same as they do before I read it.

That's how much of a change 'the book' makes when you 'get it'. You can't just explain the ideas to people, they have to read 'the book', it's just the way it's written or something but you probably won't change your beliefs or ideas without actually reading it."

"Absolutely," said Jerry, "that's why I had to go back and read it again, I knew it had triggered something in you that I didn't get, but now I do, I 'get it', it's profound if you understand the underlying philosophy or whatever you want to call it. I realise now how conditioned we are, conditioned to not ask the whys, conditioned to look at what everyone else is doing, thinking and saying and then just shrugging and sticking your head back in the sand, if they aren't really complaining then it can't be that bad, so shut it and carry on. Thing is, they are all doing the exact same thing, we are all our own worst enemy and all that does is keep the elites happy, man we've been so dumb."

"Yes Hon, but who would have thought that without actually doing anything, anything physical, that you could make such a change, I can't accept what we have anymore Jerry, I can't accept how our government acts anymore, I can't accept how we are being robbed blind every day by bankers and big business, I can't accept the spying on us, the losing of our freedoms and rights, it has to stop, it has to change and this organic system, organic economy is a good place to start. We have always known these things but we just plod along living our lives, working to pay the bills, doing everything we can for our kids, but when you actually stop and think about it, we aren't doing the right thing for our kids because we are always turning a blind eye to what is going on. At the rate Canada is going, the world is going, there won't be anything left for our kids at all unless we do something. I want our kids to have a chance Jerry, the world right now is an awful place and getting worse by the day, I have lain in bed at night not being able to sleep because I'm so worried about what the kids are going to inherit and I know lots of mothers who feel the same way.

"Jobs are getting harder and harder to get, education is ridiculously over-priced and never stops increasing, and the poor kids having debts they don't realise will screw them for decades, if not their entire lives because there won't be jobs for them to pay it off. We keep hearing there will be no money left when we retire, that there are already too many retirees using up the medical budget, what does our future hold Jerry, what are we working our butts off for, what will we end up with? I'm just so frustrated at it all and always feel so helpless, we get this little ray of hope at election time but nothing changes, it just continues to get worse, and you look at what is happening to the other countries and you know it's only a matter of time before we are in the same boat. But, finally, a real ray of hope, I can see it, something I could never before imagine, there is a future for our kids, for us, for everyone, I'm elated Jeff, elated that there is another way because I couldn't conceive of one before. I actually feel positive, positive for the future, for us and the kids, positive for the first time in years, and all it took was a change of belief, we can do this Jeff."

As Dawn Approaches

"I hear you Andrea," answered Jerry, "I really do hear you. It's kinda crazy, you know, all this stuff, the garbage that goes on in this world today, the direction the country is heading, it's in your face every day but you push it to one side, you have to or you'll go nuts. You work hard, you struggle to do all the right things as a family, raising kids the best way you can but in the back of your mind it's always there, we know things are not right and we have no idea how to make 'em right either, you just keep hoping and hoping that someone's gonna come along and wave their magic wand and save us, even though you know that's baloney. Then you read 'the book' and presto, the light goes on, we are the ones we've been waiting for, we are the ones who need to change, change a belief and your world changes, I see it too Andrea, I really do."

"Oh Jerry I'm so glad you do, now you know how relieved I am that there is a light at the end of the tunnel after all, I can sleep at night now knowing there is a very good chance our kids may have a decent world to live in after all."

"Yeah, it sure feels good don't it?"

"Jerry, I've never been the philosophical type as you well know, but now I have 'woken up' to what kind of world we have really been living in. I have racked my brains trying to figure out why we, the people, the taxpaying voter, have been so blind to what's going on, why we are so trusting of our government, our politicians, our systems. But I see why now, I get why we just work away, pay our bills, always looking forward to something, always looking ahead to that vacation or new gadget that will make us happy, that will give us temporary relief from the grind, the economic prison we're all part of."

"Yeah you're right Hon, never heard you talk so...so deep like this before...what is it you see, why do we just work, pay bills and all that, enlighten me oh wise one."

"No need to make fun," Andrea pushed at Jerry's arm in jest.

"Just kidding Honey, you know me," Jerry said as he smiled reassuringly.

"Well, if you think about it it's the culture. Nothing wrong with culture, every society has to have a culture, a system of some kind or it wouldn't be a society would it, well not a cohesive society I wouldn't think."

"But don't we like our culture Hon, what's wrong with it?" Jerry asked Andrea.

"No there's nothing wrong with our culture or most other cultures as long as the people are free. The inherent problem with any culture is how it boxes in the mind of those raised within it.

It kind of sets up invisible walls in the mind, it sets the limits to what is acceptable, to what is normal, don't you see that?" asked Andrea.

"Well, yeah, kinda," Jerry replied, "but it's all we've ever known and.."

"Exactly," replied Andrea, "and when someone or something different comes along we don't like it, we don't understand it, it's alien to us, that's how boxed in our minds are!"

"Yeah, yeah I get that but where does this fit in with what you were saying about our lives, our daily lives, the working, the paying bills and all?" asked Jerry.

"What I'm saying," Andrea explained, "is we have been raised in the same system as our parents, we grow up hearing them talking and dealing with the same things we are, working, paying the mortgage, paying the bills, raising the kids, our minds are being set in the same ways as theirs, we subconsciously accept things for what they are and instead of looking up, seeing what is going on and asking questions, we carry on like good little tax paying citizens. When you think about it, we even help keep the box in place! Anyone who dares challenge it by saying something outside the norm, dressing in what we call weird clothes or has a weird hair style with different colours, or wears nose rings and has tattoos, are usually thought of as weirdos or something. And anyone who dares challenge the system is called a radical or troublemaker and the public shuns them, when in reality they are more original than most of us, they 'believe' in a different way from the way we do, their box is a much bigger box, actually they probably don't have a box, they are refusing to be kept inside a box. They aren't afraid to live outside our box Jerry."

"Ok Hon I get that but where does thinking outside the box help us in the big picture...oh hold it, I think I know where you're going with this. It's the belief thing isn't it?"

Andrea nodded. "Inside the box we can't actually believe there could possibly be another way to exist successfully, our minds, well I know mine does, let me correct that, did, think that way before reading 'the book'."

"You're right Hon, the culture kinda programmes us not to even think of making big changes, it seems impossible, even if those changes could be the best thing to ever happen to our society, it's all down to the belief again, isn't it?" Jerry added.

"Yes you clever boy, working that out all by yourself," Andrea mocked Jerry with a nudge and a wink.

"No seriously Jerry, that's what I'm talking about. I must admit I was ticked at first that Davina and Leanne at work didn't get what I was saying, to me it makes so much sense. But their minds are still inside the box, like mine was, it just needed me to talk with them after 'waking up' to realise it. So, what I'm saying is our culture, our systems, limits our outlooks, determines the possibilities for us ahead of time, does that make sense Hon?"

Jerry was really engrossed in this conversation. It had been quite some time since they had talked about things other than the kids, bills, work and the usual everyday challenges a family deals with. What Andrea was saying was becoming increasingly clear to Jerry but these ideas certainly took some expanding of the mind. Jerry had a mental vision of a mind inside a box, it was an old saying, he knew that. 'Thinking outside the box' was a fairly well known term in society and now it made complete sense.

"Yeah it makes sense Babe, the box thing, I know it's a common enough saying and all, but you know me, I have my own way of seeing things, but I get it now. All the box really is, is your own beliefs."

"You know, that old grey thing between your ears never ceases to surprise me," Andrea laughed aloud then added, "that is a better way of looking at it. Didn't 'the book' say something about beliefs filter your perception?"

"That's my point," Jerry continued, "as you said, our culture programmes us, it instills certain beliefs, and Gandhi was successful because he changed people's beliefs. There is no box, the so-called box is merely our collective beliefs, our culture cannot help but brainwash us with certain beliefs."

"You're dead right Babe," Andrea continued, "The problem with that though is we get stuck don't we? We get into a rut and can't see our way out. Our beliefs restrict what is actually possible because they filter our perception. Hmm, change the beliefs about what is possible and the perception changes, that's from 'the book', perception changes Jerry, that's why Davina and Leanne looked at me like I was insane," Andrea laughed aloud again. "Ok I see it now, it's how we perceive everything isn't it? Before reading 'the book' I perceived things in a different way. I read it, it changed my beliefs in what is possible, which in turn broke the hold of the cultural brainwashing or programming and freed my mind to perceive what is actually going on in our country, our world. That's why you won't understand the ideas until you've read it, they seem way too radical when just told to you by someone."

"Sure thing Andrea, let's get that bottle of wine and

celebrate, I think there's a few things we need to discuss about all this, it's exciting, the people having the say in what goes, what's best for the country and the people, never thought we would ever be talking this way."

"Yes it's exciting," said Andrea, "I know what we have to do now."

24 – The Judge

The Judge had been at Anthony Carsdale's party for an hour and a half and had met everyone present. The mood was certainly upbeat, there was definitely an electricity in the air, people were excited, change was the talk of the evening, real change. The music had stopped and Anthony Carsdale stood on a chair and tapped his wineglass with a spoon to gain everyone's attention.

"Ladies and Gentlemen, firstly thank you all for coming tonight, as you know we usually throw a party around this time of year but this time there's an added element of excitement. I know everyone present is familiar with how our world is changing and that together we will all do everything we can to prevent our beloved Canada from suffering a similar fate as that of other nations. I am honoured and humbled to be among the true patriots here this evening, patriots who represent many of the main sectors of our present institutions such as; education, finance and politics. It would appear that people really are waking up and understanding the dangerous direction in which Canada is heading and this will certainly help our task. Tonight we are fortunate to have among us Shirley Dickinson, a leading banker who tells us she has many colleagues who understand the nation's looming predicament and whose allegiance is unfalteringly to Canada. These people will be an integral part of the transition to the new banking system and they are ready to go into action to implement things as smoothly as possible when the call comes. We also have with us Frank Miller, Professor of Political Philosophy at the University of Toronto who tells us he will be bringing ideas from 'the book' to his lectures, something we know the government is opposed to but also understands that the power of popular opinion is definitely on side with the ideas of 'the book'. Frank is convinced that once he begins using the ideas in his lectures that other educators will follow and this can only help increase public acceptance of an organic economy. Last but not least we have member of parliament Timothy Rendall, who, I am very pleased to say, in the spirit of an organic economy, wishes to be called Tim and not 'The Honourable'"

The room burst into laughter, applause and many cheers. This was what the new way was all about, people being people and not hankering after self-important titles which really mean nothing. Anthony waited for the cheers to abate then continued.

"Each one of the people I have just introduced also has a network of colleagues who feel the same way as we all do and are ready to do their part in the transition. When the time is right you will receive a call with the code word, which as you know will be the date and time at that moment. You can then commence to make the calls to your own list of people. The movement, for lack of a word, is swelling in ranks and it is becoming apparent the government understands it is on very shaky ground, however, we must all remain vigilant and be careful with whom we discuss our plans. We have people in every sector ready to put into operation that which they deem necessary for a smooth transition. These people have sworn an oath that everything will be done with the best interests of Canada and her people as the basis for all decisions and that they are only temporary custodians facilitating the transition until the new constitution is presented, modified as required and voted on by the people. Friends, please enjoy the remainder of the evening and learn as much as possible from each other regarding the roles you all shall play. Let us raise our glasses and toast the new Canada and 'The Organic Economy'."

The Judge could hardly believe this, yes this is what he expected to hear but actually hearing it was to him historical. He never would have dreamed just a few years ago that his fellow Canadians, including so many in strategic positions of society, would be poised to take such action. This was exciting stuff and he, the old Judge was to partake. His role being to assist assemble and facilitate the countries best lawyers in assessing the legal and financial positions Canada had with other nations, groups, central banks and all international treaties that affected Canadians, including the complete separation from the British Monarchy and the City of London banking cartel. This was the real deal, this was going to be real change as it should be, purely in the best interests of the country and her people, the ones who actually create the prosperity for the nation and each other. For many, these were frightening times, for some they were the greatest opportunities ever presented to the people.There were so many deals that were entered into by previous politicians which were to the overall detriment of Canadians. The Trans Pacific Partnership (TPP), the Transatlantic Free Trade Agreement (TAFTA), the Transatlantic Trade and Investment Partnership (TTIP), NAFTA and other free trade agreements, deals with other countries, the United Nations and many other abbreviated agencies, central banks and corporations, which mainly benefitted a handful of elites at the expense of Canadian prosperity and rights. The entire food industry from farming to purchase which was at the time controlled by a handful of mega corporations would be returned back to the people to produce organic, genetically modified free foods. The farmers would never again be held to ransom by the despicable antics of the likes of the GMO (Genetically Modified Organism) seed suppliers, their despotic reign would be over. Yes, the foods would be more expensive initially, but the long term savings in health care costs would more than offset the cost of natural, healthy foods. People themselves will be encouraged to grow their own foods and buy locally to reduce transportation costs and pollution. The next generation will be taught more practical skills such as; growing vegetables and this will become second nature to them as they will only know this system.

The Judge was 'old school' and was raised to appreciate what he had. 'The Organic Economy' was all about the getting back to what really mattered instead of the destructive forces of materialism and greed. With the transition to an organic economy, corporate and banking control would all be coming to an end and from then on the people would decide what is best for the nation, a truly democratic way, direct democracy for the first time. The teams of lawyers would provide the evidence that any deals and treaties which did not benefit Canada would be null and void. The Judge knew there would be outrage from those affected but this was not about petty politics, this was real, this was history in the making, this was about casting off the old and evolving to a completely new way, the Judge could barely contain his excitement, the thought of what the country would be was in itself intoxicating and for him to not only be alive to witness it, but to actually play an important role, was a dream coming true. This was actually happening, people had started to believe, not just a few people but en masse, the beliefs had changed, the tide had turned, there was no going back now and he could feel it in his old bones that the government knew it also.

CHAPTER 6

25 - Professor Francis 'Frank' Miller

University of Toronto Professor, Frank Miller, had prepared his upcoming fourth year political philosophy class and was quite excited to be 'letting the cat among the pigeons' so to speak. The Professor knew he had to tread carefully. He could not upset his employers lest he lose tenure or his coveted position. Even though a university was historically accepted as a bastion of free speech, one could only rock the boat so far these days, true free speech did not exist any longer and like everything else today, there was control in any direction one wished to look. Frank knew that even science itself was owned to some degree by corporate interests and anyone who dared disagree or question what was the accepted and controlled versions of science were ostracised from the scientific community and their careers were either derailed or ruined. Free speech had no place in science today, not if you wanted an academic career. Frank was well aware of the subtle misuse of certain words, words most often misused in a negative way and he would begin his lecture on that note. The fourth year students took their seats and the Professor began.

"Good day everyone, hope you all enjoyed the long

weekend, today's class is titled 'Conspiracy Theories', yes, I thought that would raise some eyebrows. Good, I would like to jump right in as there is much to cover. Unfortunately some of our words have been misused over time and given different meanings. Some have been misused to the advantage of those making a particular point. For example, the word 'anarchy', the mere mention of which tends to conjure up the idea of lawlessness, riots, robbery and senseless murder. The true definition of anarchy as I am sure most present here will already be aware is to be without a ruler or controller, 'an' meaning 'without' and 'archy' meaning 'ruler'. The word conspiracy has and continues to be misused, people today shrink away from the term 'conspiracy' and shudder at the thought they may be called a ....wait for it.....conspiracy theorist! The term 'conspiracy theorist' was weaponised by the CIA to counter skepticism against the Warren Commission's findings of John F. Kennedy's assassination in CIA document 1035-960. A CIA directive called "Countering Criticism of the Warren Commission Report" successfully utilised the term 'conspiracy theorist' against anyone questioning the government or its secretive programmes. Thus the term 'conspiracy theorist' has itself become something to avoid, conjuring up images of an unstable person making outrageous claims that should not be believed. The main stream media has also been complicit in the use of this term and will often employ it as a cheap shot knowing well the person in question will be immediately dismissed as a 'tin foil hat wearer'."The Professor waited for the sniggers to subside.

"Of course there are people who make false accusations about governments and certain departments, especially concerning the more secretive programmes and it is apt to use the term but nevertheless, the term 'conspiracy theorist' is a valid term in its own right regardless of where it may have originated. This class is called 'Conspiracy Theories' because today we are going to look at speeches made by public figures through recent history to see if there could possibly be a conspiracy to control the world by certain people."

Eyebrows again were raised.

"People conspiring for gain whether monetary or control is nothing new. But could it be possible for a group of people to plot to control the entire planet? Corruption often follows money and power as we know but the power that corporations and bankers now wield has never been greater. Could this all have been part of a greater plan, a plan to mold the populace into one world governance, was there a conspiracy to force the world into a totalitarian global state?"

The Professor had a laptop computer set up to project the material he had prepared onto the whiteboard background for the students to see.

"During the last ten years we have seen great changes in the western world. Democracy was taken for granted and accepted as something which was here and would always be here. In effect, people became complacent about democracy and many voters who were disillusioned with politicians decided to not even vote. However, I should not have to explain to anyone here the changes which have been ongoing in many of the western countries, countries which are under various levels of dictatorship, albeit a very cleverly veiled one due to total media control. Long before this happened there were people who were trying to warn the world that this was going to happen, that concerted and coordinated efforts had been in effect for many years. They constantly warned that a group or groups of people had a plan to rule the world, a plan which was widely known online as the One World Order or New World Order. That this cabal or cabals hungered for a one world government, one world bank, one world currency, one army, one police force totalitarian dictatorship. They have even announced it to the world, they would say, the Georgia Guidestones spell it all out, in ten languages too. For those who are not aware, there is a marble monument in Georgia, USA called The Georgia Guidestones which have the ten principles of a new world order carved into them, the first being the world's population must not exceed half a billion people. Who paid to have this monument prepared and erected? No-one knows, the customer, who called himself or herself, R.C. Christian, was anonymous. Naturally those who tried to raise the alarm were dismissed as conspiracy theorists, the tin foil hat wearers. However, now we have seen and continue to see the direction the world is heading, were the conspiracy theorists correct all along? Should the term 'conspiracy theorist' revert back to a level of credibility? Most of the following statements deal with the United States because of the ideals which it stood and supposedly fought for.

Let us begin with a quote from James Warburg who was a very successful agent for the Rothschild banking dynasty, I am certain everyone here is familiar with this family so I shall continue. The quote is as follows;"

'We shall have world government, whether or not we like it. The question is only whether world government will be achieved by consent or by conquest.'

The Professor continued, "That quote from James Warburg was made in 1950. Warburg certainly had the inside track on the ambitions of his employers the Rothschilds and we know how powerful and wealthy they were and of course, still are. There is little on this planet that they do not have an interest in where money and power is involved.

"Warburg says *'we shall have world government by consent or conquest'*

"Why would a man of his knowledge and standing say such

a thing? This is no mere trifle, by consent or conquest we shall have world government. Was this an idle threat or a response to a barbed question?

Next quote is from the memoirs of David Rockefeller, again, I am certain everyone here is familiar with the Rockefeller dynasty also."

The Professor displayed the next quote on the screen and read it out to the class.

"Some even believe we are a part of a secret cabal working against the best interests of the United States, characterizing my family and me as 'internationalists' and of conspiring with others around the world to build a more integrated global political and economic structure - one world, if you will. If that's the charge, I stand guilty and I am proud of it."

"Now keep in mind the influence this family has. They own or have interests in all the major areas of industry, commerce and banking and fund many of the institutions which exert influence on society. He himself used the words *'secret cabal'*, *'conspiring'* and *'one world'* to describe his ideals of political and economic control as well as *'working against the best interests of the United States'*. Was this quote taken out of context or is this proof of a conspiracy?

"In 1975 Congressman Larry P. McDonald wrote the following;

'The Rockefeller File is not fiction. It is a compact, powerful and frightening presentation of what may be the most important story of our lifetime - the drive of the Rockefellers and their allies to create a one-world government combining super-capitalism and Communism under the same tent, all under their control.......not one has dared reveal the most vital part of the Rockefeller story: that the Rockefellers and their allies have, for

at least fifty years, been carefully following a plan to use their economic power to gain political control of first America, and then the rest of the world. Do I mean conspiracy? Yes I do. I am convinced there is such a plot, international in scope, generations old in planning, and incredibly evil in intent'

"Was this merely the ramblings of an embittered politician or a serious attempt to expose a conspiracy? He certainly had no fear in using the term conspiracy in connection with the Rockefellers and their allies. As fate would have it Larry P. McDonald was a passenger on the Korean airliner which in 1983 supposedly strayed into Soviet airspace and was shot down with all lives lost." The Professor paused to let this sink in.

"Strobe Talbott, Former U.S. Deputy Secretary of State in 1992 stated;
'In the next century, nations as we know it will be obsolete; all states will recognize a single, global authority. National sovereignty wasn't such a great idea after all.'

"Senator Talbott was obviously quite positive the world would be heading in the Rockefeller's preferred direction.

"Congressman John R. Rarick had the following to say;
'The Council on Foreign Relations (CFR) is dedicated to one-world government, financed by a number of the largest tax exempt foundations (i.e. Rockefeller), and wielding such power and influence over our lives in the areas of finance, business, labor, military, education and mass communication media, that it should be familiar to every American concerned with good government and with preserving and defending the US Constitution and our free-enterprise system.

Yet, the nation's right-to-know machinery, the news media; usually so aggressive in exposures to inform our people, remain silent when it comes to the CFR, its members and their activities. The CFR is the establishment. Not only does it have influence and power in key decision-making positions at the highest levels of government to apply pressure from above, but it also finances and uses individuals and groups to bring pressure from below, to justify the high level decisions for converting the US from a sovereign Republic into a servile member of a one-world dictatorship.'

The Professor added, *"The nation's 'right to know machinery', the news media; usually so aggressive in exposures to inform our people, remain silent when it comes to the CFR, its members and their activities."*

"Could there be truth in Congressman Rarick's accusation? Are the media complicit in keeping quiet regarding the CFR? How could that happen, who is powerful enough to persuade the media from reporting on information which will affect our national policies and overall global direction? It has only been quite recently that the media reported anything to do with the Bilderberg meetings also, and that was only after the exposure by the alternative media. Is there a conspiracy to keep the dealings and outcomes of these groups secret and away from public scrutiny? Should the public be entitled to know about the decisions these groups make, for these groups consist of the world's top industrialists, bankers, politicians and even royalty?

"Dr. Johannes Koeppl, Former official of the German Ministry for Defence and advisor to NATO stated this;

'The interests behind the Bush administration, such as the CFR, the Trilateral Commission - founded by Zbigniew Brzezinski for David Rockefeller - and the Bilderberg Group have prepared for and are now moving to implement open world dictatorship within the next five years.'

"Moving on to William E. Dodd the U.S. Ambassador to Germany in 1937 said;

'A clique of U.S. industrialists is hell-bent to bring a fascist state to supplant our democratic government and is working closely with the fascist regime in Germany and Italy. I have had plenty of opportunity in my post in Berlin to witness how close some of our American ruling families are to the Nazi regime. They extended aid to help fascism occupy the seat of power, and they are helping to keep it there.'

"And General Douglas MacArthur had this to say;

'I am concerned for the security of our great Nation, not so much because of any threat from without, but because of the insidious forces working from within.'

The Professor then said. "Of course he did not divulge to whom he was referring.

Let us now move on to some statements made regarding the central bankers for they are front and centre of any one world government."

"President Andrew Jackson, 1834 speaking to bankers;

'You are a den of vipers! I intend to rout you out, and by the Eternal God, I will rout you out. If the people only understood the rank injustice of our money and banking system, there would be a revolution by morning.'

"Henry Ford stated;

'The one aim of these financiers is world control by the creation of inextinguishable debts.'

"So Henry Ford had no doubts as to the game plan by the bankers, was Henry Ford a conspiracy theorist?"

John Reid

"John Hylan, 1922, Mayor of New York;
'The real menace to our Republic is the invisible
government which like a giant octopus sprawls its slimy length
over the city, state and nation. Like the octopus of real life, it
operates under cover of a self-created screen. At the head of this
octopus are the Rockefeller Standard Oil interests and a small
group of powerful banking houses generally referred to as the
International bankers. The little coterie of powerful international
bankers virtually runs the United States government for their own
selfish purposes. They practically control both political parties. It
seizes in its long and powerful tentacles our executive officers,
our legislative bodies, our schools, our courts, our newspapers,
and every agency created for public protection'

"Franklin D. Roosevelt in a letter to Colonel E. Mandell
House in 1933;
'The real truth of the matter is, as you and I know, that a
financial element in the large centers has owned the government
of the U.S. since the days of Andrew Jackson.'

"Congressman Ron Paul in August 2003 said;
'I think there are 25,000 individuals that have used offices
of powers, and they are in our Universities and they are in our
Congresses, and they believe in One World Government. And if
you believe in One World Government, then you are talking about
undermining National Sovereignty and you are talking about
setting up something that you could well call a Dictatorship - and
those plans are there!'

"As you are all familiar with the book called 'The Organic
Economy', I think you will agree the author erred in missing this
next quote which would be so very apt. This was published in The
London Times in 1865:

As Dawn Approaches

'If this mischievous financial policy, which has its origin in North America, shall become endurated down to a fixture, then that government will furnish its own money without cost. It will pay off debts and be without debt. It will have all the money necessity to carry on its commerce. It will become prosperous without precedent in the history of the world. The brains and wealth of all countries will go to North America. That country must be destroyed or it will destroy every monarchy on the globe."

26 – The Cottagers

Andrea and Jerry sat down to relax with a bottle of wine and Jerry asked Andrea,

"So, what do you think about having no interest on loans, ain't that something, it's huge, my head spins just thinking about it?"

"Yes, it's crazy, good crazy, that part is still sinking in Jerry. It affects us so much through our lives that to think of life without it is, well, like a dream or something. I would never ever have thought that a system could exist like that, you know, borrowing money without paying interest."

"Yeah that's kinda how I'm thinking too Honey. Imagine that, a mortgage without interest..."

"I know," Andrea continued, "we would have had this house paid off years ago."

"Or maybe not," Jerry added, "we may have opted to do something different with the extra money, like take more expensive vacations or buy better vehicles or something."

"Yeah that's true, who knows, we never had that choice to make, yet," Andrea replied.

"And car payments, no interest there either," said Jerry.

"And credit cards, no interest on those," Andrea answered.

"You kinda have to re-arrange your way of thinking about money," Jerry said.

"How do you mean?" Andrea asked.

"Well, without interest payments to afford, would we have bought a bigger house or saved the money and bought more expensive vehicles? What would we do with a more disposable income?"

"Good point," said Andrea, "I suppose it depends on what we want from life."

"To be debt free would be a good place to start," Jerry added.

"Yeah but if we were debt free would we buy more things and just get ourselves into debt anyway?" Andrea asked.

"I don't know Honey, if we had everything paid off I would like to keep it that way and save our money for when we wanted to buy something. Like the old fashioned way, if you want something then save for it, nothing wrong with that but society has made it perfectly acceptable to buy things immediately, with credit, instant gratification."

"That's true," Andrea replied, "and how often do we get behind on card payments meaning we are stuck with interest payments."

"Happens all the time," Jerry said, "just can't be helped."

"I wonder if we will ever get away from being a consumer society, you know, buying things we don't really need just because you think it's cool to have or your friends have it?"

"I hope so," Jerry replied, "I really hope our kids can grow up in a world where they are just happy with what they have instead of relying on 'things' to make them happy, cause they'll never really be happy."

"Can you imagine that," Andrea said, "people content with what they have, not trying to keep up with the neighbours, the friends, a different world for sure."

Jerry stared at his wine for a few moments then said. "You

know, I think we, society, has been played like a fiddle. When you really think about it, how things went from a society that used to save up their money to buy things, to one that uses credit cards and borrows to buy, how the banks made it all acceptable and so easy to do. They knew that a percentage of those people would be paying late and they would make a killing on interest payments. In cahoots with the consumer corporations that spend billions in advertising to make people want to buy their unnecessary products, what a brilliant scheme."

"Yeah, good point, and if you really get down to it Jerry, a lot of the things we buy, do they actually make us happier within ourselves or are we like, falsely happy because we are gratified from knowing that others know we have them, did that make sense or is the wine getting to my head?" Andrea said with a short laugh.

"Oh yes Babe, it does make sense and if we are honest with ourselves there definitely is a part of us that feels good about having some things just because we know other people want them, maybe it's a human ego thing or something, hey look at me sitting behind the wheel of my shiny new Corvette."

"That sounds about right," Andrea said, "funny animals aren't we? Imagine how much simpler life would be if we just bought the things we needed or wanted, you know, wanted for our own purposes. Would save a lot of money too."

"Maybe that's all part of this organic economy thing, it does talk about greed and materialism doesn't it?"

"You're right Hon, it does. If the next generation can grow up with that mentality then the world will be a much better place."

"I'll drink to that," said Jerry with a wink and a smile then added,

"And what about getting rid of politicians, love the sound of that," Jerry said.

"So sick and tired of our politics Jerry, we all know it's a joke but we let it go because, well, we didn't have any ideas how to change it, did we?"

"No we didn't but we do now. To me that's the one thing in 'the book' that I haven't gotten clear in my head, well not yet anyway."

"How do you mean?" asked Andrea.

"I agree we have no more use for politicians and I agree the people should have as much say as possible, which the new voting system would allow. I'm just not clear on how we run the provinces and country without a leader of some kind," Jerry replied.

"I don't see it as a problem," Andrea said, "I think it's something we have to get used to, it'll be a completely new way of doing things and there's always going to be challenges with something that's never been tried before, well, on such a scale as this at least."

"Yeah, you're right Hon, I'm sure there will be problems, but hey, I solve problems every day."

"Exactly!" Andrea replied, "so do I and we get things done so to me all these new ways, new ideas, yes there will be lots of challenges but it'll be well worth solving them. Anyway, the truth is the current ways, the political system has, as it says in 'the book', proven to be useless, it has to change to protect us from these bully boy corporations and bankers, we don't have much choice to do anything but change, move on, try new ways, that's pretty obvious to me now and I for one welcome it. I didn't realise how sick and tired of it all I was, it's such a relief to have new ideas, real hope for the future, for the kids Jeff."

"Absolutely Honey," Jerry said as he touched glasses with Andrea.

27 – The Newly-Weds

James and Julie Young had returned from their honeymoon in Jamaica two months ago and were settling down to a life together. They had finally found time to accept an invitation from Mark and Sarah Jenkins to enjoy a barbeque at the Jenkin's house. The weather was warm and sunny but less humid than it usually was in July or August in southern Ontario. Mark was barbecuing steaks, burgers and hot dogs listening to James regale him about his honeymoon in Jamaica. The ladies were in the kitchen preparing salad and vegetables and talking about the wedding, marriage and the honeymoon. Mark and James began talking about what was happening in Canada.

"Remember what you told me about the military stepping in to help save the country from becoming a dictatorship?" Mark asked James.

"Yes, barely," replied James, "I wasn't feeling much pain by that time," he laughed.

"What's the latest and greatest on all that then?"

"Well, by all accounts there are many more military personnel ready to join the movement and help prevent Canada from becoming a dictatorship," said James.

"Good to hear," Mark added, "still hard to believe we're

actually talking this way, you know, Canada, dictatorship, military takeover, blows my mind."

"Agreed Mark, the world is certainly not the place we knew even five years ago, rapid changes for sure. Did you read 'the book' by the way," James asked.

"Yes I did and I hope to dear God we can steer Canada in that direction," Mark replied.

"Glad you read it," James added.

"Me too, thanks for mentioning it, it made things pretty darn clear to me and we can see now we don't have much choice but to change our systems, our ways."

"Who would have thought our own Prime Minister would stoop so low as to sell out his own country," said Mark.

"Same as the rest of them, the US, UK, Australia, Germany, France, Italy, but the truth is they have little choice Mark."

"Little choice?"

"One day, hopefully soon, the truth will all come out and people will finally understand what has been happening for many years, it will be a shock to most I can tell you that but they need to know."

"Can you elaborate James? I would like to know."

"It would take too long Mark, but let's just say the true controllers of most of the world are not who we think they are, it isn't the national leaders that's for sure."

"Yeah 'the book' mentioned something along those lines, so hard to take in though. So that's why they don't have much choice, they're following orders or something?"

"Yes, something along those lines Mark," James replied, "the US has its own story because of what the US is. Being the power they are, the industrial, financial, corporate and military power they have made them the focus of the, let's say cabal, the real controllers. The US needed to be broken, economically and financially and its military controlled by the cabal, which as we have seen, has happened. It also needed to be broken socially which is why they allowed so many illegal immigrants into the country via the Mexican border. The UK has also been taken over but the tactics were different because the challenge was different. Australia went the same kind of way as the US but Europe is trickier being there are so many countries, however, because of the EU it has been made much easier which was the plan from the beginning, consolidate the countries, share the same currency, the same governing body, exactly the reason the EU idea was dreamed up in the first place, as was the Canada, US, Mexico Union, by the same controllers that are now going all out for a one world dictatorship.

The EU was formed to make the eventual shift to global dictatorship that much easier, basically it was the forerunner for the New World Order. The basic plan, as I have learned, is to destroy the western world socially, economically and financially. People would be so desperate for anything other than what they have, no food, no water, no safety, just a kind of hell on earth, which of course, was intentionally planned by the elites. Then the elites come to the rescue as the saviours of mankind and propose a New World Order and everyone thanks them from the bottom of their hearts. It's a well-practiced formula Mark and always works like a charm, it's called 'problem, reaction, solution', also known as Hegelian Dialectic. First there is the goal, the result you want, second, you create a crisis so bad that people want anything other than the crisis, third, you offer the very solution which was your goal all along. 'Problem, reaction, solution', works every time."

"Oh man," said Mark, "we really do have to wake up and smell the coffee don't we? There's nowhere to hide now, no pie in the sky dreaming that it won't happen to me, to my wife, my kids. We really do have to get up and fight back or we lose everything including our freakin' freedom!"

"Got that right Mark," James replied.

"But what about us, Canada, where do we stand James?"

asked Mark.

"We think because of our location being next door to the US that the 'powers that were', sorry Mark I won't refer to them as 'the powers that be' because they ain't ruling us, anyway, they think they could take us any time. But the US has not been easy for them, they introduced martial law after the food and water shortages led to the riots, but it's been a wake-up call for them. The American people now have their backs up, they understand the big picture, that this is for real, that those who do survive will end up as slaves, the Americans have finally woken up and are now acting more like the Americans they always thought they were, the people mean business and the fight is on. So the battle for overall control by the cabal is taking longer than expected, and as far as we are concerned, it will never happen, now."

"That's good isn't it? Doesn't that mean we in Canada have longer to prepare?" Mark asked.

"Oh yes, any delays can only be of benefit to Canada and as the true news about what is taking place in the US filters through to Canadians, they are waking up by the thousand each day, it's just that our main stream media are so controlled by the cabal and man are they doing a number on us Canadians, trying to paint a rosy picture of everything happening in the US and elsewhere. And that's the only reason the entire population of Canada isn't up in arms, the media propaganda." answered James.

"Any idea when the party starts here then?" Mark asked.

"It's kinda strange James. The movement to prevent a tyrannical takeover began a year or two ago and at first it was all very hush hush, then as more and more people saw what was happening in the world, especially across our own border, combined with the fact so many Canadians had read 'the book', it seemed the government had almost silently conceded to the fact we weren't going to just sit back and be taken over." James replied.

"But our governments aren't going to simply step down are they?" asked Mark.

"Highly unlikely," James continued, "they are bound to the globalists and their rules and will have to stay in place until the end, which means following the dictates of the globalist controllers."

"I just don't understand how the leadership of a sovereign nation can be so controlled by outsiders, outsiders who aren't even Canadian." Mark stated.

"Remember those international agreements, the Trans Pacific Partnership, the TPP, TTIP, TAFTA, etc. The global elite have so much power and already pretty much owned most senior politicians in every country. The countries by that time were in no position to argue their way out of it, it tied everyone together and put a stranglehold on the various country's powers and sovereignty.

These deals gave the elites an added quantum leap in power and control and severely weakened national sovereignty to the point the political leadership really were puppets of these elites, the cabal if you like." James responded.

"Aha!" Mark cried, "now that makes sense James, I didn't realise how weak our leadership was, I couldn't understand why they never publicly condemned the tyranny in other countries, why they kept quiet on the subject."

"Truth is they haven't a chance Mark and anyone who dare stand up against these despots would wish they hadn't."

"What do you mean, threats, that sort of thing?"

"Oh for sure Mark, that's standard practice, threats against you, your family, that's nothing, just business as usual for these cretins."

"But why James, why would people who have all the money and power they could ever need, want to do this, I just don't get it?"

"And neither will any sane, rational person Mark. Let's just

say that these people do not think like the everyday
person. Their minds are wired differently, they get their
kicks from controlling humans, controlling everything they can
control.

As ridiculous as it sounds, they're like a pack of Dr. Evil's
hungering for world domination, they have no empathy for the
human race whatsoever and think of us as a waste of food and
resources, resources which by some insane divine right they
think are theirs. They still believe in the divine right of Kings, just
that they think they are now the Kings. Don't even bother trying
to understand what makes these despots tick, just concentrate
on keeping them out of our lives once and for all, they've been
riding the gravy train on our dime for a hundred years too many."

"James, I don't mean to pry or to stick my nose into your
business but you know a heck of a lot, my gut tells me you don't
really work as a weapons trainer."

James looked away, sighed, looked back at Mark and said,
"Mark, you're as dear a friend to me as anyone I know, we go
back to our childhood days together, you're like a brother in my
eyes and I won't lie to you. Yes I actually do engage in some
weapons training and with the armed forces, other than that I
won't lie to you, so I won't say anything more. Make of that as
you will."

"Nuff said," Mark replied, "but what I find comforting is
you are in the know and it sounds like we have enough military
and others in the right places to keep hold of our great country."

James smiled and nodded without saying a word.

28 – The University of Toronto

Three of the students who had attended Professor Frank Miller's conspiracy theory class the week previous were enjoying a coffee at the campus cafeteria before their next class with the Professor.

"What did you make of the Professor's assignment, is there a conspiracy for a New World Order?" asked Suzy Ho, an overseas student from Hong Kong. The first to answer was Robert Campbell, a Canadian who had migrated from Jamaica with his parents when he was 12 years old.

"I don't feel comfortable using the term 'conspiracy theory' because it's always linked to garbage or supposed garbage, but, when you see what has happened to the world and what continues to happen, I have a hard time believing that this could all take place without a plan, some kind of master plan. It's too big to just unfold the way it has without some kind of long term plan, so yes, I think there must have been a big conspiracy for all this to happen, but I still don't like using that term."

"Good points Robert but I don't think there was a conspiracy. These power hungry people usually can't agree on anything, they all want it their way. I don't believe they could organize such a thing, it's too big." said Erica Schwartz, a

Canadian student from Ontario.

"So how do you think it all happened Erica?" Suzy asked.

"My guess is it was a gradual thing, the corporations became increasingly powerful as did the bankers and they continued on the path of globalism which morphed into fascism, which is what we are seeing now." replied Erica.

"But what about the tyranny, the police state, the loss of privacy and freedom, people disappearing, the use of NDAA, the FEMA detainee camps, you think that all just happened naturally as a consequence of globalism?" asked Robert.

"I see your point Robert but, well, I just can't buy into this conspiracy theory thing." Erica replied.

"I understand Erica," Suzy added "but that's what this assignment is about. Has the term 'conspiracy theory' been twisted to ridicule people who are making a nuisance of themselves by publicising things certain people want to be kept quiet?"

"It is a possibility Suzy. I am under no illusions of how the CIA goes about its business and I wouldn't put it past them to do such a thing, I just can't believe that what has happened is a true conspiracy."

"Even with the quotes the Professor gave us Erica? People in the know who tried warning the world what was going to happen?" Robert asked.

"I just can't see it," said Erica, "I just can't."

"What's your take Suzy?" asked Robert.

"I'm the opposite, I don't believe this could all happen without plans. I believe this was planned decades ago or even longer. If you understand who is behind it all, the elite families who have been here for a long time. They run the world one way or another and the Presidents and other leaders have to follow along also. Therefore I believe this was a conspiracy because it was planned and the term 'conspiracy theory' was weaponised by the CIA." Suzy replied.

"Elite families, where did you get that idea Suzy?" asked Erica.

"I have been interested in global economics for some time and I see a pattern of who controls the important things, the money, the energy the large corporations. Certain families are often behind it, families that are very powerful.

These families have great influence, even over agencies like the CIA"

"The CIA," Robert smiled, "Criminals In Action, indeed."

Both ladies chuckled at Roberts quip then Suzy spoke.

"I read that the CIA funded the women's liberation movement too."

"What, no way!" cried Erica, "why would they do that?"

"Because it suited someone's agenda maybe," Robert said, "I read that too Suzy."

"I don't get it," said Erica, "why would they do that, why help empower women?"

"If I'm correct, it was to increase the tax base, you know, get women into the workforce," Robert answered.

"That's a good thing, empowering women, I'm all for that, but why would the CIA be funding that and not the government?" Erica said.

"Don't know but it can't be good if the CIA are behind it. Actually I also read that it was to get children into school earlier," Robert said.

"And why would the CIA care about that?" Erica asked.

"To get the kids early, you know, the state gets the kids early and can mold them, indoctrinate them," Robert replied.

Erica laughed and Suzy briefly looked away. "Now that's a 'tin foil hat' statement, not you Robert but whoever said that," Erica said.

"I know Erica but have you noticed the school curriculum and how it has changed?" Robert asked.

"Conspiracy theories again," Erica replied.

Suzy spoke up. "Even though I more or less agree with Erica about the schooling, we must not write everything off as conspiracy theories. There may be some truth, we shouldn't write it off completely without verification or we are the fools."

"That's right Suzy," Robert continued, "conspiracies are real, they happen every day, to be more accurate there should be a different term to describe people with outlandish ideas. But we must always keep an open mind."

"Well, yes of course, open minded but not naive," said Erica.

"Skeptical but not close minded," added Robert.

"That's cool," continued Suzy, "skeptical but open minded, open minded without naivety."

"I like it!" Robert cried.

"Yeah that works," Erica continued, "anyway, what's so wrong with having a one world government, wouldn't that be more efficient, wouldn't that end wars and poverty? Wouldn't life be better for everyone, all under the same system, same currency, same laws, what's so bad about it?"

Robert and Suzy looked at each other in surprise, then Suzy answered, "Have you researched anything about the One World Order or New World Order Erica?"

"No, not particularly, I've kinda read some things here and there," replied Erica.

Robert spoke next. "Well for one thing, those who have been proposing a one world government have no plans for democracy Erica, there would be no vote, no choices and you know what that means?"

"Well, er...ok... I see, a dictatorship is that what you mean?"

"Bingo!" Robert replied, "a dictatorship with absolute power, absolute control, global control."

"And that is just the beginning," Suzy added, "it's bad enough today the way we are spied upon, they already watch everything we do and they aren't backing away. Can you imagine what that would be like if we had zero say, no voice whatsoever, I shudder to think of what that world would be like. Who could stop them from doing whatever they want, torture, slavery, they could do anything and no-one could stop them, no-one."

"She's right Erica, maybe do a little research on that, the only people who are amped for a new world order are the very last people on earth you want owning a new world order, and that's what they'd be, our owners."

"Really, I think you guys are full of crap, but I will check it out properly now," Erica said with a chuckle.

CHAPTER 7

29 – The Patriots of 'The Movement'

History informs us that things are rarely stable for long periods. The geopolitical map of the world has been changing for many a year. But after the Second World War people in the west in general believed that what they were now experiencing, the lifestyle, employment, vacations, health and retirement in dignity, were immovable, this was it and it could never be taken away. The standards had been set and most people knew what to expect in life, gratefully, there were few major surprises anymore as life was more or less stable. Physically and mentally the evolution of mankind had reached its zenith, our knowledge and technology could keep us alive for almost a hundred years, life was secure and stable, many could find employment which matched their own personal skillsets. Food and shelter were for most a given. What more could there possibly be, how much further could mankind go as a mammal?

People always feel more sophisticated than their ancestors, a little smarter, lessons have been learned from the past and, well, there is democracy, law and a civilised society. Armed forces protect the people and nation so nothing would really go wrong, really change for the worst. Yes the occasional overseas war but that could be dealt with, that's what the armed forces are for, send them. But things did change. They changed slowly, stealthily, almost to the point no-one saw it encroaching, no-one except the usual 'tin foil hat' wearers whining about things such as; Bohemian Grove, the Georgia Guidestones, the Council on Foreign Relations, the Trilateral Commission, the Bilderbergers, the police state, UN Agenda 21 and a new world order dictatorship.

No-one would listen, barely anyone lifted their head high enough to take a look around the world and see what was happening, to learn from history as it gradually repeated itself. Yes the latest generation usually enjoys the pinnacles of knowledge, technology and education but the one thing which never changes is the human being itself. People seem to forget that, at their peril. The people collectively made one glaring error of judgement. They did not factor in that with respect to the human race nothing had changed from the past, power hungry psychopaths continued to lust for control, they never went away, they were always there, just that the times had changed, their outward appearance had changed and their methods along with it.

What would it take for the general populace to wake up and realise their way of life was over. Not just unemployment, not just hardship, but poof! Disappeared, gone forever, the western lifestyle, the American dream, gone, just another chapter in history that the future generations would definitely not be reading about should the tyrants have their way and rewrite history to suit their agenda. The off-spring of the people who were left would have nothing with which to compare, nothing to hope for, nothing to dream for, they would know no different and overt slavery would be considered 'normal'.
For most of the other western nations it was almost too late. Tyranny was in place which would make any fighting back orders of magnitude harder than had the people realised years earlier.

The founding fathers of the United States for example,

implored their people to forever remain vigilant and keep a watchful eye on their government but they, like most others in the 'civilised' western world, grew complacent and refused to believe tyranny could be lurking around the corner. Canadians were more fortunate. They had the advantage of seeing what was happening to other nations even though their own media did their utmost to camouflage the desperations, as ordered to by their globalist masters. A critical mass of Canadians had woken up, had understood the gravity of the situation and added to that was the fact that a critical mass proportion of the populace were familiar with the ideas of an organic economy, they understood its message loud and clear and the importance of birthing a system which also protected them from potential future tyrants. The network of Canadians ready to participate in a transition from the present government and constitutional monarchic system, to a new system, a system based on 'The Organic Economy', was nothing short of astounding. People were coming together, they wanted to participate. The numbers had swelled significantly and every major area of concern such as money and banking, energy distribution and public services were covered. The transition would be as smooth as they could possibly make it happen. They all understood this was a form of mutiny, but a form of mutiny in which they knew in their hearts was the right and only thing to do, it was more of a duty, a duty to the country, to their children and to themselves. The alternative option was to lie down and cede their country to a puppet government completely controlled by a foreign dictatorship which would rapidly become a one world global dictatorship. No, this was worth fighting for, it was all or nothing time and they understood they had everything to lose unless they helped take back their nation.

The patriots of the country were just about ready for the challenge, for the transition. An atmosphere had developed that was almost electric. The knowing that one was to be an integral part of, not so much a revolution but a liberation, for when the moment came they knew the country would be under the iron grip of martial law or a similar form of military control as her sister nations had been for some time. They also knew that that was when the liberation would begin and the military would preside over all major news outlets, issuing statements to the people about exactly what was happening.

The nation would be glued to their television sets and radios. As soon as the announcements had been made the various heads of government departments would be summoned to meetings and informed that they would remain in place but would be reporting to a committee instead of a minister or political department head. All current serving ministers would be offered a role in the committees primarily as consultants during the transition to an organic economy but they would no longer hold any form of power and would be considered an equal among colleagues on the various committees. This would ensure the country and provinces remained cohesive and efficient. It would be business as usual as much as possible under the circumstances.

The Governor of the bank of Canada would also be offered a role as consultant but those in the know thought he would not accept. An organic economy hinges on three major points, one is true democracy, devoid of useless, obsolete politicians, two, the nation issuing its own currency and three, a total ban on all usury or interest on loans. The governor of the bank of Canada having played the borrowing game with the central bankers for years was thought not to want any part of an organic financial system. However, the offer would be open to him to join in his countries historical leap to liberation from the leeching debilitation of the central bankers. The Judge had been working with a team of top lawyers with expertise in the areas of international law, finance law, commercial law and related disciplines that would assist in easing the passage toward a new system of finance and commerce. A system which would benefit the nation and her people, instead of a privileged few.

The major challenge would be the eradication of usury, or interest on loans, keeping the money supply flowing and ensuring confidence in Canadians that life would not come to a crashing halt. The lawyers had already prepared documentation to prove the fraudulent nature of loans, where the 'money' originated and how the public had been tricked into paying interest on something that did not actually ever exist. However, keeping the money supply flowing, keeping the wheels of industry turning would take a little more persuasion as would preventing people from panicking and trying to withdraw all their cash from their bank accounts. That would create chaos but also prove how fallible and fake the financial system really is, for there would never be enough actual cash to give everyone, it never existed.

The money outlets, the banks, were corporations and not government controlled so to keep them open and facilitating the flow of money, a banking state of emergency would be overseen by the military. The banks would eventually have the choice of remaining in business under their corporate names, but they would not be allowed to lend money using the fractional reserve system or charge interest on loans of any kind. They could instead become investment houses but it is expected they would cease to operate. Although these measures appear somewhat extreme, what will be happening is the birthing of a new system, a new nation ruled by the people and not by money and greed. This would not be a half-hearted attempt at a revolution but the metamorphosis of a nation breaking free of the oppressive clutches of political, financial and economic systems that only served the privileged elites.

The banks have enjoyed healthy profits for many a decade, the elites have hoarded immense wealth, much at the expense of the people, but their time will be over. A new nation will be born, a nation ruled only by the people, a nation that will learn to enjoy life as it should be instead of the economic slavery it is today. A brilliantly clever, cunning and deceptive economic slavery championed by the 0.01 per cent who gained so much at the people's expense. Over the following months the lawyers will also present their findings to the foreign central banks and explain why the people of Canada do not owe the billions of dollars in interest that is claimed.

All loans to Canada will also be terminated as Canada will issue her own currency. All international trade deals that are deemed unbeneficial to Canadians will be scrapped immediately and wound down to facilitate the completion of current contractual obligations. An organic economy absolutely requires a strong manufacturing base which supplies its nation.

The announcement of liberation will also include a statement confirming the abolishment of all British royal involvement in Canadian affairs. As there will be no government, royal representation will not be required. A vote by the people will decide if Canada detaches completely from the Commonwealth. A new system based on the ideas of 'The Organic Economy' is as it should be, so simple and straightforward that anyone could understand how it works. It should be quite apparent that nations built on manufacturing would crumble when that very same manufacturing was shipped away overseas. That unemployment would increase, tax revenue would decrease which would increase the pressure on the government purse. The government would eventually fall behind in its debt payments to the central bankers and have its credit rating downgraded, further increasing the pressure on the government purse. When the pressure becomes unbearable, more money is loaned from the central bankers who can barely contain their glee, rubbing their hands knowing that it is only a matter of time before they step in and run the country, the script would be played out flawlessly, everything going to plan and the financial grim reaper would land in Canada swinging his scythe of austerity, slashing services and benefits and anything that aids the poor and needy, reducing a once strong and proud nation to almost third world status, a status needlessly created by corporations and bankers, a status which resulted from pure greed. The new system however, would bring back manufacturing and place a tariff on imported goods to match the true cost of the products had they been manufactured in Canada. Goods would be more expensive to buy yes, but it is all relative. A nation with healthy employment levels, a nation that issues its own debt free currency based on a tangible value and a nation that does not charge interest on anything will in time become a prosperous nation.

Remember the last quote the Professor stated, the quote from The London Times, 1865;

"If this mischievous financial policy, which has its origin in North America, shall become endurated down to a fixture, then that Government will furnish its own money without cost. It will pay off debts and be without debt. It will have all the money necessity to carry on its commerce. It will become prosperous without precedent in the history of the world. The brains, and wealth of all countries will go to North America. That country must be destroyed or it will destroy every monarchy on the globe."

Taxes on income would, in time gradually decrease. Services such as healthcare would be second to none and post-secondary education would eventually be free. The new system would also see stability in prices. Inflation and growth are only necessary evils to fund the unnecessary interest paid to the central bankers. No interest, no inflation, stability. The interest paid by banks for your deposits only assist in hedging against inflation anyway, so no inflation, no need to hedge.

The new system, a new economy, simple, straightforward, self-perpetuating, organic.

CHAPTER 8

30 – The Judge

"The usual?" Jeff asked the Judge as he settled himself on a bar stool near the Guinness pump, his favourite spot.

The Judge had had one of those days. He had to turn away an applicant for Canadian citizenship, a twenty one year old man who had come to Canada with his parents when he was six months old.

"If you insist," answered the Judge, "And better keep it company with a Brandy too please."

"Tough day at the office?" Jeff asked as he knew the Judge well enough to know when that was the case.

"Nothing we can't handle Jeff, but it does tick me off when an applicant who wants Canadian citizenship doesn't know anything about the country."

"Aren't they supposed to learn about Canada, you give them books to learn from don't you?" Jeff asked.

"Oh yes, we really make it as easy possible. Some people though seem to think if they've lived here long enough they should automatically be given citizenship or that's how it seems anyway," the Judge answered.

"So what do you do in that situation?"

"Told him to come back when he had learned something

about the great country he wishes to be a citizen of," the Judge replied.

"Good for you Judge!" Jeff added, "Good to know you people are standing up for our country."

"Thanks Jeff, we do try our best," the Judge said as he lifted his pint of dark ale. "Cheers," the Judge said and took a welcome mouthful.

"Does that happen often, people not knowing what they are supposed to know?" Jeff asked.

"Not really, most are very good actually and take it very seriously, which they should, but I do have to turn some down for being charged with a federal offence."

"Really!" Jeff replied.

"Yes, I had a young man in my office, an applicant who had applied at the same time as his wife to be, who waited outside my office for her turn. They both had professional careers so were well educated, the process is usually a breeze for a couple like that.

"However, when I asked if he had been charged with a federal offence since the background checks we always do through the RCMP, he answered in the affirmative. Then he explained what had happened. He was out with his friends drinking in a bar and decided to proposition a lady sitting at the bar, he offered her money for sex but it was an undercover police officer," explained the Judge.

"Oh no," said Jeff, "what happened, what did you say?"

"I told him we had to cease the application there and then. He hadn't told his fiancee either so I offered to him that I would fail her which would give him time to explain things, but he said she knew everything about Canada, there was no way she could fail the questions. I never saw or heard of them again."

"Wow," Jeff remarked wide eyed, "Imagine that, she must have been fuming when he told her. You're all excited about getting your citizenship then you find out your fiancee propositions hookers! How awful for the poor girl," Jeff said shaking his head.

"Yes I'm sure it was. But we also have some nice surprises from time to time."

"Oh yeah, like what?" Jeff asked the Judge, who didn't usually talk too much about his work.

"Well, from the age of fifty five upwards, an applicant doesn't need to be tested. But I had a lady applicant who was seventy two, she was from the Far East and she gave me two letters. I looked at the first one, it was a letter showing she had completed an English as a second language course, something she didn't have to do as an applicant for citizenship at her age. The second letter was proof she had successfully completed a course about Canada, another thing she didn't need to do.

"Now here was a senior citizen who didn't need to spend the many hours that she did, learning our language and about our country, I was very impressed and proud as a Canadian that she wanted to be a citizen of our country."

"That's awesome Judge," Jeff exclaimed.

"Yes I thought so too Jeff and she was obviously very proud of her achievements, so I decided to ask her a couple of questions anyway, to allow her to display her knowledge, which she seemed eager to do."

"Really, how did she do?" Jeff asked.

"I have pictures on my office walls, the Prime Minister, the Ontario Premier, the Queen and the Governor General.

I pointed to the Prime Minister and asked her if she knew his name and she did, she rattled of his correct official title and full name, I was impressed. I then asked her if she knew the name of the lady, which of course was the Queen and she replied correctly using her full Canadian royal title, again I was very impressed and I could see she was enjoying herself so I asked her if she knew the name of the man in the picture next to the Queen, which happened to be the Governor General. She answered that it was the Queen's husband, so I just said yes that's correct," laughed the Judge.

"Oh nice, that was decent of you Judge," said Jeff.

"Thank you, I appreciate that, anyway how is my favourite barman today?"

"I'm good Judge thanks," replied Jeff, but the Judge had detected something wasn't quite right with Jeff, something the Judge had said.

31 – Jeff the Barman

Jeff moved along the bar to serve a customer, he took a clean pint glass and began to fill it with lager as requested. Jeff's mind drifted off as he waited for the glass to fill but his mind was on something completely different, for the Judge had just mentioned immigration and that took him back to the march he attended four days previous, what the Judge had just said took Jeff straight back to the 'moment'. The moment he encountered someone who had not been born in Canada. It was four days previous, it was late August and Jeff was in St. James park in Toronto among the crowds gathered to hear the speeches before the march against the GMO (Genetically Modified Organisms) corporations.

The crowd was large and people were packed together in the small park like sardines, waiting to hear the speakers in the bandstand, who lined up to say a few words about what the march and protest was all about. Many held placards as did the smaller man beside Jeff who held a large home-made version. The first speaker began and Jeff felt a tap on his shoulder from someone behind him, it was difficult to turn around because of the squeezing crowds and before Jeff could turn a female voice with an English accent said.

"Could you possibly move your placard a little please, it's blocking my view?"

Jeff cocked his head to his left to save turning fully around and said. "It isn't mine, I can't move it."

The young woman behind Jeff had misunderstood and thought he was holding the placard for someone else, then said.

"Can't you move it, just for a few seconds, I'm trying to take pictures of the speakers?"

Jeff cocked his head to his left side again and replied, "I can't move it, it isn't my placard."

The young woman thought Jeff was being obstinate and said to her friend beside her. "Some people are so inconsiderate."

Jeff was usually a calm, mild mannered young man and it took a lot to get him going, but having someone accusing him falsely of being inconsiderate was enough to raise his ire a little and this time he was determined to turn around and address her face to face, eye to eye.

As he began turning his head, Jeff said, "inconsiderate, what part of 'it isn't mine' don't you....under....stand."

That was the 'moment', as Jeff uttered the word 'you' he saw her face and his life would never be quite the same again. He never really knew what his own version of perfection was, but in an instant he now did. It wasn't physical perfection, perfect skin or perfect hair, it was something far deeper than that. Their eyes met and for two long seconds Jeff could not hear anything, what could only be described as a warm electric glow filled his entire being, he felt as if he were plunging into her beauty. He had always thought this purely the stuff of movies and romance novels, but here he was, completely absorbed by this young woman. Added to the experience was the feeling he had that she felt the same for him, for she did not look away but seemed as mesmerized as he was. That was the moment, the moment Jeff knew there and then that he was head over heels in love.

Nothing could possibly prepare anyone for a moment like this for it transcended any and all other feelings he had ever experienced.

An ear piercing screech of feedback from the public address system shook them from their momentary trance and Jeff turned around to face the person now talking to the crowds. His heart pounding, all Jeff could think of was how to approach the young woman behind him. As a young barman in Toronto he never had problems meeting and dating pretty young women but right now he was almost trembling with nervous excitement and anticipation. Jeff hadn't felt this way since he first asked a girl to date him at the tender age of fourteen. He racked his brains for the best way to introduce himself knowing they had already started out on shaky ground, he knew he only had one chance to get this right or she would be gone forever. So engrossed in thought was he that Jeff hadn't heard anything the speakers had said but the speeches were over and people were gradually peeling off toward the street where the march started from. Being so close to the bandstand it was still crowded where Jeff stood. He had decided on a conciliatory and humble, but not a weak approach. He took a deep breath and began to turn around to address the young woman.

"This had to be done right," he was thinking as his legs shook from nervous anticipation. "I must face her eye to eye, with a smile,"

As he turned ready to explain things he opened his mouth to speak, but to his horror it was someone else standing there, she had vanished, other people had filled her vacated position behind him, it was as if she had never existed. Jeff was stunned, momentarily shell shocked by her disappearance. "Was she ever there?", he thought to himself for a second, "yes of course she was," and he took off through crowds to the street where the march started.

Jeff scanned the crowds but realised he didn't know what

she was wearing, didn't even recall the colours she wore, it had all happened so quickly. The only positive identification he could make was that she had brown hair, not light but more of a darker brown colour, but only the colour, he couldn't recall the style or length. He also realised that as stunningly beautiful as she was to him, he wasn't even certain he could pick her out of a crowd, wasn't certain he would recognize her, it all happened so fast. Jeff was usually a calm man but he scurried between the crowds and scanned his brain furiously trying to picture her face and make a match. He did recall a flash of blonde hair when he had turned around to speak to her, yes, the girl with his dream girl, her friend, had blonde hair, that would be more efficient to look for. Jeff swiftly sidled up to each blonde girl he saw who was with others, hoping with all his heart that a brunette, a beautiful brunette would be walking with her. He found three such blondes who matched his image and moved near them but only received dirty looks as he scanned the blonde women's brunette friends. People were walked in lines across the street, chanting slogans, some were banging drums, others blowing whistles. Jeff heard none of this, his mind was frantic and his heart beat rapidly as he snaked his way through the protesters. Jeff had made his way to the front of the march but had failed to find her.

"She may have stopped in at a coffee shop or something," he thought, momentarily bolstering his hopes.

Jeff made his way back through the protesters, it was much easier now as he could walk slowly amid the oncoming marchers as they were now facing and walking towards him. He meandered slowly through the crowd scanning every blonde woman. There were many more this time as everyone by now had left the park and joined the procession. Jeff gradually made his way through the entire march, The end of the march went by him and he stood there, in the middle of the street, dejected, defeated, shoulders sagging and head bowed. Jeff had never felt this way before. He had barely even spoke to her, didn't even know her name, but already understood the pain one can only experience with true love. Jeff again heard the drums and whistles, he looked up and saw the front of the procession coming towards him. "That's right," Jeff thought, "the march goes around the city block two or three times."

He carried on, searching relentlessly, scanning for younger blonde women with brunette friends. He continued non-stop for another hour and twenty minutes, walking and scanning from beginning to end, physically and mentally tired but emotionally exhausted. Jeff finally had to accept defeat. He had never felt this way before. It was like a part of his body had been torn away. He put his hands in his jean pockets and made his way slowly, dejectedly toward the subway. Along the way to the subway a taxi had stopped about 70 yards up ahead, one of hundreds which did so every few seconds. The rear door was opened by one of a group of three young women. As the first lady stepped into the taxi Jeff noticed blonde hair, his heart raced again and he saw a brunette enter the car, it was sudden but he just knew it was her. Jeff began to run toward the taxi and as the blonde woman stooped to climb in he shouted out to her to stop, Jeff was frantic, running toward the taxi, waving his arms and shouting to attract the blonde woman. Half inside the taxi, the blonde woman froze momentarily and looked back at Jeff as he shouted and at that instant everything slowed down for him. His heart felt like it was coming out of his chest as he knew he had found her, the woman of his dreams was just a few car lengths along the sidewalk from him, sitting in the taxi. He ran as fast as his legs could carry him, shouting above the noise of traffic and waving his arms at the blonde woman to stay. This was it, his last chance, he had to stop the taxi. But the blonde woman must have thought Jeff was calling someone else and climbed quickly into the sedan, closed the door and the taxi pulled out into the street and disappeared. Jeff was now an emotional wreck, no-one had ever had that effect on him but she was now gone forever. Everything told him he would never lay eyes on her again.

In the following few days Jeff could not get the young woman out of his mind, he never ever thought this kind of thing would happen to him, love yes, marriage certainly, but this was love on a different scale, he didn't know such feelings existed. For a few days after the march, there were several times Jeff thought he had seen her. Twice on the subway as a train pulled out of a station, once on a streetcar and three or four times on the busy streets but worst of all was in the Crown Pub, he thought she had made his dreams come true by walking into the pub but it wasn't her. His mind worked overtime straining every cell to picture what she looked like. "How strange is that!" Jeff thought, "I am head over heels in love with a girl who's face I cannot exactly remember." Jeff also began doubting his initial feeling when their eyes met that she felt the same way, and the more time that passed by, the more he doubted it.

32 – The Judge

Jeff finished serving the customer and walked back to where Judge sat at the bar.

"You look like you've just seen a ghost," the Judge said to Jeff, "Are you ok?"

"Yeah, yeah, yes, I'm fine," answered Jeff.

"You could have fooled me, come on what's up," asked the Judge.

"No really I'm fine," Jeff replied.

"Look Jeff you put up with my nonsense, you always listen to me now I think it's my turn, so come on, out with it."

"Ok Judge, but it's dumb really, there's nothing to tell, it's just..."

"Girl trouble?" the Judge noticed Jeff's face, "I'm right aren't I?" said the Judge.

"Yes and no."

"Yes and no? Can't make up your mind, well let me make it for you, I'm guessing the answer is yes," said the Judge.

"Well, yes but it's going to sound dumb," Jeff replied.

"Try me, I've got time."

"Ok when you mentioned the march it took me back, back to a moment, a moment I met, well kinda met this girl," Jeff answered.

"Ok so you kind of met a young lady, that's a start now pray continue," the Judge asked.

"She stood behind me and tapped me on the shoulder, asked me if I could move my placard but it wasn't mine. I told her I couldn't move it, that it wasn't mine but for some reason she thought it was. I guess from where she stood it looked like it was me holding it. She asked me again and I told her a second time it wasn't mine, then she said something to her friend, something about me being inconsiderate so I turned around, fully around this time because I was ticked you know, to tell her, tell her it wasn't mine, that I wasn't being inconsiderate." Jeff said as he stared into open space, then paused.

"And?" the Judge asked.

"That moment Judge, that moment, I can't get it out of my head," Jeff said starry eyed.

"Would this by any chance be the moment you set eyes upon her Jeff?"

Nodding slowly Jeff said quietly. "Yes, yes, that moment."

"Sounds very similar to when I met my wife Jeff. I didn't think anyone would ever know that feeling I felt, only the very lucky ones ever do, but you do now. So what's the problem, doesn't she feel the same way?"

"Our eyes met and, and it was indescribable, I'm sure she felt the same way Judge but when I went to turn around again and ask her for a date or something she was gone!" Jeff said in despair.

"Gone, you mean she had left before you could speak with her."

"Yes Judge, I turned around and nothing, someone else was standing there, she had disappeared," Jeff replied.

"My oh my I can understand your pain young man, if that happened to me when I met my wife I ......well it didn't I'm very pleased to say. So, you went looking for her I take it?" the Judge asked.

"Yes I looked everywhere, I've never done anything like that before, except when our dog went missing when I was a kid, it felt like that, desperate.

I searched and searched through the entire march several times, then after I gave up I walked to the subway and saw her again, getting into a taxi with her blonde friend and another girl. I screamed at them, the blonde girl to stop, she did, looked my way then got into the taxi and it drove off," Jeff said with a big sigh.

"So that's it, you have given up?" asked the Judge.

"Does it matter now, I'll never find her again, I'll just have to learn to get over her."

"No no that's not the spirit, have faith, if it's meant to be then it's meant to be and all that, so come on, what was she wearing, what do you remember about her, you said she had a friend, anything noticeable about her?" the Judge quizzed Jeff.

"Were you a detective at one time or something?" Jeff asked the Judge with a smile.

"Just tell me what you can, you never know Jeff."

"All I know is she was English, about my age and had brown hair, that's it, see what I mean, it's ridiculous, I'm just being dumb."

"And she had a blonde friend you said."

"Yes but what's that got to do with her?" Replied Jeff.

The Judge picked up his drink, deep in thought.

CHAPTER 9

33 – The US Dollar Crashes

Due to the lobbying and bribery of politicians to de-regulate the financial systems, the bankers had the green light to raid the markets. Between them they wrecked everything for the people, their quality of life, their net worth, everything. The US Dollar, which had been printed furiously for so long after the bank bailouts, the quantitative easing as they called it, finally crashed after the BRICS countries of Brazil Russia, India, China and South Africa decided to go their own way. The BRICS nations had set up their own banking system and reserve currency which almost finished off the US Dollar completely, for the US Dollar had for so many years been kept artificially solvent by its direct linkage to oil. The 'petro dollar' was now history and the people of the US would now understand the true cost of living as would Canada and other nations in step with the US Dollar.

As painful as this would be, it needed to happen for this was the only way the people would ever understand the entire financial system was based on a flawed premise, usury and infinite growth to sustain that usury. Should the people dare to wake up and understand what truly happened, they would insist a new system be installed so that the nation could be rebuilt on a solid, organic foundation and not a false economy designed to enrich a microscopic minority of elites.

In a measure designed to save the system, the US devalued the dollar by a staggering fifty percent, wiping out the net worth and savings of millions of Americans as well as Canadians. They did this in the second week of September which now also meant winter hardship especially for those living in colder climates. This caused the cost of living to double, even triple overnight and so began the painful awareness of the insanity of printing colossal sums of 'money'. This also had a debilitating effect on the Euro and British Pound and all western nations suffered. This currency disaster was devastating for the people of these nations. For many, everything they had toiled honestly for, over decades, had disappeared overnight. The hardest part to swallow was the fact it was all created by a relatively small group of people whose greed knew no bounds. It would be years or even decades before any semblance of what the western populations once had, would be enjoyed again, and that's if a recovery were even possible. Without a strong manufacturing base the high levels of unemployment would never abate. Tax revenue would never be able to provide for the less fortunate and everyone needed to brace themselves for a very rocky road ahead. The sole focus being survival.

As much as everyone knew it was inevitable, the crash of the US Dollar still sent shockwaves around the world which would reverberate for a long time. Things would never be quite the same again, for many it was like the end of the world, for others it was a blessing. For those who could not 'awaken' to the approaching tyranny and believed everything was just fine, the crash spelled disaster. For those who knew, who could see what was happening, who had read and were familiar with 'the book' and a new system, the crash was the best scenario they could hope for. The crash was a golden opportunity to dismantle the corrupt systems which had created this very mess and bring in a new way.

Sometimes it takes a monumental disaster to facilitate real change, to truly grasp the situation and understand the systems were flawed and like most things had a 'shelf life'. People in the west had become so mentally comfortable, so complacent, so entrenched with the state that it became a kind of all-in-one mother and father figure. So wilfully blinded were they that most could not even grasp the atrocities the various western nations undertook on a daily basis around the globe in the name of democratising nations that didn't want to play in the financial sandbox with the western machine.

The world had never before experienced such bullies, which left millions of corpses, maimed and devastated victims in its wake. The US was only ever supposed to protect its own soil but fell prey to what can only be described as 'monsters', monsters which distorted everything the nation, the people and its constitution stood for. It was blatantly obvious that the US and most western nations of strategic value had been covertly taken over and the true reins of power lay in the hands of a cabal of elites with designs on the world and over mankind which defied any semblance of humanity. Included in those who could see what had been going on were various organized groups which had identified every possible person they knew that had involvement with anything deemed criminal. This included politicians and decision makers who had in any way contributed to the deaths and injuries of innocent people and the plundering of land and resources in any nation including their own. The lists were extensive and the groups responsible for collecting them were determined these criminals of humanity would one day soon answer to their crimes and be punished accordingly with long sentences of incarceration. The US was already under martial law but the dollar crash was about to take things to a new level. The looting, rioting, mayhem and violence before martial law was enforced was bad enough but the nation was bracing itself for what was to come. People were now going to be desperate and survival would be the only thing left on their minds, survival and whatever it took to survive. The law of the jungle had returned to America.

Those deemed responsible by the people for the dollar crash were in grave danger. So many had lost everything, they had nothing left to lose and made it their sworn oath to see those responsible hang or be shot. This included bankers, investors and politicians but others such as; corrupt judges, police chiefs and officers had targets painted on them. It was payback time for many who had experienced or witnessed glaring injustices. So frightened were those identified as enemies of the people that they chose to pay armed guards to protect them, for the protection provided by the state was often inadequate. Canada, being so interlocked with the US economy would also feel great pain. The devalued dollar resulted in almost everything becoming two to four times more expensive than before.

However, these difficult times were also the catalyst for a new level of cooperation between neighbours and even strangers. This was also happening in all of the nations affected by extreme hardship. People from all sectors of the population began learning how to grow their own vegetables inside and non-GMO seeds were almost as valuable as currency. Because of the extreme prices of food and energy, the food banks could not keep up and communal soup kitchens sprang up everywhere. People had to begin sharing food with family, friends and neighbours but although challenging at first, this forced-sharing of resources created a renewed human spirit, people had to come together to survive and materialism had to take a backseat. Discussions of what led to this mess were frequent and many and people began discussing and dissecting the failure of the systems and quickly 'the book' was brought up as a future reference for a remedy.

'The book' had in layman's terms explained the root causes

of what had happened and now the painful realisation was being experienced, in person, by everyone. They were now waking up to the fact that the systems were flawed all along. This was not just a natural effect of market fluctuations or a market correction. This was the predictable result of a corrupt and flawed system, compounded by greed. It wasn't difficult to predict either. And as complex as the expert economists tried to make it sound, it wasn't rocket science, it was merely the smoke and mirrors of squeezing blood from a stone, extracting every ounce of profit from a system which had nothing left to give. There were no complex mathematical formulas left to bamboozle the public with, in spite of the efforts to do so.

CHAPTER 10

34 – Jeff the Barman

Jeff was still working the bar at The Crown pub which, due to a strong clientele of regulars had managed so far to stay open after the dollar was devalued forcing many such establishments to close. Most of the regulars worked in sectors which although certainly affected by the devalued Dollar, were not overly threatened by it, they would survive. So it was for the most part business as usual. Jeff was still smitten by the young brunette woman he lost at the march. He thought he may be able to put her out of his mind but he could not. His heart still missed a beat when he saw a brunette who, in his mind's eye, could be the lady in question. It even missed a beat when he heard things like GMO or when he heard a female English accent. They brought memories flooding back, he couldn't help it, that was just the way it was at the moment. The harder he tried to put her out of his mind the harder it became.

It had been over three weeks since the moment, that moment at the march, the moment which he had re-lived countless times since. Jeff would go to bed at night trying to remember her face exactly, but it all happened so fast. What he did know though was he would recognize her in an instant if he ever saw her again, which he had to admit to himself would never be likely. The Judge though, wouldn't hear any of it and would tell Jeff not to give up hope. "If it was meant to be, it was meant to be," he would say. Jeff realised the Judge was an old fashioned romantic soul at heart and now he knew what that felt like as Jeff himself had recently learned, albeit painfully, that he was too. Jeff hadn't seen the Judge for three days but it was Monday afternoon and he knew it was likely he would be coming in for a pint.

He had just finished serving drinks to a group of regulars, swapping the usual niceties and commenced to wash some glasses. The main door had just opened and closed so either someone had just left or someone just entered. Jeff knew the timing and after about thirty seconds looked up from the glass washer to the bar to see if anyone needed serving. What happened next, completely and utterly floored Jeff, for standing at the bar looking directly at him was to him nothing short of a miracle. The young lady, the young brunette lady, the girl of his dreams, was standing there, there, at Jeff's bar waiting to be served. He walked over to her in a daze and simply said, "hello."

At that very moment the young lady herself then recognized Jeff and her eyes widened in shock, amazement and joy. They both stood there temporarily frozen in time, as if in a dream. A million things flashed through their minds in a nano-second, both of them were stunned and speechless. They both spoke at the same time, a confusing utterance of words which neither understood. They were fumbling and mumbling, then they both smiled and both said "No, you go ahead," they both laughed and then were interrupted by Jack Finlay, the owner of the pub who said to Jeff, "Jeff, take your break I'll cover for you."

Jeff answered back. "But my break isn't for a couple of hours Jack."

"Take a bonus break Jeff, I'm in a good mood and it looks like you have something to take care of," Jack replied.

That's when Jeff finally managed to speak to the young

woman and said. "Would you care to join me at a table, it's my break?"

"Yes, I would love to," came the southern English accent which sent that warm electric glow coursing through Jeff's entire being again. Jeff was still in a daze as he walked out from behind the bar and made his way with the young woman to a free table, what was going on, the girl of his dreams had just walked in and his uncle, his boss, had very conveniently shown up and told him to take a break, something that never happens. However, there were far more important things to take care of right now, the other things could wait. As they both sat down Jeff said to her, "I know this sounds kinda dumb but do you remember me from the march?"

"Yes of course I do," replied the young woman, looking into Jeff's eyes.

"Oh that's great, that's really great," Jeff continued, "I'm Jeff," Jeff said as he awkwardly extended his hand to her.

"Hi Jeff, I'm Nicole but please call me Niki, nice to finally meet you," Niki replied, "I never thought I would see you again."

Jeff let out a huge sigh of relief. "Me neither Niki, me neither. When I turned around and saw you I...."

"I know," Niki interrupted, "I saw you, I felt the same way."

"You don't know how much those words mean to me Niki, I couldn't get you out of my mind."

"Me too Jeff, I've been going crazy, I can hardly believe I'm actually sitting here with you hearing you say this, it's like a dream."

"That's how I feel too, I'm so glad you came here, and you feel the same way. I thought you did when I turned around and our eyes met, but as time went by I began thinking it was just my imagination," Jeff said.

"Same, same, oh my God I've never experienced anything like this before, we don't even know each other yet, it's crazy but I love it," said Niki.

"Oh my, where do we start, I want to know all about you Niki."

"You will, you will and I want to know everything about you too Jeff," Niki said his name again, "Jeff, so your name is Jeff, I kept wondering what your name would be but I didn't think of Jeff, I love it...Jeff."

"That's exactly what I was thinking, I love the name Jeff," Niki laughed out loud and tapped Jeff on the arm in mock punishment which Jeff adored.

"Just kidding Niki, wow I do like your name Niki," Jeff said pronouncing 'N-i-k-i' slowly.

"Would you two like a drink?" Jack asked as he passed their table.

"I can't I'm working Jack," Jeff replied.

"Not anymore, you can have the night off Jeff, looks like you could use it," said Jack.

"Jack what is going on, you never do this but you couldn't have done it at a better time," Jeff asked. Jack flicked his head toward the bar where the Judge sat on his stool, leaning around with a big grin as he raised his glass to the ecstatic couple. Jeff raised his arms and shoulders to display his being dumbfounded but the Judge just winked and spun back on his stool to face the bar again.

"I don't get it Niki," Jeff said, "Something's going on and the Judge knows something."

"Oh the Judge," said Niki, "You know the Judge?"

"Yes I do he's a regular here and, well, like a good friend to me, hold it, how do you know the Judge Niki?"

"I didn't until today," Niki continued, "I am applying for my Canadian citizenship and I got a letter from immigration for an appointment with the Judge."

"So it was the Judge then, oh my God and I thought you had just walked in off the street!" Jeff said in amazement.

"But, but how, I mean what, I mean how could he know,

it's impossible, but it's not because I'm here," Niki exclaimed.

"I don't know Niki but I am forever in his debt for this, I will never be able to thank him enough."

"Yes Jeff and me as well." Niki was trying to take it all in, so was Jeff but they couldn't stop looking at each other. Jeff slowly slid a hand across the table and placed it on Niki's who held Jeff's hand with both of hers. Jeff then placed his other hand on top, both their hearts beat with a rhythm of pure joy.

"You know at the march, at the park, I was going to ask you out on a date or something, but when I turned around you had gone," Jeff said.

"Yes I wanted you to ask me out or I was going to find an excuse to talk to you but my friend, Kelly, the girl beside me, had a text from a girlfriend who was waiting for her so she just grabbed my arm and said, "quick we have to go," and before I could say anything we were off in the crowds towards the street. I kept looking for you as well but I couldn't see you," Niki explained.

"I must have spent an hour and a half walking up and down through the marchers trying to find you Niki, I was desperate," Jeff said.

"Ahh Jeff that's so nice to hear," Niki said as a tear formed in the corner of her eye. "We did spend about half an hour in a café but I sat by the window and kept looking for you there too."

"I can hardly believe my ears," Jeff continued, "Not only have I found you, but to know for sure that you really did feel the same as me all along, it's a dream Niki, it's a miracle."

"Yes it is Jeff. I'll never forget this day as long as I live."

"Me too, me too," replied Jeff then continued, "Did you take a taxi home that day by any chance Niki?"

"Yes I did, well the three of us did."

"I was right, that was you Niki. After the march when I finally gave up and stopped looking for you I saw three girls getting into a taxi and I was sure you were one of them. I started shouting at the blonde girl to stop but she got in and I watched you drive off, it was a killer."

"Oh no you poor thing, poor Jeff," Niki patted Jeff's hands and stroked his cheek which felt like heaven to Jeff. "Yes she told me someone was shouting and running but she didn't recognize you and thought you were trying to get the attention of someone else."

"Didn't you look yourself?" asked Jeff.

"No, she didn't tell me until the next day. Kelly's a bit of an airhead Jeff, I love her to pieces, she's great fun and a brill friend but she's in her own little world bless her."

The new couple finished their drinks and made their way arm in arm to a nearby restaurant, a favourite of Jeff's. The ground beneath them felt like they were walking on air. They had a lifetime of things to learn and share about each other and a lifetime ahead to look forward to together.

35 – The Judge

The next day, the day Jeff and Niki would never forget, Jeff was working the bar as usual except he was a very happy young man today. He couldn't wait for the Judge to show so he could ask him how he did it, how he pulled off the miracle which brought Niki into the pub. The Judge came in around his usual time and sat at his favourite bar stool near the Guinness pump.

"Evening!" Jeff said to the Judge. "The usual?"

"Good evening Jeff, yes please that sounds like a plan," the Judge replied.

Jeff brought over the drink to the Judge and said, "This one's on me Judge."

"Thank you very much but there's no need to do that Jeff," the Judge remarked.

"It's the very least I can do, you worked a miracle, you brought Niki here. I haven't a clue how but you did and we both thank you from the bottom of our hearts Judge, we really do," said Jeff.

"Think nothing of it, it was quite simple really and to know you two lovebirds are happy together is reward enough for me I can assure you," the Judge remarked.

"May I ask how you did it, we are both baffled?" Jeff asked.

215

"Certainly Jeff," the Judge continued, "being an immigration Judge means I am in regular contact with the RCMP who undertake the background checks on those applying for Canadian citizenship.

"You told me the young lady had an English accent and she was with a blonde friend, remember?"

"Yes but that surely isn't enough to go on, is it?" a puzzled Jeff asked.

"You were at a march, a protest and almost all of them are monitored by the RCMP and certain undercover personnel. They take thousands of photographs and there were at least two drones filming and photographing the crowds too," said the Judge.

"But how..." Jeff was lost.

"They have had facial recognition software for some time now and it can identify anyone in the database instantly, even if the photo isn't that good, but these were. It was a bright, clear day and your name was tagged beside your face,"

"What database Judge, I have never been arrested or anything, where did they get my photo from?" Jeff asked in surprise.

"Oh Jeff, privacy disappeared years ago, almost everyone's face is recorded somewhere and the facial recognition software is excellent, it hardly ever makes mistakes. In fact they have had pre-crime software for a while now too. If it flags someone in the crowds as likely to misbehave, the police on the ground are notified immediately and they watch the person," the Judge said.

"They don't arrest them?" Jeff asked.

"Not in a protest situation Jeff, too potentially volatile. Arresting someone for doing nothing wrong at that moment could spark a serious problem that need not have happened. No, the police and drones will just monitor them,"

"Wow, who would have thought all that was going on?" said Jeff to himself, then asked, "but what about Niki, how did you....oh I get it now, you saw a photo of me and saw her blonde friend Kelly behind me, and then you saw the brunette and her name was flagged by the facial recognition software, right?"

"Bingo! said the Judge. "There she was and her name beside it. I checked my own database for migrants from England and Niki was there. I saw she had applied for citizenship and took her case, really quite simple you see," the Judge replied.

"Ok that works, wow, I never would have thought of that Judge. Niki told me how you got her to come to the pub, that was really clever too, trying to help her get a job at an English pub, making the call to Jack and telling him what was going on. I couldn't figure out why he gave me the break and the night off either. I really can't thank you enough Judge, we are both forever in your debt."

"Don't be daft," the Judge replied. "trust me, with my dear wife now departed the pleasure is all mine, and your uncle's too Jeff."

"Honestly Judge, sometimes you just don't know how good people can be to you," Jeff said.

"Just take care of that young lady and treat each and every day as special, they pass much quicker than you think," said the Judge.

"I promise you Judge, I will, I will."

CHAPTER 11

36 – The Newly-Weds

Mark Jenkin's door bell rang. Mark went to the door and to his surprise James stood there.

"Hey James, come in, come in, what a surprise, how's things buddy?" Mark asked enthusiastically.

"Good Mark thanks, in spite of the economic situation, but we're all in the same boat so can't complain, you?" James asked Mark.

"Good, well except for the price of things now, but like you said, we're all in the same boat, anyway to what do we owe the pleasure of your presence my friend?" asked Mark.

"Well, I've been away for a few weeks.."

"Yes I know bud, I've tried calling and Julie said you were away and not sure when you would return, that must be tough on a new wife," Mark said.

"Ouch," James replied, "Yes it is but Julie understands my work and it won't be like this forever I can promise that. Anyway, I was in the area and thought I'd drop by for a coffee and a chat with my old buddy Mark," James said as he wrapped an arm around Mark's shoulder.

The two friends walked into the kitchen "Take a seat James, anywhere you like," said Mark.

"How's everything with you guys, Annie, the kids?"

"Yeah we're good, obviously things are tight moneywise what with the devaluing of the Dollar but we're lucky. Both Annie and I still have our jobs but the kids, well we may not be able to put them into winter sports this year, don't even know if there's a league this year for either of them," Mark replied.

"What sports are they into Mark?"

"Brandon plays hockey and Sarah wanted to start figure skating," Mark replied.

"We've got all that to come, I hope," said James.

"Oh you will bro, you will, it's hectic but you wouldn't swap it for the world."

"Yeah we can't wait, Julie will make a great mother and I'm looking forward to being a father," James replied.

"Any news on that front, I know it's early but..."

James chuckled and said, "well the practicing part is fun, but nothing to show I'm accomplished yet."

"Ah you'll be a father before you know it James," Mark continued, "Anyway, what's the scoop with the movement, the liberators?"

"Well, they're as ready as they'll ever be is what I'm told. I think they want it to happen as soon as possible too," James replied.

"Why's that, what difference does it make?"

"Well, imagine if you were part of it and had a role to play. There's still a big risk that it doesn't play out exactly as planned and those involved could be arrested and charged with treason if it backfires, not that it will though but the stress is always there from the possibility," James replied.

"Oh yes, jeeze I didn't think of that, that would be stressful."

"They thought the dollar crashing would speed things up, that maybe the protests and marches would heat up and martial law brought into effect but it hasn't yet. I think people are still adjusting and haven't realised how bad things are going to get for them." said James.

"Things are pretty bad though aren't they? I mean, we are ok but many jobs have been lost in the service industry and people are struggling to get food and pay bills. Our community isn't too bad because most have jobs and they formed a neighbourhood committee to collect food for the soup kitchens that are springing up everywhere." Said Mark.

"Yes they are and the good thing as you said is people are coming together now, they're helping out not just family and neighbours but strangers. There's a real spirit of humanity coming alive. But for the patriots, the movement, it just helps prolong the liberation. The timing doesn't help either, being it's now fall people won't want to protest in the cold so the likelihood of martial law being imposed looks remote until next year," James said.

"Then again I hear they may devalue the dollar another twenty five to thirty percent in the near future, that may force people out into the streets to protest or loot and riot," Mark added.

"Yes that is a possibility too, but we, I mean they, cannot make a move until the time is exactly right. The Prime Minister has to announce the enforcement of martial law first, so the people know it's real, then they make their move to liberate. There are still a number of people out there that believe in the government, the systems, and nothing will shake that belief so we need the people to experience maximum effect from what Martial Law means, then they can know without doubt the choice they have when they vote for the new system or to stay with the old."

"Hmm didn't think of that James, that's right though, people could still elect to continue the old way, that is stressful for the movement. So there will be a vote soon after then?" Mark asked.

"Oh yes there has to be Mark, I think they said a vote for a new system will be held one month after the liberation. The vote will ensure Canadians they have free will and that it is not a coup and it will also placate the rest of the world and the likes of the US or UN not to intervene."

"Ok that makes sense, I didn't think about what other countries might think especially the US."

"They won't like it one tiny bit. The cabal who controls everything including the US and UN want us all under martial law so we have to be as visible and open as possible to show the world we are liberating Canada and not taking over, as in a coup."

"Yes, yes I see that now. Is there anything I can do to help?" Mark asked.

"Yes, it's absolutely imperative that people try and continue on with their lives as normal as possible, not be tempted to buy more than they need which empties the stores and for you Mark, you can relay what I have said to you, tell people what this is all about, it's about freedom, it's about them, for real this time," replied James.

CHAPTER 12

37 – A Long Cold Winter

The winter cared not for the additional hardship suffered by those who usually just made it by.

The devalued dollar caused the price of food and energy to skyrocket and many of those less fortunate souls, the pensioners, the poor, those living on government cheques and those making minimum wage found themselves in full survival mode. Food, water and heat, were the only things on their minds and for many, that simply could not happen without additional help, help from family, friends, neighbours and even strangers. The soup kitchens were always busy, as many would stay there just to keep warm and save money on their own energy bills. Recreation centres, churches and halls were made available for people to keep warm and the homeless were allowed to sleep at designated buildings.

The government, as an emergency measure, had rushed through a bill to supplement those who relied on the government purse. They were given an additional payment to help with the crushing rise in the cost of living. However, it was never going to be enough to make up for the higher costs and so the people suffered. If there were ever a time the Canadian government could help the needy it was now. But most gave the government a failing grade for their responses. It was common for many to only have enough food to eat once per day which weakened immune systems and created overflowing crowds at doctor's offices, clinics and hospitals. Severe colds, influenza and pneumonia became epidemic and many elderly people succumbed. But the true, kind nature of people experiencing hardship together shone through. A new spirit of helping one's neighbour, meaningful donations of food and water and volunteering time at the various places which catered to those in hardship and desperation became clearly apparent. The power of the human spirit knows no bounds.

38 – The Banks

One would prefer to think that when times are hard or severe, that when people, through no fault of their own, cannot possibly afford to make mortgage payments, that they can barely afford to stay alive, that the bank they have faithfully paid each month year after year, would show some humanity and offer some leeway. A mortgage is a long term commitment, what difference does it really make to a bank if you could put your payments on hold for a year or two?

They could charge an additional fee which could be added to the mortgage, which would eventually be paid by the owner. But no, not only did the banks evict their clients from their homes, they again for some insane reason paid their executives obscene bonuses. When the rest of the country were experiencing untold hardship, the banking world again rubbed salt in the wounds. Did this provide them with a kind of demented power trip? "Look what we can do, just because we can!"

The Canadian people had had enough, the hardships were one thing but this was a step too far. Christmas had come and gone, New Year came and went with people saying a big "good riddance" and wishing, hoping and praying the new year would bring them better fortunes. Protests began in the cities, protests against the banks, against the lack of help from the government, against globalisation which they blamed for the situation.

39 – The Protests

It can be said that there are those who attend protests and marches merely to cause trouble or are sworn anarchists looking for trouble. But in the biting cold when winter has Toronto firmly in its grip, the protestors who brave those conditions are genuine and focused on the issues at hand. Protests spread across Canada. The major cities saw an ever expanding number of people that demanded the government do more to help people. People were dying, they needed either financial aid or a break from their energy bills and food. The situation left hardly anyone untouched. Most people were either directly affected or had family or friends that were suffering.

The protests in the main had been peaceful. Most of the police themselves had family and friends who were affected and understood the protestors grievances. But in Toronto, four weeks into the protests, two police vehicles had windows smashed and four bank branches were vandalised. The police responded by boxing in an entire section of protestors, rounding them up and arresting them.

The same as happened years earlier at the Toronto G20 conference in 2010. And as in the 2010 protests, it was agent provocateurs who actually did the vandalism and not the protestors themselves, who, as was witnessed by television camera crews, tried in vain to stop the vandalism. This in turn created a backlash and the protestors grew in number, the people were in no mood to be set up and treated this way.

Whenever they could, Jeff and Niki would also join the protests but Jeff implored Niki never to go by herself, it was becoming too risky because if by some chance she was arrested and convicted on some false trumped up charge as had happened to innocent people at the G20 protest, she could be deported. Niki had to be careful until she had citizenship.

CHAPTER 13

40 – The Cottagers

Jerry had been talking to Nick on the phone and they were discussing the present situation.

"How's your job situation then Nick, is it safe?" asked Jerry.

"Funny enough even with the present situation we are busy as hell Jerry," Nick replied.

Nick was a millwright in a specialist rubber manufacturing plant, they supplied the rubber component to companies which manufactured specialized equipment to the Canadian armed forces and other militaries. The constant war against terror was a money machine for such companies and the devalued dollar seemed to have no negative effects.

"Well that's good to hear, you certainly landed a safe job there it seems," Jerry said.

"You're darn right there Jerry, the last two companies I worked for went under even before this mess," Nick added.

"So you're all coping then, the food, the bills, you're getting by ok?"

"Yeah well it's tough, had to tighten the belt like everyone else, I mean, there's just enough for food and heat and gas for the truck, but we are feeling pretty darn lucky to be honest, you know, when you compare with a lot of the others. How about you Jerry, you ok, you and Andrea and the kids?" Nick replied.

"Yeah about the same as you Nick, we're getting by but work is getting slow. Thankfully Andrea works for Revenue Canada and that's a safe income. I'm lucky in that I do upscale renovations and my clients are loaded, but as I said it's slowing down some."

"You spoke to Ron at all lately, just wondered if there was any news about you know what," asked Nick.

Nick was well aware of the total surveillance the government employed, albeit illegally, even though they always denied it.

"I called the other day but Ron is working a lot of hours in Toronto, he's part of the police lines keeping an eye on the protestors," Jerry replied.

"I was just wondering if there was the likelihood of any action coming down the pipe, know what I mean Jerry?"

"Yes I know what you mean but haven't heard anything myself, I'll let you know if I do ok."

"Yeah and I'll do the same if I hear anything," Nick said.

"Actually I'll try Ron again after we finish, see if he's around tonight," Jerry said.

"Ok bud, you let me know if there's any news then."

"Will do, talk later Nick." said Jerry.

"Yeah thanks for the call Jerry, goodnight bud."

"Goodnight Nick," said Jerry as he hung up the phone, then walked into the front room to see Andrea.

"How's Nick and the family?" Andrea asked Jerry.

"Nick says they're fine, they're surviving ok and his job is safe, they're real busy as usual," Jerry replied.

"Thank heavens!" said Andrea. "What about Ron, any luck getting a hold of him?"

"No but I'm just about to try him again, I want to know if they're ok and if he's heard anything through the grapevine," replied Jerry.

Jerry picked up the phone and dialled Ron's number and

Ron did pick up.

"Hi, Ron speaking."

"Hey Ron, Jerry here, how are ya?"

"Jerry, good to hear your voice pal, yeah good thanks, we're good and you guys?" Ron asked.

"Surviving Ron, surviving," replied Jerry.

"Yeah it's been a tough winter for everyone Jerry, some of the sad things we are seeing, real sad," Ron added.

"Yeah I don't doubt that bud. You're on duty at the protests then Ron, Natalie was saying?"

"Yes I am Jerry, yes I am," Ron replied with a tone that Jeff knew meant that Ron wasn't exactly a happy camper.

"You don't sound too thrilled about that," Jerry prodded.

"Protests are never the first thing you want to be doing, then the fact it's freezing cold and usually at night for me, no I can think of many other duties I would prefer."

"I hear ya, listen Ron, I was wondering if you'd heard anything, you know, what we talked about before, 'the book' and all that," Jerry asked.

"Can't say too much right now as you know Jerry but I thought folk would have been rioting by now, the cost of food, gas, all that, but people are sticking together, helping each other out, real neighbourly and all," Ron replied.

"Yes that is good to see, turns out we care after all, gotta like that eh?" Jerry said.

"Yeah, it's real good to see," Ron replied.

"Ok so nothing doing yet then?"

"No, well except the military are on alert, that's all I heard so far. But if I hear anything more I'll let you know ok," Ron offered.

"Sure thing bud, you take care down there ok?" said Jerry.

"Will do, no worries Jerry, thanks for calling," Ron said, then shut his phone off.

41 – The Newly-Weds

Mark Jenkins had been busy this particular winter. Never had they as paramedics had so many calls from worried neighbours about seniors and those with mobility issues. As it turned out, many of those calls were justified and the crew had saved several people from either freezing to death or starving in their own homes. But they were the fortunate ones as many had perished. Mark had often wondered what the situation was, if things were still on track with the 'movement'. He was fascinated by what James had told him and he hadn't been able to touch base with James for weeks but he was calling him now.

"James Young speaking," said James as he answered his cell phone.

"James it's Mark, how are you buddy?" Mark said enthusiastically.

"Mark, it's good to hear you, I'm great and you?"

"Good James, busy as hell but good, anyway long time no speak, how is everything?" Mark asked.

"Well, can't say too much but Julie and I have our fingers crossed if you know what I mean?" James replied.

"Oh that's fantastic, let's hope everything is fine, if it all looks ok we'll have to celebrate bro."

"Darn right Mark, darn right," said James.

"So, Julie ok then?"

"Oh yeah, couldn't be better really, and Annie and the kids?" James asked.

"Fine, fine. Hey James, I know we can't say much over the phone, but any news on the 'situation', anything on the horizon with the 'movement' if you know what I mean. I kinda thought something would have happened by now?"

"Yeah me too. Remember I said before, we hoped it would happen sooner rather than later, but it's later already. However, I do know they're on alert, the guys in the 'movement' that is, if you get my meaning?" said James.

"Oh yes, I get it James. So they're on alert, just waiting then I suppose?"

"Yes, the protests are likely to be the catalyst as we see it right now. Did you hear that there are foreign armed forces now in the US, Mark, the cabal who run everything really mean business."

"No I didn't, foreign soldiers in the States, what in hell's name for?" Mark asked.

"This is it, it's the beginning of the end game. Like I said before, they had to destroy the US financially which they did, then instigate problems to force martial law on the country, then once that was under control bring in foreign troops to run things. They will be wearing UN insignia but it'll be no peace keeping mission I can assure you."

"Holy crap, and that's what happened James? I haven't seen anything about that on the TV or anything," Mark said.

"Of course you won't, the media is all controlled like I said months ago, they will make it seem like things are hunky dory, just to prevent folk from worrying," said James.

"Oh man, things are happening just like you said they would, so where does that leave us now James?"

"They will be looking to bring foreign troops into Canada soon, after we are under martial law but they will have a surprise coming, can't say any more than that Mark, not now, ok?"

"Yeah, yeah sure James, sure, thanks for the heads up. Look I better be off, thanks buddy and take care, talk soon."

"Yeah, you too Mark, you guys take care." and they both hung up.

42 – Jeff the Barman and Niki

Jeff and Niki spent as much time together as possible. They were hopelessly in love and were in the process of learning about each other, their lives, their passions, their pasts, their hopes, their dreams. Niki learned that Jeff enjoyed working at his uncle's pub and meeting people, and that although intelligent and capable, Jeff had no desire to climb any corporate ladder or be caught on the 'hamster wheel of modern life', or as Jeff would say, "existing." Jeff wanted to call his own shots, be his own person, follow his passions and enjoy life one day at a time. For him, life meant now, enjoying the now instead of thinking about what may happen in fifty years, and apparently many of his peers were thinking the same way. Jobs were becoming so hard to come by, careers even more so, and so many get bogged down in student debt and couldn't even find work in their preferred field. No, Jeff wanted nothing to do with that.

Jeff lived above the pub also, which was a huge bonus as his uncle Jack wanted no rent from him. Being a pub, his food was also provided so Jeff did quite well for a barman especially with his tips. The arrangement suited Jack perfectly as he had experienced his share of dishonest employees either helping themselves to money from the cash register or giving away free drinks to friends. Jack always knew his brother's son was an honest person and the longer Jeff ran the bar the better as far as he was concerned. Jeff learned that Niki was a lively, street smart, twenty four-year-old woman who had left England for Canada four years previously with her parents. Niki had attended art college in England before migrating to Canada and photography was her passion. She lived in a small studio apartment in Toronto in which Jeff gradually began filling with such belongings as; a toothbrush, deodorant and other male necessities.

Niki had been raised by very open minded parents and she grew to be a confident, free thinking person with an open mind prone to asking questions. Although as a freelance photographer, Niki's work took her to many different locations and events, she soon learned that she loved nothing more than photographing events of passion such as protests and marches. There was just something about being at these events, a different energy maybe, a raw energy. Whatever it was, Niki fed off it and found she always came away with great photographs. Photos which captured that same energy. Jeff also learned that Niki was somewhat of an activist and held firm views on the current political and financial situations. Niki and Jeff had talked about such things many times but Jeff wasn't always convinced about Niki's points of view, until the crash and devaluing of the US dollar that is. The crash of the dollar had the effect of waking many people to the cold, hard reality that things really were going from bad to worse and that the future looked anything but rosy. There were the usual bleatings from the expert economists on the TV shows and in the newspapers, but the devaluing of the dollar brought such hardship that people were not going to be fooled that easily, for now at least, however hard the mainstream media tried.

"So you think we need to start over, the economy and the systems?" Jeff asked Niki.

"You read the book Jeff, 'The Organic Economy', didn't that resonate at all with you, the new systems, the new way, that's what he said, we need to start afresh and I absolutely agree as do many others," Niki replied.

"Yeah you're right he did say that, but what if we gave another party a try, why wouldn't we try that before dismantling the entire system?" Jeff asked.

"Because the political systems do not represent the voting taxpayers as a whole and it's always vulnerable to corruption and being taken over by the elites, and when that happens we are under fascist rule, which is what has happened, is this what you want Jeff?" Niki answered.

"No of course not, I just get concerned that we may give up systems that have worked for so long and we end up regretting it, you know, we may look back and think it wasn't that bad after all and wish we had it all back," Jeff replied.

"Understandable, and the systems worked quite well for a few decades but that's all changed now, we know we are being sold down the river to corporations and bankers, and that's because they lobbied and bribed our 'supposed' representatives to de-regulate the banking structure and allowed corporations to have the rights of a person among other things."

"Yeah I get all that and you're right, I suppose I just don't like big changes Niki," said Jeff.

"But that's the point, we are seeing big changes, huge changes, things aren't like they used to be and with the systems we have, the old systems, they never ever will be again either, it's gone, it's over, and it will get much worse than what we have right now Jeff. The dollar as we know it, issued by The Federal Reserve, will probably never recover and even if it did we will be back in the same boat in the future or our children will be dealing with it all. It's time to clean house Jeff, start anew, I mean, look around you, you know how there will be so many retirees without enough money to live on because their savings were wiped out by the system and we, the country won't have enough money to support them and their expensive medical bills. The political system allowed corporations to move our manufacturing overseas and who held the door open for them and watched the prosperity which it all was built on, vanish, our representatives did. The working man and woman, the ones who pay the taxes and vote have been screwed blind Jeff. Plus we now see our taxes being used to bloody well spy on us, take our freedoms and rights away in the name of security, great deal for us that is. I know big change can be a bit scary but don't you see, it will be far more scary if we don't change?" Niki replied.

"Yes, yes, I just needed it spelled out to me I suppose Niki, its such a big step though isn't it, but you're right, the fact is we are already going through big steps, big ugly steps with no guarantees it won't get worse in the future at any time. We can't continue this way, it has to change, I don't want to live under martial law like they do in the US now either. It's time to get real and face the facts, we do need a lot of things changed and who has any idea how to do that except what's in 'the book', and people seem to like those ideas so why not," Jeff said.

"Well if anyone else has ideas bring 'em on, that's what this is all about, us having the say, we call the shots. Think of that Jeff, no more lobbyists bribing our representatives, no old boys network looking out for the privileged classes, no more paying billions in interest to central bankers for nothing, no more secret, under the table deals with globalists that steal our countries assets and resources. If we had a say in any of that do you think we would allow it? No we wouldn't, so why would we ever want anything to do with these systems? Niki said passionately.

"I've had many chats with the Judge about these things too Niki, he's on side with what you're saying as well."

"Really, so the message is really getting out there then, to all age groups and levels of society, that's great to hear Jeff," Niki responded enthusiastically.

"Yeah I was surprised by what he told me, how things really are, who runs things, how the mainstream media is controlled, scary stuff Niki, at first anyway," said Jeff.

"Yes it is at first, then you get angry, then you want to tell everyone and then you realise they are like you were before you woke up, it's like two completely different worlds," Niki replied.

"Yeah, and I like the first one and wish it could just go on but I am seeing now that it has run its course, it can't continue, we just have to face up to it don't we? Jeff said.

"That's right but the change isn't going to make life worse Jeff, it will improve our lives, things will eventually pick up and flourish and when they do we will look back and be grateful we rid ourselves of these systems," Niki responded.

"I know, I know Niki, I can't fault what you're saying at all, it's time isn't it? We are the ones who will see history being made."

"Yes Jeff, you and I, we will be a part of it all, paving the way for a future for all of us to enjoy, it's so exciting," replied Niki.

"But I have friends who don't see it yet, who can't accept that we can change the system and when they tell me how they feel, I find I tend to start agreeing with them. Then I see you and you convince me again that we will change it all, it's strange Niki, I sometimes find it hard to argue the point with others who don't believe it can happen, you know, the changes and all," admitted Jeff.

"I know Jeff, it's a challenge it really is. I've had the same experience with some of my friends, believe me," Niki added.

"So how do we do it, how do we get people to see there isn't a choice, the systems don't work for us, it has to change, how do we do that?" asked Jeff.

"That's the biggest question of all Jeff. If everyone woke up and realised what was really happening, what has been happening for a long time, the long slow decline from most people having a decent standard of living to what we have now, people barely surviving, even with a good job, the lies, the wars, the corporate and banking control of everything, if they all just woke up together it would be over, they wouldn't put up with it, never. I sometimes think they must be spraying something at night that stays in the air and we breathe it in all day and it stops the mind from processing what is really going on," Niki said laughing but also shaking her head.

Jeff chuckled too, "I see what you mean, or maybe it's a secret frequency they transmit through the cell towers that controls the brainwaves," Jeff said pretending to be a demonic madman.

They both laughed at that and Niki said, "I know, it sounds bloody loopy but it really is like people are asleep, in some sort of a trance, and do you know what, this has been known for thousands of years, it's nothing new, Plato covers it in 'The Republic' in the parable of the cave and that was what, three hundred years before Christ or somewhere around there."

"The parable of the cave, I vaguely remember that Niki, what was it about again?" asked Jeff.

"It's along the lines of what we are seeing now, when people are raised in a system or systems, it is almost impossible to think outside those systems. The parable of the cave sort of goes like this;

Imagine there are some people who since early childhood have been chained in such a way that they can only look forward, they sit there looking at a cave wall and that's all they see, they don't even see those beside them. There is a fire that is always burning behind them which throws shadows on the wall of the people who walk back and forth between the fire and those sitting chained looking at the wall. That's all they ever know. They hear the voices, but only ever see shadows of people on the cave wall, so they only have a two dimensional experience, the shadows. Then one of them has the chains removed, he turns around for the first time and sees the fire which hurts his eyes, he then goes outside the cave where he sees the sun which also hurts his eyes as he gets accustomed to sunlight for the first time. He sees trees and people and mountains then goes back to tell the others chained in the cave that the shadows on the cave wall are not reality but a poor version of reality. The chained people notice the free guy can hardly see in the dark as he has to wait for his eyes to adjust again. They won't listen to his nonsense about reality and think that he is worse for having been freed as his eyesight is poorer than theirs. The point is the shadows on the cave wall are all they know and they get angry and defensive when it is challenged.

Just like people today who believe everything is fine, the media tells the truth, the government is our friend and the bankers and industrialists are just doing what they always do. When you see what is going on and try and explain it they too get defensive and angry," stated Niki.

"Ok that's a good analogy Niki, so how do we wake people up, any ideas?"

"As it stands Jeff, you can't. All you can do is talk about certain things at the right moments, mention websites to check out, that sort of thing. Short of a gun in the face from a tyrannical government employee or the military, I have no idea how to get people to see what is going on and that the net is closing in on us, it won't be long before we have no freedoms and rights at all, but you can't make people understand that."

"So that's it then, there's nothing we can do," Jeff said.

"No, not really, what is helpful though is things like 'the book', because a lot of people have read it or seen it discussed on TV and it has opened so many minds to new ideas, that will be immensely helpful when the collapse comes," replied Niki.

"You have no doubts there'll be a collapse then?"

"Oh no, no doubts about that at all, something has to give,

the financial system is screwed, the dollar is a basket case, isn't that obvious, the devaluing should be a clue?" Niki asked.

"Yeah I suppose it is. There I go again, I know you're right but I don't like facing the idea of what might happen, you know, with a collapse and all that," said Jeff.

"But always keep in mind Jeff, the collapse means we may get the one and only chance to get rid of the old system and start again with a new system, it's the most exciting thing I can imagine with respect to Canada, don't you think?"

"Yep, you just have such a way of putting your point across Niki, your confidence it will all work out for the better is really inspirational I have to say," Jeff replied.

"Thanks darling, it will!" Niki replied as she leaned over and kissed Jeff on the lips.

CHAPTER 14

43 – The Riots - The Catalyst

It was the second Tuesday in February when it happened, just after eight o'clock in the evening. Maybe the patience of the police had worn thin, but a scuffle broke out when the police attempted to arrest a protestor who appeared to be doing nothing to warrant arrest. Other protestors tried to pull their colleague back and the police pepper sprayed those in the vicinity. More protestors rushed in to help and the police let loose with their batons. A full on brawl began with no side backing down until a protestor was shot by one of the snipers on a rooftop. The sniper had aimed to injure the protestor but she was killed instantly.

The word spread back to the crowds immediately and the touch-paper, the fuse of the powder keg had been lit. The protestors went on a rage fuelled rampage, a rampage that Toronto, even Canada, had never seen the likes of. As the snow fell the protestors ran riot through the streets smashing windows, setting fires, looting stores and overturning and torching vehicles. News of the rioting, looting and vandalism reached other Canadian cities and all hell broke loose there too. This was what certain members, a very small group of the federal government was waiting for, they could now invoke martial law.

As Dawn Approaches

John Reid

44 – The Prime Minister's Speech

The very next day after the rampages, the Prime Minister's office announced to the media that there would be a very important announcement made that day at noon. Most people thought it would be to condemn and promise swift action against the protestors, and to commiserate with the injured police personnel and thank them all for their bravery. The Prime Minister did just that but went one step further.

"My fellow Canadians, we have all suffered greatly since the devaluing of the dollar. Many people have suffered great hardship especially through the cold weather and we in the government understand that emotions can run high in such trying times as these we face today. However, we cannot and must not allow our cities to be attacked, looted and burned as was witnessed last night. Our brave and wonderful police have also had to endure these hardships and have always set exceptionally high standards even when under immense provocation. An incident which is still under investigation was in no way an excuse for the complete breakdown of civility which spread across the cities of our nation, unnecessarily resulting in colossal damage to property and a danger to innocent people's lives. My cabinet has met and discussed this dire situation and have unanimously agreed that we have no alternative but to invoke martial law. The armed forces will be visible and patrol the cities and towns of Canada to maintain law and order. The safety of all Canadians being paramount. The Secretary of Defence will be making an announcement soon after this and will explain the

rules of conduct. We expect martial law to be temporary and we ask all Canadians to comply with the military's orders. Thank you for your anticipated cooperation."

The vast majority of the nation were in shock. Canada under martial law, what was the world coming to? Was the situation that bad that it warranted martial law, soldiers patrolling the streets, checking identification, like they had already been doing in the US, UK and other countries. What was happening to the world, where was this leading to?

But there were others who were celebrating martial law for this was exactly what they had been waiting for. It was only a matter of time before the 'movement' would spring into action, make the announcements and liberate Canada and Canadians. But the clock was ticking and time was not on their side. The announcement of martial law in Canada had meant that another surge of foreign troops would be deployed to the northern parts of the US, from the East coast to the West, within a day's convoy drive to the Canadian border crossings.

45 – Martial Law in Canada

It was surreal, martial law was in effect in Canada. The War Measures Act was invoked in October 1970 by Pierre Trudeau in response to the Quebec seperatists FLQ, who had kidnapped two people. But Canadian troops were only deployed in Ottawa and Montreal. This time it was the entire country under martial law. The Secretary of Defence had issued a statement explaining what martial law would mean for Canadians. Basically everything continued as normal except people were to stay at home between dusk and dawn unless they were shift workers or had a proven reason for being outside. Everyone had to carry identification also. Protests of any kind were banned outright and the police also had additional powers to detain without warrant anyone considered a threat in any way to Canada. Checkpoints were set up everywhere and people were routinely arrested and taken away without charge. The mood had changed, people were genuinely afraid of the police now as well as the soldiers.

The Internet was so controlled now it wasn't even worth using and everyone knew each keystroke they made on their computers while online was monitored. Social media was shut down also, but the television continued to air propaganda that all was well in the US but that the authorities were being cautious.

As Dawn Approaches

The newspapers also spewed propaganda regaling the great efforts of the Prime Minister and his government for keeping Canadians safe in these troublesome times and some actually fell for it. Cell phones were still working but people were extra careful as to what they said. Calls were usually quick and to the point.

46 – The Newly-Weds

It had been five long days of martial law and Mark couldn't wait any longer. Rather than risk calling James he drove to his house on the way home from work hoping he would be home. Mark rang the doorbell of the Young residence and waited. James opened the door to see Mark standing in the doorway.

"Hey Mark, come on in buddy, to what do I owe the pleasure?"

"Oh nothing much James, just on my way home from work and thought I'd drop by," Mark replied.

The two friends walked into the house and Mark followed James into the kitchen.

"Honey, Mark's here," James called out to his wife Julie. "Can I get you a drink, beer, coffee, anything?" James asked.

"No thanks all the same bud but I can't stay, the curfew and all that nonsense," Mark replied.

"Hi Mark!" Julie said as she walked into the kitchen and gave Mark a hug. "How are you?"

"Fine Julie but more importantly, how are you?" Mark said as he dropped his gaze down to her stomach.

"Well, fingers crossed eh James?" Julie said as she wrapped an arm around James's waist.

"Yeah fingers crossed, too early to tell, don't want to get

our hopes up just yet do we Honey?"

Julie smiled and shook her head.

"I am on a bit of a flying visit to be honest Julie and wanted to ask James something," Mark said.

"I have laundry to finish putting away so I'll leave you guys to it, see you later Mark, lovely seeing you and give my love to Annie and the children will you?" Julie asked.

"Sure will Julie, nice seeing you and best of luck," Mark said as Julie made her way upstairs.

"Ok you want the latest on the movement, am I right Mark?" James asked.

"Yes it's driving me crazy James, it's been what, five days since martial law and nothing, I thought you said it would happen straight after the announcement of martial law. This is getting pretty scary and I don't think there's any plan in the works to end it at all, the martial law," replied Mark.

"That's right Mark, as I said to you last time it's the end game as far as their concerned. They have Canada right where they want us," James explained.

"So why aren't they making a move?"

"It was decided that it would be far more effective if they held off for a while before making a move. The reason being to take advantage of the situation, let the people actually experience martial law, let them understand what life would be like forever for them. It would help sway the undecided in the vote, that's the strategy Mark," James answered.

"Oh I see, I see, yes that's excellent. My God I was so worried, I thought the movement had given up or fallen apart or something. Yes that strategy should help big time, people are scared of this martial law already James," Mark said.

"That was the hoped for outcome my friend," James answered, but purposely did not mention the fact that the UN and thousands of foreign troops were readying for a cross border invasion of Canada. An invasion with the blessing of a small group in the Canadian Federal Government. And once they were in place, they would never leave.

The media had to spin the UN foreign troop presence in the US and other nations as a benevolent and necessary security measure, that the people should be grateful and their safety and security were the top priority. But even though the Internet was no longer a viable medium for accurate information, the truth made its way everywhere that freight was shipped. The borders around the world were still open for business. Commercial and industrial freight continued to be shipped between countries. It was crucial that life continue on, to a degree, normally, so it was business as usual as much as possible.

Business people could also cross the borders, but tourists were no longer allowed and neither would any sane person want to. Being arrested in a foreign country under martial law would be serious if not potentially fatal. The human being is incredibly resourceful and adaptable and information via written letters made its way back and forth across borders carefully hidden among the goods, food, beverages, whatever was being shipped.

A network soon formed that relayed information about what was really going on in each country and Canadians were learning of the severity of life under the so-called benevolent security of the UN troops. Which in reality was a poorly disguised invasion force. The people of the Western world now had to face the cold stark reality that a New World Order was digging in to control every facet of their lives and the conspiracy theorists, the so-called 'tin foil hat' wearers were finally proven to be correct.

CHAPTER 15

47 – The Movement

So, as Mark explained to James Young, a change of plan had been made by General Benoit 'Ben' Rousseau, the highly respected military tactician. It was risky but the payoff could be well worth the risk.

The General knew it was all about timing. To give martial law enough time to show Canadians what life would be like under the New World Order, but not long enough that the UN and its foreign troops had time to cross the border into Canada. If that happened it would be game over for Canadian freedom and likely the deaths of anyone connected with the movement. Those connected with the movement were aware of the change of plan and many were becoming nervous about it all. But it was a catch 22 situation for them, make the move to liberate straight away and risk a 'no' vote by the people, which would reinstate the present government and result in their own arrests and likely trial for treason. Or risk waiting to guarantee a 'yes' vote at the potential expense of being arrested by a new world government and be subjected to whatever they would do with renegades. Between a rock and a hard place, the earlier exhilarations of being a part of Canada's liberation had faded away under the sweat and anxiety of what they could now clearly see was a very dangerous game. A game where the stakes could not possibly be any higher. The General, as a career soldier, was quite at home

with it all and did his best to lift the spirits of all concerned. He understood these were civilians, even brave civilians at that, but they were not trained soldiers. He reminded them of the enormous significance of what they were about to do, of how they would be historically aligned
side by side with the likes of the French resistance and other brave souls who risked their lives to save their nation. The General also reminded them that the alternative was slavery or death under a New World Order, for their plan was to reduce, over time, the global population by ninety percent at the minimum. The General had also made the prudent decision to withhold from the civilians in the movement, the 'intel' he had regarding the planned invasion by the UN and their foreign troops. The stress was quite high enough without adding to it.

As a standing General he was, of course, privy to much of what was planned by the Canadian government, but he also knew the 'inner circle', who were puppets of the cabal, had other plans for Canada, plans which had to be withheld from the Canadian military, lest they refuse orders and rebel.
The plan was to invoke martial law and then allow the foreign troops under the banner of the UN to enter Canada and gradually take over the enforcing of martial law from the Canadian military. The purpose behind it being that it is easier for a foreign soldier to control people, there is a degree of separation, it is not the foreign soldiers own people he is controlling, barking orders at, arresting and processing. This is why Canadian soldiers had gradually been deployed to other parts of the world such as Europe, where they would perform similar duties and assist the execution of martial law over people that spoke a different language, again, a degree of separation. The General knew of this and he had full knowledge of the troops situation in the US. He knew they had been shipping thousands of armoured vehicles, troop carriers, tanks and everything required for such an operation. He would have first-hand knowledge of when they

were expected at the borders because he would be coordinating with them, however, they had no idea what the General had in store for them. The General knew the UN convoys would begin mobilising soon, within the next few days for certain. But he kept a watchful eye on events, he could not be caught unawares of their arrival or it would be too late, the plan would fail and he would be responsible for the consequences which would greet the members of the movement. In his own mind he had planned for the announcement to be made one week after martial law was invoked and tomorrow was day six. He planned this because he had assurances from the command in the US that they would not mobilise for a few more days at least. The patriots of the movement were simply told to be ready at any time for the code word.

48 – The Deception

The General was awakened by his cell phone just after four thirty on the sixth morning of martial law.

"Sir, sorry to wake you sir," came the frantic voice of the caller, a soldier on duty in a communications centre, monitoring among other things, activity across the border via satellite feed.

The soldier had orders to call the General at any time if movement of the UN convoys across the borders in the US began.

"Seargent Walker here sir," said the soldier.

"Yes, ok, what is it Sergeant?" said the General.

"We have visible evidence of mobilisation of the UN convoys sir, heading toward the Canadian borders in Ontario, British Columbia and Alberta and the remaining convoys are getting ready to mobilise sir," said the Sergeant.

"You are absolutely certain?" asked the General.

"Yes sir, not only have we proof from the satellite feeds but the UN command has also confirmed to us they are mobilising and to be ready for them sir," the Sergeant replied.

"Did they say why they were coming now?" asked the General.

"Yes, they said a big winter storm was expected across most of the Northern US and they wanted to avoid it so they are coming here earlier than expected. But we checked sir and we do not see anything out of the ordinary with the weather," the Sergeant replied.

"Thank you Sergeant, I am on my way," the General said and turned off his secure cell phone.

The General was very surprised but knew a game was being played. The UN troops readying to make their way to Canada could not hide their movements so their command announced it and made the weather the excuse. With that in mind the General knew without doubt that the UN command had been tipped off about the liberation, the general had a spy or traitor in his midst. It wasn't a secret that many Canadians wanted change, real change. They could see clearly what was happening in the US and around the world and 'the book' had been read by hundreds of thousands of people and had been the topic of discussion on many radio and TV shows. People were becoming increasingly open and ready for something new, the ominous facts of the nefarious direction the world's leadership were heading made such a quantum leap far more palatable. The movement were sworn to secrecy also but even if they told their spouses or close friends it either wouldn't be taken too seriously or considered as powerful as it was going to be. For everyone's protection there was also an 'on a need to know basis', and information about the movement among the patriots was compartmentalised. The only person with a finger on the pulse of the entire plan including which day the liberation would happen, was the General himself. But he had to face facts, the plan had been compromised, the occupying invading troops of the UN were rolling towards Canadian borders and the General had to act and act fast.

<u>49 – The Eleventh Hour</u>

The General called a meeting with the military section of the chain of command involved in the movement. They were to have a very short, secure conference call at seven that morning. During the call the general explained what was happening, that the UN convoy had mobilised and were on their way to the Canadian borders. They all knew what had to be done and would set things in motion hopefully before the ministry became aware.Tanks and armoured vehicles were to be hauled as quickly as possible to the borders at risk and the good news was they would reach those borders before the UN convoys. They would then be used to stand guard and prevent the crossing of any UN vehicles.

If necessary, the UN command would also be warned that the Canadian military would fight to the last man to prevent the invasion, a monumental gamble, but this was all or nothing. The one concern was the Ministry of Defence being alerted to the moving of the tanks to the borders and ordering them to stop and turn back, and the subsequent fallout from that which would include the rapid termination of the General's career to say the least. While the tanks and other vehicles were being hauled to the borders, the General made his last minute arrangements and made the first of the seven calls he needed to make. One for each of the principals of the main cells of the movement. From there the movement would relay all the necessary information downstream to the patriots. The code word, as everyone involved knew, was the date and time the announcement would be made, the date of course was today and the time was set as eleven o'clock in the morning. Those whose duty as a patriot involved being at a certain place to undertake their roles would be ready to do so. Military personnel would be evacuating and guarding all parliamentary buildings both Provincial and Federal and all lawmaking would be suspended until after the vote. An updated list had been made of the politicians who were known to be working with the potential invaders. They would be arrested and detained pending the outcome of the vote which the patriots hoped would see them charged with treason. The Prime Minister and four cabinet members were on that list also. The list had been prepared and updated with the help of military intelligence officers who were proud members of the movement. The movement was far larger and more organized than anyone had realised, except the General who commanded it all. Military personnel would also go to the major TV stations throughout the nation and inform them to air the message of liberation from the General. The CBC would permit the use of their coverage.

The military personnel would also go to the major newspapers and inform them to publish a pre-written letter by the General and on behalf of the movement, to the nation, which would explain everything in detail as to what was planned by the traitorous politicians and the upcoming vote for freedom and true democracy. The media would also be closely monitored for accuracy and truth before publishing and airing and the restraints on the Internet and many websites would be lifted. People would again be able to speak freely without fear of being monitored and possibly questioned and detained as had been happening before the Internet clampdown. The entire movement were well aware of the importance of disseminating their message thoroughly and comprehensively and to allow people to discuss everything fully with each other. The more the people understood what the movement stood for and why they took such risks to liberate Canada, the better the chance there would be a 'yes' vote.

50 – The Announcement

At ten thirty that morning the General arrived at the CBC broadcast building in Ottawa with three commissioned officers, two dozen soldiers and six members of the Special Forces. It would seem like overkill but it was more for effect and would make it easier to facilitate what the General was about to do. A stunned receptionist listened to one of the officers explaining that there was a message of extreme national importance that was to be broadcast and that she should not contact security or anyone else. Ten soldiers stayed on guard, two at the main doors, four in the reception area and the other six patrolled the building. All entry and exit doors were locked and no-one was allowed into the building until after the General had left. The same thing was happening across the nation as soldiers guarded the major TV stations which would provide the CBC announcement feed of the General's historic speech of liberation. At the same time, officers and soldiers also arrested and detained the Prime Minister, certain cabinet ministers and members of parliament as well as those in the provincial governments who were proven to have committed treason, this also included five of the provincial premiers. Some could not be arrested right there and then because they were out of their offices and that included the Minister of Defence.

The Department of Defence were eventually notified that convoys of Canadian military vehicles loaded with tanks and other heavy equipment were heading to the main borders. The infuriated Minister of Defence was notified while driving to his office and immediately sent out a directive to have them turned around and for the military to arrest and charge those responsible with treason. The minister was completely taken aback and could not understand what was happening, everything was going to plan, the white painted invasion force disguised as UN peacekeepers were almost at the first borders, it was the end game, they were home and free, the New World Order was well on its way to having full control of the US and Canada, the minister would be a part of the most powerful government the world had ever known. The minister was also on the movements list of those proven to have acted treasonous. He had not yet been arrested because he was out of his office and hadn't yet arrived. The minister was driving himself through Ottawa, infuriated by what was happening. "Who made the decision to send troops and equipment to the borders?" He thought to himself, "what the hell is happening, we were almost home and dry." As soon as the minister had sent the directive, General Rousseau was informed as was planned in advance should that happen and he immediately overrode the minister's directive. The Canadian forces continued rolling to the borders. At ten forty five all the police chiefs of the provinces were notified of the coming speech and that for the next four weeks the military would be acting as the guardians of the nation. The police would continue as normal except there would be a military officer in charge instead of a political minister.

The CBC broadcasting team were frantically re-arranging schedules to allow the General to take to the air at eleven o'clock. The staff had been through many a tense experience airing news over the years but nothing came close to this historic moment, it was surreal, no-one knew what to expect, except some of the household names who announced the news daily to the nation. They of course were present at the General's mansion for several meetings of the movement as were other media personalities from different TV organisations and journalists from various print media, such was the scope of the movement by this time. For everyone else, all they knew was a top ranking General had taken charge of their building and calmly explained he was going to make a speech concerning the future of Canada and the freedom of her people. They didn't know how this was going to go, what the General was going to say, but what they did know was they were going to be a part of history.

The General took the seat in front of the cameras, he was coached briefly on broadcast etiquette and given some tips to maximize effect. A make-up specialist applied powder to his face and the General scanned his notes, his speech, one more time to make sure the sheets were in order.

The main CBC anchorman Doug Sherbourne had already arranged with the General weeks ago that he would explain the interruption in regular programming, that there was an announcement of national importance to be made and then introduce him. The time had come and three minutes before eleven o'clock, national news anchor Doug Sherbourne went live.

"Ladies and Gentlemen, this is your national news presenter Doug Sherbourne with a very important message.

"In a few moments General Benoit Rousseau of the Canadian military will make an announcement of immense importance to each and every one of us.

"We strongly advise every Canadian to listen to what the General has to say."

The Minister of Defence was listening to some classical music in his car and did not hear what any of the radio stations were talking about, the major announcement that was about to happen. He made another call to his secretary but someone else picked up and explained that the secretary was under arrest for treason.

"Treason!" the Minister screamed, "what in hell's name is going on, I am the Minister of Defence and I demand to know now," he yelled.

"Sir, please drive to your office. There is a military order for your arrest." the soldier responded.

"My arrest! What kind of game are you trying to play here and who am I speaking to?" the minister was livid but becoming worried.

"Sir, I am Colonel Richard Wainright of the Canadian armed forces, the Prime Minister is under arrest for treason and General Rousseau is the interim leader of the liberation of Canada. To make things easier for everyone please drive directly to your office or we will be forced to apprehend you in public," answered the Colonel.

Back at the CBC studio the General looked into the camera knowing the magnitude of what he was about to announce. He had thought about this moment a thousand times. How should he look? Serious, stern, relaxed, friendly? How should he sound? Authoritative, amiable, concerned, sincere?

As hard as he tried to ignore them, these thoughts were with him night and day and were also the theme of many a dream. Should he give an impression of being too serious and authoritative it could quite easily scare many people and sway a 'no' vote. If he gave an impression of being too friendly, people may take this as a lure and not to be trusted.

The General now understood the special skillset politicians today had to have to be successful, another very good reason for a change of systems, for that skillset meant nothing when it came down to being an effective representative for their voters. The General decided he would be as natural as possible. It was time to end the acting, the dramatics, the scoring of Brownie points.

Today of all days he had to be real, the people deserved it, he would read his speech with sincerity and integrity and orate as his written words demanded.

"Here goes," thought the General.

"My fellow Canadians, my name is General Benoit Rousseau of the Canadian Armed Forces.

I am here now to make an announcement of the utmost importance to each and every Canadian, possibly the most important speech you may ever hear in your lifetimes. It is challenging to know where to begin with this announcement, but I will say as a passionate Canadian soldier that I act truthfully and faithfully on behalf of your freedoms, rights and democracy. This is not an announcement of a coup or military takeover but one of liberation and honesty. As you are well aware, Canada has been operating under martial law, a completely unnecessary martial law. But I can assure you as a serving officer with full knowledge of the future intentions of certain members of our Federal and Provincial governments, that this martial law was imposed for completely different reasons than that explained to you by the Prime Minister."

The General knew that so much hinged on timing and so much hinged on time. He knew that the powers that be, the cabal, would be doing everything possible to block his announcement from being aired around the world. The General's speech would be without doubt the biggest threat they had experienced to their ambitions and should people around the world get word that Canada had thwarted their attempts at controlling her, it would likely spark off a pushback that would be difficult, if not impossible to contain. The General was well aware that if they could have completely blocked his speech from being heard or seen, then there would have been a short war between the UN cabal run United States and Canada. A war which Canada would lose very quickly. The speech would nonetheless be heard worldwide, not by everyone but enough people that the cabal would not risk an all-out attack on Canada. They had control of much of the world but an attack against a nation such as Canada would be disastrous, for their mode of operation was stealth and covert actions, to sneak into a country under a false guise of friendliness. To be seen to outright attack a nation such as Canada would alert the rest of the world to their plans. But the General being a mastermind of tactics had fore-planned well and he made sure that Canadians overseas were also part of the movement and had copies of the speech to disseminate in the various countries around the globe where they lived. That and his military colleagues stationed overseas would ensure the announcement would be heard by enough people globally to persuade the cabal not to attack Canada. It was a risk, a big risk, but this was the ultimate fight for freedom and the General had never been beaten tactically.

The General continued,

"Martial law was imposed to facilitate a quiet invasion by foreign soldiers under the United Nations banner, as it currently is in the United States, although this news has been kept quiet by a complicit media. UN convoys are heading to our borders as I speak but we have Canadian troops ready to block their entry and invasion. All Provincial and Federal parliaments are now suspended until further notice but the duties of local government, councillors and mayors will continue.

"I declare as a guardian of Canadian democracy, to the United Nations and United States that on behalf of a free Canada, do not attempt to cross our borders with armoury or troops. We will defend to the last soldier our home and native land. This also applies to all air traffic both military and commercial until further notice by myself. I repeat, do not attempt to cross our borders with armoury, troops or aircraft until further notice by myself. This speech and all information pertaining to this liberation will be aired constantly on the CBC television network and radio stations as well as published daily in all of the main newspapers. It is imperative that everyone know as much as possible about what we are doing, why we are doing it and what we seek to achieve. Pease allow me to explain who and what has brought me to this announcement. There are, I am very, very proud to say, a great number of true patriot Canadians who understood the direction the US and other nations were going, they understood clearly the loss of freedoms and rights that were happening and knew Canada would soon follow. These brave patriots have risked their lives and joined the thousands of military personnel in what we have called the 'movement', the movement to free Canadians from tyranny. These brave civilians of the movement hail from every sector of public life including politics, banking, justice, law and order, media and other vital sectors. They will help facilitate, educate and ease the nation toward the new election which will be held in the next four weeks. The movement is not political or aligned with any ideology, it is simply a group of patriotic Canadians who wish to free Canada from potential tyranny and help bring a new system of direct democracy, a real democracy whereby we are all involved directly in the decisions which affect us.

I have irrefutable proof that the Prime Minister, certain cabinet members and members of the Federal parliament, as well as members, some high ranking, of the provincial parliaments, have acted in a treasonous manner. I will show proof that these people were willing cohorts in handing Canada and Canadians over to a UN invasion force which would have acted as the permanent police force for a One World Order. A world order in which a totalitarian dictatorship would enslave those who managed to survive it. These traitors to our great nation are currently being detained and will face trial for their actions. We have just experienced, in Canada, national martial law. You now understand how life would be under a world order, an order that is the goal of the cabal of bankers, industrialists and certain extremely wealthy families. You have been given a small taste of what was to come, which was planned to begin today with the UN invasion. From this we can learn a most important lesson, that we cannot entrust our nation, our very lives, to a relatively small group of elected representatives, for they are, as has been proven, corruptible to the point of treason. There is far too much at stake In this day and age of global power and control to entrust so much power to so few, it is to our detriment that we do so. The present political and financial systems have run their course and no longer serve the purposes for which they were intended. It has been very apparent for some time that the wealth and control of the world was quickly falling into the hands of a very powerful few and that they would stop at nothing for total global control of all money, laws, food, water, health, energy and education. The movement of patriots have bravely risked their lives to stop this from happening to Canadians and our goal is to ensure that we introduce a new system, a system which will protect Canada from these tyrants.

Each member of the movement is in agreement with the ideas set out in the book called 'The Organic Economy', and we know that many of you are familiar with this book. For those who are not we will be making it available on the various Canadian government websites so that you can fully understand what it is we wish to accomplish. The movement has proposed a new constitution which protects Canada and Canadians from the greedy hands of central bankers, mega-corporations and those who have ambitions detrimental to Canada. The new constitution is simple and straightforward and is based mainly on an organic economy, an economy which serves the very people who create by their labours, the wealth and prosperity which fuels that economy and thus deserve also to share its fruits.

We have all suffered since the US dollar was devalued and it may be devalued again. Some economists think it will never fully recover but an organic economy will not be tied to the US dollar and we would all prosper as it reaches its natural equilibrium. The era of greed and materialism has imploded, it has finally shown to us all that it was a false economic system which benefitted the elites at the expense of those who produced the wealth, namely you. The new constitution and the new proposals for an organic economy will be fully explained and discussed on the CBC radio and television network as we lead up to the election. The election will be primarily for Canadians to decide if they wish to continue with the present political and financial systems or to choose a new future by voting for an organic economy. Of course, we in the movement make no secret that we are hoping that Canadians can see clearly the direction we were heading with the present systems and elect a new system and constitution. Until the election, which we expect to hold within four weeks, martial law is revoked and we encourage everyone to continue with their lives as normally as possible. The movement will also do everything they can to help facilitate business and commerce to continue to function smoothly.

Everything will continue to run as before. All Provincial and Federal ministries will serve the people as before but there will be no government, no politicians. The positions of ministers will temporarily be filled by military officers acting as overseers. After the vote is held the military will step down and hand over to the movement or the governments. Should the people vote for an organic economy, the movement will assist in the process of putting into place that which is necessary to run the nation via direct democracy and the issuing of debt free money.

On behalf of the movement of patriots, please read and learn everything you can regarding the new organic system of economics. We are convinced it is the only way for all Canadians to enjoy true democracy and prosperity, and the only system which can protect them. Thank you for your time, please go in peace."

As soon as the General had finished his speech the cameras were back on Doug Sherbourne who had new information to share with Canadians.

"Ladies and gentlemen, for those of you who have just heard General Rousseau's historical speech, I am sure you are all shocked by what is unfolding. To recap, the Prime Minister and many other politicians, some senior, have been arrested for treason. General Rousseau claims to have irrefutable proof of this. The military is assuming control of the country until an election is held within the next four weeks. Martial law is revoked until after the election and it's business as usual as much as possible. The election is for all eligible Canadians to decide if they want to continue with the present political and financial systems or to opt for a new system based on an organic economy, as suggested in 'the book' of the same name.

"I believe we have footage, yes we do, yes we have live footage of three Canadian border crossings..."

The camera shot changed to footage from helicopters overlooking the border crossings.

"There ladies and gentlemen we can clearly see the white painted convoy of United Nations troops, it must go for a mile, maybe longer. I think we can see armoured vehicles and I'm not certain but that could also be tanks. Ladies and gentlemen this is what the General was referring to, he called it an invasion force, not a peacekeeping force. Apparently General Rousseau has information that this was to be a covert invasion. Incredible scenes, we can also see the Canadian armoured vehicles and I think I see tanks also, they have blocked the border ladies and gentlemen, our Canadian military are actually blocking our borders to what is claimed, and on good sources, to be an invasion force.This is unbelievable, we are witnessing a historical moment, I for one never thought I would see anything quite like this." Doug Sherbourne wanted the General to comment also.

"General Rousseau, from where you sit can you see the

footage sir? What an incredible sight!" Doug said.

"Yes I see it, and I must tell the audience how close we came to the invasion being a reality," the General replied.

"I think this is all still sinking in General, I think the nation will be in shock, did you have any idea it would be this close, I mean, you only made the declaration ten, fifteen minutes ago and the United Nations convoy is there now, ready to cross our borders," Doug asked.

"Yes, we knew it would be close, probably not that close, but close." the General responded calmly but inside he was sweating bullets, for the announcement was supposed to happen tomorrow. Until that phone call this morning about the convoys heading towards Canada and the frantic arrangements to head them off and make the announcement hoping the Minister of Defence didn't find out until it was too late. "How did it go? Fortune favours the bold," the General thought as he rewarded himself with a little smile.

"This couldn't have worked out better," he thought, "I couldn't have planned this better myself, the announcement coinciding with the UN at the borders and the CBC showing footage of it all. The Canadian people will definitely now understand why we did what we did."

The General was very pleased how it all went, the effect was maximized and everything was looking good for a vote for change, real change. "As long as we can hold off an attack from the UN," he thought. He knew the UN and US command would be livid at what had just happened. That they would be frantically judging and deciding if an attack were feasible. That they would be checking how far the announcement went around the world, but he knew there was safety in numbers. Safety in the number of people around the world who had heard or knew about the announcement. The General had played this game perfectly and he knew that timing made all the difference. The longer the UN held off, the stronger Canada's position. The UN missed their one chance, they were checkmated, he knew it, they knew it.

CHAPTER 16

51 – The Cottagers

Andrea was at her desk at the CRA (Canada Revenue Agency) when word went around the office that something massive was happening to Canada. The head of her department called her and told her to bring everyone to the cafeteria to watch what was going to happen on the large screen TV. Obviously no-one had a clue what was going to be said but after the announcement and subsequent scenes of the UN convoys at the borders, they were dumbfounded, absolutely dumbfounded. The department head was also in some shock and thought about sending everyone home for the rest of the day. She made a call to her boss who agreed it may be a wise idea, but then they both realised the General said to continue on as normal as much as possible. So it was decided to give everyone an early and extended lunch break so they could all discuss what had happened and come to terms with it all. There wasn't any point continuing working straight away as it would be difficult for them to focus on their tasks and costly mistakes were more likely. Similar scenarios played out in workplaces all over the nation and some employees were sent home. Andrea called Jerry who had heard the announcement on the radio.

"Hi Hon how are ya?" Jerry asked Andrea.

"Good, good, did you see the speech Jerry?" asked Andrea.

"Yeah I heard it on the radio, unbe-freakin-lievable!" exclaimed Jerry.

"I know Babe, we were all called to the cafeteria, they gave us a long lunch break to take it all in, I'm in shock, I can't believe what's happened, can you?" asked Andrea.

"Same Hon, in shock, me and the boys here we're all in shock, we don't know what to say to each other, I think it has to sink in some first," replied Jerry.

"Yes, you're right, we're the same here, I mean, what do you say to that?"

"Well it sounds on the surface that it's what we were hoping for don't it? He's talking about an organic economy so I guess it's a good thing, and then holding off the UN at the borders like that, jeeze who would have ever thought this could happen," said Jerry.

"Yeah I guess you're right Jerry, but we have to get more information and see what the media makes of it all, then we can digest it," said Andrea.

"I suppose so, even though the media can't be trusted to tell the truth it sounds like the military are making sure they do this time," Jerry answered.

"If it is all true, that we vote on a new system, like the organic system then that's the best news I've heard in a long time Hon, it's what we dreamed of isn't it, this could be it Jerry, a new system, our kids will actually have a future, I won't lose sleep worrying about them anymore, " said Andrea.

"Yes Honey you're right, this could be what we hoped for and I hope and pray that it is because this country was going straight to hell before today," Jerry replied.

"Yes it was, Jerry I'm so excited but a little scared too, it's all so sudden and so terrifyingly real,"

"No surprise there Hon, this is huge so it's bound to be a little scary, but by the looks of it, if the people vote for a new economy then we're golden," Jerry said.

52 – The Judge

The Judge continued with his responsibilities at immigration and saw Jeff at the pub as usual, except when he was meeting with the network of top lawyers and law experts in preparation for a 'yes' vote and the process of proving the banking systems as fraudulent and the trade deals as non-binding for Canada, as the people had no say in their ratification. Should the vote be 'yes' the experts would be meeting with the Treasury and the Bank of Canada to arrange how money would be issued in the future.

This was likely going to be the biggest challenge to a new system, this and the dismantling of the 'High Street' banks, the banks everyone banked with. The first time the Judge went to the pub after the announcement, Jeff was, like everyone else, in disbelief.

"Evening Judge, the usual?" Jeff asked.

"Twist my arm then Jeff," the Judge replied as always.

"What a day, I still can't believe what's happening Judge, the Prime Minister and politicians arrested, the UN convoys, we're all gobsmacked here," said an awestruck Jeff.

"Yes, it was quite something, went rather well too I feel," replied the Judge.

"You don't seem that surprised, did you know about it

then Judge?" asked Jeff.

"Actually yes, I did as it happens," the Judge answered.

"Wow, are you a member of the movement too?"

"There's no harm in mentioning it now, if the vote is 'no' they will know I'm involved anyway, so yes Jeff, I am a part of the movement," the Judge replied.

"Oh man, you really are a dark horse aren't you?" Jeff smiled in admiration, "so you've been involved in this all along, that must have been exciting?"

"Exciting is one description, scared is another, both would describe the feelings at some time or another," the Judge said.

"Ok, can I ask you some questions about it, you know, the new economy?" Jeff asked.

"Certainly Jeff, the movement is very keen to help people understand fully what it will mean to them, so yes, fire away."

"Ok, I have read 'the book' and Niki and I have talked about it many times but how do you stop corruption, I'm not clear on that?" Jeff asked.

"Oh yes that's quite a simple one to answer really. Assuming a 'yes' vote, you know there will be no further need for politicians so there will be no-one to bribe or corrupt," the Judge answered.

"Ok I get that but how do you stop a large corporation from doing something they shouldn't. Let's say they have to have planning permission for something and they bribe the bureaucrat responsible for planning, how do you stop that?"

"Good question Jeff, in place of political ministers there will be committees of citizens who will monitor the departments, one committee for each department. There will also be accountants on the committees who will monitor expenditure and together they will keep a watchful eye on backhanders and bribes. Now you do know that it is highly unlikely we will be able to stop all foul play but we will endeavour to do our utmost," replied the Judge.

"Yeah, yeah of course, but what if a committee member takes bribes, how do you keep check of that?"

"That has been addressed too Jeff. No person can serve on the same committee for more than two years and there must be at least ten years between serving on that particular committee, therefore no member will be around long enough to become too familiar with either the bureaucrats or the clients they serve," the Judge replied.

"Ok that works. So anyone can serve on a committee correct?"

"Yes, there are no specific requirements except having graduated from high school and being willing to swear an oath to serve Canada and Canadians faithfully and loyally as a guardian of democracy," answered the Judge.

"So you serve on the same committee for two years in a row, can you serve on another, for another department?"

"Certainly, the way we are looking at it now is, after the two years service you wouldn't be able to serve again for another five years, that's to give others a chance. Now, if there were a shortage of volunteers you may be asked to serve another term, in a different department. But we rather hope that there will be enough volunteers, people proud to act as guardians of democracy for Canada," the Judge remarked.

"So will there be a leader on the committee, a spokesperson or something?" queried Jeff.

"There will be a chairperson, someone always has to keep things moving along efficiently and the chairperson has the seat for four months. We do not want to give an impression the chairperson has any real power, the power lies with the Canadian people, period," the Judge replied.

"What about press releases, who does that, who speaks to reporters?"

"The departments will have their own public relations

personnel but the committee must first check all press releases as they are the overseers of the departments. Let me be clear Jeff, the committees aren't there to be a thorn in the sides of the departments, they do a good job, they are experts at what they do, we are there to make sure there is no corruption and to collect information that may be used at the next vote," replied the Judge.

"How many people on a committee Judge?" asked Jeff.

"I think it will depend on the size of the department, but these things can always be changed, whatever works best, nothing is set in stone, it is all flexible and what works best for democracy," answered the Judge.

"What if someone, a father of three children who lives way up north, wants to be on a committee, can he?"

"Absolutely Jeff, in fact that will be a factor in selection, we would want as diverse a committee as possible. Committee members who live over an hour's drive from the office will be given accommodation and expenses, as well as a generous salary. They could bring their spouses and children too if wished as we would have schooling available for them," the Judge said.

"That's awesome Judge, I still can't believe we could soon be seeing this in action, it blows me away," said Jeff.

"Yes, me too Jeff, me too," the Judge said lifting his glass to Jeff then taking a mouthful.

53 – The Newly-Weds

On the evening of the day, that historical Wednesday the announcement was made, Mark called James.

"Hi buddy, Mark here, I can't believe it, I just can't believe it bud, you were right, exactly right,"

James stood in his hallway with his phone to his ear, smiling as he listened to Mark's words.

"Yeah, kinda crazy eh? But it was a close one Mark, those suckers were ready to invade this morning, never thought I'd see this day bud I tell ya," James replied.

"No, no me neither, it's nuts, I mean, am I dreaming or something, every time I think of it it seems unreal but it's not," said Mark.

"I know, I know, it's crazy even to me and I was ready for it, well kinda, I didn't know the UN were coming so soon," James said.

"Oh man I hope with all my heart the vote is 'yes', I like the sound of the new way more and more, it makes so much damn sense," Mark added.

"Yeah it does Mark, I can't see the vote being 'no', not now, not after the martial law and then the UN at the door," James replied.

"Me neither, I mean, there's no contest is there, tyranny or freedom," Mark added.

"True enough Mark, but they never took anything for granted, too many people can't handle real change, even when they know they're being screwed, but after today's events I think enough people will vote yes," James said.

"Ok, when the vote is in and it's a 'yes' we must get together and celebrate, all of us," Mark exclaimed.

"Absolutely Mark, this is history, this is freedom, we should be all be partying in the streets and I mean that too, it's the biggest thing to happen to Canada in centuries," James replied.

"Ok bud, talk to you soon," and Mark rang off.

CHAPTER 17

54 – A Nation in Disbelief

After the General's announcement the nation was in what could only be described as shock and disbelief. Canadians could barely believe what they had seen and heard and those who missed it were quickly informed by others who had difficulty being believed and in many cases, thought of as practical jokers. Naturally it was all that people talked about, even though many people were familiar with 'The Organic Economy' book, there was so much to talk about, to come to terms with, to understand. Not only was the nation almost invaded, but the Prime Minister and many politicians were under arrest and charged with treason. But martial law was lifted which was a huge relief so maybe the General was a good guy, who could tell at this moment? Canada had never had a military coup before, in modern times at least. Ok it wasn't a coup he said but a liberation. Liberation sounds good, we were under martial law and now we aren't, and we saw the UN convoys at the border. The General and this 'movement' saved us, but did they? He said we will have a vote within four weeks, that's good, that means it isn't a military takeover, unless things don't go their way maybe and the military does take over. No, can't see that happening, Canadian soldiers would not do that. Foreign UN troops yes but not our Canadian men and women. Maybe this is a good thing after all, but who knows, what do you think?

These and many other questions were being asked and dissected, people not sure what to think.

They were in a sense, lost. There wasn't yet a consensus, more of an opinion vacuum. The next few days would see Canadians talking these things over and over, trying to find fault with what the General had said, as they should. This particular time in Canada's history would be the subject of many a sociology and psychology paper. People in a decision vacuum. People who could not form an independent opinion, they needed to hear what others had to say first, ideas were discussed and digested but it was strange because there were no political party leaders selling ideas. That would be much easier, we only have a choice of this or that. No, this required a different approach, one needed to think for themselves this time, one needed to become responsible. This was different, this was new, this was real, a new energy began to resonate, one that had never been experienced before, an energy of belonging, of mattering, an energy of self-responsibility, and after a few days a general consensus began to form. The media ran articles and new and previously shelved documentaries about how they saw life within an organic economy, the UN convoys, even how they had occupied the US, something which had been censored before now. They even aired and published information about what was happening to the UK, parts of Europe and Australia too. Canadians were appalled at what they were learning and angry at what had been held back, censored and whitewashed. The military ensured the media were fair as it was well understood that their corporate masters would always prefer the present system of government, being so easy to control and manipulate to their demands and whims.

As the days went by and life returned to relative normality, relative because people were still hurting under a devalued dollar, a sense of calm descended on the nation as the threat of a

UN invasion faded. The knowledge that an election was to be held appeased the global community, neutered the UN forces and excited Canadians. The cabal however, were infuriated, their careful plans scuppered and now the global community would be that much harder to contain. If they couldn't take Canada by stealth, the global community would begin seriously resisting the UN 'peacekeeping' forces, knowing they were being occupied. If Canada remained free it would serve as a beacon to the global community who would resist and fight for the same freedom. The cabal were snookered and they knew it. The only other thing was to do what the US has done for many decades, what they were the masters at, what even the KGB wished they could have emulated. To go undercover, create unrest and discord and destabilize a nation. Then offer a smooth talking cabal puppet as a saviour of the nation. For the CIA this was old hat, they were past masters at it, they wrote the book on it. Time to pay CIA headquarters at Langley a visit, but then again how could they destabilize a nation that doesn't have a government, doesn't have a leader to assassinate, no-one to threaten, bribe or replace when the entire nation are in effect, the politicians. If successful in the upcoming election, a new Canada would be the only major nation on the planet protected from the cabal bullies, the first time ever a major western nation couldn't be controlled by the cabal. The ability to neutralize the cabal and corruption was apparent, an organic economy inherently protects a nation from those who wish to subvert it for their own gain. Snookered again.

55 – The Proposed Constitution of a New System

The movement had acted quickly and versions of the new proposed constitution appeared in the print media as well as being aired constantly on various television shows along with discussions and debates about what it all meant. Even though many Canadians were familiar with 'the book' there were still more that were not and the movement knew it had to get the message to everyone before the election. Not only to ensure that people were fully informed on what they were voting for, but the movement were confident that people would much prefer the new system once they learned about how it would work for them. The movement had laid out the proposed constitution in an easy to follow manner. The Canadian Charter of Rights stood as before and that was followed by the three major changes to the present system, namely that parliamentary politicians and government were obsolete and everyone had to vote four times per year on all issues, money would be issued debt free by the Bank of Canada, the people's bank and usury would be abolished.

So, to clarify, there would no longer be Provincial or Federal parliaments but at the municipal levels there would continue to be elected representatives such as; councillors and mayors. Local issues should always be dealt with by those familiar with them, namely the local residents. However, improvements can always be made and the local people could always employ a similar form of voting system as the province and federal voting systems to select certain local ideas. There would no longer be a government as all forms of power, imagined or real, were to be nullified. Although the present bureaucratic departments would continue to run as before, there would be an administrative panel of civilians that would oversee each department in place of a government minister. Therefore 'Ministries' would be called 'Departments'.

All laws and decisions affecting Canadians were to be decided by Canadians and voted on four times per year. This frequency could be decreased over time if the people so decided. Electronic voting would be the preferred method with everyone having a unique encrypted code to enable voting via phone or computer. The voting process needed to be made as easy as possible as there were going to be many items on which to vote each time. All banks would be nationalised under the Bank of Canada which would issue all money debt free. Canada would no longer borrow money from central banks and interest on loans of any kind would be outlawed. The boards of directors of the 'High Street' banks were going to be informed before the election that in the event of a 'yes' vote, which was highly likely, that all banks will be nationalised and the staff at the branch level would continue to be employed, but the Bank of Canada would become their employer. The boards would also be informed that the Bank of Canada would take over all loans and deposits and that credit cards would be phased out as the new 'advance' cards were put into circulation. The 'advance cash' cards would be the Bank of Canada's version of a credit card but there would not be any interest charged. The card would act as a debit card because the bank would have pre-approved a certain amount that could be used. A formula would be used which projected future earnings against expenses and an advance limit pre-approved. Should the account holder fall behind in payments their pre-approved 'advance' limit could be put on hold or lowered.

Account holders would have a personal associate who knew their portfolio well and would always be available to help. The new way was not to punish people for over-spending, but to help them get on their feet, stay on their feet and prosper. In effect, nothing would change for the bank customer, it would be business as usual except the interest portion of any payments would be nullified. These were the main planks of the new system, the 'organic' economy. The new constitution did not go too deep into detail as it was organic and inclusive and the people needed to decide how it evolved.

The one thing in 'the book' that was left out was the idea of price and wage freezes. This was thought to be too constrictive and the movement thought it best to let the markets find their own equilibrium. The idea though, could always be introduced at a later date by citizens through voting.

Another concept that 'the book' did not cover was the tax system. It was agreed by the movement that a study group be formed to look into a new fairer system which the corporations could not evade. The matter of Canada's ties to the UK were also made clear. Without politicians and parliament and with the people using direct democracy, the Governor Generals, the Queen's representatives for the country and the provinces would also be obsolete. Canada would be a fully sovereign nation and the Queen and London would no longer have any say in Canada's affairs. Certain members of the movement had great ideas about how things should work but the new system would essentially be leaderless, that was its strength, no individuals with power, no-one to bribe, corrupt or blackmail. The people were finally protected from the greed and ambition of those who cared not for them or their nation. Therefore the movement in its wisdom held back from defining the new constitution in too great a detail or people may just think of them as the new leaders, when the idea was for the people themselves to learn self-responsibility and essentially be their own leaders. The members of the movement would lay out a framework for the people to 'flesh out' over time and the ideas of the movement's members would also be added to the voting list for everyone to decide upon. Being leaderless would take some getting used to. The various departments would continue to run as before but an administration panel of citizens would oversee them and ensure that bribery and corruption would not be tolerated. Who would make the important decisions such as which projects, sectors or causes to fund? Decisions such as these were previously made by political ministers and often the decision was affected by partisanship, ideologies and other factors having no connection to the actual issue at hand. There were to be many such questions, but the most important thing for people to keep in mind is this was to be a new system, it had to work as the old system no longer did. For every question there is a workable solution, it just needs a fresh approach and the old ways of thinking and doing things would gradually fade into oblivion as the next generation takes the reins knowing only the new system. However, things had to start somewhere so it was made clear that certain members of the movement, those with the requisite skillset, would help set things up such as the administration panels to oversee the various departments which managed the country.

THE ADMINISTRATION PANELS

The first panels would be selected from members of the public who had put their names on the list to be an administrator. The list would be available on the provincial and federal websites. The panels will consist of citizens from all age groups and as many different regions as possible so that the nation is represented equitably. Panel members must have at least graduated high school, have no criminal charges against them, be willing to undergo a background check and be prepared to take a short course on the subject matter of the particular state department they would be randomly selected for. The panel member would also be expected to state an oath that all ideas and decisions would be based on what is the best outcome for Canada and Canadians. The panel member would only serve two years on that particular panel and move on to another randomly selected panel after the two year period and only if there is a shortage of volunteer panel members. This is to counter familiarity and corruption.

The initial thought was a panel member could serve again after a five year period from the last posting.

The administrator (panel member) would be issued a competent salary and expenses and given accommodation. Family members could also live in the accommodation and schooling would be available for the children. The administration panels would consist of a number of civilians, possibly twenty or more depending on the department and the workload. Panels would also consist of accountants and longer term facilitators. The accountants would be specifically knowledgeable with regards to departmental finances and would monitor those finances and advise the panel.

The facilitator would be the resident expert and stay with a particular department's administration panel for five years or longer if deemed satisfactory by the people. The facilitator would not hold a vote or sway decisions but be on hand to advise the panel on protocol, precedent, specific issues and help to maintain continuity so that things run smoothly from year to year for the department. Facilitators would have their own special courses to take to enable qualification for their important roles and swear or state an oath to protect democracy. The facilitator would be a highly respected person in society as a guardian of democracy, but would hold no more power than any other person. Panels would consist of two, two year groups. A first year group and a second year group. Therefore half of the group would always be first year and the other half would be second year. Each year the second group which would be finishing their two year service, would move on and the first year group would become the new second year group. Again, this is to protect against familiarity and potential corruption.

After a two year service if any members go on to serve another department they will not be with their colleagues from the previous panel. It is hoped that enough people will want to serve on the panels that it would not be necessary for anyone to serve more than two years in one go. The more people that become involved as administrators, the better for the nation and democracy. The panel will elect a chairperson who will chair for four months, but should there be a shortage of willing panel members the chairperson can maintain the position for one year. The main function of the chairperson is to move things along and keep things on track. The chairperson will also be the spokesperson for the department, delivering addresses to the media as required.

The new system would initially allow each bureaucratic department to promote from within to find a Chief Operating Officer when the need arises, but the panel would decide along with department heads if an outside hire was necessary for a COO position. Second year panel members would also be involved with the selection process of a potential outside hired candidate. Duties of the panel include monitoring departmental activities to ensure the taxpayer's money is spent as wisely as possible, to ensure that there is no collusion and corruption and to collect data that may be used as items for the next vote list.

All facets of an administration panel can be changed or

adapted by the people in a proposal and vote to improve the system. The administration panel overseeing the Canadian Security Intelligence Service will consist of panel members who agree to undergo a more thorough background check and sign the Official Secrets Act. The administration panel overseeing the Department of Trade and External Affairs will also provide the national spokesperson who will report on the day to day issues and information relevant to Canadians. This panel will also deal with heads of state of other nations and a minimum of three panel members must always be present when in dialogue with other heads of state. Any national or provincial issues which require a broader perspective such as emergency situations requiring immediate attention, will call upon three second year members from every other administration panel, provincial panel members for provincial issues, federal panel members for federal issues.

EDUCATION

The school curriculum would be revisited and revised to include less homework and testing and more focus to be placed on critical and free thinking. The focus would be less on training students to becoming economic wage slaves and more on self-development. The teaching of subjects for those not as academically inclined to be geared toward reading, writing and arithmetic and more hands-on classes. All students will spend more time outside especially in the warmer months and will learn how to grow organic vegetables. In the winter months they will learn how to grow food inside.

The curriculum will also include teaching the students how the organic economy works. They will also take field trips to the departments and watch the admin panels in action.

JUSTICE & LAW

The system will remain as it stands but the people can propose and vote for changes in the laws and removal or addition of laws. The election of judges is also open for proposal. Special attention would always be paid to changes in law so the people fully understand all the potential consequences, which often are not always apparent. To be enshrined in law that the will of the people outweigh corporate interests where quality of life and the environment are affected.

DIRECT DEMOCRACY & VOTING

The most important aspect of the new organic economy is true democracy. True democracy would be achieved by direct democracy which requires voting on a regular basis and all voters becoming involved in the process, no exceptions. Those who fail to vote without good reason will be fined a percentage of their salary. There is no excuse not to participate. The voting list is prepared by a full time committee who collect lists from the departments and from the people via the provincial and federal state websites. The term 'state' is in lieu of the term 'government' and does not infer power of any kind. No one person has more power than any other. All parliament buildings will become forums for the people to discuss their ideas for the betterment of the nation and her people. These ideas will be added to the vote selection list.

VOTE SELECTION LIST

There will usually be two lists for the people to vote on. The first list is the selection list. This list consists mainly of ideas from the people and which are logged in at the state websites. New ideas require the support of twenty people to be accepted as valid. The twenty people must also log into the website as supporters of the idea and provide their names and voting password. This list is then placed on the ballot and the people can decide if the ideas are in the best interests of the nation and her people.Those ideas accepted by a majority of voters will then be discussed and debated on national television and in selected newspapers. The state websites will also archive all televised discussions and debates. The new ideas will then be listed on the next vote ballot three months later. Each person can submit one idea per vote and endorse three other ideas per vote. This is to prevent the system from being bogged down with frivolous ideas. If an idea fails to make the vote list it cannot be re-submitted to the vote selection list for one year.

VOTE LIST

The actual vote list will contain ideas and proposals from the state departments and the ideas from the people which were accepted at the previous vote and discussed in public. The vote list will be made public four weeks before a vote. This enables the people to view the list and research any items they may not be sure about. The research can be carried out on the state websites which will archive articles and recorded presentations of debates and discussions. The ideas will also be categorized by what the expected costs will be in taxpayer dollars. Some ideas will have no cost associated with them or may even save the taxpayer money. The ideas that do have associated cost will be categorized in groupings pertaining to their associated costs.

For example;

$1 to $100,000.

$100,000 to $500,000.

$500,000 to $1,000,000 and so on.

Therefore if a voter did not have time to watch the debates on certain ideas then that voter can at least see what an idea will cost the taxpayer before voting yes without knowing the financial consequences.

Any idea which will cost the taxpayer more than a certain figure, for example, $1 million for a provincial idea and $5 million for a federal idea, will be added to the treasury list and voted on when the annual budget is prepared for vote.

The annual provincial and federal budgets will be presented to the people with a certain percentage open for interpretation as new ideas are voted in. The interpretation could be in the form of, "which of the following three services would serve Canadians the best?" Or, "should we reduce the funds to service (a) by ten percent, and re-allocate to service (b)?"

The thought behind this is there is only one 'pie' of taxpayer money and decisions have to be made by the people as to which services they want or need. These are mere suggestions as to how decisions on funding can be made equitably across the nation and can also be modified and adapted as the people see fit.

There will be three potential answers to a vote item, yes, no and undecided. For those who either do not fully understand the issue or did not have time to research it via the discussions, the 'undecided' selection should be made. If a vote item did not exceed fifty percent in 'yes' or 'no' returns, and there were a significant percentage of 'undecided' returns, then the item would be re-visited, re-presented, debated and discussed in more detail and be listed to be voted on again at the next vote.

BUDGETS

Initially, the committees will analyze all revenues the province and country collects and continue to re-distribute as before. Each province will have its own budget committee, there will also be a federal budget committee. However, as the new system takes shape and new ideas are incorporated, the budget committees will offer suggestions on how to save money and where increased spending can be allocated.

The constitution will also aim to reduce college and university education fees over time until they are free. The timetable for this cannot be fixed at this time, but the budget will be open and all revenues and expenditures will be freely accessible to the people as stakeholders in the nation. The people can vote for certain issues such as free tuition to be expedited, but they will also be aware that other sectors will have a reduction in funding to enable it, that or a tax increase. Canadians will no longer suffer the burden of paying the many billions of dollars to central bankers that it has for decades. This addition to the revenues is expected to hasten the programme of reducing and eventually eliminating tuition fees for post-secondary education. The additional revenues from the mortgages and loans expected to be nationalised will also hasten free post-secondary education and enable income taxes to be reduced. This increase of disposable income is also expected to increase spending and fuel a growth in employment.

As Dawn Approaches

THE BANK OF CANADA

All banks will be nationalised as the new system will be organic and no longer based on the flawed model of fractional reserve lending, interest and infinite growth. The new system, over time, will change forever the lives of the people. It is expected that national prosperity will increase each year enabling lower taxes, lower tuition fees and more spending power. The people will finally share in the nation's prosperity.

Nationalising the banks is a mammoth step but a step which must be taken. The entire global system of banking and the issuing of money has been nothing but a smoke and mirrors paradise for the banking families. The financial systems based on fiat currency and inflation have no basis in a true, organic world, a real world based on human need instead of greed. These systems have been manipulated over and over again to line the pockets of the elites at the expense of the working taxpayer's rightful quality of life. A quality earned with honest labours.

This had to end at some point, people would wake up and see through the veil of deceit and now, for Canada, that day has almost dawned. The banks have made their billions in profits over the years using a 'sleight of hand' approach lending money they did not in fact have, but received interest payments for. The changes are drastic but imperative if the people are to survive and live with dignity.

The nationalised Bank of Canada will issue real money without interest as it did up until 1974 when Canada was basically debt free. The decision to begin borrowing from private or central banks in 1974 immediately began to mire Canada and Canadians in debt, resulting in billions of dollars per year in interest payments, payments which consisted mainly of compounded interest, which could have been used constructively for the nation itself. A nation issuing its own currency is the base on which to build an organic economy.

The new banking system will not be based on infinite growth and inflation, therefore prices will remain more stable reducing the need for wages to keep pace with ever increasing costs of living. Ideally a house purchased today would be sold for a similar price in twenty years, giving our children a solid, positive future as opposed to the bleak outlook they have faced for the past few years.

The existing bank branches will likely be purchased by the Bank of Canada and those customers who had investments through the high street banks can either continue to invest through them if they opt to remain in business or have their money refunded.

MANUFACTURING

Canada, as with other nations, lost many jobs through the trade deals which helped make the corporations much richer. Once the teams of trade and law experts explain that Canada will no longer honour traitorous deals, manufacturing will resume in Canada and we will achieve full employment. Our children will have futures and careers to look forward to once again.

CORPORATE POWER

Oligarchies formed by powerful corporations such as; the pharmaceutical, chemical and agriculture giants which lobby politicians and force policies which eradicate the small farmer and the small business, will no longer have the ability, power or laws to continue to do so.

CHAPTER 18

56 – The Pre-Election Days

The patriots of the movement were busy living their lives and helping explain to all who asked what an organic economy would mean to them. Change can be challenging to sell to people, even if that change is far more beneficial for them. A body in motion tends to stay in motion. It appears that can also apply to people. However, ten days before the election things were looking great for the movement. It seemed that the message had got through that an organic economy was the only way to go.

The CBC ran a daily show on both television and radio, which featured members of the movement who were highly familiar with the ideas of the new system. They formed a panel which answered questions and discussed scenarios sent in by viewers and listeners. People were actually so excited about it that many began wearing badges of the orange and brown sunrise logo of the original organic economy blog from years previous before the banning and shutting down of such sites. The only difference was the badge read "Say 'YES' to an Organic Economy" and underneath the motto "Enough for Everyone."

The mood was also greatly helped by the lifting of all Internet censoring and people were assured they could communicate freely with all means of social media without fear of unwarranted surveillance.

New websites appeared almost hourly extolling the virtues of an organic economy, people were abuzz about it and it was the subject of songs which were hurriedly recorded and aired on radio and TV. There had been so much censoring of the Internet, assaults on free speech and rights over the last few years that people had almost forgotten what freedom tasted like. The lead-up to the election gave them back that taste and they loved it, a new optimism filled the air. There were even music festivals across the country dedicated to an organic system.

The UN command had spoken to the General and tried to warn him that blocking the borders and allowing an election for a new system would not work and the nation would fall as planned to the UN command. The General knew it was a desperate bluff and made it clear that Canada would elect a new system and that its success would spell the end of the ambitions of the cabal for a One World Order. That other countries would watch Canada become a free and prosperous nation and want to emulate it.

He also reiterated that Canada would fight to the last man to protect its sovereignty and freedom and the general also reported the conversations to the nation through another televised address which merely served to bolster the case for a new system.

At this point though the only negatives were the job layoffs for those working for companies which relied on importing or exporting, for the borders were sealed until further notice. The rest of the world stayed quiet and watched the grand spectacle of Canada's bold stand-off, everything was on hold until after the election. Other nations knew that if Canada dumped the present systems she would be ostracised for some time. There would be immense pressure exerted from the likes of the US and UK to impose all manner of sanctions on her, things were going to be rough for a while and Canadians would need to be resilient and stick together. Should they opt for an organic economy it would be a test case as the world looked on. Many politicians around the globe were concerned but not overly worried as they knew they would be fine for a few years yet. The voters around the world would be a different matter though. Should Canada flourish under the new system, there would be a strong likelihood that they would also push for a similar system.

In the published and aired articles about the new economy, members of the movement were often included and interviewed and it was always made clear that the economy would be very challenging over the next few years. Firstly, there would be the hostilities from the globalists and bankers who would make it their business to punish Canada as hard as possible for breaking away from their clutches. Breaking free of the central bankers would likely be the divorce from hell, for the bankers that is, not for the Canadians who actually produce true wealth. However, it was made clear to Canadians that it would be a rough ride for a while, possibly two or three years, but time is a great healer and presidents of nations and chairpersons of banks change and along with it their policies. In moving forward, fear would not be a factor.

"This was the time for a new direction for mankind," the movement would say. "The old ways of greed, materialism and the debt that results from them are over. This is the time to re-assess our lives, what life means to us, what do we really want, can we see what greed and materialism has done to the world and its people? Do we wish to experience such stressful existences? Do we need to compete with each other all the time, the biggest house, expensive cars? Or can we refocus and look inward, understand that true happiness comes from inside and not from external 'things'. That it comes from our own decisions, that we can simplify our lives to such a degree that stress no longer has a hold on us, freeing us to be healthier and happier."

Some could see that this new system was far more than just a system. It would enable people to evolve away from the stresses and greed, it would change people, change their outlook on life in general. As with a school or factory, the quality of life within those walls almost always begins at the top. A good, solid, fair principal sets the tone for their school and that tone resonates through to the teaching staff and onto the students. Likewise a good, fair, plant manager sets the tone for their factory, which then filters down through the department managers and supervisors to the workers on the floor. Tones are set at the top which affect people. When the people themselves become the leaders as with an organic system, the effect is cumulative and this will change people, it will be subtle but they will change to a healthier version of themselves, healthier in mind, attitude and outlook.

This change will also be helped along by a new focus on service by the provincial and federal employees, including the Bank of Canada employees. Their mandate will be to help people as much as possible, for with the new system we are all in this together, it is we who will have the power to lead happy and fulfilling lives, to control the direction of the nation, to decide ourselves if we need to go to war instead of being led by the nose by corporate controlled nations.

We did not spend millions of years evolving to become stressed out, burned out wrecks, scurrying through impossible traffic to spend forty hours per week doing something we despise just to eke out a 'living'. That isn't living, it's merely existing, there must be more to life than this, racing to an early grave from the stress on which this existence depends.

What went so wrong? Perhaps we grew too fast, the breath taking speed of the advancement of technology coupled with 'easy to get' money from the flawed fiat financial system and the fractional reserve lending practices, creating money from thin air. The constant in-your-face commercials convincing us we need this and we need that or we will imagine we will be considered failures by society. It isn't organic, it is a manufactured system designed to suck in as many people as possible to be the consumers which drive the demands required to feed the very system which created it all. Therein lies the problem, it isn't organic. It isn't based on reality but an undying desire to keep the profits pouring in, the monster had to keep growing or it would implode and now we have witnessed for ourselves that it has imploded, it has run its course, it had a shelf life but surpassed its sell-by date.

Time for a new system. This time let us be sure it is an organic system based on reality, based on our needs more than our wants. Let us grow slowly, sure and strong and give the nation a chance to catch its breath, to stop whenever we feel like it and smell the roses. To re-learn what really is important, to remember who we truly are, to discard the rat race once and for all and be the people we desire to be.

The movement ensured that people remained focused by reminding them of how things were and where the nation was headed.

As one ex-politician who was helping implement the new system stated. "For the next few years things will be very challenging. As you all know the economy was bad, the dollar is devalued and may not yet survive. If we had stayed with the old political system we would be economically and financially bankrupt, as well as under permanent martial law."

"The new system will bring back manufacturing to Canada. It will take some time to get things running but jobs will gradually become available. The goal is for Canada to be self-sufficient, that is the essence of an organic economy, as the motto says 'Enough For Everyone'.

"We will all need to regroup and help each other, look out for each other, yes it is about survival and we need a strong spirit of community but the rewards will come and our children will only know an organic system. They will take the reins and ensure they are never subjected to the greed of bankers and usury, the corruption of politicians and the overwhelming power of corporations."

The nation was unusually quiet, and even though they were once again legal, there were no protests, there was nothing domestically to protest. The treasonous politicians were in custody, it looked certain that the vote would be a 'yes' vote for a new system and should that be the case every voter would have a say in almost everything anyway, so no real need to protest.

Even the notion that Canadians would in a way be their own politicians, created a sense of calm, the persistent anger that many people carry because of political decisions or non-decisions, melted away, it no longer existed. It gradually began to truly sink in what an organic economy meant. People understood things were going to be tough for a while, heck, they were well used to that by now anyway, but knowing that Canada would be starting over, bringing manufacturing back but with a difference this time, was fantastic. The difference being that, as the motto says, "Enough For Everyone" meant that the manufacturing model would not be all about profit but about people, about communities. Yes, profit needed to be made but not at the expense of closing down factories and laying off hundreds of people just to make a few more cents for shareholders. The focus of business would now be about self-sufficiency. Manufacturing what Canadians needed was the first priority. The idea would be to be independent from the rest of the world and should any other nation cut Canada off from certain imports it would not be a threat to the existence of her people.

To do business in Canada would mean to be in partnership

with Canadians, a concept so long overdue. Co-operatives would also be encouraged where workers could band together and own a company together as working shareholders. The emphasis again being 'Enough For Everyone' instead of greed for a few. This concept would take years to infuse into the psyches of people and the fabric of society, but a few years is relatively insignificant in a nation's long history.

It was also made clear that Canadian made goods would be more expensive at first, but that it was all relative. What is the real cost of living when the economy is based on a flawed system of infinite growth, interest and fractional reserve lending that relies on inflation? What is the real cost of living when manufacturing has been dismantled and sent overseas so our children have little hope for a career?

The standard of living is anchored to what people earn and the total expenses they need to pay to live and enjoy life, sustainable over a period of years. An organic system, once in equilibrium, where employment is at a maximum or near maximum, will allow a good standard of living which should gradually improve, not decline as the world has experienced over the past few decades. The efforts of the workforce will be re-invested back into the nation instead of leeching out and into the pockets of central bankers.

As the rest of the world watched and waited for the election, many opinions were voiced in the various media around the world, well at least those few which had the freedom to do so. Countries such as the UK, US, Australia and the major European nations under martial law dare not mention what had happened in Canada. Damage control was the name of the game which meant a news blackout lest those under tyranny rear up and fight back also.

But those countries which aired and published 'expert' opinions on the Canadian situation, saw reactions ranging from,

"Canadians will never survive this" to, "Canada will break away from the global systems and flourish."

The naysayers couldn't see Canada surviving the onslaught of sanctions from the rest of the controlled world, it would be forced to cave eventually, the people would demand it after suffering food and water shortages and having no buying power.

The optimists said that Canada was self-sufficient in food, water and even oil and had hydro-electric power in some provinces which could be hooked into the national grid if necessary. That Canadians could weather the tough times ahead and rebuild a manufacturing system which would eventually create full employment. That being rid of central bankers and issuing debt free money Canada would be a highly prosperous nation in a few years and that having direct democracy and being politician free would protect Canada from the bribery and blackmailing of the elites.

Initially many foreign pundits poured scorn on the notion of breaking away from the global systems of finance, economics and trade deals. But as the idea of an organic economy sank in, it became grudgingly accepted. The problem being all along that people could not 'think outside the box' and that included almost all the so-called experts, who it seemed were some of the most reluctant to accept a new system which had no part in the global system, "how dare they," seemed to be the consensus of the experts!

What always came up in discussion and debate was the present state of the current global system. They were so corrupted and manipulated that it was becoming increasingly more difficult to defend, hence by comparison, making Canadians appear like geniuses. Not only were they spearheading a complete breakaway from the 'millstone around the neck' global systems, they were likely going to end up a prosperity powerhouse. Plus they had seen off the cabal which almost had them dead to rights as slaves under tyranny.

As Dawn Approaches

In general the many nations admired what Canadians had done and the direction in which it looked assured they were heading. It was understood that should the new system be voted for and it became successful, it would set the standard, show the way forward and the rest of the world would likely want to follow Canada's example. The magic had started to happen and glimpses of a new world flickered into the consciousness of people around the world.

57 – Election day

It was now four weeks to the day that the General had made his historic announcement and it had finally arrived, it was election day, another historic day in Canada's history. The media had constantly published and aired information about an organic economy and what it would mean and those who weren't familiar with it were well versed by now.

The one major difference with this election was every eligible voter had to vote. Those who did not were to be fined heavily because of the immense importance of this decision. People had become so jaded with politicians that many had not voted in years, but today would be different, everyone had to vote and they could also take the day off from work if they wanted to without fear of retribution.

Even though electronic voting was now the main method of voting, the polling stations hadn't been so busy in years. Voters lined up in the cold and the lines hardly diminished the entire day and many polling stations had to stay open an hour or two longer to allow all the votes to be cast.

The patriots of the movement, although certain of a 'yes' vote and victory for a new system, were still somewhat concerned, their lives literally depended upon the outcome. The Judge had gone to his office but all citizenship interviews were postponed on this day. He cast his vote via his computer and went home. Most TV stations in Canada followed the voting and as usual the hosts of the shows kept things ticking along with theories about what will happen the next day and thereafter.

Back at his home, after dinner, the Judge sat in his favourite leather armchair and savoured a small Brandy while watching the election coverage. His thoughts drifted back to the events leading up to this day, the early days of the movement, his being asked to help put a team of lawyers together, the many meetings, watching the numbers in the movement swell. He felt a great deal of pride in not only being able to participate in the movement but at the sheer number of Canadian patriots who risked everything to also be a part of it all. His mind drifted back further.

"And with that your Honour, I rest my case." the Judge was thinking back to his days as a young up and coming prosecution lawyer, smart, ambitious, the world was his, he had been snapped up by a large law firm, he was on his way.

He thought about how ruthless he had become. He had modeled himself on his hero, Randolph Bergman, an American prosecution lawyer who had never lost a case. He was unbeatable and any defence team that faced Bergman knew the likelihood of their client being found guilty was almost one hundred percent.

The Judge thought back about the way he began treating people, he really wasn't a nice human being at all. People feared him and he learned to enjoy it, it gave him a sense of power. He abused his position because he could. He belittled people unnecessarily when cross examining and adored the feeling of control as he strutted around the courtroom like a Shakespearian actor on stage. He thought about that man on the stand, that poor, broken, destroyed man on the stand, the man who had lost his wife, the man who was accused of murdering her in cold blood. The evidence although less than solid, was more than enough for a lawyer of his calibre to have a field day with and a field day he did have. He had put the man through hell on that stand because he could, the man, totally broken wept through his cross examination and the young lawyer smugly accepted the plaudits when the verdict of guilty was read by the jury foreperson.

The Judge as a young lawyer realised afterward that he hadn't acted as a prosecution lawyer in the name of justice, but as an egomaniacal bully. He realised that it was always about him and not the case itself. What had happened to him? His parents hadn't raised him this way, they were good, fair people with a strong sense of justice. Had he let himself be seduced by this power he had discovered? Most of his colleagues seemed to think of him as a courtroom star but was that who he was now, was that what he wanted to be, a bully for the sake of being a bully?

He thought of that poor broken man on the stand, the man who was found guilty and went to maximum security jail where he was beaten several times, once almost to death, the man who had somehow managed with the help of a determined lawyer who gave his time, who cared, to prove his innocence and once again become free. The man whose family and friends, even his daughters, had disowned him. The man who loved his wife with all his heart and was falsely accused of her murder, the innocent man he took great pleasure in taking to pieces on the stand. He thought about how that man must have felt, and he thought how he had inflicted such unnecessary pain just because he could.

That was when the Judge as a young lawyer had his epiphany, something deep inside him told him this was wrong, that he could use his skills for constructive purposes. He never acted that way again and did everything in his powers to help people, he had realised that helping people was infinitely more rewarding than hurting them.

The Judge's favourite armchair soon worked its magic and

he fell sound asleep for hours. He awoke and decided to step outside for a few minutes to get some fresh air. He put on his winter coat and boots and stepped outside into the snow. He looked at his watch and saw that it was after four o'clock in the morning and realised he hadn't turned the sound back up on his TV to see if the election results were in.

The glow of the dawning Wednesday sun backlit the city sky and the Judge thought about the new day ahead. Even though he was certain the vote would be yes, he looked at the glorious colours being projected from over the horizon and said to himself, "As dawn approaches, am I free, or a prisoner in a tyranny?"

The Judge stepped back inside his house, took off his winter coat and boots and made his way back to the TV. He sat in his armchair, took the remote and turned up the sound. The TV displayed a large group of people in a hall, they were all celebrating, champagne or something was being poured into containers, people were dancing and singing, the scenes were of complete joy and the reporter with the microphone could barely hear the answers from the revellers she questioned.

But the judge did hear her question, "how do you feel now Canada has voted for a new system?"

The Judge couldn't help it, he raised his fist in the air and shouted a euphoric, "yes!"

CHAPTER 19

58 – The New Beginning

History had been made, not just Canadian history but world history, for Canada was the first western nation to go it alone and break free from the corrupt, self-serving systems of the global elite. No longer would the people be economic slaves working and paying taxes just to see much of the fruits of their labours end up in the pockets of foreign bankers. No longer would the voter be played like fools thinking their vote for a political party actually meant something. No longer would the people fund their own personal prison, being spied upon and treated like scum by puffed-up police strutting around like Rambos barking orders at those who pay their wages and benefits. No longer would Canadians be forced to sit back and watch their country be stripped of its resources by foreign corporations empowered by international trade deals, signed by traitorous Prime Ministers and politicians that never asked the people.

The election returned a result of eighty eight percent in favour of a new system. The people were now in control of their destiny, there was still a long way to go and all the real work was yet to be done. Mistakes would be made, that was fine because they could also be rectified. New things, new ideas would be tried. Some would pass the test of time and some would not and that was fine too. That was what freedom and democracy meant, the freedom to try new things, the freedom to learn new things and the direct democracy that enabled it all.

The Prime Minister and the other politicians accused of treason would all be found guilty, the evidence collected was overwhelming and they were handed long jail sentences. The new system would be based on a new financial model and the removal of government and politicians. The people would vote on all issues, this was the dawn of a new age, this would prove to be the final step in the evolution of democracy. How did it take so long to get here, how could such a miniscule minority of power hungry psychopaths control so many people for so long? It wouldn't matter anymore, it was over, for Canadians at least. To get the new system going as fast as possible the movement was going to be instrumental in setting up the requisite administration panels and overseeing the huge changes in the banking system.

Even though the banks had been informed of their nationalisation, the Judge and his teams of top lawyers, law and accounting professors, would have all the documentation ready to be published and aired proving the old financial system was fraudulent and the trade deals which did not benefit Canada were unconstitutional. That borrowing money from central banks at compounding interest and indebting the unborn was illegal and immoral. Finally a nation was standing up to the corrupt, global, elitist systems and would no longer be economic slaves to anyone. The people would be free of tyranny, free of immoral surveillance, free of the fear of prison from speaking one's mind, free of a police state, free to be free.

59 – The First Days

The movement was busy assembling the first administration panels which were randomly selected in the form of a draw from the lists of volunteers who had already began signing up on the state websites. By the following year when the next cohort of panel members would be chosen, it would be by an automatic random select application on the state websites. The movement was heartened to see how many people had already signed up to serve on a panel.

The panel members had to move into the supplied accommodation and take one week of classroom training on the specifics of the particular department they would be overseeing. Therefore it would be two to three weeks after the election before the administration panels would be in place. Meanwhile the departments were not to make any major decisions until the panels were ready.

As soon as the election results were in, the movement had instructed the banks to continue business as usual and had announced to the people not to panic and make unnecessary withdrawals or there would be a run on the banks. The financial and law experts in the movement were meeting with the banking boards to work out the nationalising of the bank branches.

Another specialist team had informed the central banks

which the previous Canadian governments had borrowed from, that Canada would no longer be paying them interest on fraudulent loans. It was quite straightforward to prove the process was fraudulent and that the central banks didn't actually have real money to lend. It didn't matter what the bankers thought anymore, their scam had run its course for Canadians and once people understood how money was created and paid for, it became natural to seek its demise.

Again it all boiled down to beliefs. The beliefs that the old systems were rock solid and couldn't be changed or even bettered. How could they? Decade after decade, Prime Minister after Prime Minister, not one person in a position of power had ever said anything negative about the systems, so they must be the best way there is, nothing else could better it. But now people could see that that thinking was wrong, they saw how things were shaping up with martial law, a police state, no jobs, no future, insurmountable personal and national debts and when a fresh idea surfaced for a new system, people saw it had merit, saw how it compared to the present systems and then they changed their belief and would no longer accept things as they were.

Voting would be held four times per year for the foreseeable future which meant the first vote selection of the ideas of the people, and the first actual vote on the new constitutional proposals should be held in June, as it was now March. The votes would be held in January, March, June and September. It was decided that December was not a good month for voting as so many people were busy preparing for Christmas.

The new system had also breathed new life into the CBC, the Canadian Broadcasting Corporation, which was in jeopardy of losing most of its taxpayer funding and possibly being forced to shut down. Now the CBC was an invaluable resource for Canadians to learn what was going on and educate themselves about the upcoming items they would be voting on. The CBC had become a very important part of the new system for the people.

60 – The General's Final Speech

After the election, General Rousseau gave what was to be his final address to the nation. This was his fifth time in the chair at the CBC in Ottawa and he now felt like an old hand at this.

"My fellow Canadians, we have all experienced recently a tumultuous period in our history. We were challenged with an unnecessary martial law and almost succumbed to an invasion by the UN convoys. However, our brave men and women of the Canadian armed forces served the people by holding the invaders at bay and keeping our great land free.

"You the people have spoken and you have chosen a new way forward for Canada. A new way which will bring democracy, fairness, prosperity and a real future for our children. The next few years will be exciting and challenging for no other nation has taken such a path, a path into a new way of life, a new way of thinking, a new way of being. Let us all work together to make the best of the opportunities which will come our way. Let us all be patient and allow the new system to work.

"Please understand that for the new system to work it will require each and every one of you to fulfill your own duties by educating yourselves and understanding the items you will be voting on. Please also participate in your nation's well-being by serving on an administration panel and helping to keep our nation free from corruption.

"It may not be apparent at this early stage but the new system will, over time, also induce a new way of thinking. The building blocks of greed will disappear and in their place a new spirit of community and cooperation. We will, over time become more relaxed and learn to be happy with what we have instead of what we think we should have, for our values as human beings will revert back to what is truly important to us, our health and our quality of life.

"This is a new era, an era of prosperity and inclusion, an era which we will find to be far less stressful than we have previously known. An era without the stresses of politics, corruption, usury, surveillance and fear. An era of employment, less taxes, less financial burdens, more affordability, true democracy and a future for our children. The new system of money and a nationalised Bank of Canada will set Canadians on the path to prosperity and democracy. As Prime Minister William Lyon Mackenzie King said in 1935;

'Once a nation parts with the control of its currency and credit, it matters not who makes the nations laws. Usury, once in control, will wreck any nation.

Until the control of the issue of currency and credit is restored to government and recognized as its most sacred responsibility, all talk of sovereignty of parliament and of democracy is idle and futile.'

"Canada issued its own currency, was essentially debt free and in control of its policies until 1974 when it was decided to borrow from central banks. This sunk Canada and Canadians into debt ever since and will now cease, the billions of dollars paid each year in interest will now remain in Canada and help raise our quality of life.

"Canadians, the world will be watching us with great interest, we will lead the way, the new way. We are the first nation to break free of the monstrous grip of the globalists. We will rise as they will fall and their people will also one day break free, one by one, nation by nation, until the world is once again truly free.

"I will now hand over to the movement who are busy putting everything together for the new organic economy. I thank them all for their bravery and patriotism for without them things may have been very different today.

"And to finish, I would like to thank you, my fellow Canadians for electing to move forward with a new system, may you all enjoy the fruits of an exciting and prosperous future."

The General had been true to his word, he had not intended this to be a military coup and had handed the next phase over to the movement who would soon hand everything over to the people and that then would be that, the organic economy would soon be in full operating mode.

61 – The Nation Gets back On Track

Within two weeks of the election, diplomatic talks began between the United States and Canada.

The UN convoys had retreated back to the US bases but the Canadian Armed Forces would protect the borders for the foreseeable future. It was agreed that the borders would open again immediately so that commerce could continue between the two nations as closed borders hurt both of them. People could also cross but many Canadians who used to cross regularly for shopping trips opted to stay in Canada due to the hostile nature of the police and border guards since the US had been under martial law.

Therefore Canadians mainly crossed the borders for business reasons.

Those who had been laid off from their jobs due to the border closings were now back at work and like every other taxpayer, eagerly looking forward to seeing how their spending power would improve as the new economy took shape with the removal of interest payments and the gradual reduction of taxes. Everyone was keen to see how it all played out, the return of manufacturing, full employment, the near zero level of inflation and how life would be when economic equilibrium was attained.

CHAPTER 20

62 – The Judge, Jeff and Niki

The Judge had settled onto his bar stool by the Guinness tap and waited as Jeff poured him a pint of ale.

"Hi Judge, hi Jeff," Niki said as she appeared at the bar and pulled up a stool beside the Judge. Niki usually made it to the pub once or twice each week to see Jeff and chat with the Judge. The relationship between Niki and Jeff had so far turned out to be all it could be, they loved each other deeply and they were enjoying learning about each other and becoming familiar with each other's habits both good and not so good.

"Oh hi Niki," replied the Judge, "and how are we today?" he asked.

"I'm good thanks, yourself?" Niki replied.

"Very good thank you and what would you like to drink?" the Judge offered.

"Just a small beer for me thanks," she replied, "so how are things moving along now, busy putting all the experts to work?" Niki asked the Judge.

It had been three weeks since the election and the celebrations seemed to go on for days at the pub. People were overjoyed at the fact Canada was going to be charting a new course, a new way forward that would greatly improve the lives of Canadians. It seemed surreal, from the bleakness of martial law to a new found freedom and true democracy, all in the space of a few weeks. The Judge had been extremely busy with his teams of experts who were proving to the high street banks, the central banks and the international trade associations that Canada had been defrauded. That Canada would cease to pay the billions in interest to the central banks, would nationalise the high street banks and nullify all trade deals which did not benefit Canada and Canadians.

"Yes Niki we are very busy doing the nasties for Canada," the Judge chuckled as he spoke.

"Nasties?" Niki asked.

"Well, let's just say that our teams are up against it, so to speak. They know they are right and they know Canada is on a new path and there will be no turning back, but the people they are dealing with, the central bankers, the Canadian banks and the trade delegates, they are still somewhat in disbelief at what we are doing, we have shattered their paradigm if you like," he replied.

"Yes I guess it has shattered it Judge, let's face it, what Canada is doing is unprecedented, breaking away from the corrupt global systems and all that, it must be a shock for them," said Niki.

"Yes it is, and what is also very interesting is the reaction our teams get from some of the foreign delegates. It appears they forget they can't use subtle threats, leverage and underhandedness against us to have things their way, as they usually do, they simply aren't used to it. Our guys enjoy telling them that no matter what they say, the Canadian people will vote on it, it is the will of the people now which determines the way things will be. Democracy is a dirty word in their world it would seem."

Niki laughed and replied, "I love it Judge."

"Hi Babe, here's your drink," said Jeff as he leaned across

the bar and gave Niki a kiss, "how was your day?" he asked her.

"Good thanks, but I think this new system with its direct democracy is going to put a dent in my photography business," Niki said with a grin.

"Why's that?" asked Jeff.

"Well, you know some of my best work was photographing protests, capturing the emotions of the protesters was my thing, my niche. But now we have direct democracy there won't really be any protests will there?" replied Niki.

"Oh I don't know about that," offered the Judge, "I'm sure there will be people protesting against certain political visitors to the country, protesting what is happening in their homelands, protesting against wars, protesting against GMOs, that sort of thing."

"Hmm, ok I see your point about wars and those who are raising awareness about problems in their homeland but not about GMOs. Surely we will vote GMOs out, someone will put it on the vote list and the people will vote them out," Niki said.

"But what if the idea doesn't get enough votes Niki? What if the message, the information, fails to convince enough people? What would the anti GMO crowd do then?" Jeff asked.

"Good point," Niki replied, "I suppose we would somehow have to convince enough people that GMOs are slowly killing us, that we are the guinea pigs for unproven foods. If the vote failed how long is it before the same issue can be listed again Judge?" asked Niki.

"One year I believe Niki," said the Judge.

"Ok, so let's say the anti GMO vote failed and we had to wait another year to vote again. Would people protest to raise awareness?" Niki said, but really asking herself out loud.

"Let's think about that," the Judge continued, "people protested before to raise awareness with politicians because it was they who had the authority to change things. But now it's the people who will change things, so, would a protest help to sway a yes vote? Would people take any notice of a protest or would it be a waste of time? It's an interesting subject Niki, I suppose we'll just have to wait and see how the new system takes shape."

"I think the Judge is right Niki," said Jeff, "we'll have to wait and see."

"Yes, you're probably both right," said Niki, "we'll have to see."

"However," the Judge added, "you are in a wonderful position now to make your mark in the world Niki."

"Really, how?" asked Niki.

"Well, you can build a portfolio capturing the first nation to break free from the globalist agenda. You could photograph people in all walks of life enjoying the new found freedom, capture the voting, the admin panels at work, people paying their mortgages and loans with a smile because they aren't being forced to pay interest, that sort of thing." replied the Judge.

"That's fantastic Judge, why didn't I think of that? And there's me feeling sorry for myself that my niche had disappeared. I have all sorts of ideas going through my head now, thanks so much Judge!" said a much happier Niki raising her glass in thanks.

"That sounds like a coffee table hard back book to me Niki," said Jeff.

"Good thinking Jeff," added the Judge, "a photographic journal of Canada's journey from tyranny to freedom."

"And I have thousands of shots to get started with," continued Niki, "yes, this will work guys, I can make it work."

<u>63 – The Newly-Weds</u>

Mark and Annie had been invited over to James and Julie's for dinner, it was time to celebrate the outcome of the election and the bright new future Canada was embarking on. The pleasantries over and with drinks in hand, the men started talking to each other as did the women.

"I still can't believe it's happened James," said Mark, "I wake up each morning and then I remember what has happened, it brings a smile to my face every time."

"Yes and me too Mark, it really is quite incredible, the events before and after, what a time in our history!" said James.

"You're telling me, I never would have thought in my lifetime we would be rid of politicians and that we, us, you and me, the ladies, the people, would be deciding our future, laying down how we want to live."

"Me neither Mark," said James, "especially after the martial law too, but then again without that short spell of martial law people may not have voted for a new system, who knows."

"Who cares," added Mark, "we have direct democracy and an organic financial system now, that's all I care about, that and the future for my kids, our kids, all of our kids!"

"I hear you Mark," said James, "only a few short weeks

back we were all worried about that weren't we, no future for our kids, heck, no future for many adults either."

"Right," Mark said, "now just to get used to voting every three months, but that shouldn't be a problem."

"Why would it be, it'll be an electronic system, easy to use app for your mobile phone or computer. You should spend a little time watching the discussions or reading up on the pros and cons, just so you make wise choices, it's pretty straightforward, just take a little bit of getting used to that's all."

"Oh yeah, no problem for me or you, but what about those who are less likely to learn about the issues we are voting on, what if they just vote any old way because they aren't smart enough to understand what's at stake?"

"Well, that's just one of those things we have to deal with in a truly free and democratic country Mark. Now keep in mind there will always be an 'undecided' choice on the vote list, therefore if someone doesn't understand the issue they can select 'undecided'." James replied.

"Ok yeah that works. But to be honest James, I don't know if I trust a lot of the people I come into contact with to vote intelligently, if you know what I mean?"

"Yes I understand that Mark, but we must always keep in mind that we are thinking about these people as they are today and we need to project into the future a little, when we are all familiar with the new system, the regular voting, the research. Keep in mind also that people will talk about these things at work, in the checkout line, that sort of thing. I think it will become a normal part of day to day talk, the vote list. This new system will gradually have an effect on people, they will change, they will want to participate in their own well-being and those that don't won't really matter, there won't be enough of them to mess things up." James said.

"Hmm, now that you've said it, it does make sense. I'm thinking about today, about now, but it will change like you said."

"Yes it will, and another thing to keep in mind is it will be the next generation who will run with this system, they won't know anything else except from what they learn in history class, and they won't want any part of the old system that's for sure. The kids will have a different school curriculum, one where they will learn about the system and how important it is to fully participate. Mind you, by the time the next generation are voting, the vote lists should be a whole lot smaller, things should be settled down by then and people should have found a happy medium to live by. That's the thinking anyway."

"James, you've made me feel a lot better my man. I will admit I was quite concerned about some of the folk who will be participating in the votes, in our future and all, but you're right, it's nothing to be concerned over," said Mark.

"No, it's small potatoes James. We have a completely new system and it will take time to get used to like anything new in our lives. We are to some degree a product of our environment, even our systems, which affect our thinking more than we might realise. So, after two or three years, maybe more, maybe less, people will change. They will change their thinking patterns, they won't realise it but that's what will happen. They will look back and think how strange the new system was at first, and realise how natural it is now."

"Yeah, I guess you're right. Hey since when did you become a professor of psychology?" Mark said with a chuckle.

"Oh, didn't I tell you about my years at Harvard," laughed James, "no it's just that I took 'the book' seriously and the part about changing beliefs made an impact on me, I realised it was far more important than I first thought, that it was the key, we are all so tied up in our beliefs, it's what kept us from asking the right questions all along, we let the politicians and bankers off the hook time and time again because our beliefs allowed them to get away with it. Once your beliefs change your world changes, that made an impact and I know now that just because today things seem new and strange, that in time they won't, beliefs will change along with the new system, it's quite a mind expanding realisation Mark. Anyway, this is getting too deep, we're supposed to be celebrating amigo."

"Yeah we are bud but you can talk like that all night long as far as I'm concerned, I love it, I love hearing about what the new system will bring, the changes in people as well as the systems, this could be the best thing that ever happened to us," said Mark.

"Without a doubt Mark, without a doubt."

The women were also deep in conversation and Julie was only drinking soft drinks. Mark and Annie had congratulated the expectant parents when they first arrived. The conversation eventually included the new system.

"Isn't it wonderful our kids now have a future Julie?" said Annie.

"Yes, yes, I cannot tell you how happy we are at what's happened, the new system and all, we think it's going to be better than we imagined," replied Julie.

"It isn't that long before Brandon and Sarah will be finishing high school and we were worried about the tuition fees for college and university, then the employment situation, would there be any jobs for them, would they be able to pursue a career. But now we can breathe, it's great it really is," said Annie.

"It is," Julie replied, "what with our first child on the way, we were so nervous when we had martial law, not really knowing if the General could pull it off. I still can't believe how close to the wire it all went," Julie said, shaking her head.

"Oh well, we made it, the General did it and now we are free and have a future," said Annie.

"The General is a hero isn't he?" asked Julie, "we should have a monument to him, a statue or something fine to celebrate what he did for Canada," looking across the room to James, she said out loud, "James, I just said to Annie that we should erect a

325

statue or something to commemorate the General, don't you agree?"

"I think you should propose that as a vote item Honey," James replied.

"Yes, I think I shall," Julie responded.

<u>64 – The Cottagers</u>

Jerry and Andrea were hosting a get together for their cottage buddies Ron and Natalie, Nick and Rose. The get together was something they tried to do at least once during the winter months and this one was also in celebration of the outcome of the vote and the new future for Canadians. Everyone was at least four drinks in, the kids were watching movies in the basement and the mood was perfect. A loud 'pop' sound caused everyone to look over to where Jerry had just opened a bottle of champagne and was pouring it into six tall glasses.

"Ok, everyone over here please, come and take a glass it's time to make a toast," said Jerry.

The other five took a glass of champagne and Jerry began.

"I would like to make a toast to the new Canada, to 'The Organic Economy', the new economy, to my beautiful friends here tonight and to a great future for us and our children."

Everyone raised their glasses and Jerry said, "to a new Canada."

"To a new Canada!" came five replies.

"So Ron was right all along then," Nick said to Jerry and Ron.

"Yeah he was, so what'll be happening with the police now

Ron, now the people have the power?" Jerry asked.

"I think it's great," Ron replied, "obviously the thug element will have to tone down and we can get back to being good old fashioned cops again. Heck, I might even learn to enjoy being a cop again."

"I'll drink to that," Nick said.

"Me too," added Jerry.

"I must admit though I was worried there for a while," Ron continued, "when that martial law was still in force after three or four days I got to thinking we were toast. But one of the guys who had a friend in the movement told us it was cool and things would start to happen in a few days. Still had me worried though."

"Well you had a right to be worried Ron, look how close things got at the borders when the General made the speech, we were almost toast," said Nick.

"Yeah I was concerned too guys, after a few days of martial law I thought this must be it then, game over, I just couldn't see it all working out the way it did, but it did," Jerry added.

"What a ride though, a few weeks back and tyranny and now the damned opposite, freedom and true democracy, feels good to be alive don't it?" Ron said.

"Oh boy it sure does," Jerry replied as Nick had raised his drink and drained it.

"It'll be interesting to see what the first list of votes will be for, eh?" Jerry said.

"Especially for us cops," replied Ron.

"Why's that Ron?" asked Nick.

"Well, we expect someone will request the death penalty be brought back for starters," replied Ron.

"Oh yeah, didn't think of that," Jerry continued, "do you think Canadians will vote it back in?"

"I'll freakin' vote it in," said Nick, "get rid of them child molesters and murderers."

"Yeah, well you're free to vote how you want Nick but I don't know if Canadians will bring it back, been too many wrongful executions in the States so I'm not convinced it will make it back here," said Ron.

"What about speed limits, you know, the limits on the highways, one hundred clicks an hour is just stupid, ok maybe for trucks, we leave it at one hundred for the trucks but cars, the cars should be allowed to do one twenty, heck that's what they do anyway, well one fifteen at least, the cops don't bug you at one fifteen," said Nick.

"Yeah I'm sure we'll see that come up for vote, one twenty seems fine to me anyway," replied Ron.

"Weed, that'll definitely come up for vote, legalize weed and be allowed to grow your own," Nick said.

"Oh for sure Nick, that's been a hot potato for years now and the pressure has been building over the last few years to do that anyway, but the States has always laid on the pressure to our government too to keep it illegal or at most, decriminalized," replied Ron.

"Let's face it, alcohol is a much bigger problem than weed Ron, the teens have been doing it for ever, we did it ourselves and now they have that device which tells the cops if you're stoned and you can lose your driving licence, it should be legalized now anyway," said Jerry.

"I hear ya guys but to an old copper it still raises the hackles when I hear about it being legal. We spent so much time trying to control it and eradicate it even though we all knew it was a waste of time. I suppose if it had of been legalized years ago it would be nothing today and we would wonder what all the fuss was about," added Ron.

A burst of laughter came from Nick who then said, "Man oh man I cannot believe we are even having this conversation, how times can change. We are talking about the death penalty, higher speed limits and legalizing weed and all three could be law this year," Nick laughed out loud again.

"He's right too," said Ron, "it's all too fantastic to take in sometimes isn't it?"

"Yes it sure is Ron, it sure is. Who needs a drink here?" asked Jerry.

"It's ok Jerry I'll get mine in a minute," said Nick.

"Me too," added Ron, "hey guys I have something to tell you, I decided to put my name forward to serve on one of the new administration panels."

"That's awesome man!" said Jerry.

"Good for you bud," Nick replied.

"Yeah, not sure if I will get picked this time or any time if there's lots of applicants but me and Natalie talked it over and she's all for it," said Ron.

"Now how does that work Ron? The way I read it you won't know which department you will be joining and you have to do some training beforehand, and you get to live wherever it is for the, what is it, two years?" Nick asked.

"Yes Nick that's about what I know too. If you get selected from the random draw, which will be done by computer next year, they randomly allocate you to a department. You then do a week or two in the classroom depending on the department, just to get familiar with how they work, what their scope is etc. Then it's two years overseeing the department, making sure there is no corruption, public's money is spent wisely, that kind of thing, I hope to get picked cos I would love to do it," Ron said.

"Yeah, sounds real neat," Nick said, "now what about staying away from home, I suppose you have to find out where the department is first?"

"That's right Nick, the departments are spread all over the place but if it's within driving distance I'll stay home, if not we get an apartment, Natalie and the kids will come too if they want to, they provide schooling but we'll have to discuss that with them. At worst I would go by myself and come home weekends, unless it's a federal posting and I'm out of province," Ron added.

"I like the sound of that Ronnie boy," Jerry continued, "maybe I'll talk it over with Andrea and see what she thinks."

"Yeah, why not. Be good to help watch over the best interests of the country or province," added Ron.

"I agree," said Jerry.

"I hope you get the call Ron but it's not for me," Nick continued, "I'm a hands on kinda guy, can't stand sitting around all day reading stuff, having meetings, drive me crazy but someone has to do it."

Jerry excused himself and went over to where the women were sitting and chatting up a storm as usual.

"Ladies, does anyone need a refill or something different?" Jerry asked.

"I think we're all ok Hon," replied Andrea, "we only just got ourselves refills, you ok ladies?"

Rose and Natalie both nodded their heads.

"So what do you think of the new system ladies?" Jerry asked Rose and Natalie.

"We love it Jerry," Rose replied, "I don't know a thing about politics and economics and all that but I think I'm gonna love this new...whatever it's called.. system thingy."

"Yeah, me too," said Natalie, "it makes so much sense, why didn't we do this years ago?"

"Because no-one would believe it possible I guess," Jerry answered.

"I was telling them about what happened at work Jerry, the directive we've had."

"Oh yes, the pledge you had to sign, you mean that one Hon?" Jerry asked.

"Yes, the pledge to the Canadian people, I love it, we had to sign a pledge that we are here to serve the Canadian people in the best way we can, that it is they who pay our wages and benefits and we must be more polite and helpful to the taxpayer," Andrea answered.

"Yes that is wonderful," said Rose, "and that's how it bloody well should be too!"

"I totally agree," said Andrea, "there are way too many in the tax departments who abuse their positions and make life hell for the public for no good reason."

"Hear, hear," said Natalie, "about time too. Is that just for the CRA or all civil servants, oops you're not going to be called civil servants anymore are you?"

"That's right Natalie," Andrea replied, "we will be known as provincial or federal employees, and yes, the pledge is for all departments to sign. It's part of the new system, treat people with dignity, especially when they pay your salary."

"That's awesome Andrea," Natalie said, "it's like a different country already isn't it, there's a new feeling about it all. I can't really explain it but I can feel it."

"You can feel the wine Natalie, that's what you're feeling," Rose said as Natalie and Andrea giggled in agreement.

"What about you Jerry, what do you think about it all, the new system?" Natalie asked.

"I'm ecstatic to tell you the truth, Andrea and I read 'the book' last fall and we could see where it was going, that it was a new way that hadn't been tried before and it was a system which would work for the people, give us back our futures, the future which was looking like hell before all this. We are over the moon aren't we Honey?" As Jerry put an arm around Andrea and kissed her on the cheek.

"Yes we are Babe, Jerry and I loved 'the book', it gave us a new hope for the future. I used to lie in bed, unable to sleep, worried sick about the kids future, like most mothers I suppose. It was bad enough then, heaven knows what it would be like when the kids left school, but we didn't know how such a system could be put into place, the politicians weren't going to hand it all over and neither were the bankers, but it happened and happened so quickly, it kinda took your breath away didn't it?" Andrea said.

"Ok, so what shall we add to the vote list ladies?" said Rose.

"That we get paid for doing laundry, cooking and cleaning," Natalie replied as the women laughed.

"We get one day per month at a spa for free," Andrea added.

"Free wine!" said Rose

"What if it was voted in!" Rose screamed with laughter as the alcohol loosened her up and the other two women laughed with her.

When they had calmed down Rose said, "So how are they, sorry, we, going to stop these kinds of things from being put on the vote list then, how do you prevent all the stupid things people think of from ending up becoming law?"

"Well, first it needs twenty people to endorse the idea, which wouldn't be a problem with these two ideas. Then it gets put on the vote selection list, so, it would then need over fifty percent of votes to make it onto the official vote list three months later. Then it gets debated on the TV and people get to see if it makes sense, if it's a good idea. But when it goes on the official vote list it will be in a category of cost, so people can see what they will be paying for. If the cost is over one million dollars per year it will have to go the budgetary panel where it will be offered as an option with other ideas that cost more than one million. But the budgetary vote is only once per year so for it to become enacted it will take about eighteen months," Andrea responded.

"Oh jeeze, so I won't be getting paid for my house work and enjoying my free spa day for eighteen months then," Rose said as Andrea and Natalie roared with laughter.

"Sorry Andrea, I missed most of that, I think the vino has

slowed my brain down, now what was that again? If I want to vote for, yes I am voting for women who stay at home and raise the kids to be paid, so what's the process again, take us through it step by step if you would," asked Natalie.

"Sure Natalie, first you need to find twenty other people to agree with your idea and agree to endorse it. Then figure out if it's a provincial or federal issue. Let's say your idea to pay stay at home moms is a provincial issue, then you go to the Ontario provincial website and register your idea, with me so far?"

Both Natalie and Rose nodded.

"So, now you have your idea registered and the twenty other people who agreed with your idea will need to register as endorsers. Everyone will enter their voter ID which should be issued soon by the way, with me girls?"

"Yes," replied Rose and Natalie.

"In a couple of days or sooner, if everything checks out, you will be notified that your idea will make the next vote selection list."

"Hold it Andrea, what do you mean "if everything checks out", what's everything?" Rose asked.

"Just that you are who you claim to be and your endorsers all check out too, their voter ID, that kinda thing," Andrea replied.

"Ok got that, please carry on," said Rose.

"Right, your idea has been accepted to make the next vote selection list, not the actual vote list, but the vote selection list, does that make sense?" asked Andrea.

"The vote selection list, now that's where I'm getting messed up ," said Natalie, "the vote what list?"

"The vote selection list," Andrea said, "there will be two lists for provincial issues and two for federal issues."

"Ok I'm dumb," added Rose, "I thought this was supposed to be easy, two lists, who needs two lists?"

Andrea knew the alcohol was fogging their brains but

continued trying to explain.

"You need two lists because every dumb idea out there would make the vote list, therefore there will be a vote selection list first. That gives people the chance to say 'no' to your idea, but if enough people think your idea has merit then they vote to accept the idea, do you understand that part?" Andrea asked.

"Ok so my idea has to get past the vote selection first, is that right?" Natalie asked.

"Yes exactly," Andrea continued, "there are two stages which every idea must go through. The first round is the vote selection round, your idea will be on the vote selection list. If enough people like the idea it makes the second round, the actual vote round, the vote list, with me so far?"

"Yes, I get it, do you Natalie?" Rose asked.

"Yep I'm good, so that means my idea will take at least six months to become law, is that correct Andrea," Natalie replied.

"Yes, that's right. It's in two stages to filter out the, let's just say, non-starter ideas. But it's also important because each idea will be discussed and debated so people can make an informed decision. So, if they had to discuss and debate every non-starter idea it would take so much time and resources for no good reason. But having the two stage process eliminates that. We select what we think are valid ideas, if the idea makes it through then we get to be informed about that idea which will be on the next vote list, clear as mud ladies?" asked Andrea.

"Oh yeah, that makes sense now," replied Rose.

"Yep, got it," added Natalie, "so my idea might make it then," Natalie said with a cheesy grin.

"Not with an idea like yours Natalie, it could well make it to the vote list but obviously there would be a huge cost attached to it for the tax payer. In that case if it's over a certain figure it has to go to the treasury and budget committee and they will analyze the cost and offer up a minimum of three options, in this case maybe more."

"What do you mean by options?" Natalie asked.

"There is only one pie, correct? One pot of tax payer money to fund everything with, so, if your idea costs the tax payer let's say, one hundred million per year, then that money must be taken from somewhere else that already has it and those people will be very unhappy about that, agreed?"

"Oh yes, that's understandable," said Rose.

"Ok, I see," Natalie added.

"So, to be as democratic as possible, instead of turning your idea down, which no-one has the power or right to do in a true democracy, they will offer up options to the voter, such as, would you accept this idea along with cutting funding to these such and such areas. They will also offer different percentage cuts in those areas too, does that make sense?" asked Andrea.

"Kind of, but maybe I need to be sober for this" Rose giggled.

"I think I get it," Natalie continued, "so they will give the voter options of where the money will come from to fund my idea, like thirty million from here and twenty million from there, but with different ratios of amounts from the different areas they now fund, so people have a choice of what is important to them, what is important to keep funding, is that it?"

"Bingo!" cried Andrea, "that is the way it was described to me, now there will also be the option of not taking money from anywhere else and instead raise our taxes to pay for your idea."

"Ooh, they won't like that will they, having to pay more taxes to pay 'stay at home moms'," Natalie said.

"But, what if it encouraged moms to stay home, it'll free up a job for someone else that may have been on social security, so that may save some money for the taxpayer too, they will take that into consideration and give the net cost to the taxpayer. An idea that costs money may also be offset by the savings it creates too," Andrea added.

"Oh yes, so my idea might fly after all," Natalie said, raising her glass in salute.

"Try it Natalie, that's what this is all about, true democracy, you have as much right, as much power as anyone in the country now," Andrea said.

"I'll drink to that!" Rose added.

65 – The Judge, Jeff and Niki

"Any idea when the new credit cards will be available Judge?" asked Jeff.

"The advance cards Jeff," the Judge corrected, "should be available in a few weeks, there's a lot of them to make."

"In the meantime we use our regular credit cards then?" Niki said to the Judge.

"Yes, you can use them until you acquire your advance card, then they will be cancelled," the Judge replied.

"And no interest will be charged correct?" Jeff asked.

"That's right, no interest. But you must keep in mind this system is different, no-one wants you to become mired in debt so you will want to make your payments. There may be late fees, nothing substantial, but the main thing is your available advance cash will be put on hold until you pay down your overdraft. You won't be allowed to get yourself too far over your head, that's the idea," replied the Judge.

"Ok I get it, I like the sound of that," said Niki.

"Yeah me too," added Jeff.

"The Organic Economy will change people's outlook, the Judge continued, "with the old system it was considered quite the norm to always owe money on one's credit cards, constantly living beyond one's means, living the way one would if they could actually afford to, but many can't and get into trouble paying the obscene interest that credit card companies charge."

"And the new system won't let us get into debt, that's why it will change the outlook, is that what you're saying Judge?" Jeff asked.

"Yes Jeff, gradually over time people will learn to live more within their means. Let's face it, before we had credit cards we had to save up for what we wanted, but credit cards provided instant gratification whether you could afford it or not. With advance cash cards it will be more controlled, your bank associate will know your status and help to keep you within your means."

"But what if I want to treat myself and book a vacation or something, will I be able to do that," asked Niki.

"Of course," replied the Judge, "you will always know your advance status, similar to a credit card with a limit. But if you try to go over you would need to call your bank associate and explain the situation. If your history bears you out then you are good to go, but if you have a history of overspending and a track record of difficulty in repaying, then quite likely you would be turned down.
The point is not to live beyond your means, overspend and struggle to repay."

"Ok no problem with that here," Jeff said.

"Sounds fine to me," added Niki, "I had a letter from my bank, or should I say, my branch of the new Bank of Canada, recently, telling me the repayments of my car loan had dropped down because of the removal of the interest, fabulous news!"

"Good to hear that the new system has kicked in already," said the Judge.

"I don't have any loans so I wouldn't know," added Jeff.

"If we don't have to pay interest now, why did we used to pay it Judge? That does confuse me a bit," Niki stated.

"The easiest thing would be to read the book again Niki, it explains it quite simply. But the truth is we never needed to pay interest at all, it was a brilliant scam to be honest and over the last couple of hundred years the banking families managed to convince the heads of state that they were the best people to control the issuing of money, but of course, at a price, the price being interest." the Judge answered.

"Ok so what is so wrong about that, if someone wants to borrow money and is willing to pay for it what is the problem?" asked Niki.

"The problem is that a system of usury, or interest on loans, is inherently doomed to failure. It is all based around growth, infinite growth, and that is impossible. We saw what happened after 2008, growth had stopped, interest couldn't be paid because there was no new money being borrowed into existence, so they printed money to get it into circulation and that just created a far worse mess, a gigantic bubble waiting to burst. They tried to give us all the economic excuses as to why, but the simple truth was the entire financial system is based on a flawed concept, it had to implode and did which is why the dollar finally crashed and may well again." the Judge answered.

"I think I'm getting you Judge," said Niki, "but why is the system based on infinite growth?"

"Think of this," the Judge continued, "the bank lends you $1,000 and you must pay interest on it of, let's say, 5%. Where does that 5% come from? The bank didn't give it to you so where will it come from?"

"It's already out there isn't it," Niki said, "I earn it and pay it to the bank."

"Yes, but what about all the other loans taken out that day, and the day after, and the day after that. Where does the interest come from if the bank didn't lend it?" the Judge said.

"Oh I see where you're going," said Niki, "the banks only ever lent me the loan money the day I took out the loan, so the interest must come from loans taken out after mine, that loan money goes into circulation and that is where I earn it, is that it?"

"Exactly!" cried the Judge, "the banks never distribute interest money, only loan money, so the only way the interest can be paid back is to keep loaning money out and that only happens when there is growth. Therefore the system requires permanent or infinite growth or people will not be able to pay the interest, then they foreclose and lose securities such as their home."

"I see, I see," said Niki.

"Anyway, check out 'the book' again, it explains it better than that."

"Ok Judge. I just wish it was all easier to understand, it seems so complex," added Niki.

"Yes it does but it needn't be Niki," the Judge said, "now with the new system it should be far easier to understand. The country issues the money without interest, the people, the businesses pay it back, simple enough?"

"Yes, but how can the country make money? How does it benefit, how do we benefit?" Niki asked.

"It benefits because of what the money is used for. People will buy things, which creates jobs and creates taxes, the country in itself does not need to profit from its people, if it did it would merely drain money from the economy. With an organic system it is like a circle of prosperity. Money starts out coming from the Bank of Canada, goes to the public or commerce in loans, circulates, creates wealth through employment and profit and returns to the bank of Canada but instead of creaming off interest, we pay taxes which benefit everyone.

"Economics should be straightforward enough for most people to grasp, but the old system was so difficult to put a finger on because of the 'bait and switch', the 'smoke and mirrors' of deceit which left the taxpayer broke and shaking their heads and the bankers rubbing their tentacles with glee. In today's world we have no choice but to use money so why should we have to pay out of pocket to use it? Even the old credit cards were interest free if paid on time so why not money? All interest ever did was to make those with money richer without doing anything to earn it, and that isn't organic, it isn't real." replied the Judge.

"So why did it last for so long, why didn't anyone pick up on this sooner Judge?" Jeff asked.

"It worked fine for a while because for many years there were strict regulations on what the banks and investors could do, it was still a flawed system and would always eventually crash but it kept things in check if you like. But the bankers and investors lobbied, bankrolled, bought and bribed the politicians and whatever they needed to do to loosen, then remove the regulations. Greed as usual was the name of the game and they devised all manner of investment vehicles which hardly anyone outside the financial system could understand, it was pure unchecked greed run amok. The result as we know was devastating and caused the 2008 crash, which was the beginning of the end for the financial system. Does that make sense?" the Judge asked.

"Yes but why couldn't someone, a president or someone, realise that and change the system?" Niki asked.

The Judge replied, "Firstly, all the western countries have been sucked into this system, even Canada, but only as recently as 1974, so one president cannot change it all, it would take a concerted effort from several countries to make that change. Secondly, the president doesn't have that power Niki, you would think he or she does but the bankers and corporations have all the power today and you know why? Because they have all the money, they control the money and that gives them all the power. Anyway, by that time it was too late to change it all, it had to crash or something big had to happen like what happened to us with the liberation and removal of the old governmental system. Things gradually got worse. Wages failed to keep up with inflation, manufacturing disappeared overseas and the Middle Class was virtually wiped out but it was gradual. Ever heard of the boiling frog scenario?" the Judge asked.

"Yes I have," Jeff answered then explained to Niki who obviously had no idea, "if you put a frog into a pot of boiling water it will jump straight out. But if you put the frog into a pot of cool water and slowly heat it up it won't notice until it's too late. The frog gets used to the gradual increase in temperature, so what the Judge is saying is we were like the frog, we didn't realise things were getting so bad because it gradually happened, gradually got worse, correct Judge?"

"Bullseye Jeff!" cried the Judge.

"I still find it strange that we don't have politicians anymore though," Jeff said.

"I love it," Niki added, "they annoyed the hell out of me most of the time, always seemed they were wasting our money."

"Yes, the system of politics in most countries is hardly democratic today. The powerful elites, the bankers, corporations, industrialists and media moguls make the policies today and the politicians carry it out, they wouldn't last five minutes if they didn't. That's why so many things have been brought into being, into law, that were never voted on by the people. One could almost imagine them thinking "will we get away with it this time?", it has been like a big dare for many years, daring the public to rear up and fight back, but we didn't and they knew it," said the Judge.

"Wow, we never knew all this crap was going on did we? Well, most of us didn't. We just kept working away living our lives oblivious to it all and not realising we were heading into a tyranny," said Jeff.

"Actually, many people at first thought 'The Organic Economy' was a communist system, the bank staff especially. When they heard their banks were to be nationalised that was their first thought," the Judge said.

"Communism, you can keep that Judge," said Jeff.

"No thanks," Niki added.

"On paper it may not be a bad thing," the Judge continued, "but the same old problem would exist, the problem we have witnessed with our own system, namely, there is a government, a control mechanism, and it is human nature to become drunk with power whether it be a socialist, communist or capitalist system, the leadership either can't protect us from the powerful globalists or they run amok themselves. The only way forward now is for the people to be its own leadership and Canada thankfully, will be the first to prove it."

CHAPTER 21

66 – The New Economy – So Far So Good

By the time the first vote period was open, everyone had their vote ID numbers and were ready to vote. The people would be voting on provincial and federal proposals from the various department admin panels as well as the provincial and federal vote selection lists, which were the ideas from the people. To ensure that the electronic voting system was secure, a team of the nation's top programmers developed a unique encryption system. The electronic votes were encrypted then sent through various routes to the main data collection terminal. To double check accuracy and security, the electronic votes were also collected by a minimum of two other terminals, and the data compared. There were five terminals and no-one knew which terminals would be in use at that time as they were randomly programmed to collect data and compare results for accuracy.

An added layer of verification was also in place. After a voter had completed voting, a printable receipt was available for the voter to verify and a number of these receipts were collected and collated by local election workers. These receipts would be used as a cross-reference to compare with the electronic vote results. Any discrepancies would be thoroughly investigated and if necessary, another vote would be called.

The proposals on the vote lists were mainly to deal with departmental by-laws allowing the new administration panels access to the data and financial records so they could monitor the departments.

The vote selection lists were another matter and there were hundreds of new ideas from the people, many of which were of a more frivolous nature which was to be expected. It was also expected that once the novelty wore off then the vote ideas from the people would be of a more practical nature.

Another idea was also incorporated to make voting even easier. The voter could click on the vote proposal which would take them to the relevant information regarding the discussions and debates about that proposal. Those pages would contain the videos, articles and information given to the people in the run up to the vote so they could make an informed decision.

The frivolous ideas did include free beer for everyone, free wine for women and many other free item requests such as free Viagra. A proposal was also made to make it legal for women to be allowed to be topless anywhere in public.

The more realistic ideas included the following:

- -Change the tax system to be equitable across the board so that corporations have to pay their fair share.
- -Ban GMOs (Genetically Modified Organisms).
- -Remove restrictive agricultural laws such as the ban on raw unpasteurised milk.
- -Pull out of UN agreements which do not work for the people such as Agenda 21 and becoming a sovereign nation.
- -Increase the highway speed limit from 100km to 120km per hour for non-commercial vehicles.
- -Legalise marijuana.
- -Legalise the growing of marijuana (two plants per household).

- -Deregulate hemp so its potential can be fully utilised.
- -Bring back the death penalty for serious crimes.
- -Open up the telecom market to foreign companies to break the collusion.
- -Increase the annual vacation for employees from two to four weeks.
- -Recognise all religious festivals including Christmas by removing political correctness and allowing the term "Merry Christmas" to be used instead of replacement terms such as "Happy Holidays" and allowing Christmas to be properly celebrated in schools.
- -End the Catholic school system and have just one public school system.

The suggestion of Sharia Law was also on the list.

Most people had no difficulty figuring out how to log in with their unique ID and simply selecting YES, NO or UNDECIDED for the vote list and YES or NO for the vote selection list. The results were tabulated as soon as the voting period ended and those who had been issued a vote ID number and didn't log in or didn't call for assistance were to be contacted and possibly fined for not voting. There would be a degree of leniency this being the very first vote, but those who fail to participate in the next vote would be heavily fined.

The frivolous vote proposals were rejected but some were closer to being accepted than one might think, such as; stereotypical gender voting on certain issues, especially among the younger voters.

After the results were compiled the vote panels went into action putting together how the discussions and debates were to be undertaken.

The CBC would be airing the debating shows and each issue would be examined and debated before the next vote.

Those ideas which exceeded the cost threshold though, would be handed to the associated Provincial or Federal Expenditures Budget Panel where it would be analysed and options prepared for the people to choose from at the annual budget vote.

All in all it went very well and by being electronic it didn't cost voters too much of their time. At this time most people had received their advance cash cards and had their credit cards de-activated. The point of sale machines had been re-programmed by the various suppliers to accept the new cards and the card user would pay a small fee for each use. The plan was to eventually replace the privately owned point of sale machines with Bank of Canada machines, which, as with the present privately owned machines, would also accept the usual credit cards for foreign accounts only. This would be to allow tourists and foreign business people to use their own bank cards.

The Bank of Canada had taken over all mortgages and loans which was a dream come true for many Canadians, especially those with newer mortgages whose payments were nearly all interest. The added bonus was they would be able to completely change their repayment schedule at the next renewal, which would lower their repayments considerably, easing the burden of the home owner. This could happen because they no longer owed interest, resulting in the total 25 year repayment amount being so much lower. They could either keep to a longer less expensive payment schedule or opt to pay more and lower the mortgage amortisation period. The same thing applied to loans. This instantly gave people more disposable incomes and it would not be too long before the demand for goods would increase.

The central banks were difficult to deal with and went away kicking and screaming and threatening that Canada would succumb to global pressure and that they would have to continue to pay the billions in interest claimed by the central bankers. However, the teams of Canadian experts proved the loans were fraudulent and made it clear that other nations would soon pull out of the global banking scam. They even countered with a threat to sue the banks for the repayment of the interest Canada had paid in the past which infuriated them further.

The bad blood continued for years, but the bankers never saw another cent from Canada and the billions each year that Canada used to pay them now filled the Canadian treasury and began to assist with state programmes and the lowering of post-secondary education fees. People could now see that although their systems had been changed dramatically, their lives continued on more or less as normal.

Manufacturing would be coming back, and as that happened, Canada would be applying tariffs to imports. From then on goods would be more expensive but there would be full employment, no interest payments for anyone to pay and a gradual lowering of taxes and post-secondary education fees which would all serve to empower the people with far more disposable incomes.

The mainstream media would be monitored by the people and a constant score issued publically for integrity and accuracy. Things had changed for the mainstream media, the corporate ownership which bought them up for personal gain were, in Canada, now just the owners of, well, newspapers, magazines and TV stations. There wasn't anything or anyone they could bias, not now that the people themselves were the power holders and they had a watchdog reporting on accuracy and integrity of the news. It wouldn't be too much longer until some owners would be selling as there wasn't anything left to persuade, distort or propagandize. Amazing how things could change when the people had the power of direct democracy, true democracy.

What was noticeable was the atmosphere. The general feeling in the air was one of optimism. People were happier and less stressed as they gradually accepted and realised the new way was one of community, compassion and humanity. For example, for those who had recently lost their jobs and couldn't pay their mortgage. Their Bank of Canada associate had explained they could put their payments on hold until they were employed. This news spread rapidly and was a major factor in the way people were feeling. True to their word, what the movement had said would happen, was happening and the old stresses of survival were beginning to abate. They could now see that the new way really was about them and not geared towards profits and greed.

Such situations and the new approach to solving them were instrumental in the positive mood and this became infectious as it was finally sinking in what the new way really meant. It truly was a new way of thinking, of feeling toward each other, an evolution of thought and belief and people looked forward to the future and the new country their children would grow up in and eventually help administrate.

CHAPTER 22

67 – The Cottagers

The three families had met up for the July 1st Canada Day weekend again. So much had happened since the last Canada Day weekend, so much in one short year. The country, like most in the Western world, had gone from a nation in decline, with growing debt, growing taxes, reduced services, increasing unemployment, lost savings and pensions, little hope for the future and even less hope for their children. To a worsened situation with a collapsed US dollar, to martial law, to liberation, to a new system. Nothing in recent history could compare and hopefully never again would. However, the journey proved fruitful and the three families were once again kicking back, relaxing and having fun at Jerry and Andrea's cottage on the lake. The women were enjoying a coffee outside on the deck while the men played with the kids in and around the lake.

"Didn't see your vote suggestion on the selection list Natalie," said Andrea.

"No, I couldn't find enough people to endorse the idea," Natalie replied.

"Well, you didn't really expect to, did you Natalie?" Rose asked.

"Wasn't sure really Rose, never know til you try," Natalie

said sheepishly as Andrea and Rose laughed.

"What did you girls vote for the topless idea?" asked Rose.

"I voted no," Rose answered.

"I voted yes," said Andrea, "who cares, I prefer more freedom personally, less rules the better as far as I'm concerned."

"Hey Natalie, how is it going with Ron being on the admin panel?" Rose asked.

"He loves it, says he's learning a lot and really enjoys playing a role in helping to watch over the people's interests," Natalie replied.

"That's great Natalie, how are you with Ron being away all week?" Andrea asked.

"Oh, no problem there. Ron's hours and shifts as a cop were worse really. He's only in Downsview so I can always pop down and spend the night, which I have had to do after a little shopping at Yorkdale," Natalie said with a wink.

The men had been diving off the dock with the kids and generally having a good time, then sat on the small beach to catch their breaths.

"Who would have believed what we have just been through this past year," Jerry said.

"Unbelievable," Nick replied, "just unreal."

"Hard to imagine ain't it, that we were here one year ago and I brought up the subject of 'the book', not having a clue that we would actually be living by its ideas within a year," said Ron.

"Close though wasn't it?" Jerry said.

"Close ain't the half of it Jerry," Ron continued, "straight up, at one point I thought we were toast."

"Ditto" Nick added.

"So you got on one of those admin panels Ron, cool," said Nick.

"Yeah, glad I did too, I'm really enjoying it," replied Ron.

"How did you get selected Ron, how does it all work?"

Jerry asked.

"Well, I put my name on the provincial website and they called me a few days later to say my name came up. It's a random draw, it doesn't matter what your background is, they just base it on age, gender and address, so they get a good cross section of people," answered Ron.

"Then what happens?" enquired Nick.

"You get all the details online, which department's admin panel you're gonna be with, where you will be staying, the salary and expenses and all that, it's well put together," Ron replied.

"They put you through some classes too, don't they?" asked Jerry.

"Yep, did a week of classes, got to learn how the department works, very enlightening too."

"Which department are you with?" Nick asked.

"Department of Transport, based in Downsview, pretty easy to get to and I can go home easily enough if need be. Natalie stays with me too when she goes shopping, it's all worked out quite well," replied Ron.

"What do you actually do Ron, what goes on with a panel like that?" asked Jerry.

"Mainly we monitor where the money goes, who gets the contracts and why they get the contracts. We watch over the people's or taxpayer's money," replied Ron.

"Sounds good to me," said Jerry.

"I like it," added Nick.

"Once in a while when there's a big decision to be made in a hurry, from any department, three people from each admin panel are randomly selected to join a video conference call to make a decision. If it's something that affects the people long term then it would go to an emergency vote," said Ron.

"What kind of big decision Ron?" asked Nick.

"Usually to do with a national emergency of some kind,

when a decision has to be made that changes the status quo. As you know, everything affecting the people is voted on by the people, but once in a while there obviously isn't time for that and that's why they try and make it as democratic as possible by having three people from every admin panel vote on an emergency action. The emergency could be from any department but all department admin panels will have a say, and it would be public knowledge immediately too so everyone knows what is going on," replied Ron.

"That works Ron, I kinda like that. It's understandable there will be snap decisions to be made and that is a democratic way of doing it, yeah that's cool man," replied Nick.

"Have you had to do that yet, make a decision like that?" Jerry asked.

"No, not yet, if we did you would have heard about it through the media, anything like that would be made public as soon as possible. Canada is a true people's nation now, nothing can be done without the people agreeing to it, but it sure does take some getting used to after being treated like second class citizens forever. "

"Who needs politicians eh Jerry?" Nick responded.

"Not us, not anymore. Hey what happens if Canada were under attack though, unlikely I know but what's the strategy there?" asked Jerry.

"From my understanding The Armed Forces and The Department of Defence would deal with that automatically but if it were something like, let's say, Canada was asked to join in a conflict, then an emergency vote would be called and the people would decide. As I said, this is a people's nation now, we can't be led into conflicts by media propaganda and bought governments any longer." replied Ron.

"Awesome!" Nick replied.

"No more sending our people to needless deaths and injuries to protect corporate and banking interests, about God damned time too," said Jerry.

"So Ron, you will serve what, two years, then back to the force?" asked Nick.

"Yeah, but we don't call it that any longer, it's the Police Department now, we're all equal, no government, authority or force anymore, nothing to infer power to any group. Anyway, I have to wait five years before I can apply again to serve on a panel. Natalie could apply but it would be a different department from the one I served in. It's all to do with minimising familiarity which could lead to corruption," answered Ron.

Back up at the deck the women were still talking about the new system.

"What's the latest on a new tax system Andrea, I heard they were looking into a fairer way of taxing everyone?" Rose asked.

"Yes there is talk of looking into a different way of raising revenues through taxation. Now we don't have a government with vested interests, it's a great opportunity to do that," replied Andrea.

"It was on the vote selection list too and passed with a big majority didn't it?" asked Natalie.

"Yes it did, but we had already begun to do that so it's all good," replied Andrea.

"Do you have any idea how it would change, how it would be fairer on us?" asked Rose.

"We hear talk of bank transaction fees, additional goods and service fees, but I think it will take a while because it really is a big undertaking. It has to change though because the big corporations are getting away with so much, it isn't fair at all," Andrea replied.

"Changing the subject, I love the new media ratings system, don't you?" Rose asked.

Andrea clapped her approval and Natalie replied, "Yes isn't

it wonderful? Why didn't they do that before? It will force the newspapers to be more honest and accountable."

"We'll see Natalie, we'll see how that all pans out. Keep in mind that some of the news sources like Reuters and Associated Press are controlled by the banking interests, so if the source news is inaccurate you can't really blame the newspapers," said Andrea.

"Yeah you're right, just when you think you're rid of those cretins they still have some control over your life," Natalie replied.

"Yeah true," continued Rose, "and what about the vote idea that we get four weeks vacation per year, that made the next vote, gotta love that. Well maybe not you so much Andrea, working at the tax department you get lots of vacation time anyway."

"Yes, but I'm still pleased that people may get more vacation time Rose. They have done so for years in Europe. People need more than two lousy weeks per year, it's high time people had more time with their families, more time to relax," replied Andrea.

"I don't think the four weeks will happen in one go though," Natalie said, "I heard possibly three weeks at first, then four, to give industry a chance to absorb the costs."

"Well that's a good start," Rose replied.

"Yes I heard that too, so many positive things are happening to our society, why didn't they allow this before?" Andrea asked.

"Doesn't matter now does it, it's history," answered Rose.

"Hallelujah to that!" said Natalie.

68 – The Judge, Jeff and Niki

The Judge sat at his usual favourite position at the bar enjoying his first pint of the day which Jeff had just poured.

"Niki will be in shortly Judge and I think she has something to show you." said Jeff.

"Wonderful" cried the Judge who had a huge soft spot for both Niki and Jeff, especially as he was instrumental in their re-union, although he always played that down.

"Everything going ok with the lawyers and the trade talks?" asked Jeff.

"Yes, as a matter of fact they are almost done and dusted. Took a while but the other nation's finally got the message that the new Canada is here to stay," replied the Judge.

"I still can hardly believe you managed to pull that off, it used to bug the hell out of me, foreign corporations having more rights to our resources than the people, being able to sue Canada, which means us the taxpayer, for lost profits if we stopped them from ruining our land and water as per our environmental standards. The power the corporations had was out of order Judge," said an agitated Jeff.

"I concur," the Judge continued, "it gives us immense pleasure to tear up those monstrous deals Jeff."

"I would love to be at those tables, I bet they can't believe we are doing this Judge, pulling the rug from underneath them, how did they get away with it, how did we agree to it all?" said Jeff.

"At the end of the day Jeff, they are all just people, but they became more and more powerful, more and more greedy until they were immune to the consequences of their actions, many of us would be the same if we had that power, trust me, it's human nature I'm afraid," replied the Judge.

"You think so, I would like to think I would care about the environment, about the effects on people's lives," Jeff said.

"And I am certain you would too Jeff. But money has an effect on people, haven't you heard the stories about families fighting over wills, never talking to each other again just because cousin Mary received more than cousin Billy, money has that effect I'm afraid and most of us can be susceptible," said the Judge.

"Yes, I suppose you're right Judge."

"But, of course, the good news is the country has more or less taken that out of the equation. As fantastic as it seems, the new system has negated the power of the corporations and bankers and on that note I think we should celebrate with a Brandy. Just then, Niki walked into the bar.

"Hi Niki, what's your pleasure young lady?" the Judge asked.

"Hello Judge," said Niki as she sat on an adjacent bar stool to the right of the Judge. Jeff had seen her approaching and had also fixed Niki's usual choice of a small beer.

"Hi Babe," said Jeff as he put down their drinks, leaned across the bar and kissed her. Jeff made an obvious motion of staring at Niki's left hand then turning his head toward the Judge.

"Oh yes," Niki said, "thanks for the drink Judge. I, or should I say, we, have something very special to share with you Judge," Niki said as she lifted her left hand and waved her fingers to display an engagement ring. Jeff held her right hand as she did this and said "we have decided to get engaged and we.." Niki broke in and said "we wondered if you would marry us, perform the ceremony for us Judge?"

The Judge was elated and his eyes misted a little as he replied, "I...I would be honoured to do that, nothing would give me greater pleasure."

"Perfect!" said Niki, "thank you so much Judge, it would make everything so special for us to have you marry us."

"Jeff do you have any kind of bubbly behind your bar by any chance?" the Judge asked.

"I only have this sparkling wine Judge." Jeff replied as he held up the bottle.

"That'll do for now," the Judge continued, "let's open it up, I would like to make a toast."

The Judge toasted Jeff and Niki and they both began to tell the Judge of their future plans together. They told the Judge they were looking at getting married the following summer, then taking off for a honeymoon somewhere in the Caribbean, likely Jamaica. The Judge was so happy for them both and he could see parallels between them and when he met his wife which warmed his heart. Eventually the talk between Niki, the Judge and Jeff, when he was available, went to the new system.

Niki and Jeff were always keen to hear how things were progressing with the trade talks and the banking talks but they were almost completed. The results of the first provincial and federal vote selection and vote had not long been published and naturally this became the topic of many a discussion. Niki was thinking about something that had concerned her with the vote selection in June, a couple of weeks earlier.

"Judge, in the vote selection list there was a proposal for Sharia Law. It didn't make it through to the next vote list but what if there were enough people in favour that did want it, I mean, where do we stand in a situation like that?"

"That's a very good question Niki and that has been discussed by the movement.

As an immigration Judge I have witnessed the joy and elation of people from all over the globe who have become Canadian citizens. I am a humanist and my dream is to see everyone live in peace and harmony, respectful of each other's beliefs, without borders between us. But it will be up to the people how we move forward and I would not be surprised to see a follow up proposal calling for a controlled limit of Muslim migrants because of the birth rate compared to the average Canadian birth rate today. Now I'm not saying I agree with that but due in part to statements made by Islamic leaders in Europe, I wouldn't be surprised at all to see such a proposal."

"Yes, coming from England the talk there is it isn't a matter of if, but when, the UK becomes an Islamic state because of the demographics. But wouldn't an immigration limit be considered racist Judge?" Niki asked.

"Of course, many would call it racist, but there is the issue, will the people want to maintain the status quo, the same culture, the same Canada, or risk being an Islamic state in the future by not demanding immigration limits. That is how I think many will look at it Niki." answered the Judge.

"It's the political correct thing isn't it? We don't wish to offend people, however, we can become our own worst enemy," offered Niki.

"I'm afraid so," the Judge said looking thoughtfully into his drink, "Canada has always been high on the list of desirable countries to emigrate to and the new system will likely make it the number one desired destination. Of course that will add pressure to our immigration department and I can see it likely that extra caution will be placed on long term demographics."

"I suppose it makes things easier to do that now because there aren't any politicians concerned about being re-elected, it's purely down to consensus, political correctness won't matter," said Niki.

"True Niki, this is where we will gradually learn the true nature of the Canadian people for it is they who will shape how things progress. We have always had politicians and leaders tell us who we are, what makes us who we are, but that will no longer be the case. It truly is a fascinating time for the world to watch and learn from our new system," the Judge said.

"I just wish we could all just get along and not impose our will on any other person, live and let live Judge'" Niki said.

"One day Niki, one day perhaps, but I certainly don't see it happening in my lifetime. Just seeing Canada set her new course, with the people controlling their own destiny will allow me to die a happy man'" The Judge added.

CHAPTER 23

69 – September and the Second Vote

The summer came and went, it was a little cooler than usual but as for the new system, things were moving along smoothly. The successful results of the vote selection list from June had been compiled and the new vote list for September had been published on the provincial and federal websites. The people could now see what they would actually be voting on in September, the proposals and ideas from the people which, if garnered over 50% approval, would become law.

The CBC (Canadian Broadcasting Corporation) had been busy working out formats for the best way to present the proposals to debate and discuss every angle so the people could make an informed decision. The debaters were not typically disposed personally to any one side of a proposal but were masterful at making a point and presenting possible future problems should a particular proposal become law. The presentations would all be archived on the state websites for future viewing for those who could not view the broadcasts. Everything was more or less going to plan, the frivolous proposals had been eliminated from the vote list and people looked forward to seeing the vote results.

Would the top highway speed limit increase to 120km/h?

Would the death penalty be reinstated? Would marijuana be legalised? Would the Catholic school system be abolished? So many major proposals would be on the vote list this first time.

The people had been informed by the administration panel overseeing the treasury that the tax system was under scrutiny and a task force were looking for fairer ways to raise revenues, however, it was thought that it would take a year or two to complete before being debated on television prior to a vote. Education was also under scrutiny. There were going to be changes coming that would be tailored more toward practical and life skills, more outdoor activity including sports and field trips and certainly comprehensive studies in how the country now worked. Students would soon be fully knowledgeable about The Organic Economy and aware of the past systems, how it used to be so controlled and at the people's expense. Students would also learn how to be more self-sufficient, how to grow vegetables, they would learn basic cooking and water purification techniques and other practical skills as well as critical thinking. The past emphasis geared to indoctrinating students into becoming fodder for the economic slavery system would cease and the focus would be toward self-responsibility and making intelligent personal choices geared to an individual's perspective. These ideas would, when finalised, also be on a future vote selection list.

It was also decided by the treasury in conjunction with the overseeing administration panel, in partnership with some of the universities, to run computer models of the nation's revenues, how much money was being raised and where the money was being allocated. The purpose of this was to undertake a study to see if it would ever be viable for a computer to make decisions regarding tax revenue allocation. For example, a new proposal from a voter may incur extra costs and the panel would offer various options of taking revenue from other services or raising taxes to pay for the new proposal.

The university computers would also be programmed to give options based on pre-programmed criteria and over a period of time checked and compared to the options the panel will have compiled. If the computer results matched the options the panel compiled over a five year period, it could be put to the people that the computer output data be the source of the options as it may be more accurate. It was just a way of finding new efficiencies in the system.

The September vote, which was the second vote since the new system began, was open for one week as would now be the standard vote period. Voting went without a hitch, the new round of proposals and ideas were listed on the appropriate provincial and federal vote selection lists and the actual accepted proposals from the previous vote in June were now on the appropriate provincial and federal vote lists.

There had been complaints of confusion over the terminology 'vote selection list' and 'vote list', so it was decided by the vote panel to call them list 1 and list 2. The provincial vote selection list would be called P1 and the provincial vote list P2. The federal vote selection list would be called F1 and the federal vote list F2. Therefore the initial proposals and ideas would first be on list 1 and if they were accepted by the people for consideration, they would then be added to list 2 at the following vote three months later.

The results of P2 (provincial vote) and F2 (federal vote) were published and aired immediately on the television news shows and would be enacted as soon as possible. The Ontario provincial highway speed limit was voted to be increased to 120kmph but for passenger vehicles only. Commercial vehicle speed limits would not change.

The Ontario provincial catholic school system would remain for the present. The federal voting returned a 'no' for reinstating the death penalty and a 'yes' for legalising marijuana and the right to grow marijuana plants at home. The federal vote also returned a 'yes' for increasing statutory vacation time from two to three weeks per annum beginning the following year, increasing to four weeks per annum two years afterward. A surprise also came in the federal vote that opted to legalise euthanasia.

Federal voting also returned a resounding 'yes' to open the telecommunication markets to foreign companies to break up the control enjoyed by the present oligarchy.

GMOs would be banned and the powerful influences of the big agriculture, pharmaceutical and chemical corporations would be reigned in allowing smaller community type farming to flourish.

Raw milk was again legal to sell and the suffocating rules and regulations lobbied into law by the big corporations to kill off the little guy were gradually being scrapped, however, to compensate, there was to be an increase in health inspectors.

The proposal to end the silent ban on Christmas in schools and public buildings also returned in the positive, and all religious festivals would be encouraged to be celebrated by all people.

The September federal F1 vote selection list did include a proposal to closely control the influx of immigrants from any religious groups who by birth rate posed a potential threat to Canada's demographics, which could potentially threaten the present culture and systems. This proposal, if successful, would be debated and discussed as all proposals and voted on in the January vote. There was also a proposal to erect a statue of General Rousseau who had saved and liberated the nation, and another to forever enshrine in history, that unforgettable day in February by having a national statutory holiday. As there was already a statutory holiday in February in four provinces called Family Day, it was also proposed the name be changed to reflect that day. The proposals were voted to be on the next F2 vote list and it was decided by the Federal Vote Administration Panel to offer a selection of names for that day, the day Canada was saved.

From that first actual vote came so many talking points. People who were previously jaded with political elections featuring parties that broke so many promises, now saw real change. They could clearly see that they had the power to create the change they desired and this power had the effect of raising the future hopes of the people. It was real, it was tangible and it had a calming effect. It appeared that having real control over their lives reduced stress and increased happiness. The old ways of politics and finance were fast becoming like a distant nightmare never to be repeated. There were those who had said from day one, that an organic system, once in equilibrium, in balance, with full employment and lower taxes, and little or no inflation, would enable people to only need to work thirty hours per week.

This could happen if the people changed their outlooks from one of materialism and greed to learning to live with what they have, to learn to enjoy life with 'having enough', as opposed to the previous ways of incessant consumerism, which was destroying not only the environment but society as a whole. Having a less stressful existence was also thought to aid in the process of that particular path of evolution.

The first Thanksgiving of the new system had another meaning this particular year and the vast majority of the population who celebrated it gave thanks for the bravery of the movement and the freedom and prosperity the new system guaranteed.

As the first Christmas of the new system approached, the country was still struggling due to the devalued dollar but very slowly things began to pick up again. One by one, the restaurants and bars in the cities re-opened which further buoyed the spirits of the people. Canadian cities were beginning to recover and the new financial system was a major help because of the removal of interest on all loans. People now had more disposable incomes which didn't yet fully compensate for the devalued dollar, but did help with the onset of the overall economic recovery of the nation.

Each year Canada would now gain in leaps and bounds due to the retaining of the billions of dollars it used to pay in interest to central bankers. This would eventually result in the long hoped for lower taxes and increased disposable incomes for the people. The hope among many was, rather than just spend it all, people would work less and enjoy more free time with their families and friends, this is where the old would give way to the new. The changing of the mindset from greed and materialism, to enough for everyone. This is where the people could find the balance of living a good life, with a good standard of living, without having to be a stressed-out wage slave to do so.

Christmas and New Year came and went and the January vote went smoothly. Even though direct democracy was in place and no bloc or special interest group could bias the voting, advocacy groups began to spring up on the Internet. These groups would give their opinions on upcoming votes and occasionally make very good points about the possible effects a new proposal may have. But the new system could not be perverted by anyone or anything, such is the power of direct democracy and the power of the people.

The people elected for the Family Day holiday in February to be renamed Liberation Day in honour of General Rousseau and the members of the movement.

The proposal to monitor and limit the immigration levels of those from religious groups or cultures which could pose a threat to Canada's present culture by birthrate demographics, was voted into law.

The winter hit hard again and food and energy continued to consume a major portion of most people's budget. The soup kitchens remained busy but the general atmosphere was very upbeat. People were helping one another more than ever and they talked a lot about the next vote. Direct democracy did more than just give the people power over their lives, it also created many talking points and people were interested in others opinions and viewpoints which only served to increase the sense of community.

The third Monday in February, on what used to be called Family day, the first Liberation Day was celebrated. It was a huge celebration and the General was implored to make a speech but declined due to ill health. The nation was an ocean of red and white as Canadian flags were flown and waved everywhere. There wasn't a Prime Minister to make a speech and no-one cared. A randomly selected spokesperson from the general public gave an address to the nation and it was as good as anyone could have done. The new system had created a renewed optimism for the domestic economy and applications for commercial loans for new business were on the increase. New manufacturing facilities began ramping up to make goods for Canadians and gradually replace imports which would be more costly as import tariffs would be imposed. It was a win-win for Canadian commerce but the Bank of Canada had made it clear that inflation must be kept in check and the price of goods would be monitored for gouging, which could happen due to the lack of competition from tariff added imports.

These early days of the new system would be a boon for those starting up a manufacturing business that provided Canadians with the basic needs of life. They would receive full support from the Bank of Canada as they were providing employment and playing an integral role in the organic system.

The full legalisation of hemp also initiated a flurry of industry and new products would soon be available which could replace plastics, help the environment and lessen the demand for oil.

There was the occasional sabre rattling from the

international community, which in reality was from the globalist cabal who were still hurting over their foiled plans to enslave Canadians. The central bankers continued to bleat about the interest they claimed Canada owed them, but Canada always countered with threats to sue the banks for what they had paid, which as Canada had proven was fraudulent on the bank's behalf.

The tearing up of all the trade deals which did not benefit Canadians did create a rift which would take a couple more years to begin to heal, but that was of no consequence to Canada. The real problem for the globalists and their one sided trade deals was not so much that Canada herself had opted out, but that it would encourage other nations to follow suit and destroy the gravy train for them. Canadians accepted they would be in the globalist bully's bad books for a while, but also knew well that their nation was back on track and on her way to a prosperity that would, this time, be enjoyed by everyone.

Now that politicians were obsolete, the corporations could only bribe the upper echelons of the various departments. However, the departmental administration panels of citizens who had sworn, as guardians of democracy, to protect Canada and Canadians, kept that in check also. The only way a law could change now was through the people and not by lobbying, bribing or threatening a politician or senator.

It was a wonderful feeling being in control of one's life, of one's country, and the knowledge that the nation's prosperity would remain in the nation and eventually be enjoyed by everyone, was heartening to say the least.

"Why didn't we do this years ago?" was a common statement among people. But even though an organic system works better than any other for the people, it's the getting there that is the biggest challenge.

Before the liberation, the General had ensured that the word of its happening would be heard around the world despite the control of the media in other countries. The General managed to do this through an extensive network of friends and colleagues he had met from his various overseas postings. People would be pleasantly surprised to know how many serving officers in the various militaries of the world are 'white hats' or opposed to the controlling cabal and the unnecessary wars. The flow of news continued to leak through and many people around the globe hoped and prayed that the new system would work out as promised.

For Canada had led the way and had finally broken free of the system of economic slavery imposed so skillfully by the banking families. For economic slavery it certainly was, and the system of usury finance had, as many a wise man foretold, syphoned off the prosperity of many a nation and left its rightful owners in poverty, destitution and in the end, under tyranny. The free people of Canada could now read the statements made years previous by the so-called leaders of the world who talked of a New World Order, and by the likes of David Rockefeller who espoused a world run by a 'supranational sovereignty of an intellectual elite and world bankers' and thank their lucky stars that they themselves now controlled their destiny instead of those who for so long had desired and planned to do so.

The cabal of the New World Order were still in control of the US, UK, most of Europe, Australia and New Zealand. But the people were resisting in larger numbers especially with the knowledge that Canada had not only broken away but was enjoying more freedom than ever, her economy was recovering and the people would rightfully share in her prosperity. This was a huge shot in the arm and gave them a renewed hope that their own lives and countries were worth fighting and even dying for. The March vote came and went successfully and many things had changed in Canada in the first year of voting. It was expected that after a couple of years or so that the vote list would shorten until it consisted of a just a few proposals and amendments to previous proposals that were enacted, and yes, the March list was considerably shorter than the previous January list. Surprisingly, the concerns of the movement regarding the replacement of leaders such as; the Prime Minister, provincial premiers and their cabinet ministers, proved to be unfounded. If anything, the oversight administration panels and the systems of emergency voting between them were proving unnecessary, but would remain in place for the present.

For generations we have had leaders, good and bad, but Canadians were the first to cut the umbilical cord of leadership, they had finally left the womb of government. Ridding themselves of the parasitical central banking system was welcomed. Pulling out of all the odious trade deals was celebrated. Having direct democracy was a dream come true. But having no official, powerful leader was the real evolution of the new system. This was the mental quantum leap that needed to be made and made it was, and as with any evolution, once that step was taken there was no going back.

The people had grown accustomed to the new leaderless system far, far quicker than was previously supposed. It was quite apparent to people now that politics and politicians were nothing but a drain on a country and the people could take care of it all themselves, once they had changed that belief.

CHAPTER 24

70 – The Judge, Jeff and Niki

Jeff and Niki had decided to wed in the coming June and had made all the arrangements. The Judge would marry them at a small banquet hall near the pub. Neither Jeff nor Niki had any great desire for a big white wedding and preferred to save their money for a good honeymoon and for future travel. Jeff's Uncle Jack, who was widowed after his wife Doris had succumbed to a heart attack five years previous, had offered them his huge bedroom and living room space above the pub and he would take Jeff's smaller living area. Jeff and Niki were overjoyed at the offer as it would also save them from paying for an apartment in Toronto. Niki could also give up her apartment too.

Jack also told Jeff he was 'getting older' and would gradually ease away from running the pub and he asked Jeff if he would be interested in taking over. Jeff loved working in the pub and after discussing it with Niki, agreed to begin taking over more of the day-to-day running of the business. Jack had no children and told Jeff he would leave the pub to him in his will. In the meantime Jack just wanted a small income as he already had money saved and was going to start travelling around the world and checking things off his bucket list.

Things just couldn't get much better for Jeff and Niki.

As Dawn Approaches

Having their own pub, the partners of their dreams and a new organic system, which would propel the nation into prosperity and help secure a bright future for their children.

Jeff, dressed in his best suit, walked along the narrow carpet, the aisle, between the chairs in the banquet hall with his best man, a long-time friend called Dave Judd. Up ahead, stood there with her maid of honour Kelly O'Shea, looking like an angel, was Niki, and behind them stood a very special man, a special man in both Jeff and Niki's lives, the Judge.

The ceremony went without a hitch even though it was the Judge's first and only time he had ministered a wedding. A reception for seventy guests followed after the picture taking and the next day the newly wedded couple flew to Jamaica for a ten-day honeymoon.

71 – The World Fights Back

One year had passed since Jeff and Niki were wed and everything was going well. The economy had picked up quickly, the pub had never been busier and apart from the usual occasional spat, married life was working out great. Niki was busy with her photography and helped out at the pub whenever she could. Jeff had made some changes including bringing in live music twice weekly which swelled the patronage as well as the takings.

The organic system, now two and a half years along, was now well established in the minds of the people and had become as natural as breathing. Even the regular voting of four times per year did nothing to dent the enthusiasm for the new system, in fact it was welcomed.

The one sad thing for Canadians was that the saviour of Canada, the man whom history would never forget, General Benoit Rousseau, had passed away from complications of an illness. The General was buried with full military honours amid a national day of mourning.

Many a public building, street and park would be named in honour of this man and a commemoration statue was commissioned to be made and would be situated in Ottawa outside the proposed Liberation Museum.

Manufacturing was beginning to boom and Canada had not experienced anything like it since the GATT free trade deal with the US and Mexico in 1994. After which for years there were convoys of trucks backed up for miles at the Mexican borders, loaded with the machinery and equipment torn out of Canadian factories which remained idle until today. By someone's logic, that deal was supposed to be good for Canadians.

The Organic Economy had settled very well but it would still be several years before equilibrium. The point whereby there was full employment and the treasury could assess revenues and expenditure and begin lowering taxes and lowering post-secondary education tuition fees. The goal was still to eradicate post-secondary education fees and to find a new way or formula for fairer tax collection, but in the meantime, the tax bracket for lower income workers was reduced and the minimum wage increased. Meanwhile, student loans were interest free which helped enormously plus those parents that helped their sons and daughters with their expenditures, themselves had more disposable income due to the removal of interest payments.

Therefore, overall Canada was easily out-performing all other world economies, admittedly, many of those economies were under the shadow of tyranny and martial law. The peoples of these nations had watched Canada closely and many had had enough. They were angry and becoming increasingly defiant and a tipping point had been reached in Australia, people unafraid to die, were now openly confronting their UN oppressors. The foreign UN soldiers could contain a riot here and a riot there, but a concerted effort was made across all the major cities as a people's army revolted and took back control of some of the government buildings. That was the catalyst for hundreds of thousands of Australians to march fearlessly to the government buildings in the cities and demand their freedom. The news of this backlash had reached other countries such; as the UK and the US and they also began fighting back. They all knew it was all or nothing. Now was the time and failure was not an option lest the punishment be final. At this point for most, living under tyranny was as good as being dead anyway so the fight was now on.

The General had always known that what he did was a gamble. The cabal could have easily overpowered the Canadian forces but he guessed correctly that they just might back off due to what the rest of the world would think.

Canada being attacked by the UN or the US was globally unthinkable and the General knew that. He knew that they would not be able to contain millions of people in different countries fighting full on for their freedom. It was all about will, the will to fight to the death and at that time, with the UN claiming to be on peace keeping missions, that will wasn't quite there. The General also knew that the new economy would thrive well and when the rest of the world saw this it would rear up and fight back. Otherwise, yes, in time, once the New World Order was in full control of most of the rest of the world, they would strike and take Canada. It was a gamble, but the General in his mind had no other choice, for the UN convoys were approaching the Canadian borders as he made his famous speech.

The fighting for liberation continued in Australia, the UK and US and spread into Europe. The cabal had not anticipated the people had so much fight in them. UN soldiers were beginning to desert for they could sense defeat and knew there would be little mercy from those they had oppressed so brutally over the past few years. Then the call came, the call that signalled the world was changing. A phone call to the Department of Foreign Affairs came from Australia. Australia had fought back and defeated the UN 'peacekeeping' forces. The people were now back in control of their nation and were not wasting a second of time.

"Hi, this is Steve Armstrong from The Australian Resistance Movement, can I speak to someone knowledgeable about 'The

Organic Economy' please?"
The call from Steve Armstrong was also historical for his request
was for a team of Canadians who were well versed in the new
system to go to Australia and help set up an organic economy
there also.
Sadly, the General was not alive to hear this but it would have
been poetic justice if he had.
The dream of a peaceful planet was becoming a reality. Another
nation, having freed itself of tyranny, had decided to also rebirth
anew by implementing a different system. The Australian people
were to know the same freedom as Canadians.

72 – The Cottagers

At around the same time that Australia had overcome tyranny and the UK and the US were also fighting back, the three couples and their children, were enjoying the last weekend of the summer at Jerry and Andrea's cottage. It was the Labour Day weekend at the end of August and the weather cooperated wonderfully. The children made the most of their time at the dock and beach, swimming, diving and generally having fun. Outside on the deck the women were enjoying a drink before dinner. The salad, potatoes, corn and bread were prepared and the men hung out around the barbecue where Jerry was tending the meat.

"Don't you just love all this?" Rose said to the other women.

"Yeah, just a shame it's all over for another year though," Natalie replied.

"At least we don't go back to a stressed out existence anymore," continued Andrea, "I used to dread it, the hamster wheel of existence."

"Me too," Rose said, "but so much has changed, life is so different now."

"It is," Natalie agreed, "even the schools are different, the way they teach the kids."

"Yes, that's true," continued Andrea, "I remember being so worried about them, their future and all that but it's all changed now, the emphasis has changed, it's very different."

"I've noticed a difference at work too," Natalie added, "it just seems more laid back. We still do the work, get things done but the atmosphere is different."

"Same with us," agreed Andrea, "we are completely different at CRA from how we were before the new system. The days when we hounded the poor people for unpaid taxes and frightened them half to death and we still get the money from them, there was never any need for it."

"Do you girls have any more ideas to put on the next vote list?" Rose asked.

"Not really," Natalie said, "I think most of the changes we want have been put into place, don't you?"

"Yes Natalie, I don't really have anything to add, Jerry and I are very happy with how things are. How about you and Nick, Rose?" replied Andrea.

"Same, we love the way things have changed, love the new system." Rose answered.

Over at the barbecue where Jerry was carefully watching and turning the meat.

"Anyway Ron, you've finished your two years on the Ministry of Transportation Admin Panel then, how was it?"

"Yeah Ron, tell us all about it," added Nick.

"Loved it guys, really loved it. Felt real good to be doing what we were doing, looking after the taxpayer's money and making sure there were no underhand deals going on," replied Ron.

"So what did you do on that panel Ron, what kind of things, I know you told us before but I forget," Nick asked.

"Mainly keeping an eye on expenditure, checking out the contracts, who gets them and why they were chosen, plus watching supplies and making sure no-one is ordering things that aren't necessary then selling them for cash, that kind of thing," answered Ron.

"Did you catch anything, find any shady deals going on Ron?" Jerry asked.

"With the help of the accountants on the panel we found things alright, but that was from before the new system and the panel," Ron continued, "but we called in the brass, sat them down and told them in no uncertain terms that we knew what was going on and if we saw one more irregularity then charges would be laid."

"So, you kinda let bygones be bygones and started over?" asked Nick.

"Yeah, well the truth is, it would have taken a huge effort to prove who knew what, so we just told them to keep everything legit and to let the entire department know we would be watching things. The truth is guys, just being there, just having a panel is enough to keep them honest," replied Ron.

"That makes sense Ron, the panel itself is a deterrent," said Jerry.

"Yes Jerry, but we also told them we weren't out for a witch hunt either, we don't want good, highly qualified, experienced people quitting because of micro management from a panel of people who don't know the job like they do. We made it clear we were looking for obvious fraud, kickbacks, that kind of thing," Ron said.

"How's things at your plant Nick, keeping busy?" asked Jerry.

"Yeah, we're always busy, nothing different there, we stayed busy right through all that martial law mess and the start of the new system, how about you Jerry?" asked Nick.

"I survived through it all too and now we are steady, not booming but steady. The devalued dollar really hurt us but things are easing off now that Canada is finding its feet with the new economy," Jerry replied.

"What about you Ron, seen any changes after being away from the police for two years?" asked Nick.

"Yeah, things have changed a lot, and in a good way I'm pleased to say," answered Ron.

"In which way Ron?" Jerry asked.

"Well, after the new system was voted in and we couldn't call ourselves a force anymore, we also had directives from the top that the aggressive approach thankfully had to stop and any aggressive behaviour would be dealt with. They fired a few of the thug types and rehired with an emphasis back to good policing rather than lower IQs and muscle," Ron replied.

"So the police are kinda getting back to how they used to be, like when we called them Toronto's finest," said Nick.

"You got it Nick, it's a pleasure again to go to work now, good to be a cop again," Ron replied.

"What about marijuana being legal, how do you feel about that?" Nick asked Ron.

"It is what it is Nick. Did seem a little strange for a while especially as I had been away for two years, then coming back and seeing folk smoking dope in public and us not doing anything about it. But to be honest it's no big deal and doesn't give us any problems. Alcohol gives us far more problems," replied Ron.

"Figured as much," added Nick.

"Ok this is all ready to go," said Jerry as he started loading up a large plate with the spoils from the barbecue.

The three families sat down and filled themselves on the final meal at the cottage for that year.

<u>73 – The Judge, Jeff and Niki</u>

The Judge had just sat at his favourite spot in the pub and took a welcome mouthful of beer from the pint Jeff had just poured.

"What's new Judge?" asked Jeff.

"Oh nothing, nothing at all Jeff. You know, normality is bliss," the Judge replied.

"Normality is bliss, what do you mean?" asked a puzzled Jeff.

"We often forget to appreciate how good it is when things just run along smoothly Jeff," the Judge answered.

"Can you elaborate Judge?" queried Jeff.

"Certainly, It's Monday morning and you get into your car and drive to work. You arrive and colleagues ask you how you are and you tell them you are fine, same old, same old. The next morning you drive to work but your car breaks down on the way. You call CAA and a tow truck takes you to a mechanic and along the way the tow truck driver tells you the repair could possibly cost hundreds of dollars. The mechanic finds a loose wire and charges you for one hour's labour and you are very happy and relieved. You get to work three hours late and when a colleague asks you how you are you say you are very happy because a potentially expensive problem only cost you one hour of a mechanic's time. So, you have lost three hours pay and had to pay a mechanic one hour for his time, but you arrive at work and are happier than the previous day, even though the previous day didn't cost you anything. Did you follow that?" the Judge asked.

Jeff smiled and nodded, "I never thought of it that way."

The Judge continued, "my point being, be appreciative when everything is going as it should, don't wait for a problem to appear to realise it."

"Good advice, normality is bliss, I'll have to remember that one Judge," said Jeff as he went to serve a customer.

Niki had just come into the pub and walked up to the bar.

"You look wiped Niki," Jeff said.

"Yeah, did a lot of walking today, I'm knackered," replied Niki, "I'll be with you in a minute if you need help love."

"No, I'm fine right now Babe, take a load off and have a drink," replied Jeff.

"Ok, I think I'll do just that," said Niki as she pulled up a stool beside the Judge.

"How's my favourite Judge today?" asked Niki.

"Wonderful Niki, just wonderful," the Judge replied.

"Crikey, that sounds good Judge, is the beer that good then?" joked Niki.

"Always Niki, always, but I was just saying to Jeff how normality is bliss."

"Is it, ok I didn't realise," replied a puzzled Niki.

"Sorry, I have just been boring your husband with my take on certain things and I won't bore you, Jeff can explain later," said the Judge.

"I think I get what you're saying, appreciate things when they are going well, something like that?" Niki asked.

"Yes, exactly," replied the Judge.

"Here's your drink Mrs Summers," Jeff said with a wink as he passed Niki her beer.

"Cheers Babe," Niki took a sip and said, "this pub seems to get busier by the day."

"I know," replied Jeff, "I'm going to need some extra help soon, it's the economy, everything is getting busier, have you seen the 'help wanted' ads at the stores and restaurants?"
"Yes I've noticed them popping up," replied Niki.

"Looks like The Organic Economy is serving us well," said the Judge.

"Yes it does, I know the city feels busier these days," agreed Niki.

"I just hope that we as a society take a different route from now on," the Judge thought aloud, "I hope that people treat people properly now. The old system of greed and materialism bred a master and slave mentality in so many companies," said the Judge.

"That's why we needed union's though, to balance things, it's a shame but that's human nature right," said Niki.

"Yes, quite right Niki, if owners and management treated workers properly then unions would never have been necessary. That's my point really, I hope now, with the new system that a new mindset means we can all get along, workers and management alike and we don't need to have unions. Nothing against the unions mind, it's a dream I have of a new humanity Niki, a new world if you like," said the Judge.

"Would be nice, no doubt about that and I think it's possible Judge," Niki answered.

"I do too, but it may take the next generation, the generation raised in the new system for it to happen," said the Judge.

"I think all people want is to have a comfortable existence without having to kill themselves with stress to do so," Niki offered.

"Exactly, and you would think that should be possible

wouldn't you?"

"I do now Judge, not before the transition though, it was going downhill fast. Wages falling behind inflation, no jobs, everything costing more and more. But it's so different now, everything is different," said Niki.

"Well one thing that will help is the fact that the shoe will be on the other foot, so to speak. Employers always preferred a certain level of unemployment, the demand for jobs kept wages down and workers more subservient, afraid to lose their jobs. That will change soon, we will have full employment and the workers will be in demand so the employers will need to be careful how they treat their employees, but I'm hoping it won't need to be that way anymore," said the Judge.

"That's why I've always tried to work for myself, I can't stand being treated like someone's slave Judge," Niki said as the Judge laughed.

"No Niki, I bet you can't," he said.

CHAPTER 25

74 – Equilibrium

Two more years had passed, it had now been four and a half years since the new system was voted into being and the Canadian economy was running like clockwork. Manufacturing had bounced back and the needs of Canadians were being met domestically. There was full employment and a wide range of careers were always available.

Post-secondary education tuition was now half what it was at the time of transition and would continue to lower until it was free. A new tax system had not been introduced as yet, but taxes across the board were being lowered each year. The organic system gradually filled the state coffers as predicted and the Bank of Canada had begun purchasing and stocking gold as an investment for the future.

The new system had caused people to rethink about their futures and retirement. The system was different, there was barely any inflation at all and with no interest payments on savings, because it was now unnecessary, people either just saved their money or invested. As always, investments were risky and the Bank of Canada lent money at no interest, so corporations went to the bank now as much as they raised money from stocks.

As Dawn Approaches

A bold new plan was proposed to be voted on. Build retirement villages, real communities which had amenities and care systems including small specialised hospitals which could take care of most issues the elderly may experience. These communities would be built all over the country and would be managed and ran in such a way that retirees actually looked forward to living there. The idea was for people not to have to worry about retirement, but people were free to invest and make money to retire however they wished. The retirement villages were just an option, a very attractive option. Through the voting system many laws and regulations had been changed or removed and the people were living, in the main, as they wished to.

The world had again shifted in direction. Australia was now free and had, with Canadian help, successfully introduced the organic system and New Zealand was following in their footsteps. The UK, Europe and US had fought back long and hard against the UN troops and many lives had been lost, it was an awful period in history for these nations. But the battles were well worth fighting for, the UN eventually capitulated and the people of these nations were again free. They also realised the folly of allowing the old systems to remain and instigated organic systems, again with the assistance of Canadians. The UN building in New York City was demolished. No-one there wanted any reminder of the oppressors who were nothing more than the cabal's army.

To many Canadians it seemed almost impossible to think how much grief they used to endure with the old systems, and even harder to believe was why they put up with it all. As for the cabal of elites who wanted global control, they would learn that they had made a great miscalculation. The forces of control were where they planned to be, where they expected to be and everything was shaping up well for the ultimate intent. A central system of global control, a totalitarian dictatorship or New World Order as many a politician had called it. Be it a human flaw, a mistake by nature or an evolutionary anomaly, there have always been psychopathic personalities devoid of empathy that hunger for control, having zero regard for humanity or anything else save their own pleasures and desires. Through all history these psychopaths have left a trail of human devastation. How such a miniscule percentage of people can cause such monumental grief is barely believable but history is there to prove otherwise. History also teaches that the human race is highly adaptable and will quickly evolve to survive. People may fall prey to oppressors but will, through ingenuity and resourcefulness, find the ways and means to fight back when it means survival.

The cabal had been decimated and the people had won. The new system was gradually going global and the Judge's dream was becoming reality. The hope was eventually for the new organic nations to begin trading equitably, which would always, as with everything, be controlled by the people of those nations and not by the greed of corporate and banking interests whose power and reach had been completely neutered.

The world would be a different place, the daily news no longer spread doom, gloom, fear and negativity. People were stress free and happier and were re-learning who they really were and what really mattered in their lives. Violence was almost unheard of and the prison systems took a different approach depending on the crimes, but the emphasis was on rehabilitation instead of turning out worse criminals than went in. Those who were guilty of violent crimes or serious crimes of a sexual nature were incarcerated indefinitely.

Different nations proposed different things in their votes but each nation enjoyed the freedom and rights they wished for. Ideas were also shared between nations and lessons were also learned from ideas that didn't work out quite as expected. As these shared ideas came into being it was clear that the nations were becoming closer to each other, the different cultures were to some degree merging from afar.

As Dawn Approaches

Of all the changes proposed in the book 'The Organic Economy', the book which changed so many minds, the one thing which people seemed to have the most difficulty with was the fact they would no longer have a leadership figure or even a government in the true sense of the word. Which is understandable when you consider that we are raised with parents who protect us, guide us, tell us what to do and give us permission for things we wish to experience. But it doesn't end there, it continues on in a similar way through school and into our working lives. And in the background, constantly, is the womb of the state playing the same role. We have consistently had leaders in our lives and the belief in the state is largely ingrained by the state itself. The state and our belief in it are a self-fulfilling prophecy for it, it depends upon it, upon our unchallenged belief in it. Without that belief, our belief, the state and the systems within it would not survive, it could not survive as we would see it for the beast it really is.

We grow up within it and it is very difficult to think of life without it. With most it is akin to asking a faithful churchgoer to change his or her belief. We had never really experienced true freedom and subsequently, true self-responsibility, because we had always handed it over to a government. People have, since birth, been programmed to place more belief in the state than in each other. In fact it is in the state's best interests to keep the people insular, to keep the people arguing, squabbling and fighting between themselves over trivial matters. Matters such as left and right politics which essentially mean nothing, for the same controllers win regardless of which party is elected. When the people realise they hold the real power, when the people change and place more belief in each other than in the state, then everything changes and the people become masters of their own destinies.

The only way to truly change our systems and be free then was to change our fundamental belief in the state, in leadership.

It would be difficult for many to do so but once they did, a new world would open up to them and they would not wish to go back, for they would have evolved. And that was exactly what happened. It didn't take long for people to completely forget about leadership and government and that took many an observer by surprise.

The people of the western nations that had been under occupation by the UN forces had, unknowingly taken the long route to freedom. If they had taken note of the overt signs of what was happening to them and their nation, they could have taken back their power and changed the system before their brutal occupation.

But that was all water under the bridge and the world was now set to move forward into the golden years. After thousands of years enduring war, torture, poverty and starvation, the people would now experience the dawning of an age of humanity, peace and harmony.

CHAPTER 26

75 – The Judge

The Judge was relaxing at home. It was Sunday and he had cut the grass and tidied the garden, the Judge loved pottering around in his garden. He had his dinner and was playing his favourite classical music tracks, humming to the instruments as he readied himself for a Brandy and possibly a little nap in front of his television.

The Judge loved to look at the framed portraits and photographs on the shelves facing his favourite leather recliner. He walked over and looked at them one by one, first the portrait of himself with his beloved wife Harriet, who he missed so dearly. Then the family portraits with Harriet and Sabrina, there were five of those which spanned twenty years. There were five more of Sabrina with David and their children, the Judge's beloved grandchildren Samantha and Gareth.

Then the most recent one, which was now over three years old, the one taken of him ministering the wedding of Jeff and Niki, something he was so proud and so honoured to do. The framed picture was a heartfelt thank you gift from the happy couple. The Judge carefully picked up the portrait of him with his wife and sat down in his leather recliner. He could remember everything about that day, even how he felt, "how could one ever forget the feeling of being in love?" he thought to himself.

He took a sip of Brandy and sat back, thinking of the roller coaster of events which had occurred since he joined the movement.

The liberation, the UN convoys at the borders, the vote for the new system, the talks with the banks and trade delegations, helping to find Niki for Jeff, ministering their wedding. He felt so fortunate to be around to see the world fight back, finally defeat the cabal and rebirth anew with an organic system, a real system anchored around the people themselves and what they produced.

He thought how Harriet would have been so happy to see what had happened. She was such a people person and always fought for the 'little guy'. And the motto rang in his mind "Enough for Everyone".

"Yes," he thought, "enough for everyone now."

He looked again at the portrait with Harriet, she looked so beautiful, so radiant. He drifted away into that day, he could hear Harriet's voice, could even smell the perfume she wore and he felt her hand in his. His eyes closed slowly.

"Darling let's go," she was saying, "come along now let's not keep them waiting," he loved her voice.

"Yes my dear," he replied, "I'm coming," replied the Judge with a loving smile.

"Darling, we'll be late, you don't like to be late, do you?" he heard her say.

"No sweetheart, I'm right there, right there with you..... I've missed you so much."

As Dawn Approaches

John Reid lives in Wasaga Beach, Ontario, Canada with his wife Mandy.

They originate from The Isle of Sheppey in Kent, England and emigrated in 1988 with their two daughters.

Website:
www.theorganiceconomy.ca